A Jedi's strength flows from the Force. But beware of the dark side...

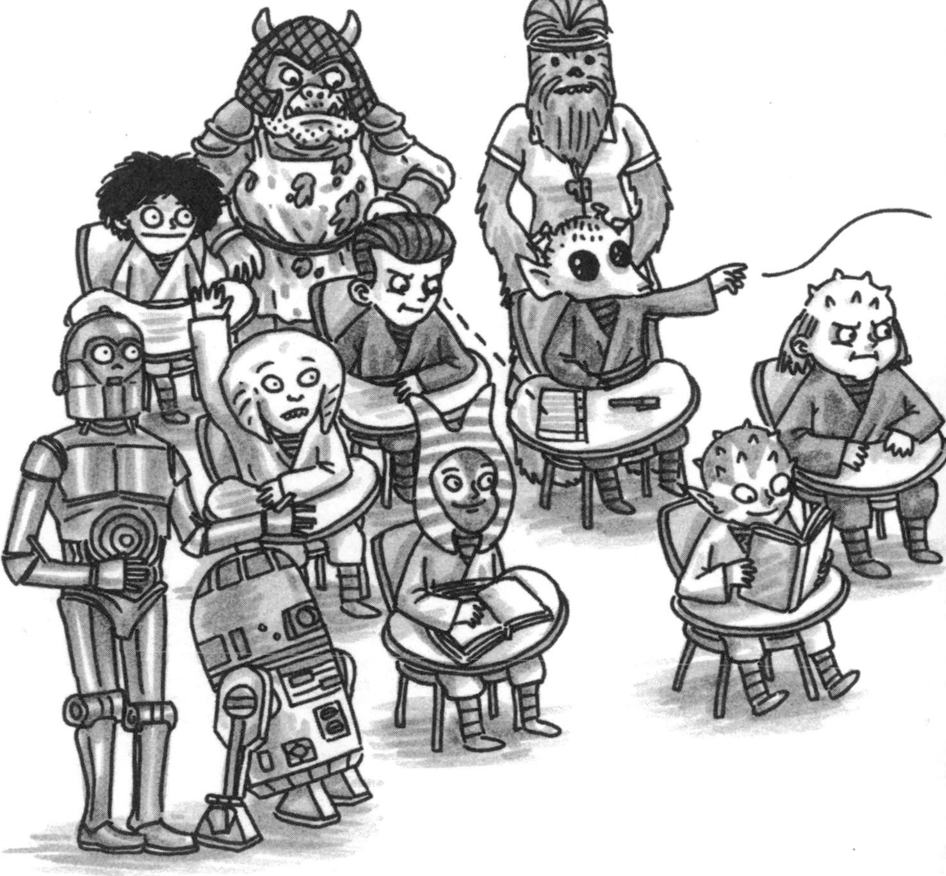

JEDI ACADEMY

RETURN OF THE PADAWAN

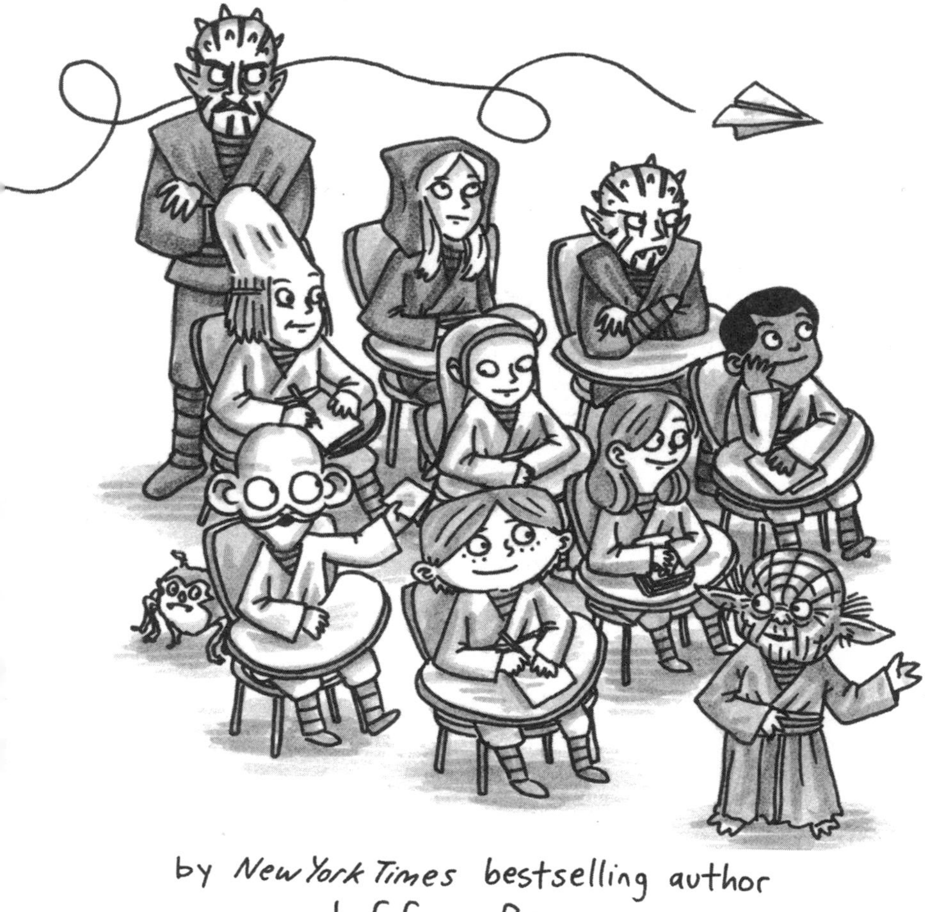

by *New York Times* bestselling author

Jeffrey Brown

Scholastic Inc.

Thanks to everyone who helped make this book not only possible, but better: Rex, Sam, Rick, and everyone at Scholastic; Joanne, Leland, Carol, J.W. Rinzler, and everyone at Lucasfilm; Marc Gerald, Chris Staros, Brett Warnock, Steve Mockus, my readers, friends, and family - especially Jennifer, Oscar, and Simon. Thank you!

WWW.STARWARS.COM

SCHOLASTIC.COM

© & ™ 2014 Lucasfilm Ltd.

Published by Scholastic Inc., Publishers since 1920. SCHOLASTIC and associated logos are trademarks and/or registered trademarks of Scholastic Inc.

ISBN 978-1-338-55257-7

10 9 8 7 6 5 4 3 2 1   19 20 21 22 23

Printed in the U.S.A.   23
This edition first printing 2019

Book design by Rick DeMonico

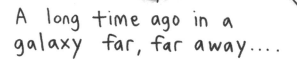

A long time ago in a galaxy far, far away....

There was a boy named Roan Novachez (that's me) who ALWAYS wanted to be a pilot but ended up at JEDI ACADEMY. His first year started off REALLY BAD but ended up great! This school year will definitely be the BEST YEAR EVER!

me when I first got to Jedi Academy

me, when I start Year Two: Jedi Pilot training!

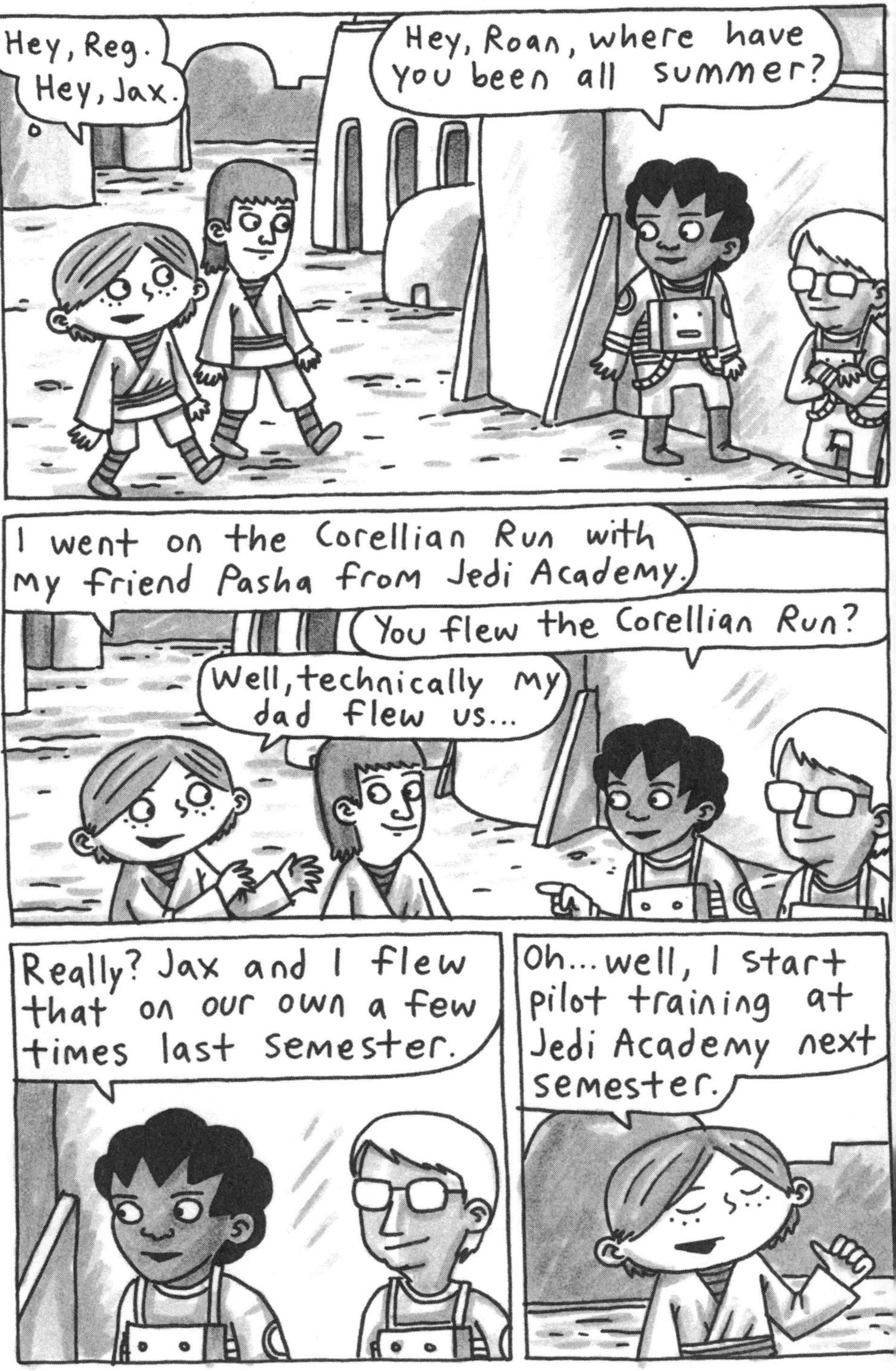
Hey, Reg.
Hey, Jax.
Hey, Roan, where have you been all summer?
I went on the Corellian Run with my friend Pasha from Jedi Academy.
You flew the Corellian Run?
Well, technically my dad flew us...
Really? Jax and I flew that on our own a few times last semester.
Oh... well, I start pilot training at Jedi Academy next semester.

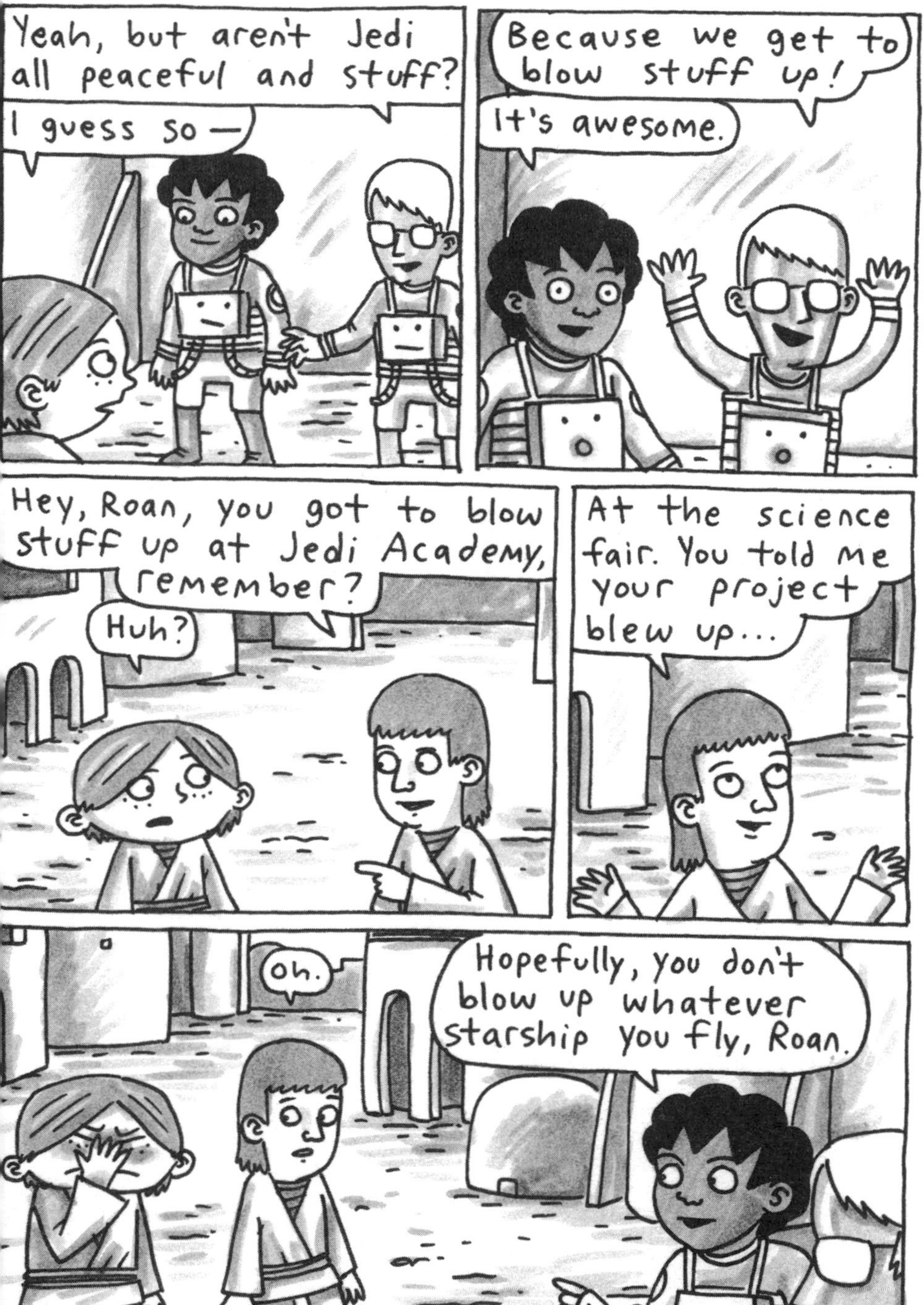
Yeah, but aren't Jedi all peaceful and stuff?
I guess so—
Because we get to blow stuff up!
It's awesome.
Hey, Roan, you got to blow stuff up at Jedi Academy, remember?
Huh?
At the science fair. You told me your project blew up...
Oh.
Hopefully, you don't blow up whatever starship you fly, Roan.

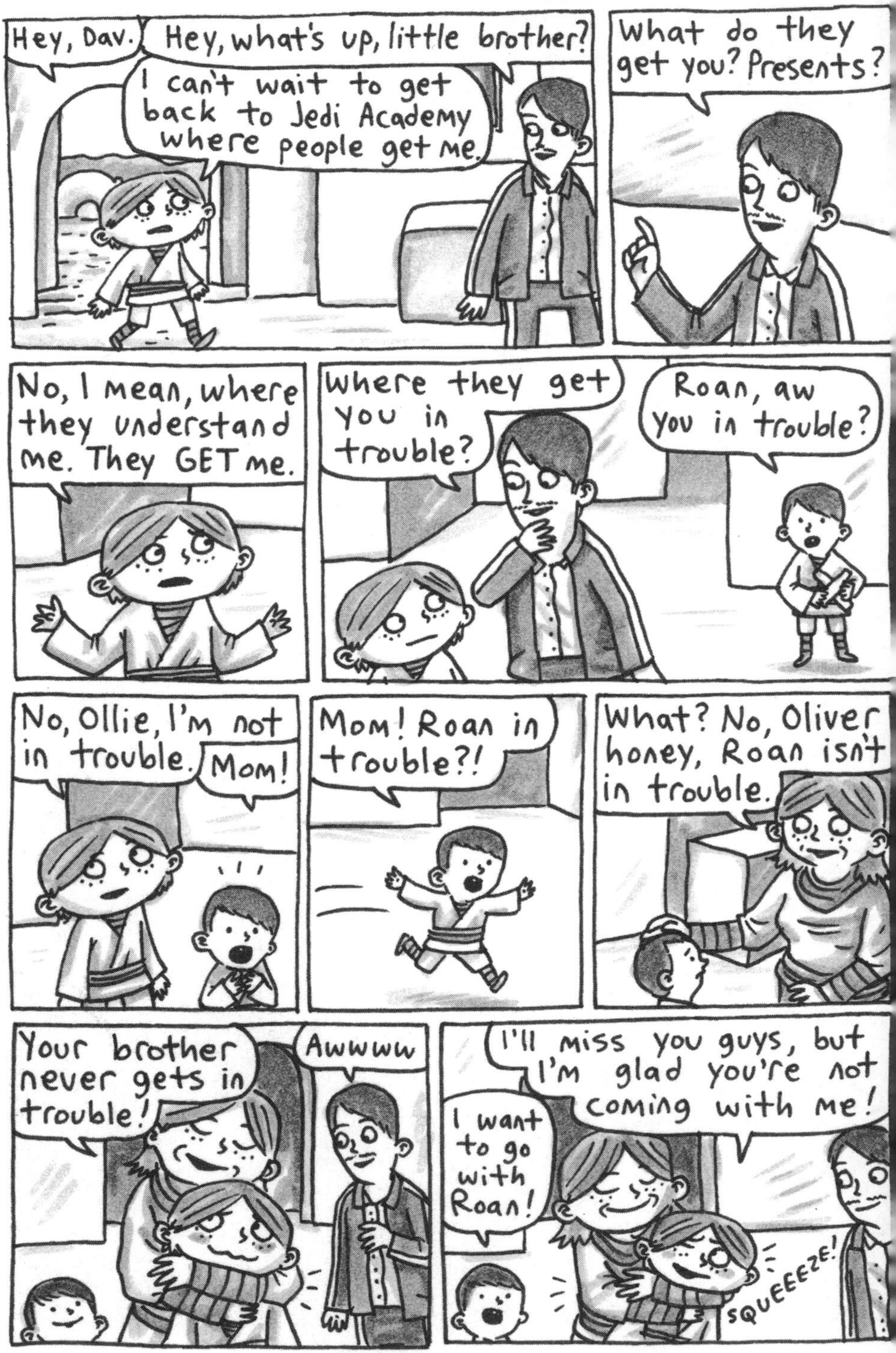
Hey, Dav.
Hey, what's up, little brother?
I can't wait to get back to Jedi Academy where people get me.
What do they get you? Presents?
No, I mean, where they understand me. They GET me.
Where they get you in trouble?
Roan, aw you in trouble?
No, Ollie, I'm not in trouble.
Mom!
Mom! Roan in trouble?!
What? No, Oliver honey, Roan isn't in trouble.
Your brother never gets in trouble!
Awwww
I'll miss you guys, but I'm glad you're not coming with me!
I want to go with Roan!
SQUEEEZE!

WELCOME BACK TO JEDI ACADEMY

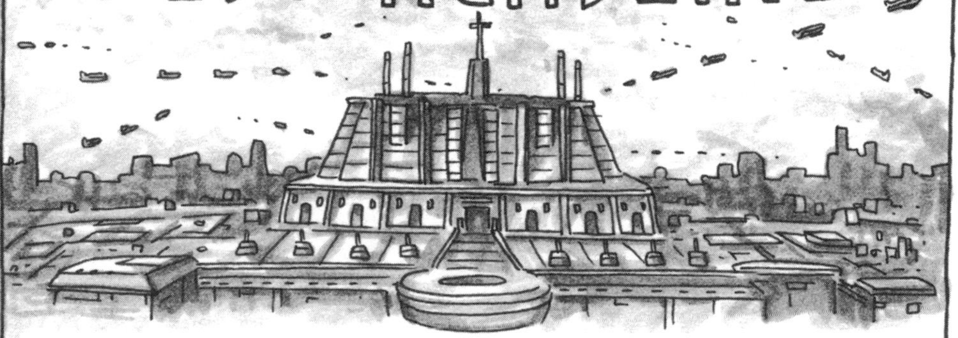

As students return to Coruscant for another year at Jedi Academy, they can expect to continue the best Jedi training in the galaxy, under the instruction of an experienced Jedi staff, including Master Yoda. This year, students will enter an exciting new phase of their training, as they learn to pilot Jedi starfighters in state-of-the-art flight simulators, continue learning to use the Force, and resist the dark side.

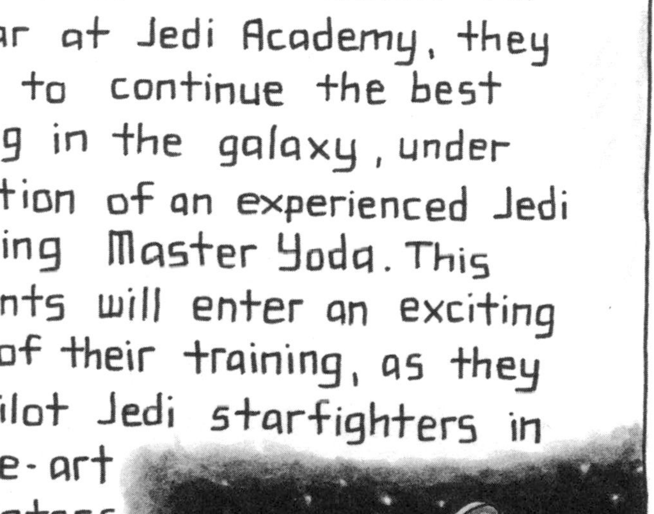

MEET OUR NEWEST STAFF MEMBER, GAMMY! Our new cafeteria chef, Gammy, is the first Gamorrean to achieve the rank of galactic gourmet after spending years training at some of the best

restaurants on the planet Lamaredd. He will be introducing a number of delicious new meals to the cafeteria, including traditional Gamorrean mushroom, liver, and eyeball recipes.

THIS YEAR, our Padawan will enjoy the opportunity to care for a class

pet, this voorpak from Naboo. Students will make sure the voorpak's soft fur stays clean and feed the voorpak its diet of live insects.

TRIDAY

I can tell Mom is really going to miss me this school year because she's been very huggy this summer whenever I've been at home. The best thing this summer was definitely going on the Corellian Run with Dad and Pasha. Dad showed us some tricks and even let us help with the ~~maitenance~~ maintenance checks on his starship. Dav was taking summer classes so I didn't see him as much, but we holochatted a bunch. I tried to holochat with Gaiana but kept missing her. She went on a family vacation to Naboo. She sent me a colo claw fish tooth, which is pretty cool. I drew a picture of a colo to send back to her.

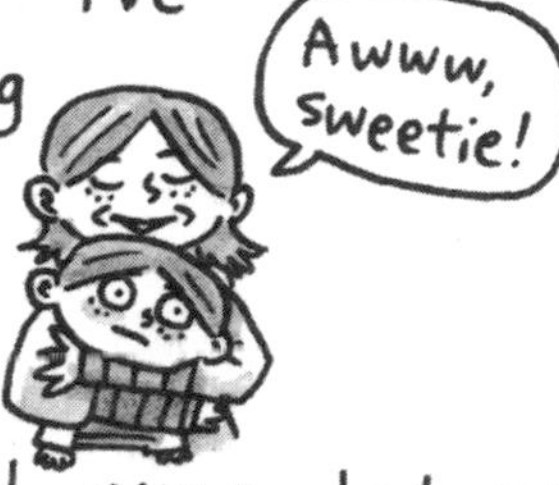
Awww, sweetie!

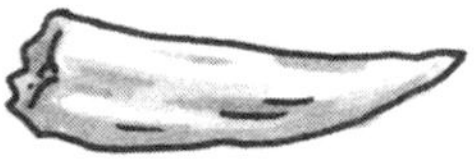

It'll be really good to see her and Pasha back at school, especially since we'll get to flight train. Finally, a class about something I'm good at! The only downside is the food at Jedi Academy.... The cafeteria food ended up being edible, but it's not nearly as good as Mom's food. And Mom never makes me eat ANYTHING that stares at me before I eat it!

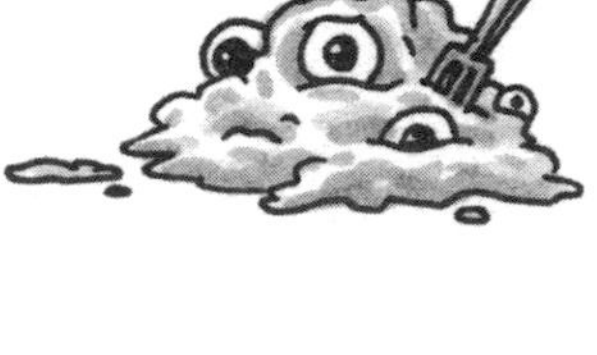

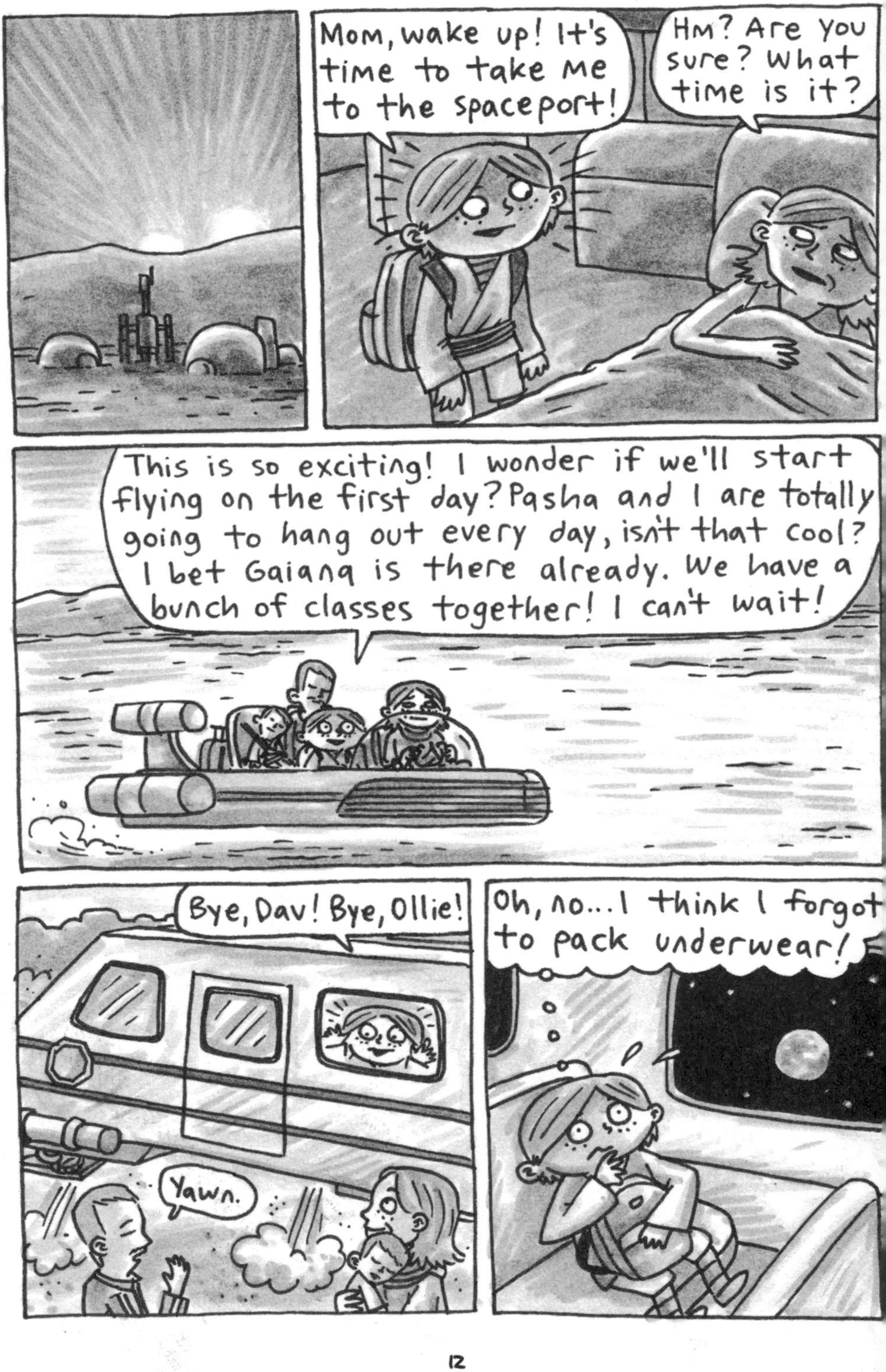
Mom, wake up! It's time to take me to the spaceport!
Hm? Are you sure? What time is it?
This is so exciting! I wonder if we'll start flying on the first day? Pasha and I are totally going to hang out every day, isn't that cool? I bet Gaiana is there already. We have a bunch of classes together! I can't wait!
Bye, Dav! Bye, Ollie!
Yawn.
Oh, no... I think I forgot to pack underwear!

MONODAY

I can't believe how boring Jedi Academy is. Nobody else is here yet. It turns out I got here a couple days early. I guess I was too excited and didn't look at the calendar right. Fortunately, Master Yoda has been around, getting ready for class. At least, I think he's getting ready for class... he's just shuffling around, going through stuff in cupboards and taking things out.

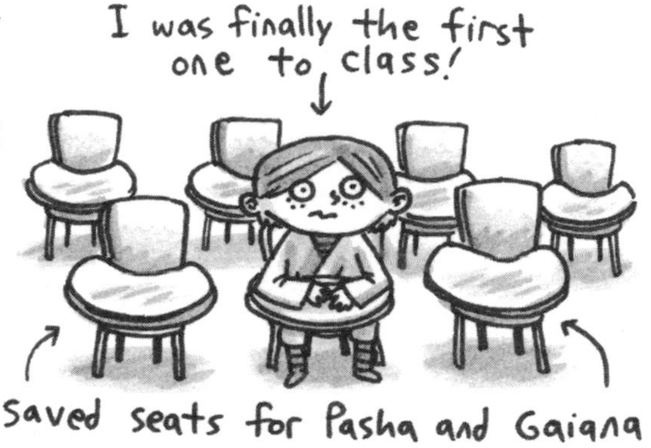
I was finally the first one to class!
saved seats for Pasha and Gaiana

He started me on some new exercises using the Force, so I've been getting back into the swing of things. Everyone else should start showing up tomorrow. I'm so ready for school to finally begin!

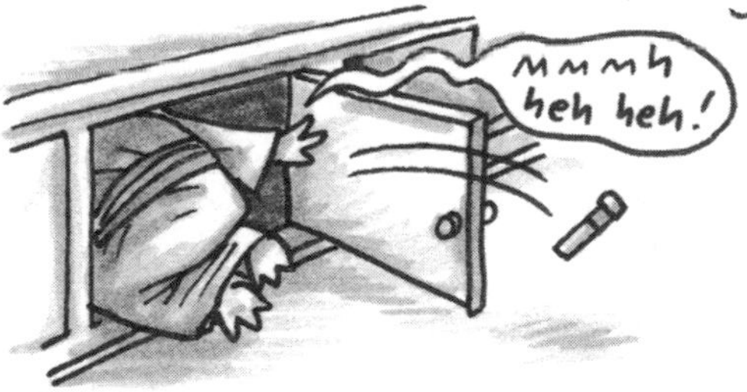
Mmmh heh heh!

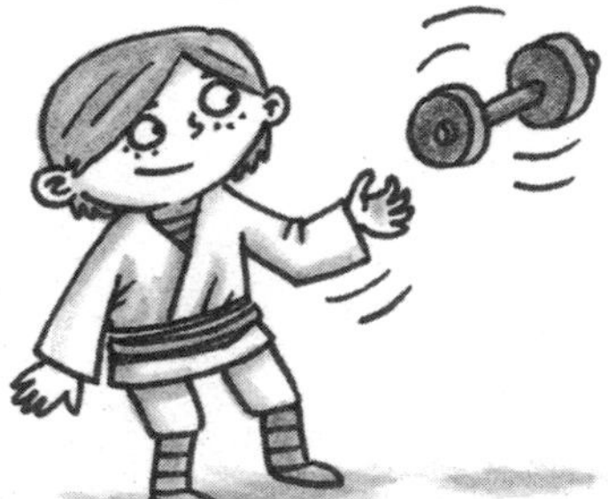

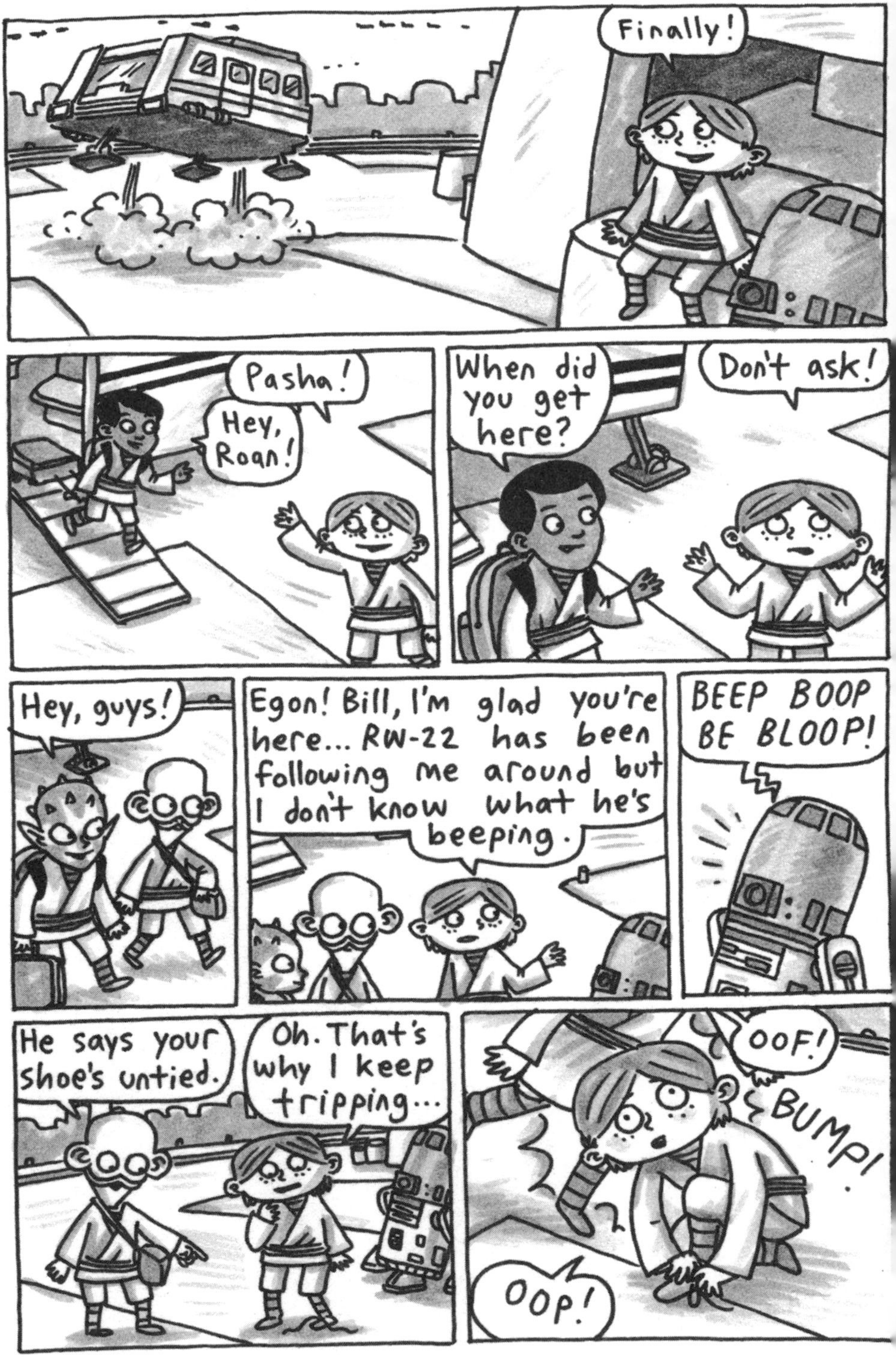
Finally!
Pasha!
Hey, Roan!
When did you get here?
Don't ask!
Hey, guys!
Egon! Bill, I'm glad you're here... RW-22 has been following me around but I don't know what he's beeping.
BEEP BOOP BE BLOOP!
He says your shoe's untied.
Oh. That's why I keep tripping...
OOF!
BUMP!
OOP!

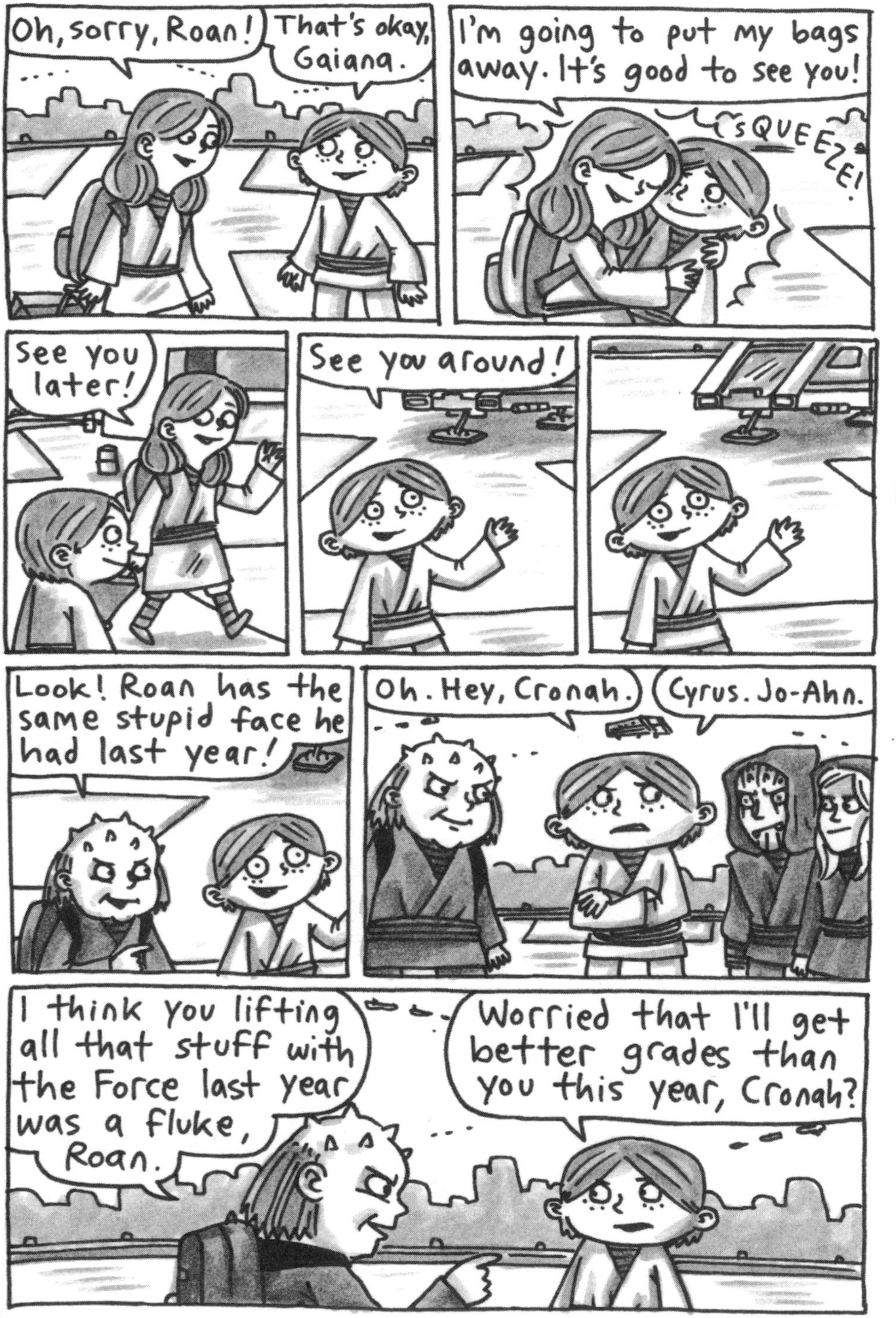
Oh, sorry, Roan!
That's okay, Gaiana.
I'm going to put my bags away. It's good to see you!
SQUEEZE!
See you later!
See you around!
Look! Roan has the same stupid face he had last year!
Oh. Hey, Cronah.
Cyrus. Jo-Ahn.
I think you lifting all that stuff with the Force last year was a fluke, Roan.
Worried that I'll get better grades than you this year, Cronah?

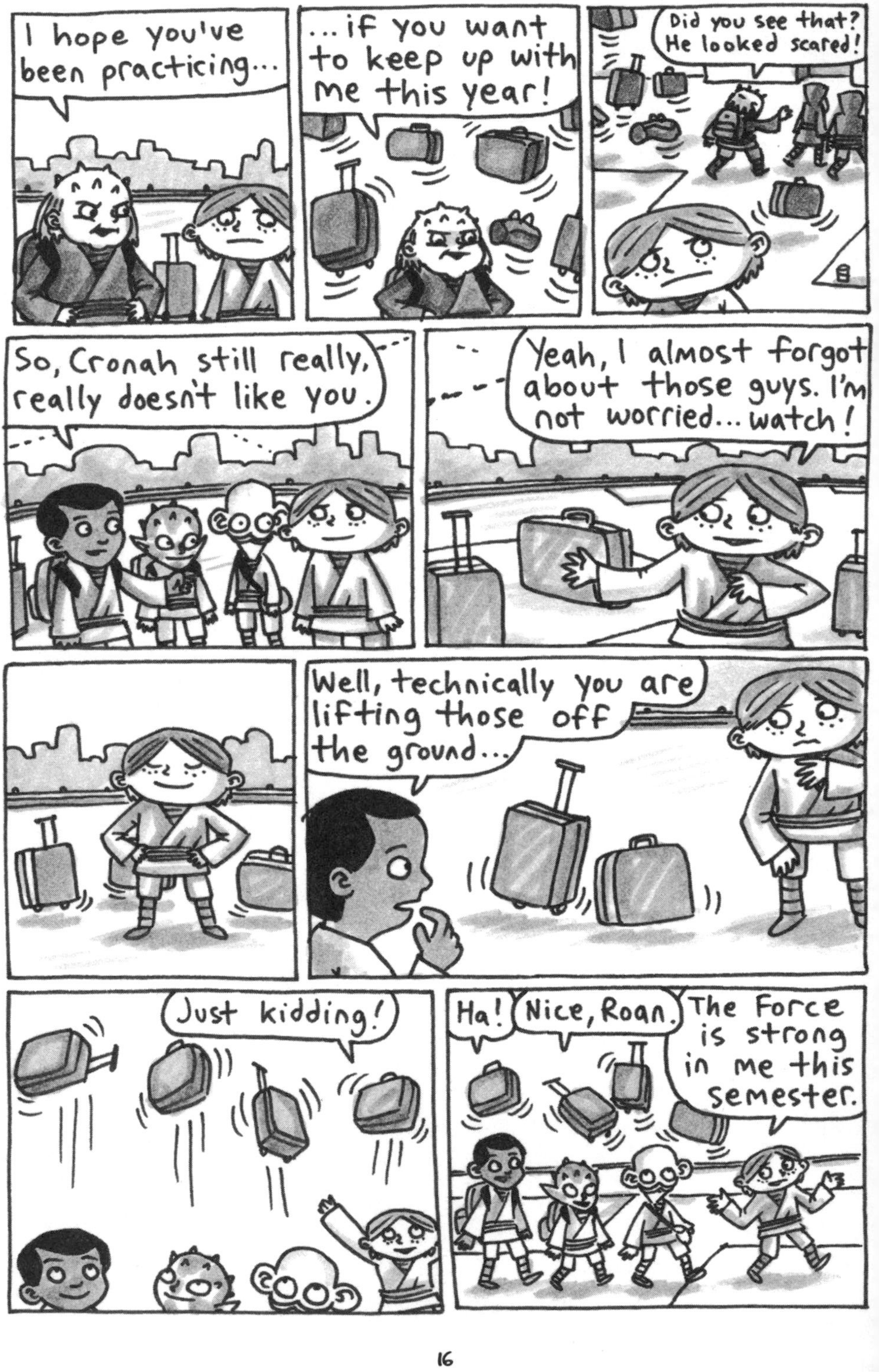
I hope you've been practicing...
...if you want to keep up with me this year!
Did you see that? He looked scared!
So, Cronah still really, really doesn't like you.
Yeah, I almost forgot about those guys. I'm not worried... watch!
Well, technically you are lifting those off the ground...
Just kidding!
Ha!
Nice, Roan.
The Force is strong in me this semester.

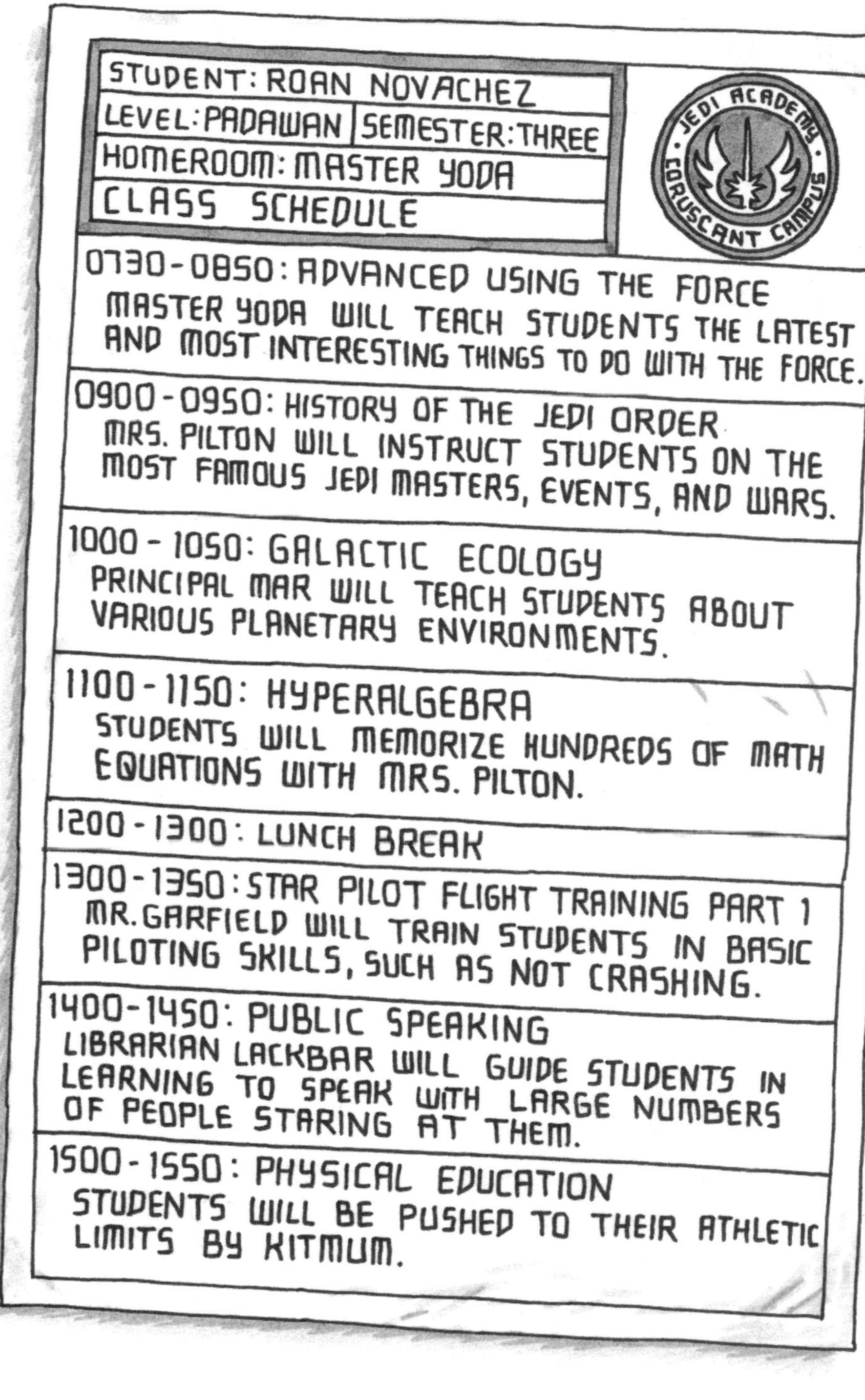
STUDENT: ROAN NOVACHEZ
LEVEL: PADAWAN | SEMESTER: THREE
HOMEROOM: MASTER YODA
CLASS SCHEDULE

JEDI ACADEMY · CORUSCANT CAMPUS ·

0730-0850: ADVANCED USING THE FORCE
MASTER YODA WILL TEACH STUDENTS THE LATEST AND MOST INTERESTING THINGS TO DO WITH THE FORCE.

0900-0950: HISTORY OF THE JEDI ORDER
MRS. PILTON WILL INSTRUCT STUDENTS ON THE MOST FAMOUS JEDI MASTERS, EVENTS, AND WARS.

1000-1050: GALACTIC ECOLOGY
PRINCIPAL MAR WILL TEACH STUDENTS ABOUT VARIOUS PLANETARY ENVIRONMENTS.

1100-1150: HYPERALGEBRA
STUDENTS WILL MEMORIZE HUNDREDS OF MATH EQUATIONS WITH MRS. PILTON.

1200-1300: LUNCH BREAK

1300-1350: STAR PILOT FLIGHT TRAINING PART 1
MR. GARFIELD WILL TRAIN STUDENTS IN BASIC PILOTING SKILLS, SUCH AS NOT CRASHING.

1400-1450: PUBLIC SPEAKING
LIBRARIAN LACKBAR WILL GUIDE STUDENTS IN LEARNING TO SPEAK WITH LARGE NUMBERS OF PEOPLE STARING AT THEM.

1500-1550: PHYSICAL EDUCATION
STUDENTS WILL BE PUSHED TO THEIR ATHLETIC LIMITS BY KITMUM.

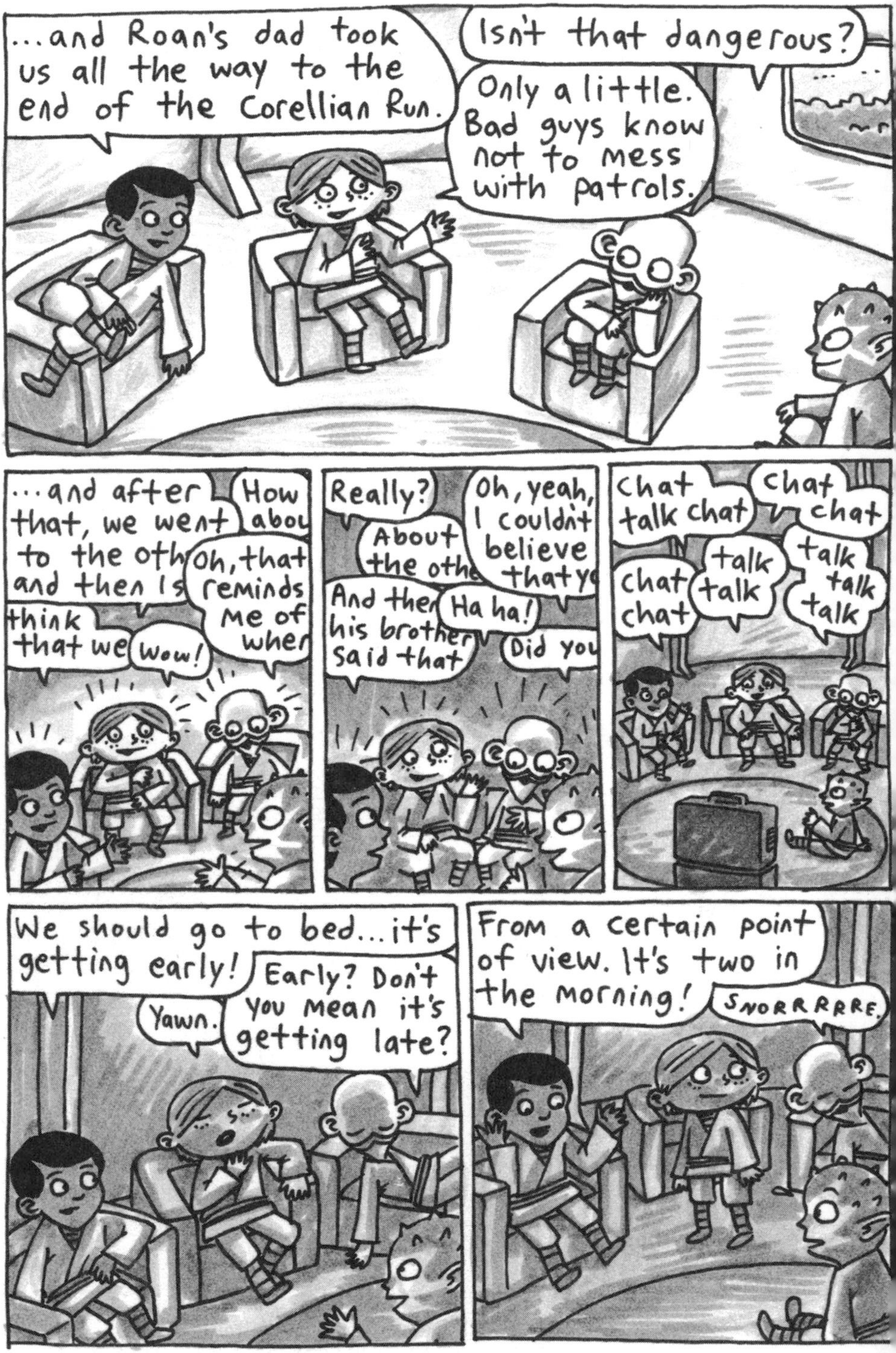
...and Roan's dad took us all the way to the end of the Corellian Run.
Isn't that dangerous?
Only a little. Bad guys know not to mess with patrols.
...and after that, we went to the oth and then I s
How abou
Oh, that reminds me of wher
think that we
Wow!
Really?
About the othe
Oh, yeah, I couldn't believe that y
And then his brother said that
Ha ha!
Did you
Chat talk chat
Chat chat
Chat chat
talk talk
talk talk talk
talk talk
We should go to bed... it's getting early!
Yawn.
Early? Don't you mean it's getting late?
From a certain point of view. It's two in the morning!
SNORRRRRE.

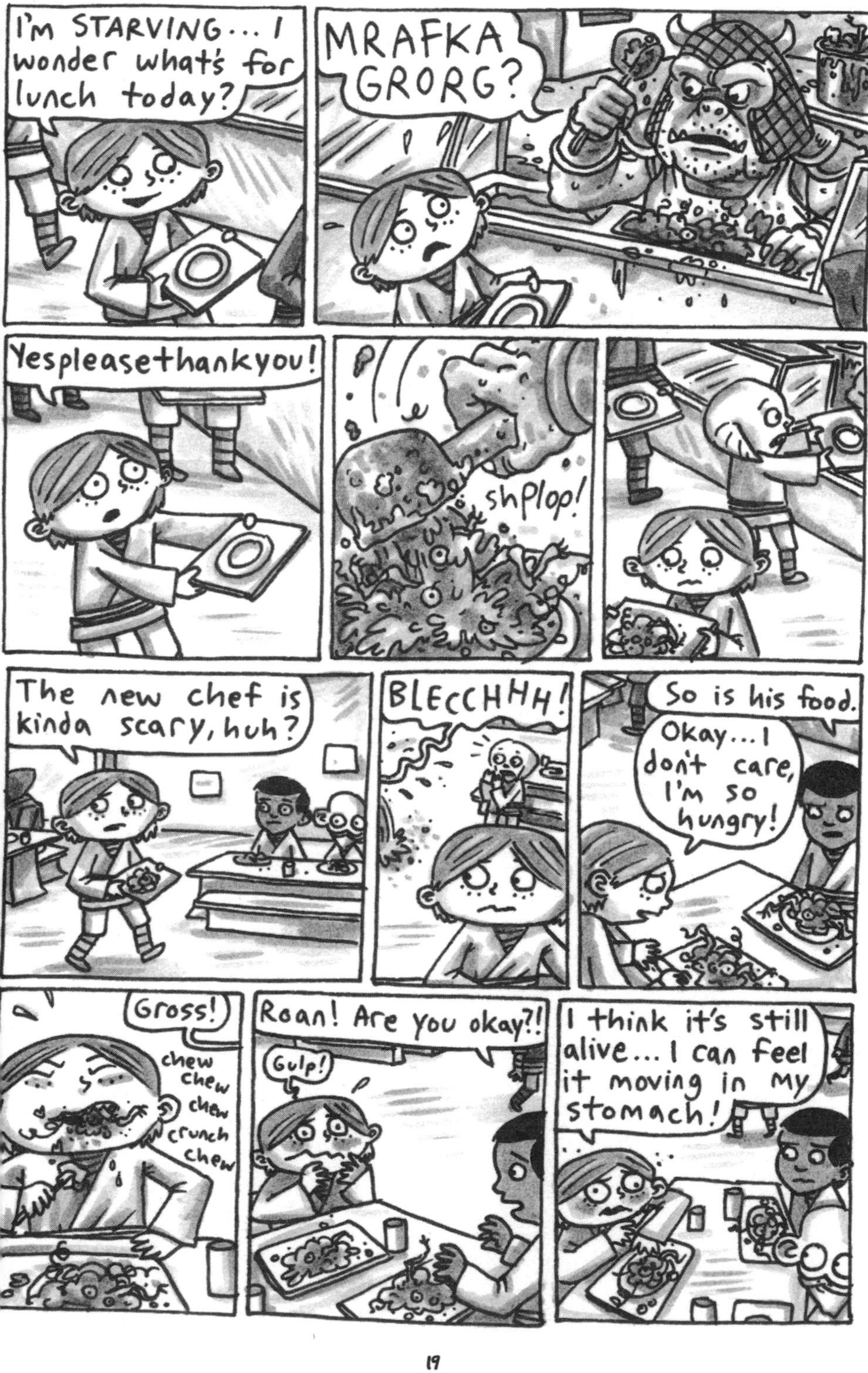

I'm STARVING... I wonder what's for lunch today?
MRAFKA GRORG?
Yespleasethankyou!
shplop!
The new chef is kinda scary, huh?
BLECCHHH!
So is his food.
Okay... I don't care, I'm so hungry!
Gross!
chew chew chew crunch chew
Roan! Are you okay?!
Gulp!
I think it's still alive... I can feel it moving in my stomach!

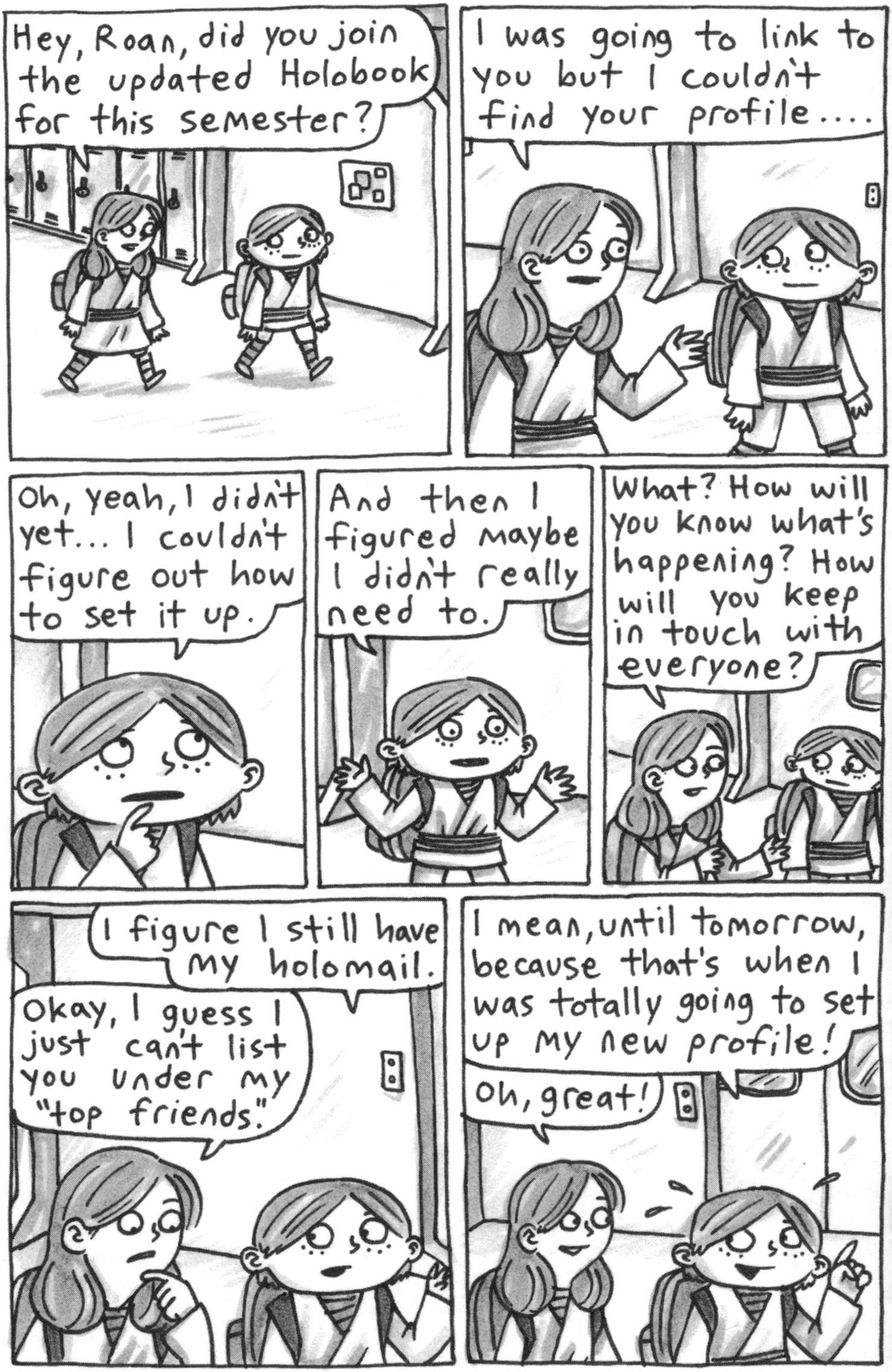
Hey, Roan, did you join the updated Holobook for this semester?
I was going to link to you but I couldn't find your profile....
Oh, yeah, I didn't yet... I couldn't figure out how to set it up.
And then I figured maybe I didn't really need to.
What? How will you know what's happening? How will you keep in touch with everyone?
I figure I still have my holomail.
Okay, I guess I just can't list you under my "top friends."
I mean, until tomorrow, because that's when I was totally going to set up my new profile!
Oh, great!

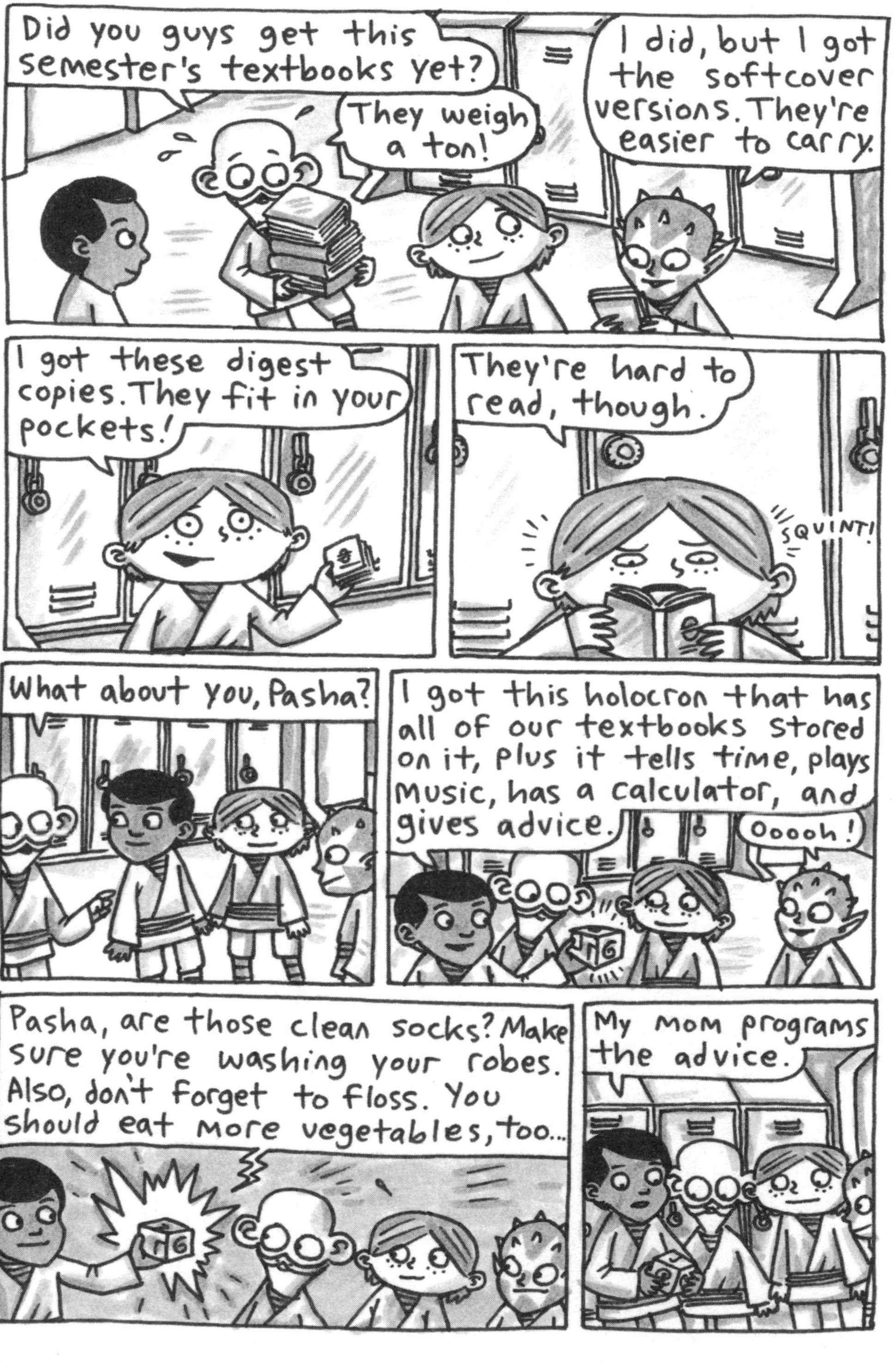
Did you guys get this semester's textbooks yet?
They weigh a ton!
I did, but I got the softcover versions. They're easier to carry.
I got these digest copies. They fit in your pockets!
They're hard to read, though.
SQUINT!
What about you, Pasha?
I got this holocron that has all of our textbooks stored on it, plus it tells time, plays music, has a calculator, and gives advice.
Ooooh!
Pasha, are those clean socks? Make sure you're washing your robes. Also, don't forget to floss. You should eat more vegetables, too...
My mom programs the advice.

TRIDAY

It's been good to finally catch up with Gaiana and Pasha this week. I think not hanging out with them so much was really what made the summer seem like it was a super-long time. I've been looking forward to pilot training ~~all summer~~ <u>my entire life</u> and now that we're starting training, I find out I still have to wait to do any flying!

me, waiting ← waiting waiting waiting

The only thing we're doing for the first couple weeks is reading through the Galactic Pilot General Instruction Flight Training Manual and Workbook, which weighs more than our class pet, Voorpee. In fact, it probably weighs more than Egon!

MATH

Normal textbook

GALACTIC PILOT GENERAL INSTRUCTION FLIGHT TRAINING MANUAL AND WORKBOOK

9th ed.

G.P.G.I.F.T.M.A.W.

Egon holding the manual

Mr. Garfield says we HAVE to learn EVERYTHING in the book backward and forward before we even step into a flight simulator. That's RIDICULOUS. Reading a book can't

THIS IS IMPORTANT!

(Mr. G. thinks EVERYTHING he says is important.)

give you the feeling of what flying is like! I think you can't understand something unless you really ~~experiense~~ experience it. It's not like flight simulators can put us in any actual danger. At least this isn't a super-boring or super-hard class for me, or I'd be even more frustrated. Of course, I have to spend so much time reading the G.P.G.I.F.T.M.A.W. that I haven't come up with any ideas to draw for Ewok Pilot comics for the school paper. A couple people have ~~alreddy~~ already asked if I've drawn any new ones, so I'll try to come up with ideas soon...

Hey, Ewok Pilot, here's the updated flight manual.

I think it'll be really useful to you!

sniff sniff

Bugdoo!

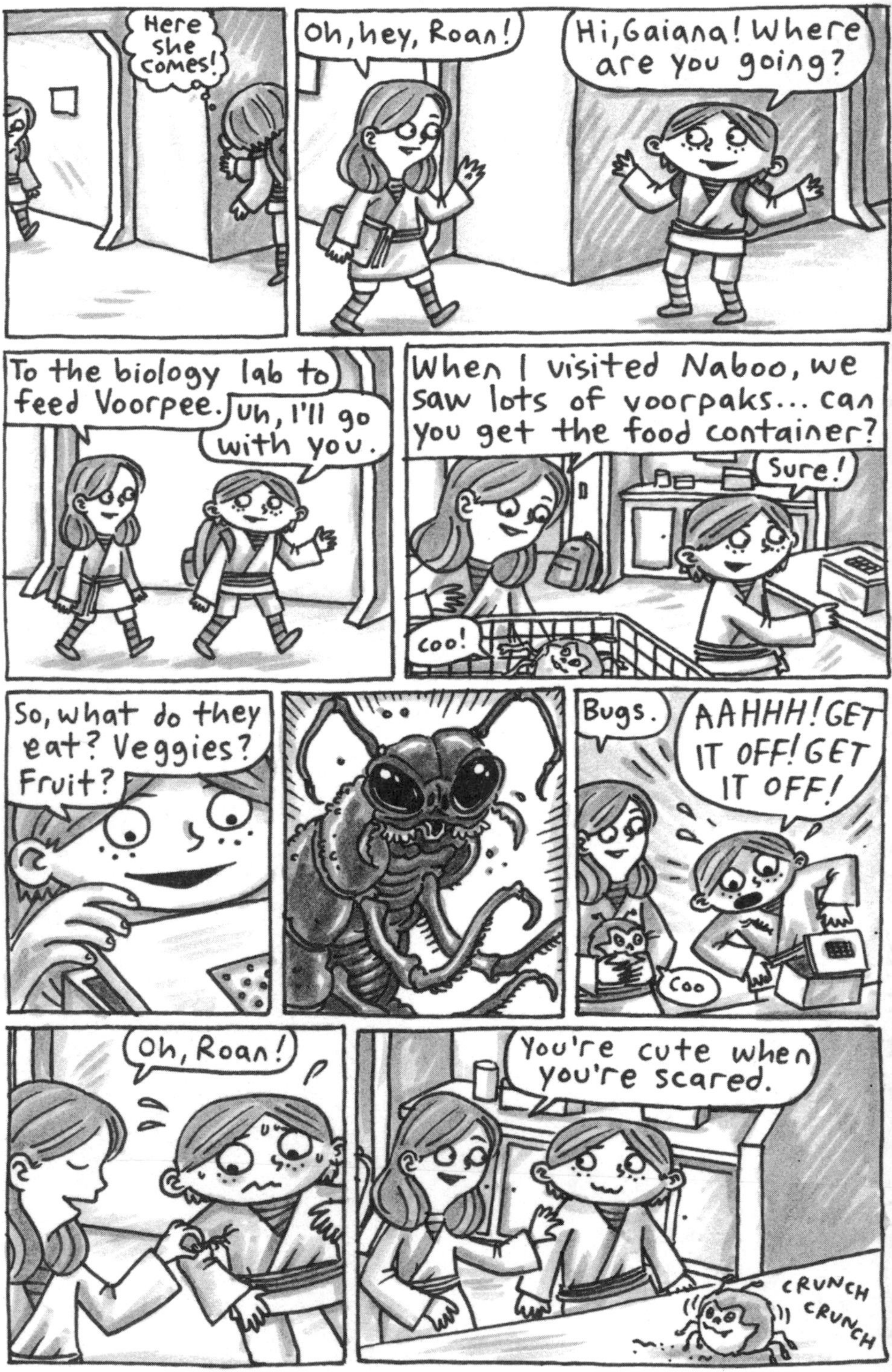
Here she comes!
Oh, hey, Roan!
Hi, Gaiana! Where are you going?
To the biology lab to feed Voorpee.
Uh, I'll go with you.
When I visited Naboo, we saw lots of voorpaks... can you get the food container?
Sure!
Coo!
So, what do they eat? Veggies? Fruit?
Bugs.
AAHHH! GET IT OFF! GET IT OFF!
Coo
Oh, Roan!
You're cute when you're scared.
CRUNCH
CRUNCH

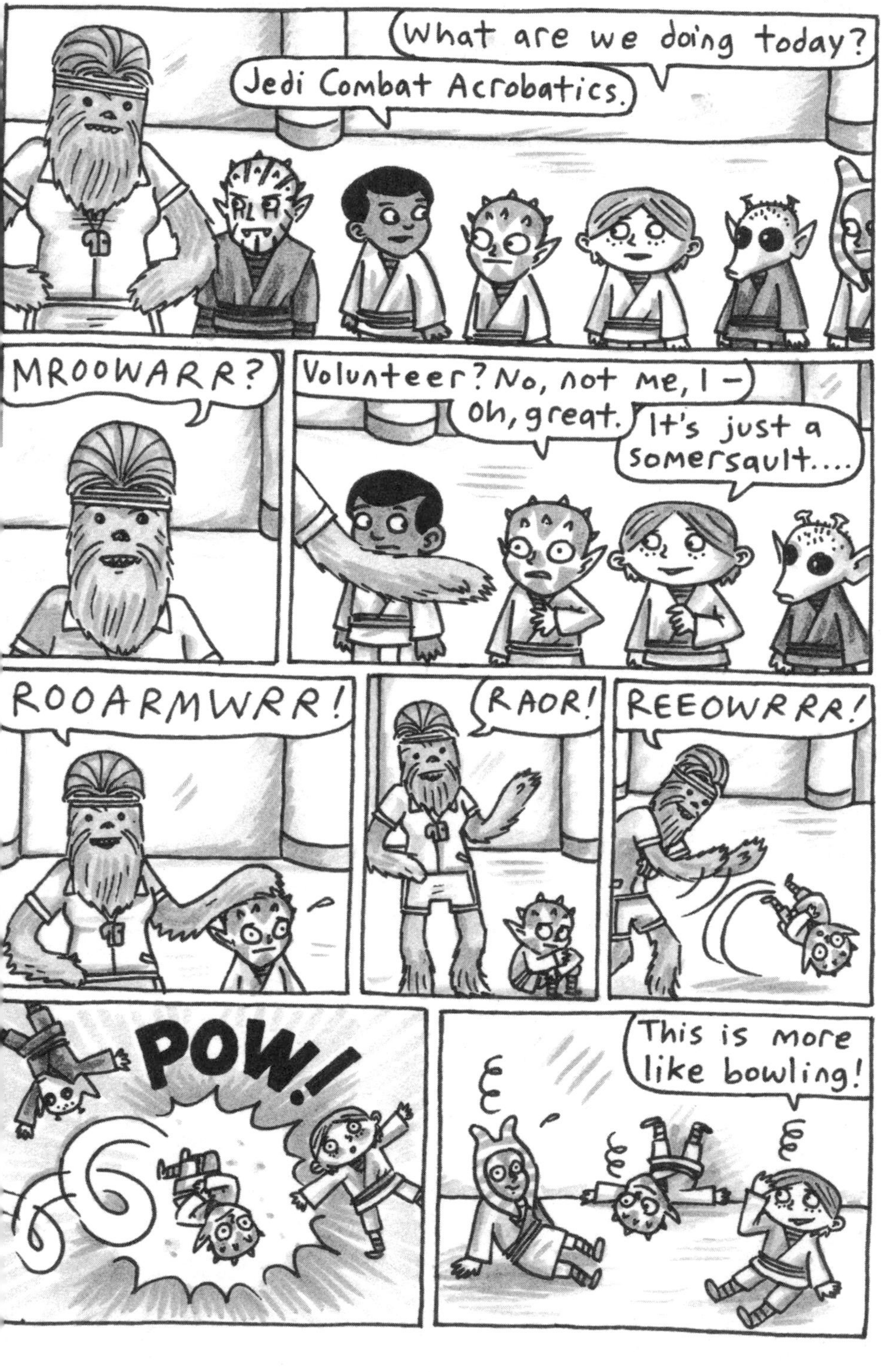

What are we doing today?
Jedi Combat Acrobatics.
MROOWARR?
Volunteer? No, not me, I —
Oh, great.
It's just a somersault....
ROOARMWRR!
RAOR!
REEOWRRR!
POW!
This is more like bowling!

The Padawan Observer

EDITED BY THE STUDENTS OF JEDI ACADEMY · VOL. MXIII #1

WELCOME BACK!

The Padawans of the Coruscant Jedi Academy returned for an exciting first week. Students were reportedly extremely excited for star pilot training, as shown by instructor Mr. Garfield's request for additional air sickness bags. Master Yoda was pleased with his first class, except that "lifting things with the Force all the time, too many students were."

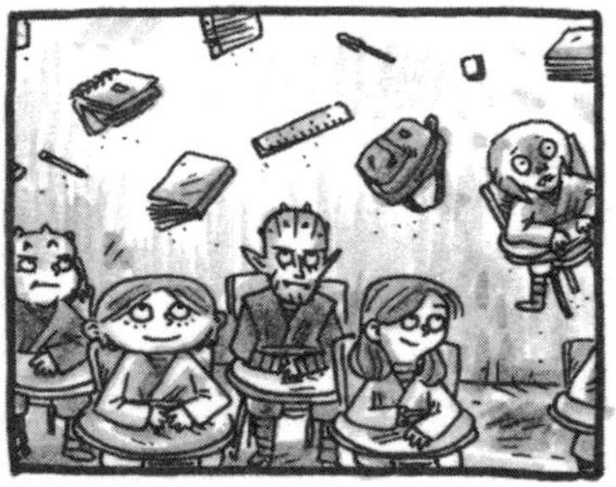

Meanwhile, Librarian Lackbar announced the first student social activity. "It's a dance!" she said. "It will be a Satine Hawkins dance, where girls ask boys." Padawans are asked to avoid wearing extra robes, which can be dangerous if the dancing is overly energetic.

INSIDE:

News.................2,7
Opinions.............3
Sports...............4
Holoreviews..........5-6
Ewok Pilot returns!...8

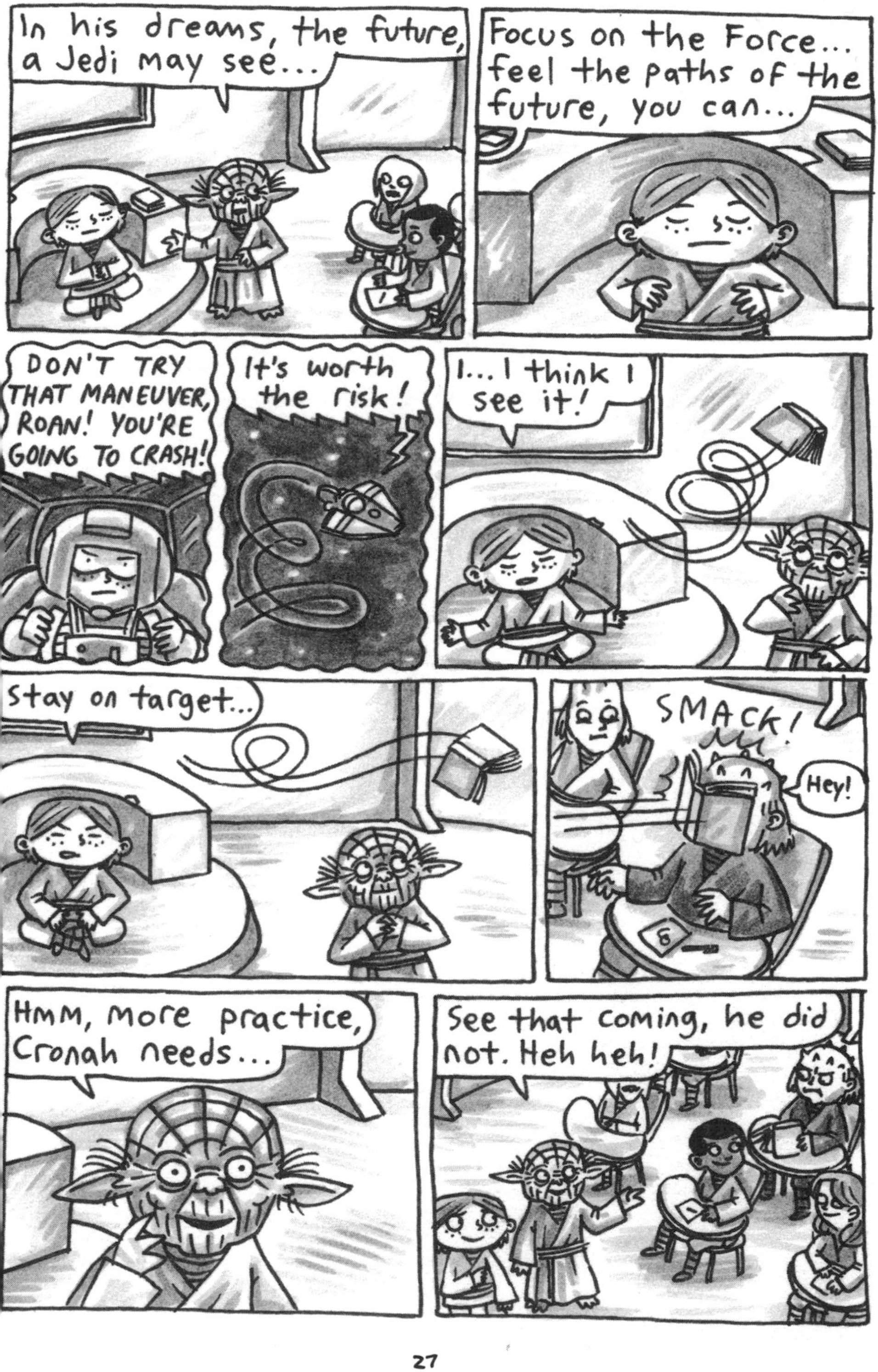
In his dreams, the future, a Jedi may see...
Focus on the Force... feel the paths of the future, you can...
DON'T TRY THAT MANEUVER, ROAN! YOU'RE GOING TO CRASH!
It's worth the risk!
I... I think I see it!
Stay on target...
SMACK!
Hey!
Hmm, more practice, Cronah needs...
See that coming, he did not. Heh heh!

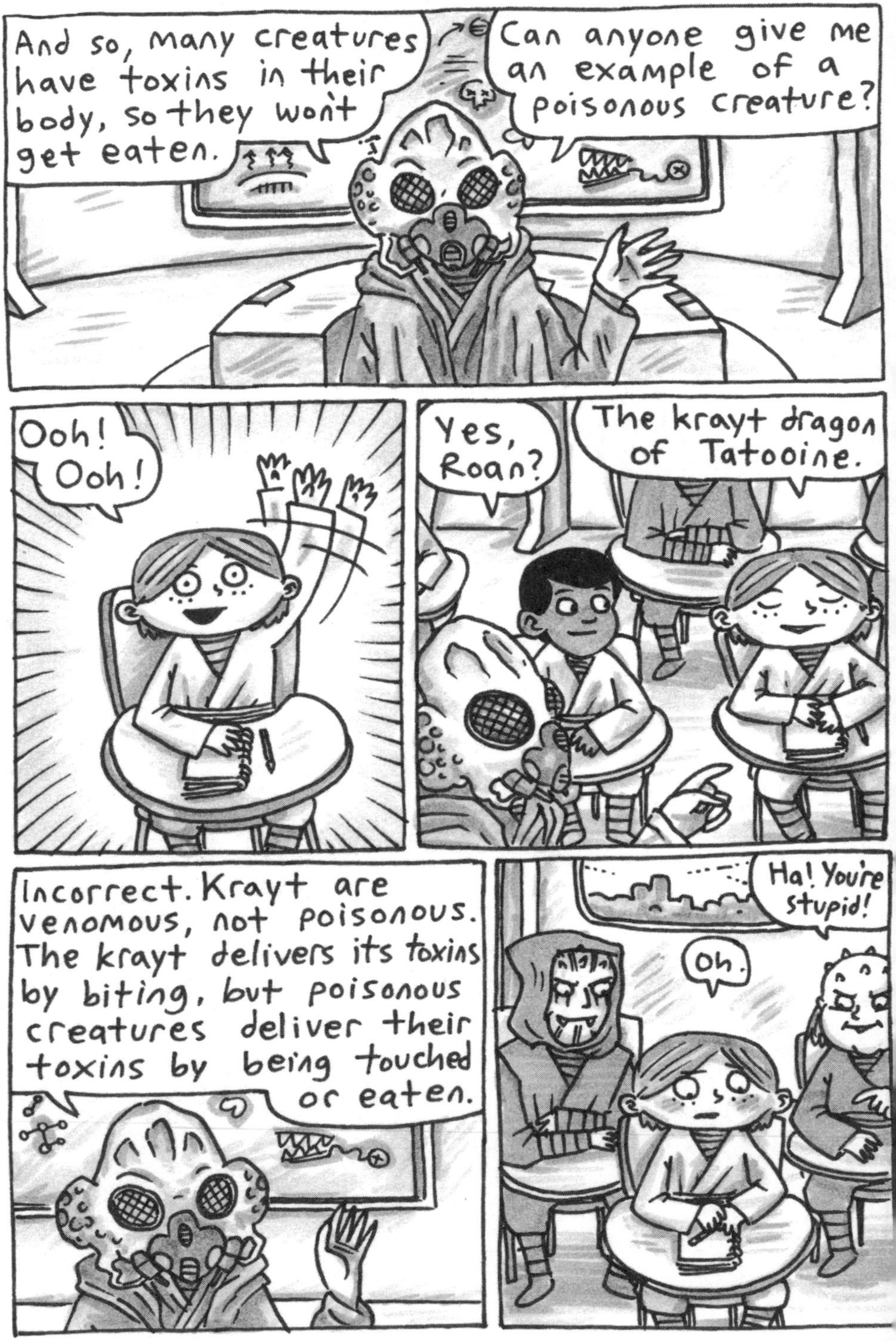

And so, many creatures have toxins in their body, so they won't get eaten.
Can anyone give me an example of a poisonous creature?
Ooh! Ooh!
Yes, Roan?
The krayt dragon of Tatooine.
Incorrect. Krayt are venomous, not poisonous. The krayt delivers its toxins by biting, but poisonous creatures deliver their toxins by being touched or eaten.
Ha! You're stupid!
Oh.

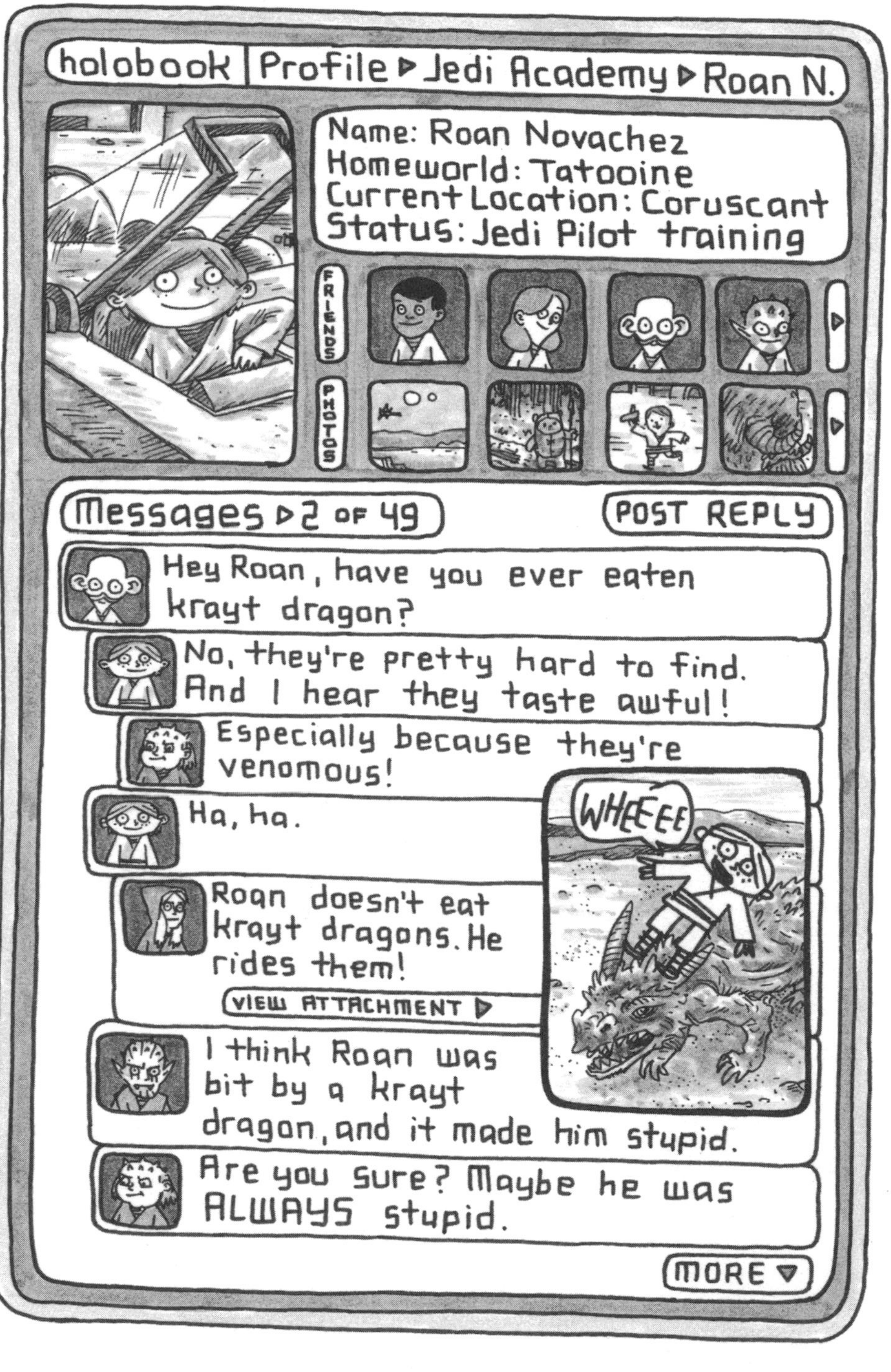
holobook
Profile ▸ Jedi Academy ▸ Roan N.
Name: Roan Novachez
Homeworld: Tatooine
Current Location: Coruscant
Status: Jedi Pilot training
FRIENDS
PHOTOS
Messages ▸ 2 OF 49
POST REPLY
Hey Roan, have you ever eaten krayt dragon?
No, they're pretty hard to find. And I hear they taste awful!
Especially because they're venomous!
Ha, ha.
Roan doesn't eat krayt dragons. He rides them!
VIEW ATTACHMENT ▸
WHEEEEE
I think Roan was bit by a krayt dragon, and it made him stupid.
Are you sure? Maybe he was ALWAYS stupid.
MORE ▾

MONODAY

Everyone here is really into Holobook but I'm starting to think the only thing it's used for is making fun of me. I also don't know how anyone has time to update so much, with all of the homework we have. I thought I might save some time by signing up for tutoring sessions with T-P30, but I found out he actually makes

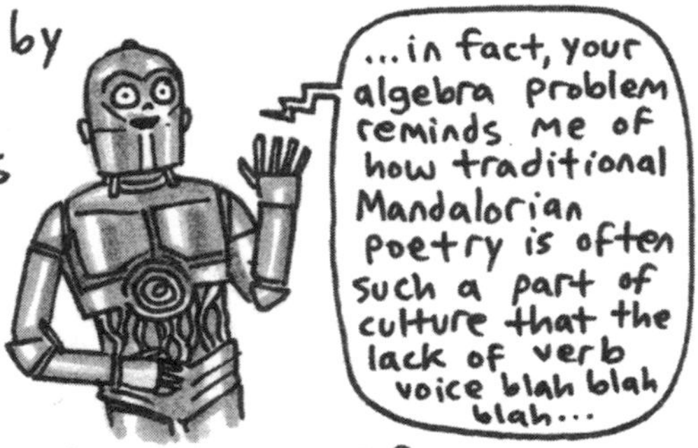
...in fact, your algebra problem reminds me of how traditional Mandalorian poetry is often such a part of culture that the lack of verb voice blah blah blah...

doing homework take LONGER. I think the teachers are giving us more homework this year, too. Maybe that's why they're giving us a school dance so early in the semester? It'll be good because I'll have a chance to spend time with Gaiana. We hung out a little last week, I guess, but it would be cool to see her at the dance. We could even hang out afterward, if she's not doing anything else.

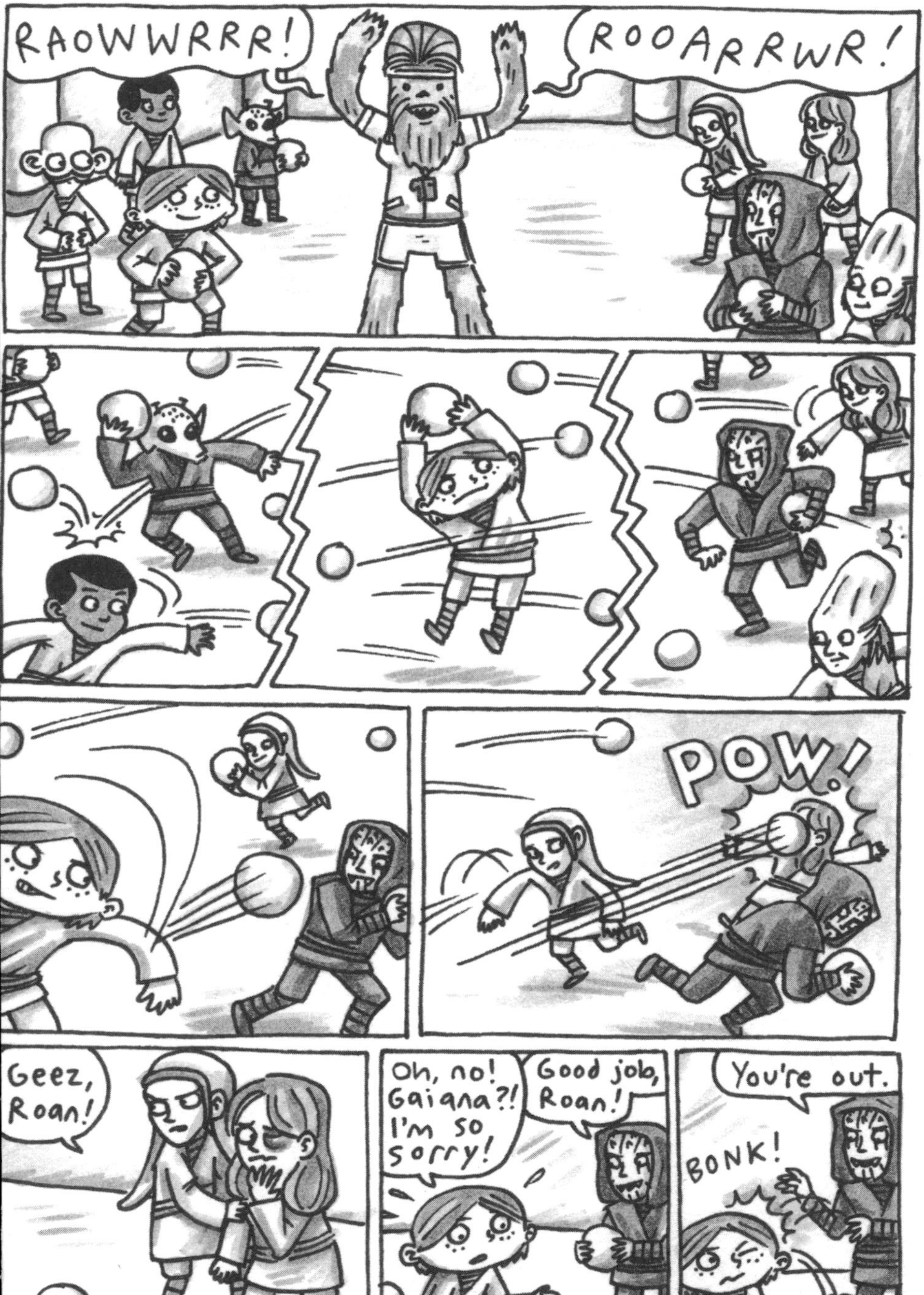
RAOWWRRR!
ROOARRRWR!
POW!
Geez, Roan!
Oh, no! Gaiana?! I'm so sorry!
Good job, Roan!
You're out.
BONK!

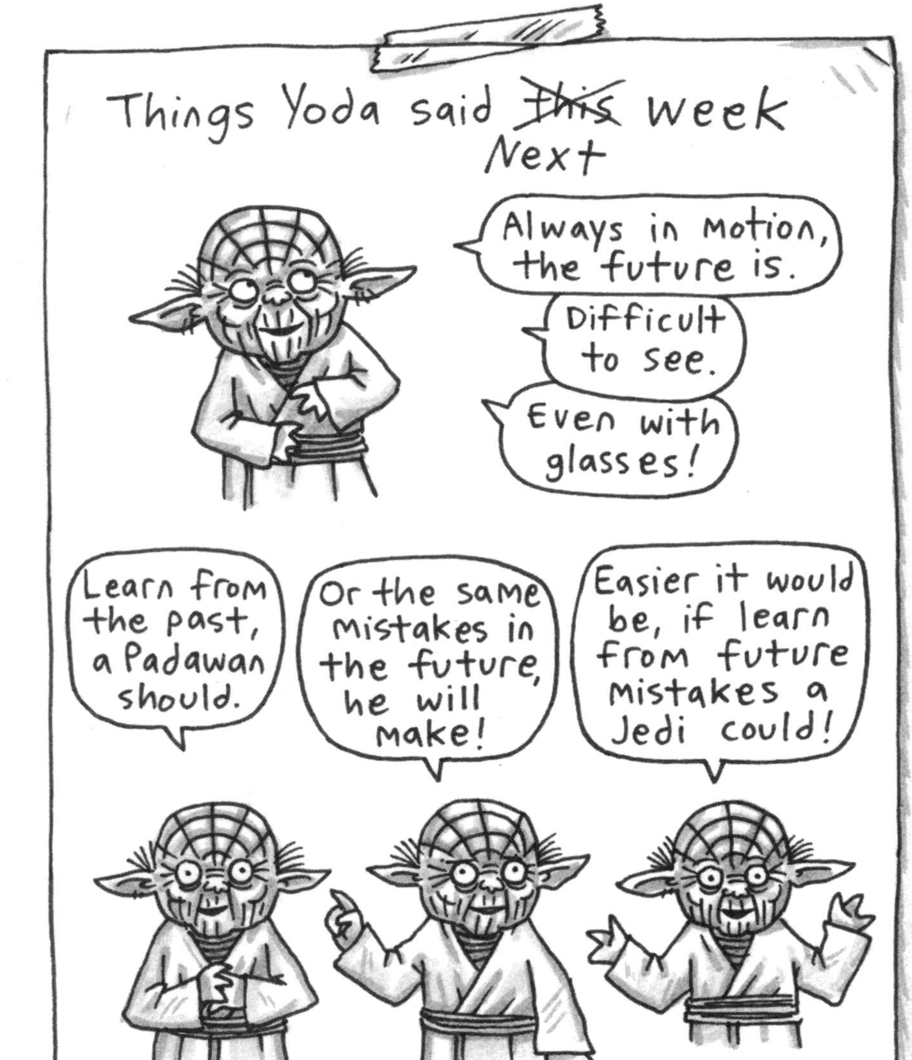
Things Yoda said ~~This~~ week
Next
Always in motion, the future is.
Difficult to see.
Even with glasses!
Learn from the past, a Padawan should.
Or the same mistakes in the future, he will make!
Easier it would be, if learn from future mistakes a Jedi could!
Yoda in the future (will be even MORE wrinkly and have MORE ear hair)

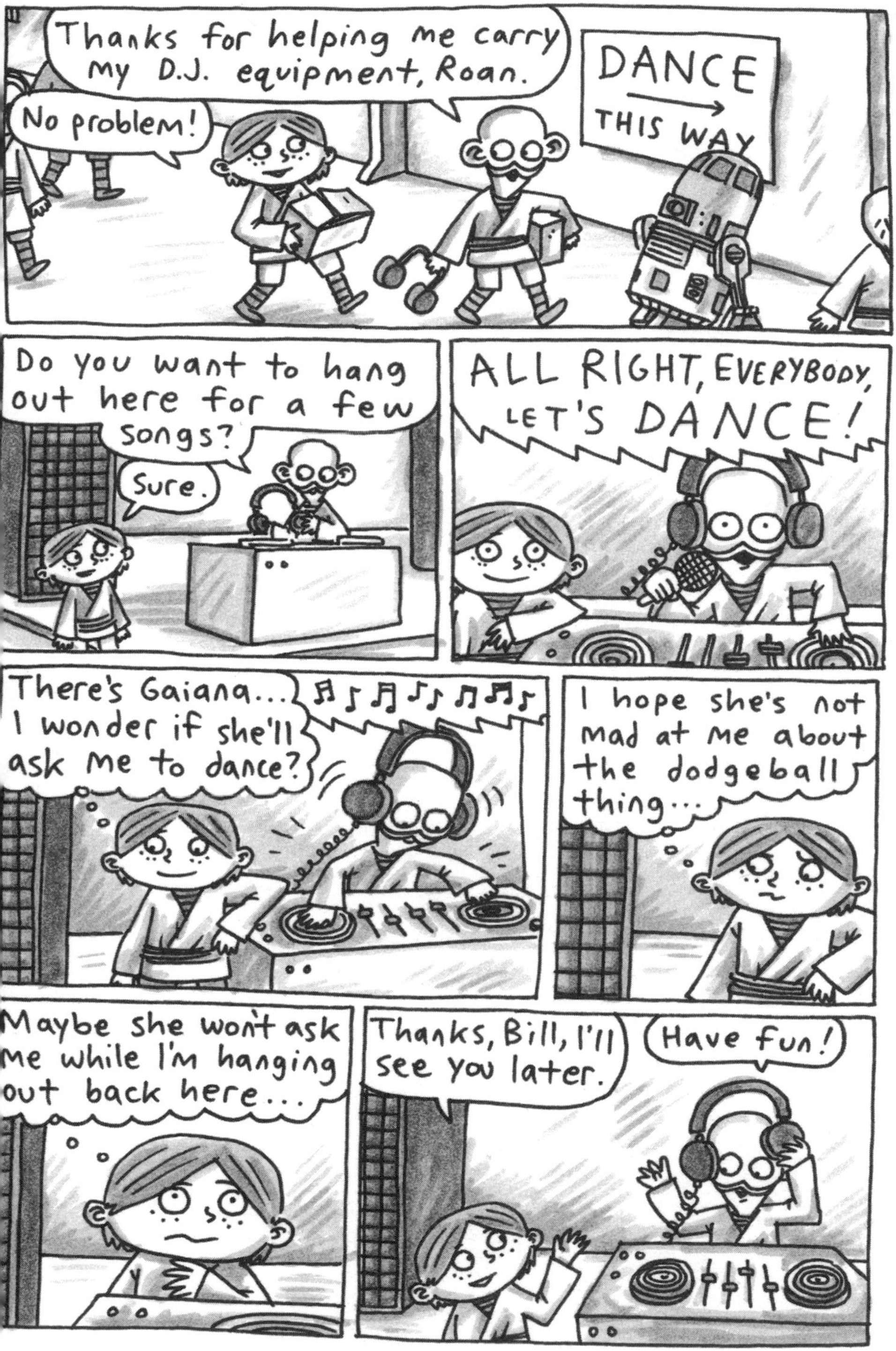

Thanks for helping me carry my D.J. equipment, Roan.
No problem!
DANCE THIS WAY
Do you want to hang out here for a few songs?
Sure.
ALL RIGHT, EVERYBODY, LET'S DANCE!
There's Gaiana... I wonder if she'll ask me to dance?
I hope she's not mad at me about the dodgeball thing...
Maybe she won't ask me while I'm hanging out back here...
Thanks, Bill, I'll see you later.
Have fun!

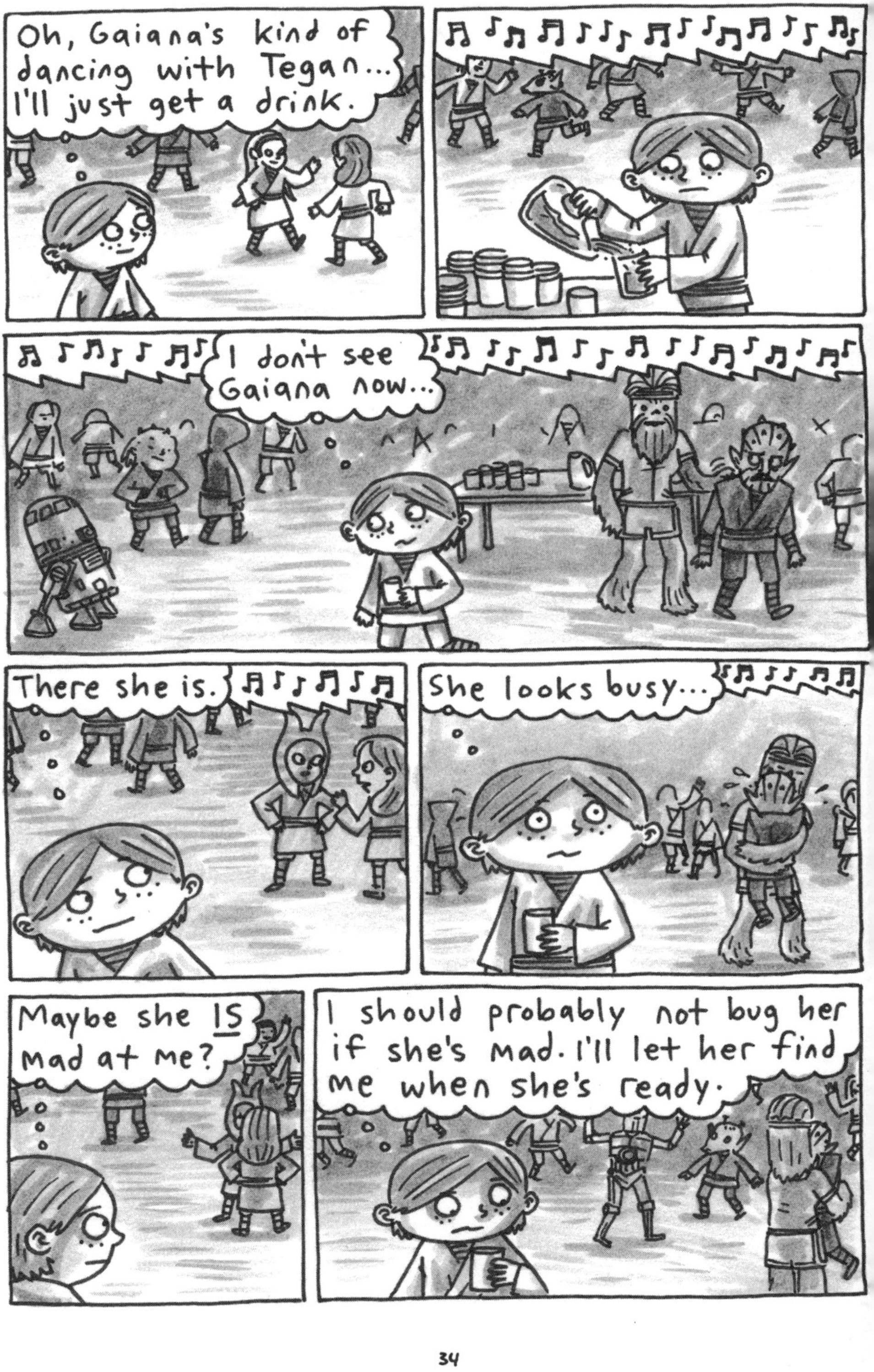
Oh, Gaiana's kind of dancing with Tegan... I'll just get a drink.
I don't see Gaiana now...
There she is.
She looks busy...
Maybe she IS mad at me?
I should probably not bug her if she's mad. I'll let her find me when she's ready.

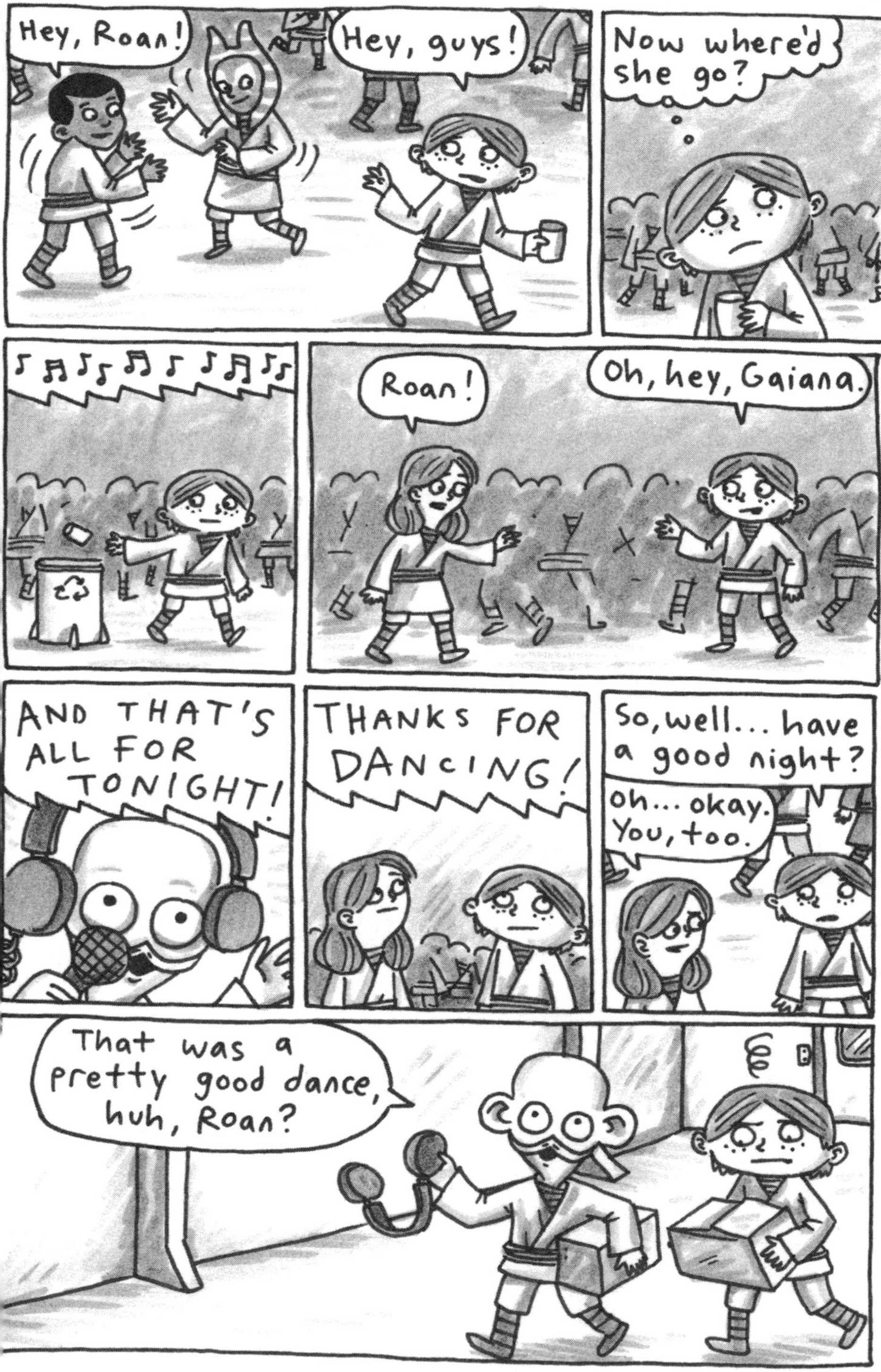
Hey, Roan!
Hey, guys!
Now where'd she go?
Roan!
Oh, hey, Gaiana.
AND THAT'S ALL FOR TONIGHT!
THANKS FOR DANCING!
So, well... have a good night?
Oh... okay. You, too.
That was a pretty good dance, huh, Roan?

Roan—
Gaiana thinks you're avoiding her.

I'm not. I thought SHE didn't want to dance with ME.

Why don't you tell her that?

I just said I wasn't avoiding her.

No, you just wrote that in a note to me.

Can you tell her?

You should talk to her.

So, will you tell her?

QUADDAY

After the dance, Gaiana asked to switch seats from next to me in homeroom. She must be mad at me, but I didn't do anything. The dodgeball thing was an accident. I hope she wasn't changing seats because of me. Maybe it was because of Cronah, who's been shooting spitballs at me, but his aim isn't great and sometimes they hit her. Pasha sits on the other side of me, but he learned how to use the Force to deflect the spitballs.

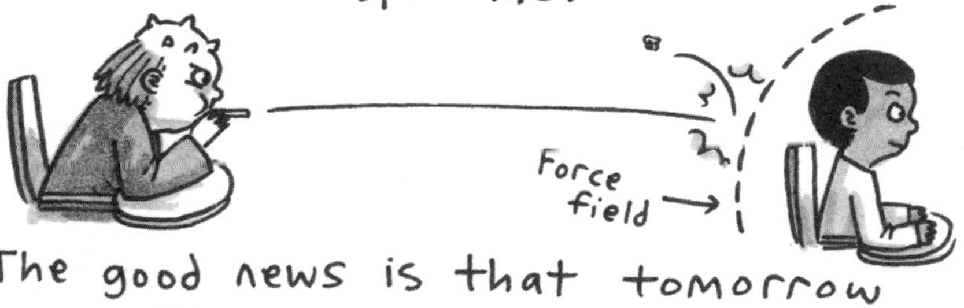
Force field

The good news is that tomorrow we're FINALLY going to get to use the star pilot simulators in flight training class! Finally, something I'VE been preparing my whole life for. After this, no one will look at me the same, because I'm going to beat all of their test scores by a whole bunch. I'll show them!!

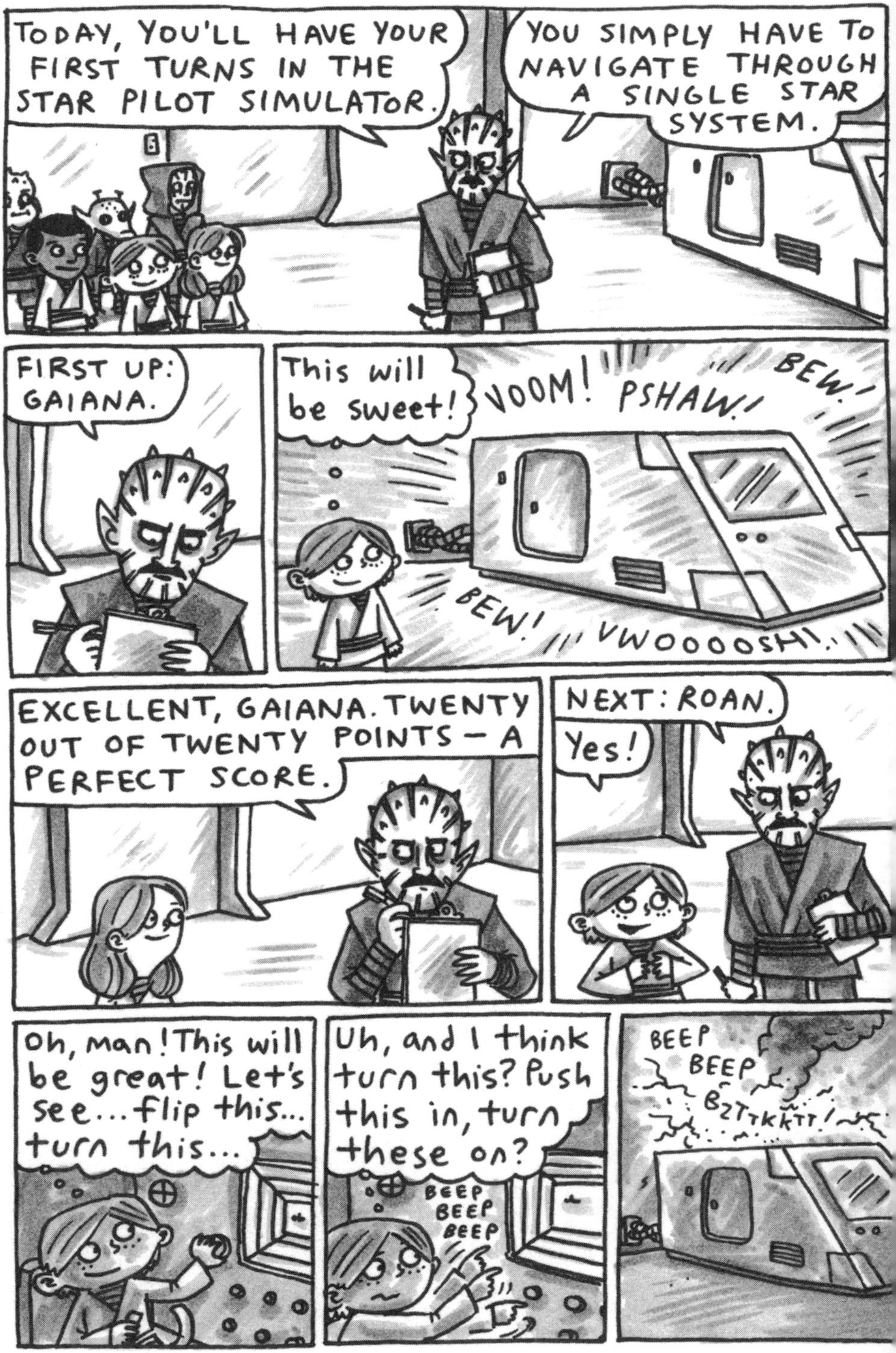
TODAY, YOU'LL HAVE YOUR FIRST TURNS IN THE STAR PILOT SIMULATOR.
YOU SIMPLY HAVE TO NAVIGATE THROUGH A SINGLE STAR SYSTEM.
FIRST UP: GAIANA.
This will be sweet!
VOOM! PSHAW! BEW!
BEW! VWOOOOSH!
EXCELLENT, GAIANA. TWENTY OUT OF TWENTY POINTS — A PERFECT SCORE.
NEXT: ROAN.
Yes!
Oh, man! This will be great! Let's see... flip this... turn this...
Uh, and I think turn this? Push this in, turn these on?
BEEP BEEP BEEP
BEEP BEEP BZTTKKTT!

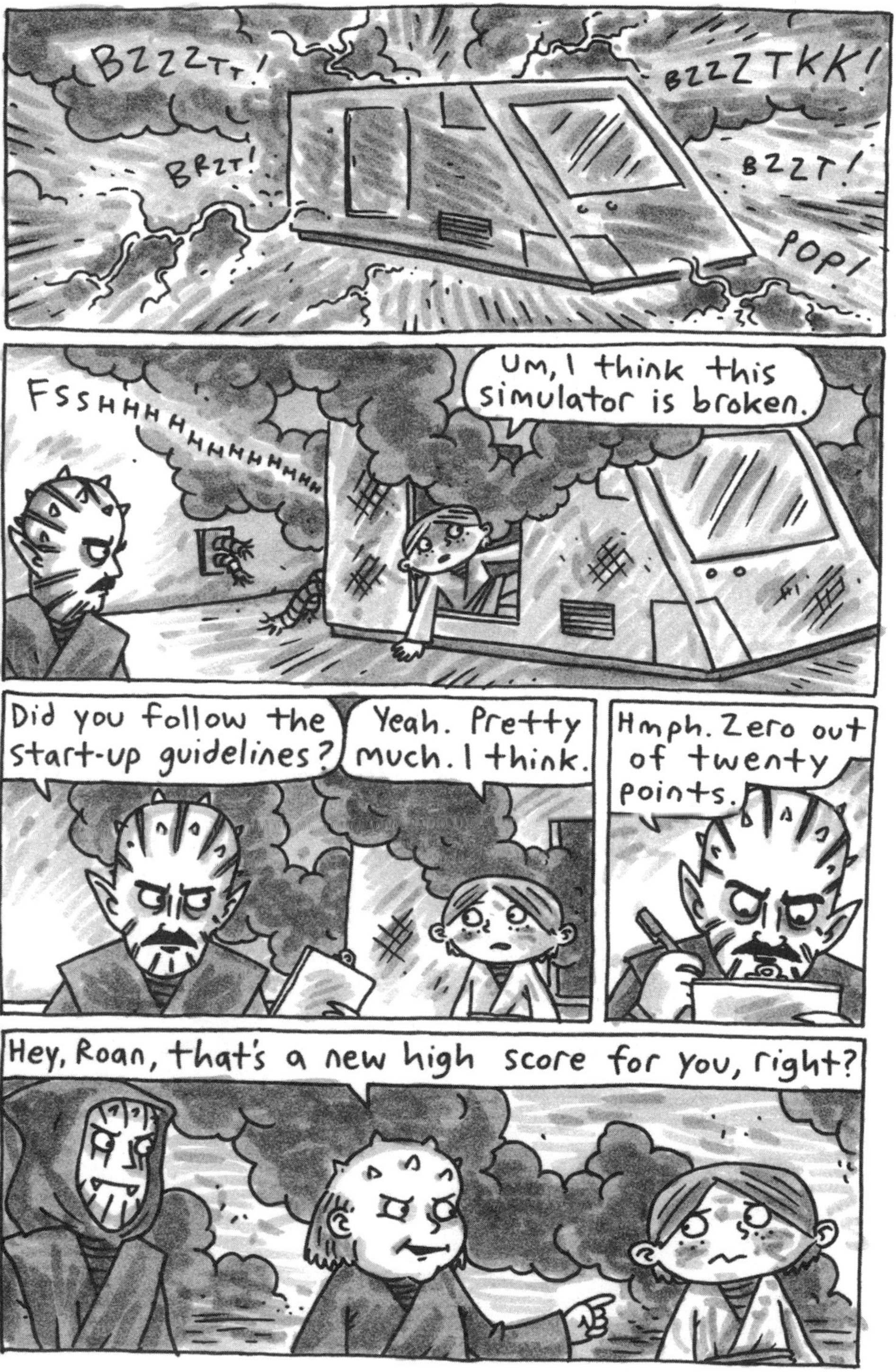
BZZZTT!
BRZT!
BZZZTKK!
BZZT!
POP!
FSSHHHHHHHHHHHHH
Um, I think this simulator is broken.
Did you follow the start-up guidelines?
Yeah. Pretty much. I think.
Hmph. Zero out of twenty points.
Hey, Roan, that's a new high score for you, right?

HEPTADAY

Star pilot training has so far <u>NOT</u> been going according to plan. It turns out reading the G.P.G.I.F.T.M.A.W. is important, because Mr. Garfield makes us take a quiz on it every other day. I bet he has to spend all night thinking of questions for them. Then there was the ~~incidint~~ incident with the flight simulator, which totally CAN'T be my fault. Everyone was looking at me like I was a doofus, but that thing was already old and falling apart. No one will believe me because now it's even more broken down.

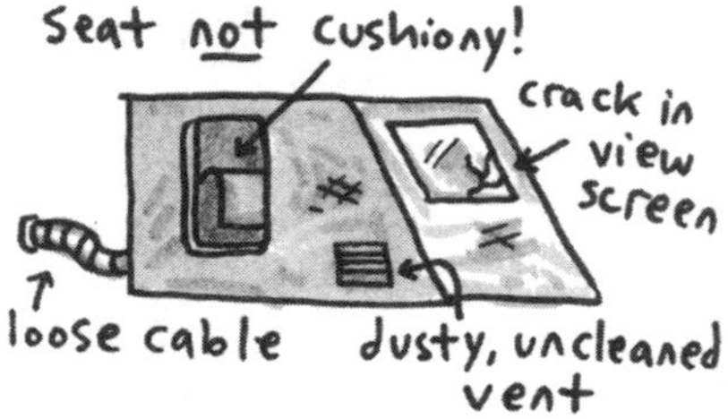
Seat not cushiony!
crack in view screen
loose cable
dusty, uncleaned vent

When we get to use the simulators again, everyone will expect me to be perfect, or they'll give me a super-hard time. I'm going to have to work harder than anyone, which isn't fair.

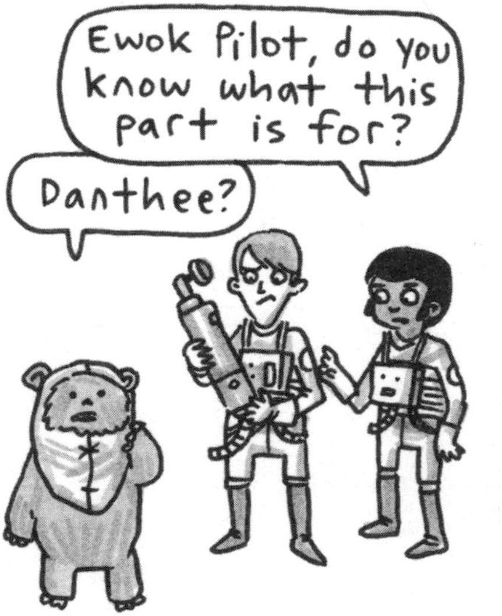
Ewok Pilot, do you know what this part is for?
Danthee?

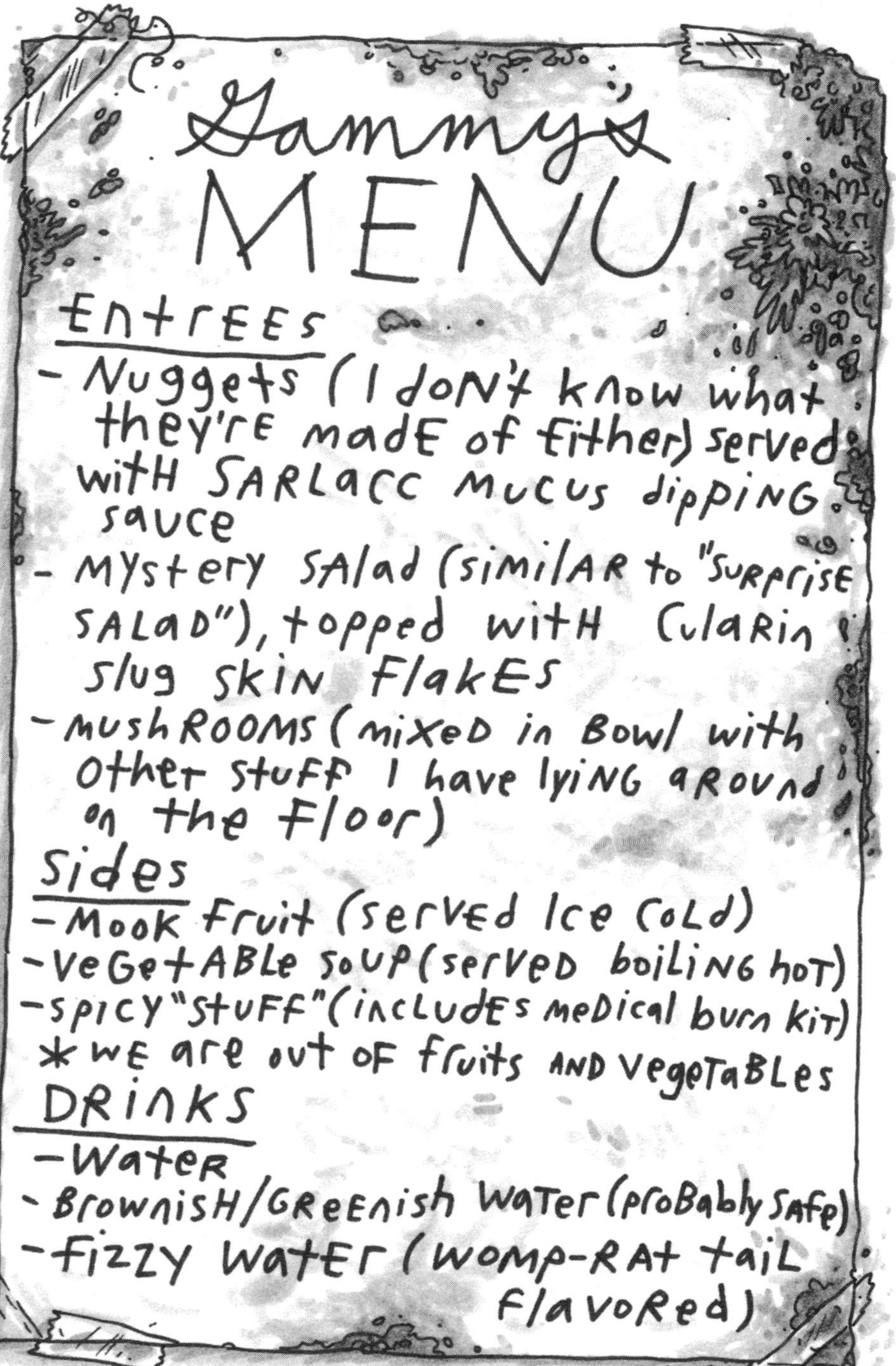
Gammy's
MENU
Entrees
- Nuggets (I don't know what they're made of either) served with SARLACC MUCUS dipping sauce
- MYstery SAlad (similAR to "SURPRISE SALAD"), topped with Cularin slug skin FlakES
- mushROOMS (mixeD in Bowl with other stuff I have lying aRound on the Floor)
Sides
- Mook Fruit (served Ice Cold)
- veGetABLe soup (serveD boiling hoT)
- spicy "stuff" (includes meDical burn kit)
* WE are out of fruits AND vegetaBLes
DRINKS
- Water
- BrownisH/GReenish Water (proBably Safe)
- Fizzy water (WOMP-RAT tail flavoRed)

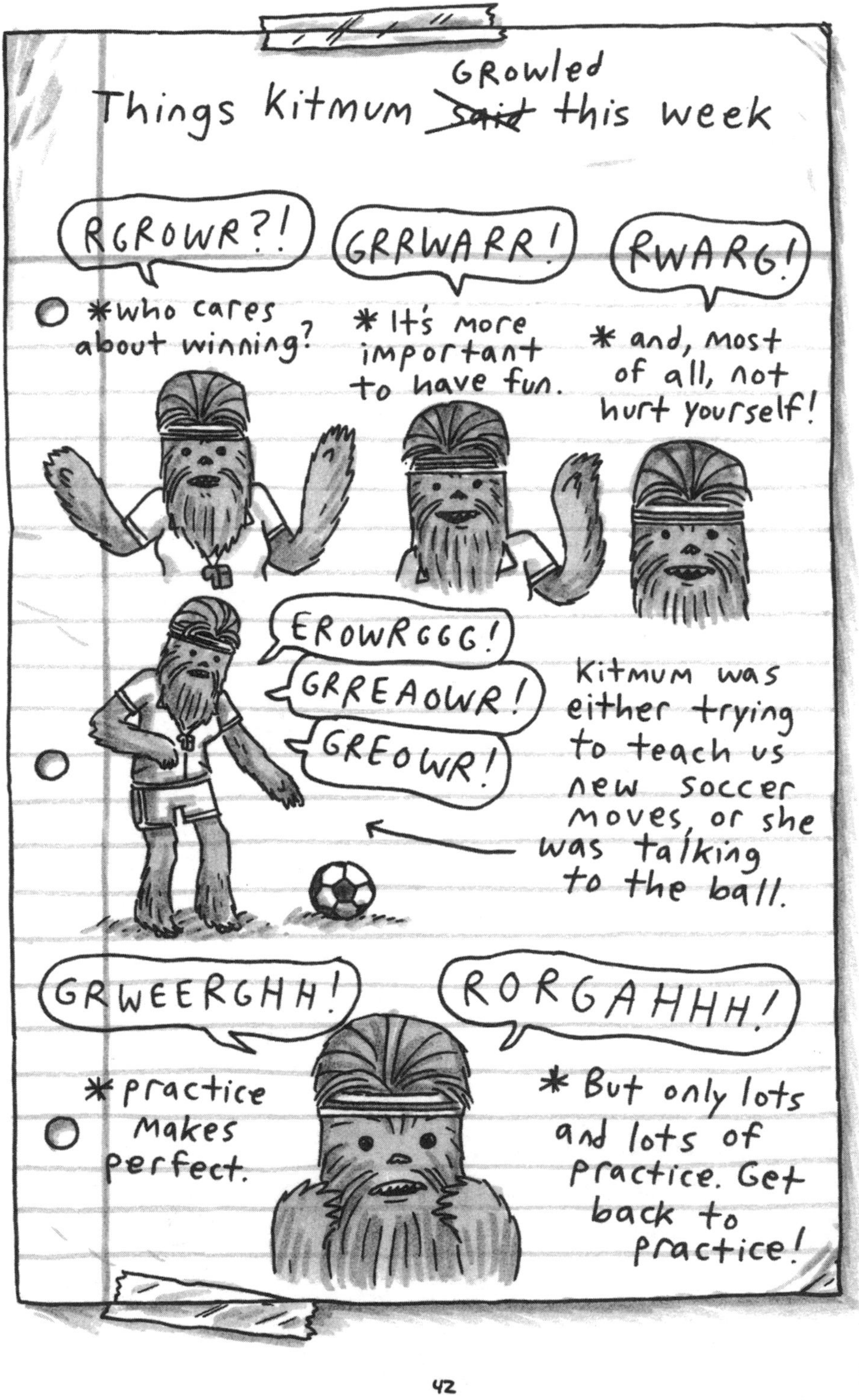
Things Kitmum ~~said~~ GROWLED this week
RGROWR?!
*who cares about winning?
GRRWARR!
*It's more important to have fun.
RWARG!
*and, most of all, not hurt yourself!
EROWRGGG!
GRREAOWR!
GREOWR!
Kitmum was either trying to teach us new soccer moves, or she was talking to the ball.
GRWEERGHH!
*practice makes perfect.
RORGAHHH!
*But only lots and lots of practice. Get back to practice!

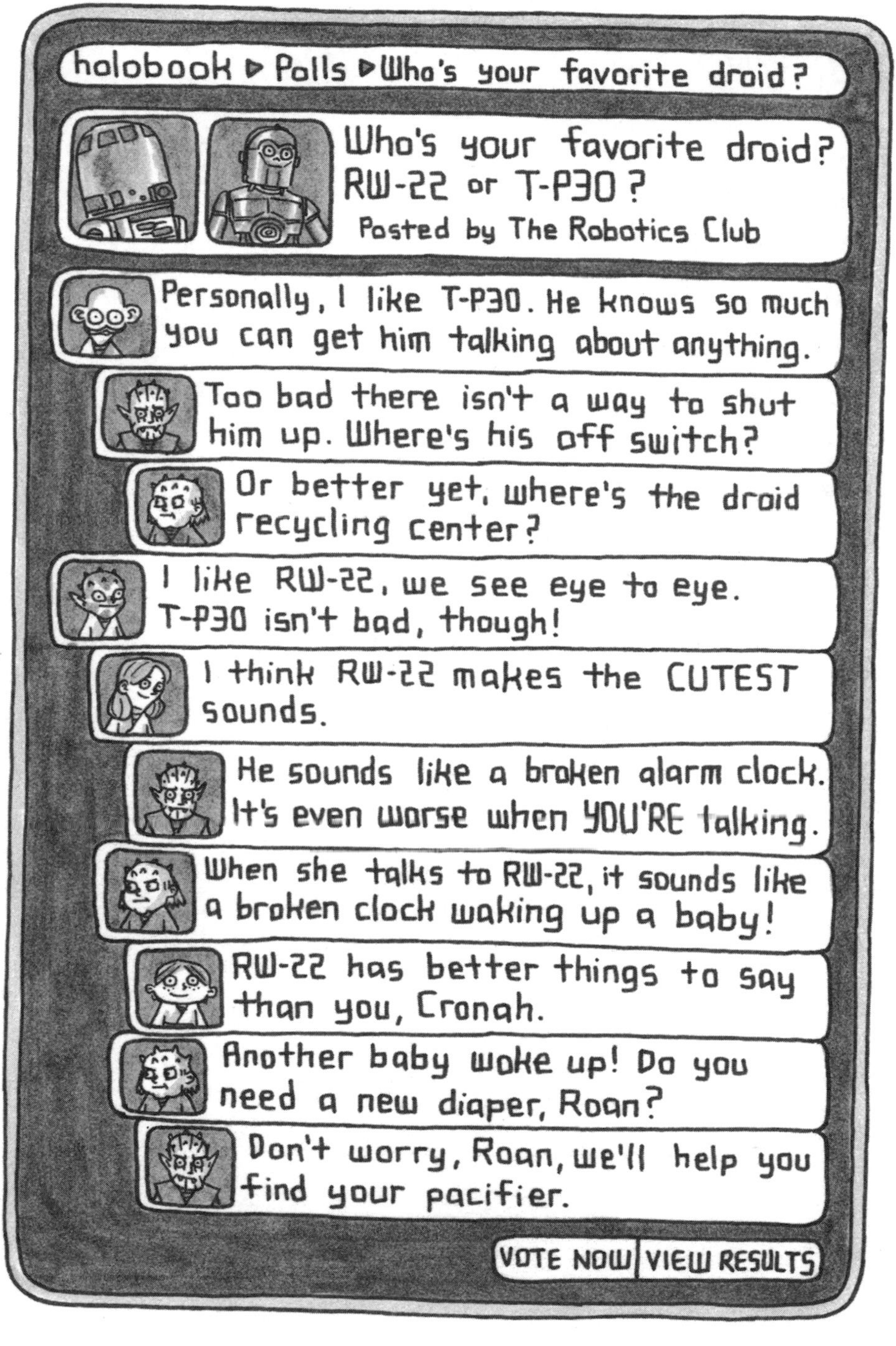
holobook ▶ Polls ▶ Who's your favorite droid?
Who's your favorite droid? RW-22 or T-P30?
Posted by The Robotics Club
Personally, I like T-P30. He knows so much you can get him talking about anything.
Too bad there isn't a way to shut him up. Where's his off switch?
Or better yet, where's the droid recycling center?
I like RW-22, we see eye to eye. T-P30 isn't bad, though!
I think RW-22 makes the CUTEST sounds.
He sounds like a broken alarm clock. It's even worse when YOU'RE talking.
When she talks to RW-22, it sounds like a broken clock waking up a baby!
RW-22 has better things to say than you, Cronah.
Another baby woke up! Do you need a new diaper, Roan?
Don't worry, Roan, we'll help you find your pacifier.
VOTE NOW
VIEW RESULTS

DUODAY

It turns out we're getting new star pilot simulators. We were already scheduled to get them, so the simulator that exploded when I was in it must have already been old and broken. No one seems to think that, though. I don't know how just pushing a bunch of buttons could break it! I've been re-reading the G.P.G.I.F.T.M.A.W.

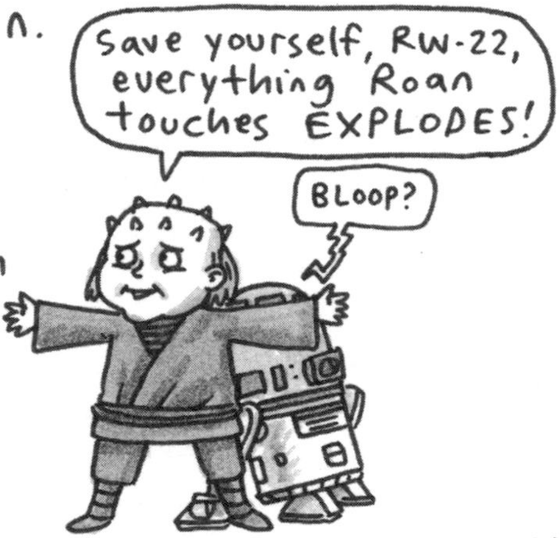
Save yourself, RW-22, everything Roan touches EXPLODES!
BLOOP?

and I'm sure I entered all of the codes in the right sequence. Well, pretty sure. I'm going to keep studying until I can show everyone that I really know what I'm doing. I'm also starting work on my project for Librarian Lackbar's public speaking class. We all have a solo project where we stand up and give a "how-to" speech in front of the class. Which kind of sounds like the teachers getting us to do their work for them, even if Librarian Lackbar says it's so that we'll learn about speaking in public (which Jedi have to do as peacekeepers) and working alone (which is how Jedi have to work sometimes). It's funny that Librarian Lackbar is teaching this class, because she sounds like she's talking underwater. I think I've got a good idea for my presentation. I'm going to give a speech about ~~Medatating~~ meditating. I'm going to make it funny and entertaining, everyone will enjoy that. Maybe I'll even make a minicomic

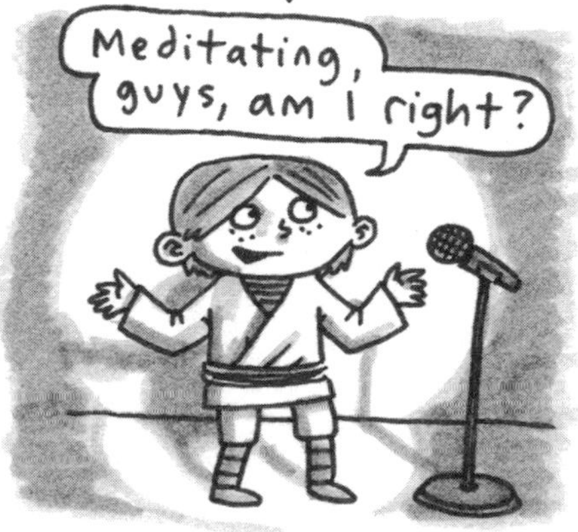
Meditating, guys, am I right?

to hand out with my talk. I could also check out the Jedi Archives. There's some great books I could find with information that Master Yoda hasn't taught us yet. The neat thing is that if everyone falls asleep during my speech, it means I gave a good speech, not a boring one!

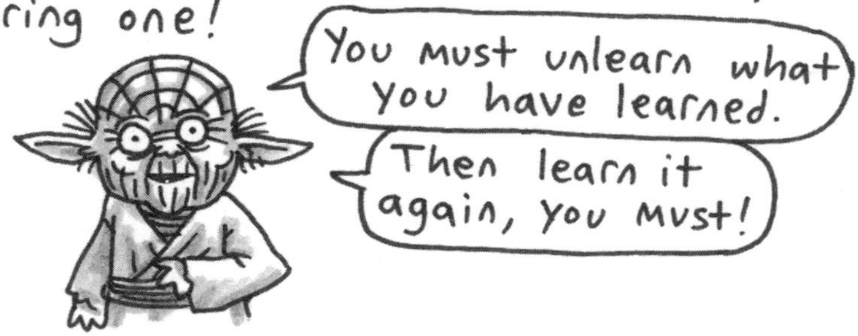
You must unlearn what you have learned.
Then learn it again, you must!

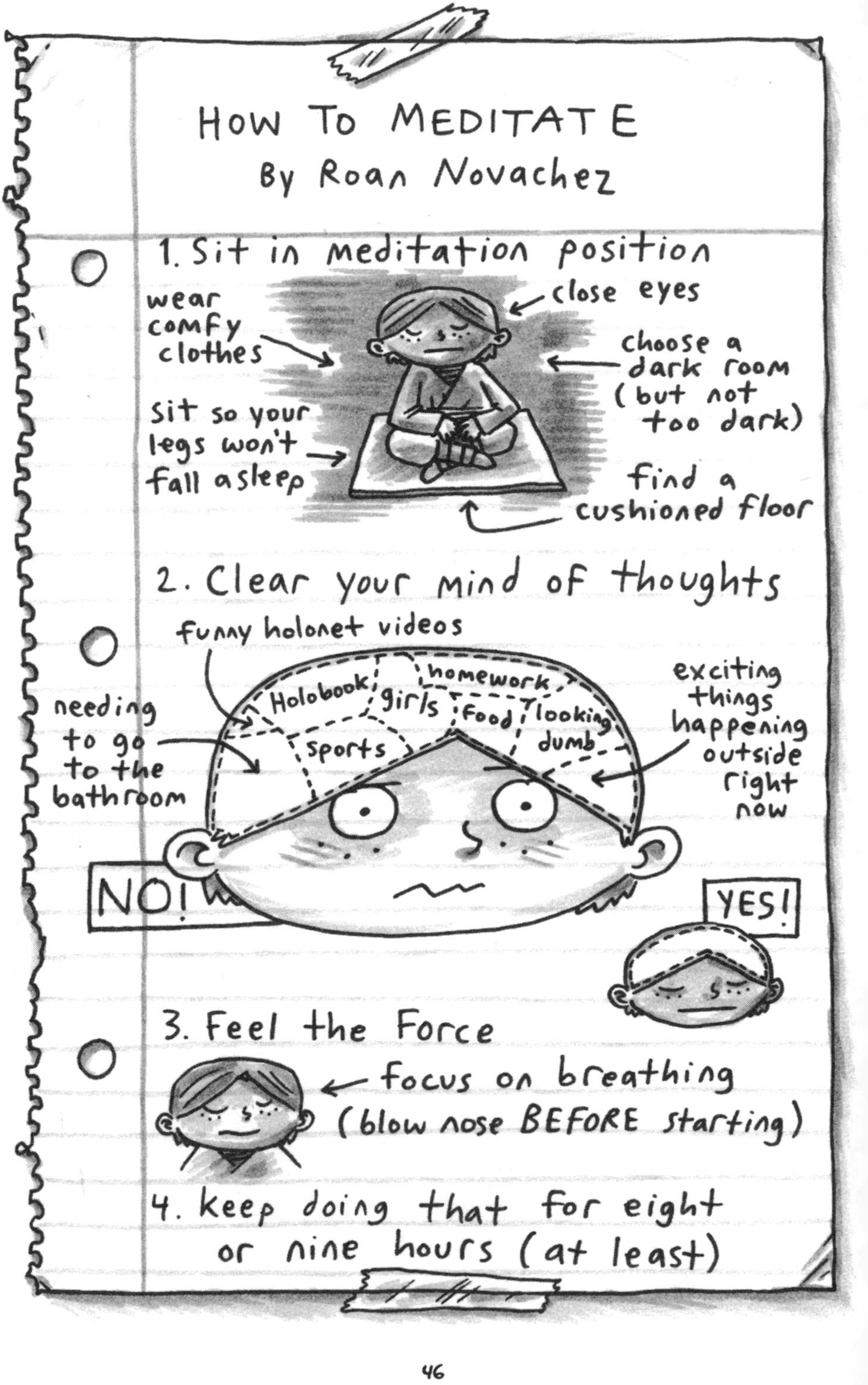
HOW TO MEDITATE
By Roan Novachez
1. Sit in meditation position
wear comfy clothes
close eyes
choose a dark room (but not too dark)
sit so your legs won't fall asleep
find a cushioned floor
2. Clear your mind of thoughts
funny holonet videos
Holobook
homework
girls
Food
looking dumb
sports
needing to go to the bathroom
exciting things happening outside right now
NO!
YES!
3. Feel the Force
focus on breathing (blow nose BEFORE starting)
4. keep doing that for eight or nine hours (at least)

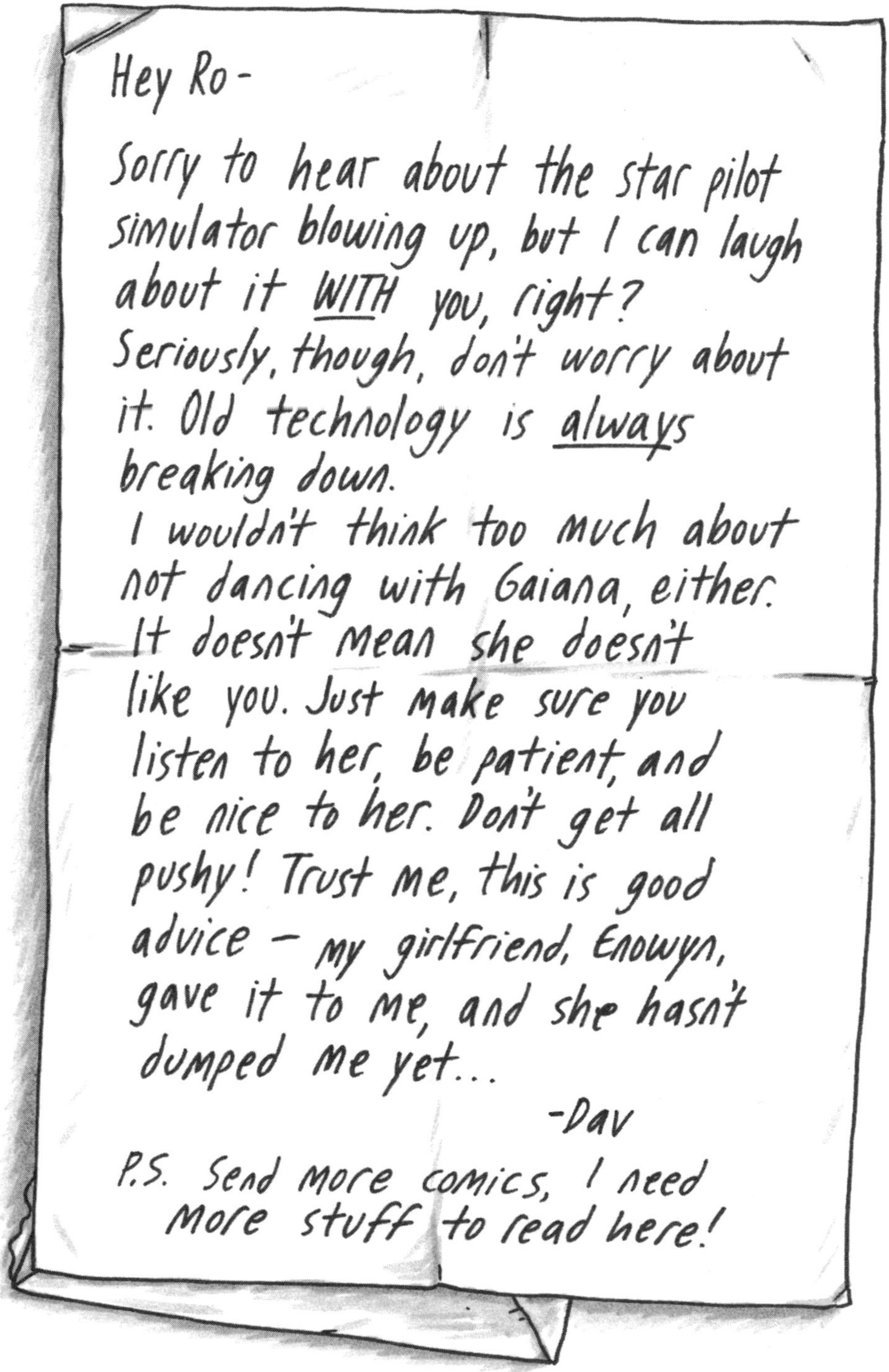
Hey Ro-

Sorry to hear about the star pilot simulator blowing up, but I can laugh about it WITH you, right? Seriously, though, don't worry about it. Old technology is always breaking down.

I wouldn't think too much about not dancing with Gaiana, either. It doesn't mean she doesn't like you. Just make sure you listen to her, be patient, and be nice to her. Don't get all pushy! Trust me, this is good advice - my girlfriend, Enowyn, gave it to me, and she hasn't dumped me yet...

-Dav

P.S. Send more comics, I need more stuff to read here!

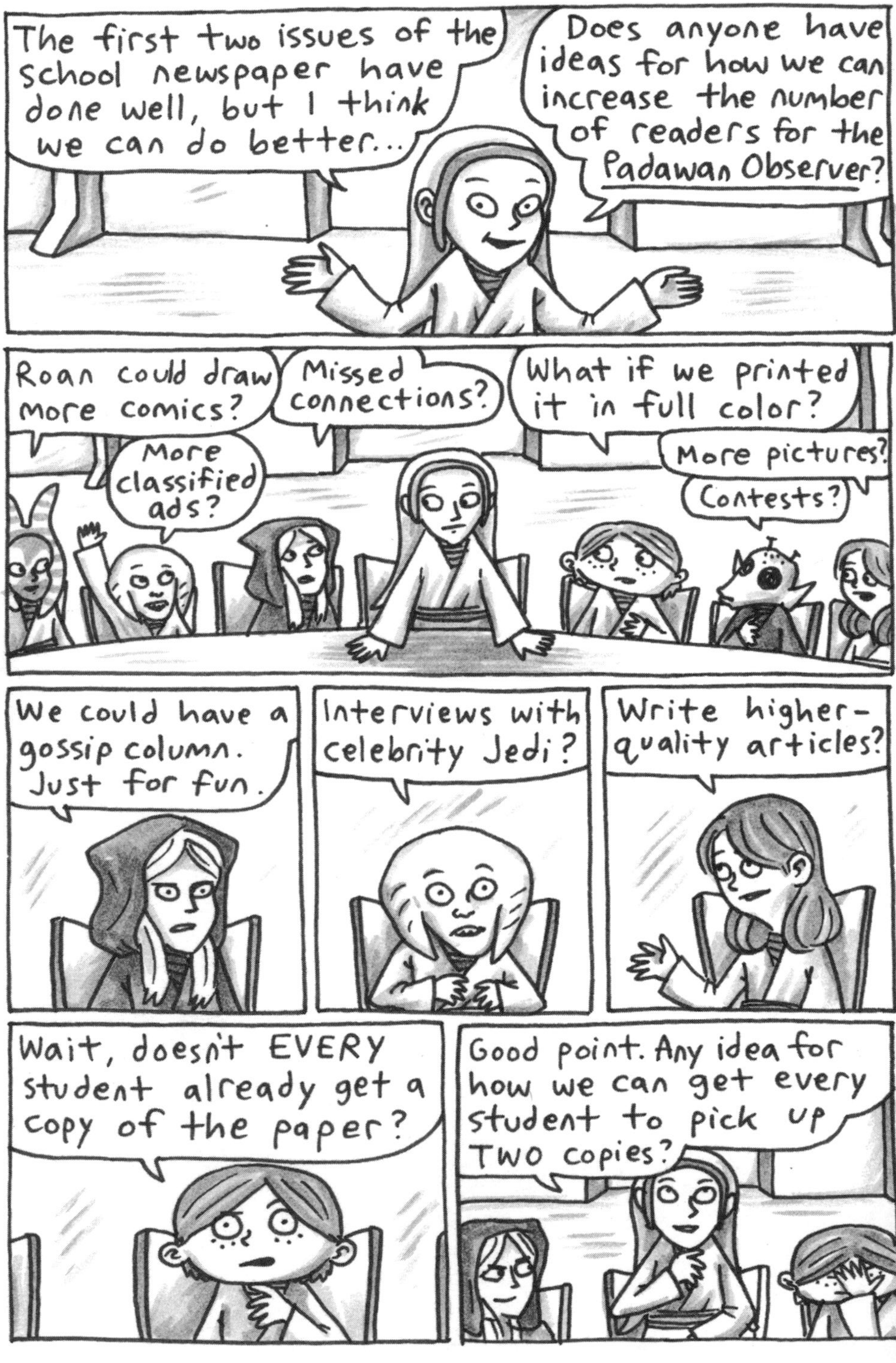
The first two issues of the school newspaper have done well, but I think we can do better...
Does anyone have ideas for how we can increase the number of readers for the Padawan Observer?
Roan could draw more comics?
Missed connections?
What if we printed it in full color?
More classified ads?
More pictures?
Contests?
We could have a gossip column. Just for fun.
Interviews with celebrity Jedi?
Write higher-quality articles?
Wait, doesn't EVERY student already get a copy of the paper?
Good point. Any idea for how we can get every student to pick up TWO copies?

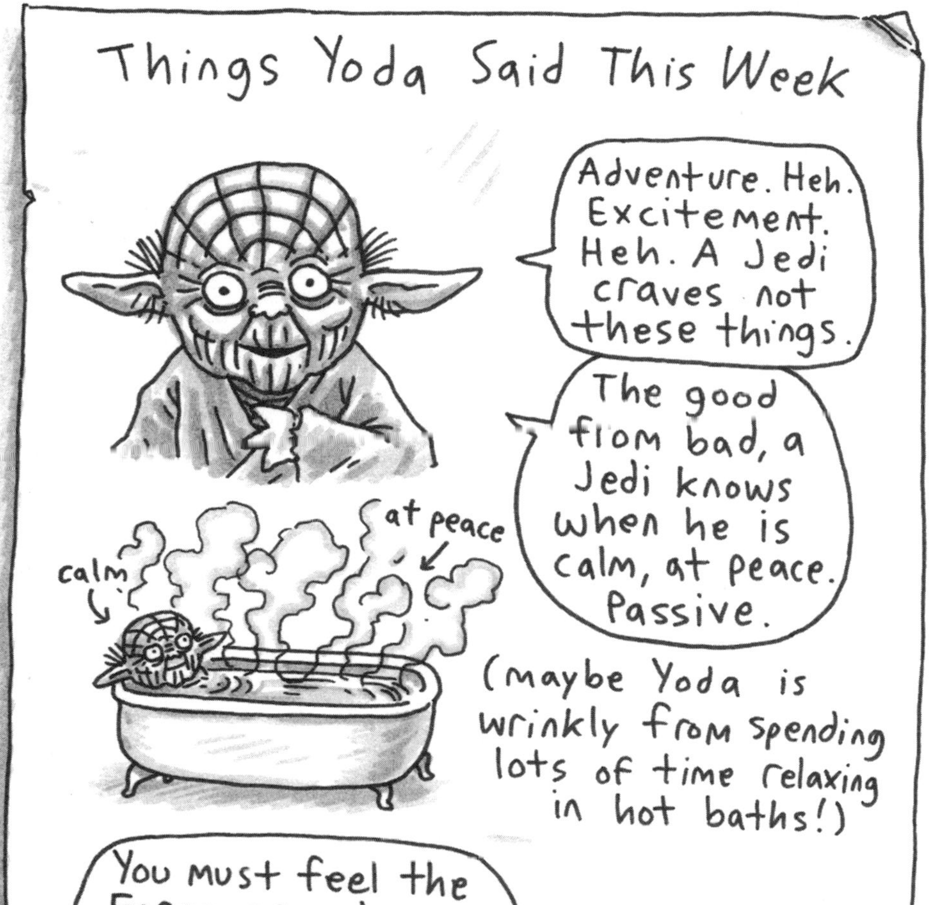

Things Yoda Said This Week
Adventure. Heh. Excitement. Heh. A Jedi craves not these things.
The good from bad, a Jedi knows when he is calm, at peace. Passive.
calm
at peace
(maybe Yoda is wrinkly from spending lots of time relaxing in hot baths!)
You must feel the Force around you; here, between you, me, the tree, the rock, everywhere.
Even between your desk and your homework.

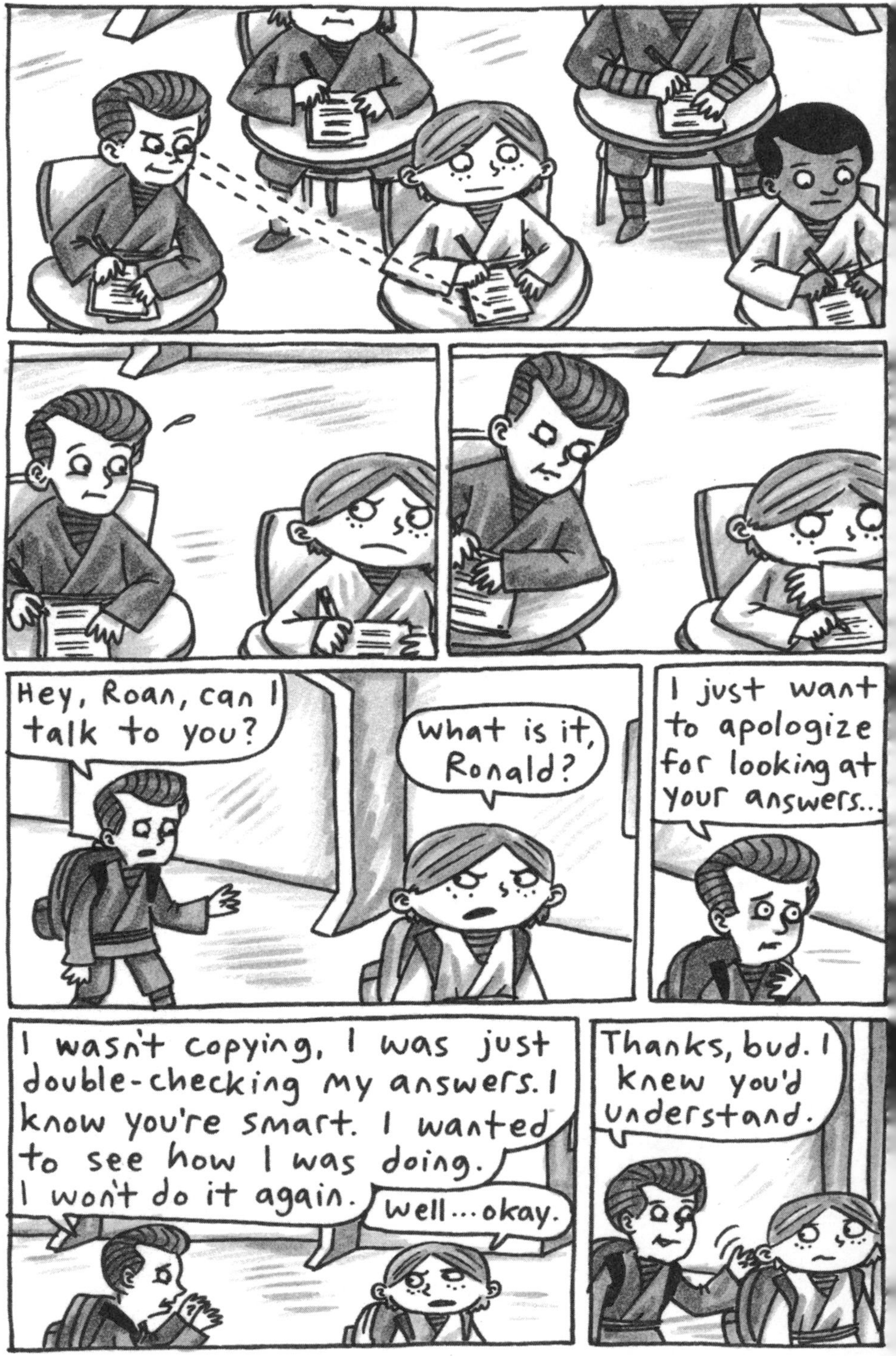
Hey, Roan, can I talk to you?
What is it, Ronald?
I just want to apologize for looking at your answers...
I wasn't copying, I was just double-checking my answers. I know you're smart. I wanted to see how I was doing. I won't do it again.
Well... okay.
Thanks, bud. I knew you'd understand.

PENTADAY

Yesterday, I caught Ronald looking at my quiz paper AGAIN. He gets okay grades, so I bet he cheats all the time. At first I wondered why he would need to cheat if he's getting okay grades, but now I think it's WHY he gets okay grades. It's weird that our class student council president isn't a better student. Or maybe not focusing on his classes is what makes him a good president? I don't know, but it's REALLY ANNOYING. I should probably say something and get him in trouble, but then everyone will think I'M the jerk, when he's the jerk. For my solo presentation, I finished putting together my minicomic handout. Bill, Egon, and Pasha helped me put them together.

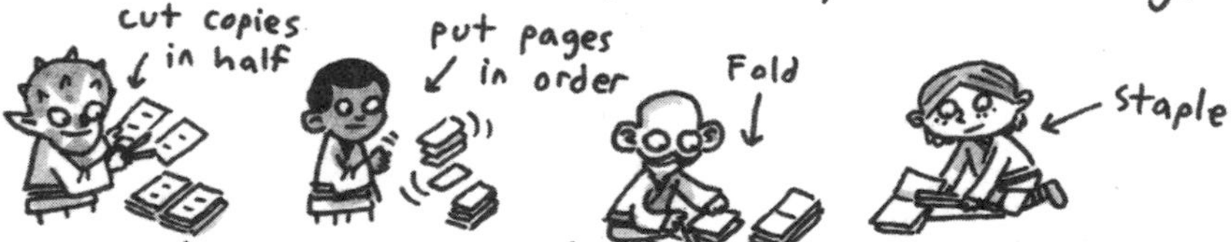

cut copies in half
put pages in order
Fold
Staple

I've got notecards to study for my speech, but I doubt I'll even need them, because I know the material so well.

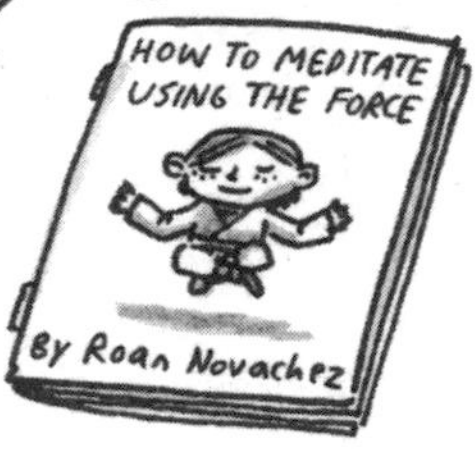

HOW TO MEDITATE USING THE FORCE
By Roan Novachez

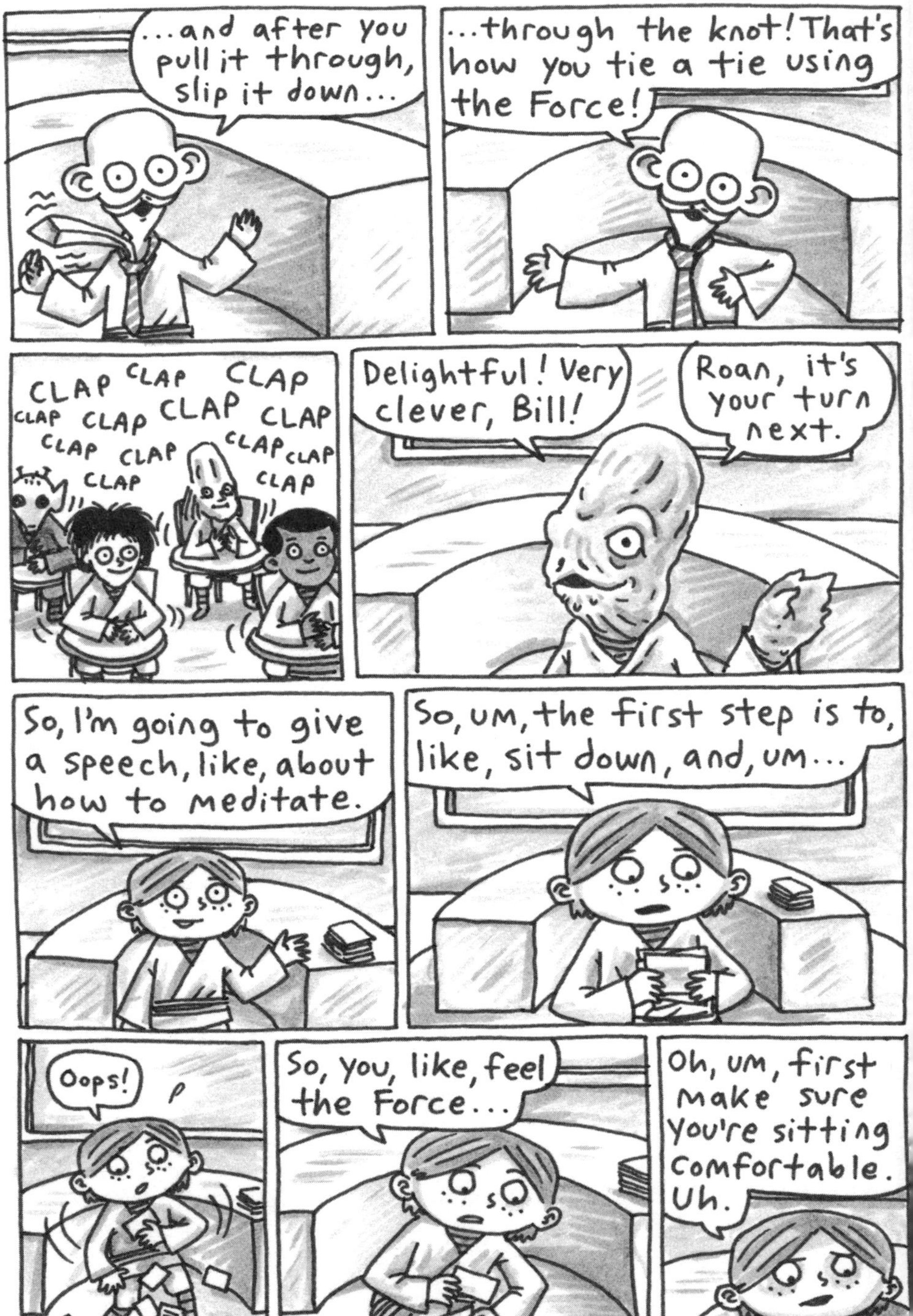

...and after you pull it through, slip it down...
...through the knot! That's how you tie a tie using the Force!
CLAP CLAP CLAP CLAP CLAP CLAP CLAP CLAP CLAP CLAP CLAP CLAP CLAP CLAP
Delightful! Very clever, Bill!
Roan, it's your turn next.
So, I'm going to give a speech, like, about how to meditate.
So, um, the first step is to, like, sit down, and, um...
Oops!
So, you, like, feel the Force...
Oh, um, first make sure you're sitting comfortable. Uh.

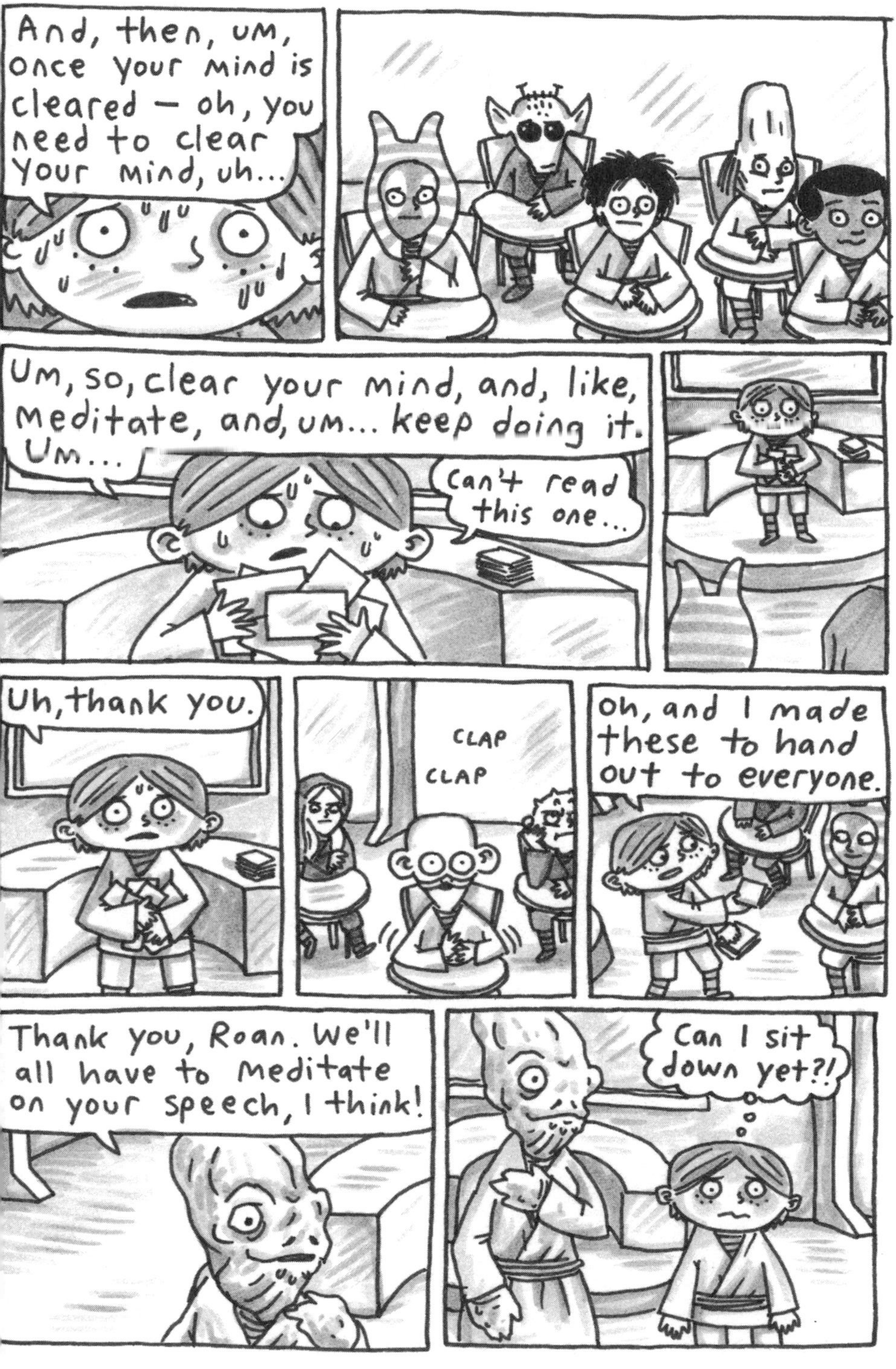
And, then, um, once your mind is cleared — oh, you need to clear your mind, uh...
Um, so, clear your mind, and, like, meditate, and, um... keep doing it. Um...
Can't read this one...
Uh, thank you.
CLAP
CLAP
Oh, and I made these to hand out to everyone.
Thank you, Roan. We'll all have to meditate on your speech, I think!
Can I sit down yet?!

QUADDAY

Apparently the most successful part of my speech was my minicomic handout, which everyone liked. Except Cronah, of course. He said if other people helped me put the minicomics together, then it wasn't really a "solo presentation." I asked Pasha how he thought my speech went, and he said it was good but that I said "um" and "like" a lot. I got a "B" for my grade, so it wasn't a total disaster. Bill asked if I used the Force to focus while I was giving my speech, but I was too distracted by my notecards being all out of order.

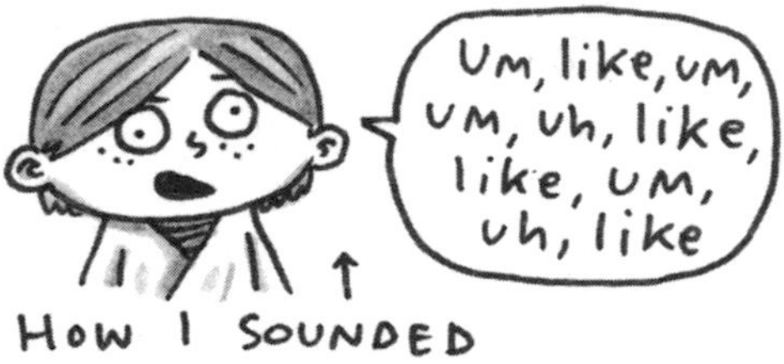
Um, like, um, um, uh, like, like, um, uh, like
HOW I SOUNDED

I think the best speech was Gaiana's, about how to sense great disturbances in the environment by using the Force. She's great.

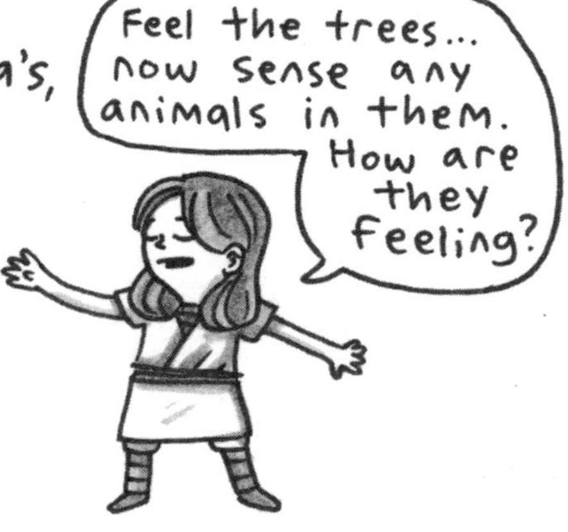
Feel the trees... now sense any animals in them. How are they feeling?

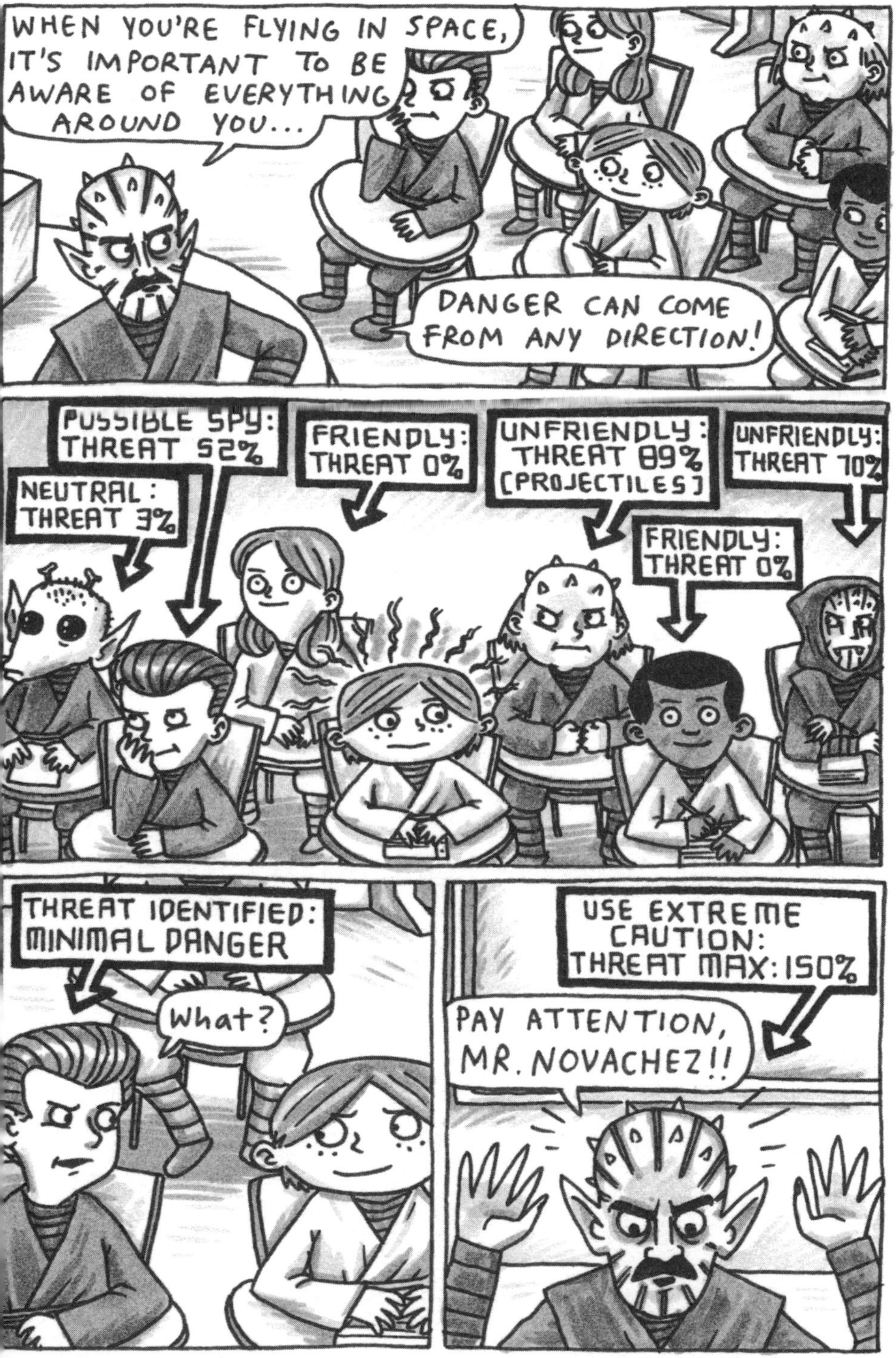
WHEN YOU'RE FLYING IN SPACE, IT'S IMPORTANT TO BE AWARE OF EVERYTHING AROUND YOU...
DANGER CAN COME FROM ANY DIRECTION!
POSSIBLE SPY: THREAT 52%
NEUTRAL: THREAT 3%
FRIENDLY: THREAT 0%
UNFRIENDLY: THREAT 89% [PROJECTILES]
UNFRIENDLY: THREAT 70%
FRIENDLY: THREAT 0%
THREAT IDENTIFIED: MINIMAL DANGER
What?
USE EXTREME CAUTION: THREAT MAX: 150%
PAY ATTENTION, MR. NOVACHEZ!!

CUTE

CLASS PET "VOORPEE" DELIGHTS AND TEACHES

This year at Jedi Academy, students have been enjoying taking turns to care for a voorpak, from the planet Naboo, which the Padawans have named "Voorpee." Gaiana, who organized the class pet program, says students will "study Voorpee's behavior and mannerisms, learning about diets and natural habitats." Voorpee is on loan from the Naboo Zoo.

EWOK PILOT

By Roan Novachez

Ewok Pilot, we have news.
kush?
We love having you as a wingman, but it's time for you to have your OWN wingman!
Meet Jawa Pilot!
Taa baa!
Yukusu kenza keena!
Tyehtgee thin?!

THE PADAWAN OBSERVER VOL. MXIII #4

holomail

FROM: master_yoda_642
TO: Padawan Class Group
SUBJECT: Important Field Trip
Information

OPTIONS
◀ REPLY
▶ FORWARD
□ PRINT
○ POST TO HOLOBOOK

WHEN: WEEK SEVEN

WHERE: THE PLANET HOTH

PURPOSE: To study animals surviving on the frozen planet in order to learn how to adapt to extreme conditions.

ACTIVITIES: Camp in the ice caves below the surface, observe herds of tauntauns, and search for any vegetation.

NOTES: As always, students will be accompanied by Jedi chaperones, who will most likely be more than capable of handling problems such as ice scrabblers, wampas, pirates, smugglers, and ice worms.

CHAPERONES: Master Yoda, Mr. Garfield, T-P30, AND RW-22.

ITEMS TO BRING: Extra clothes, waterproof boots, snowshoes, long underwear, gloves, sunglasses, ice cube trays, scarf, hat, Hoth chocolate mix.

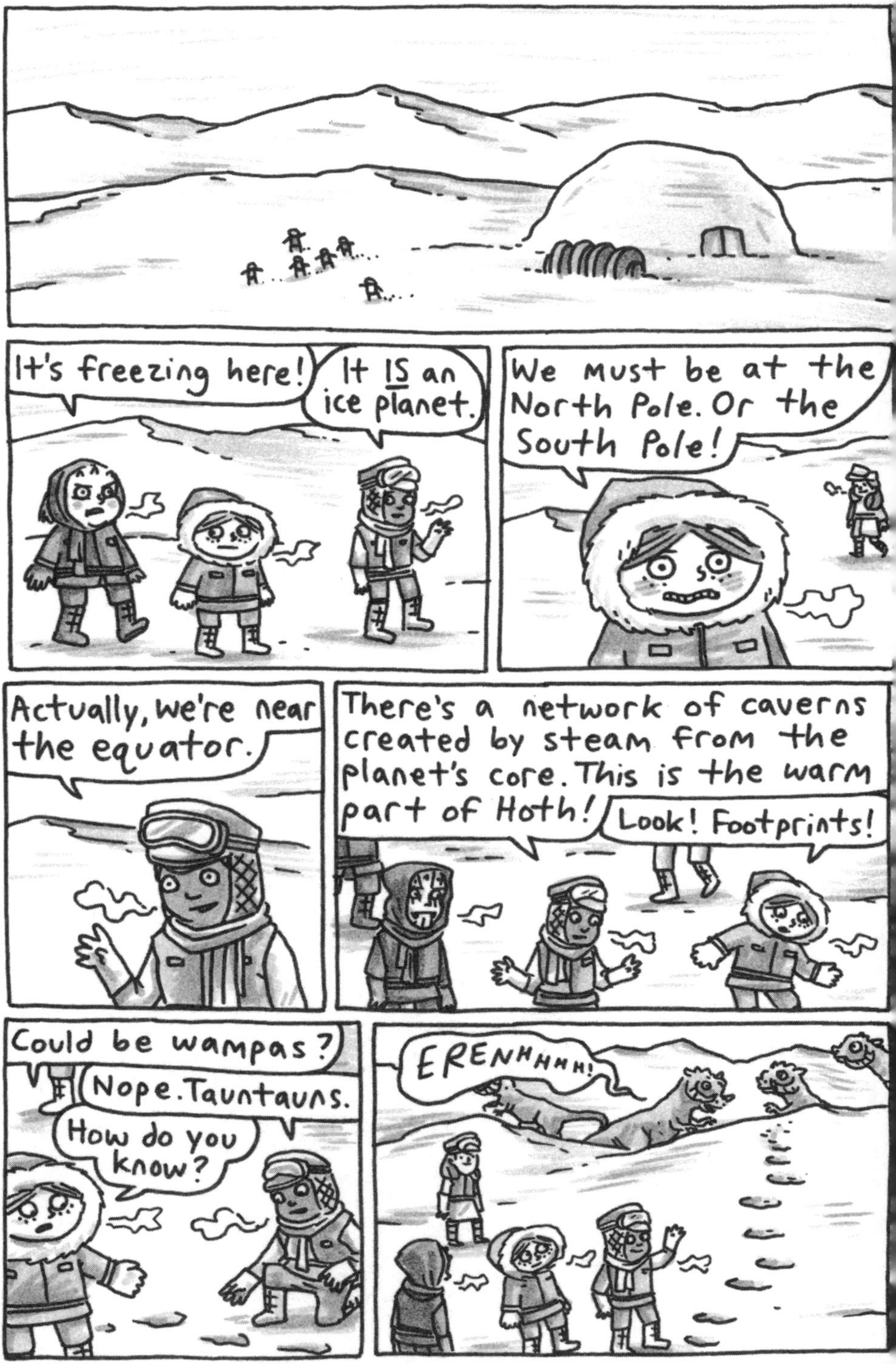
It's freezing here!
It IS an ice planet.
We must be at the North Pole. Or the South Pole!
Actually, we're near the equator.
There's a network of caverns created by steam from the planet's core. This is the warm part of Hoth!
Look! Footprints!
Could be wampas?
Nope. Tauntauns.
How do you know?
ERENHHHHH!

DUODAY

The field trip to Hoth was a lot of fun, although at first it looked like it was going to be super-boring...

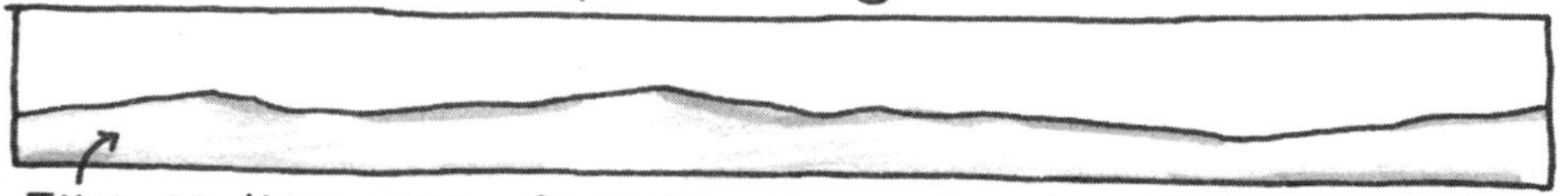

THIS IS HOW THE PLANET HOTH LOOKS EVERYWHERE

Growing up on a desert planet, I had no idea how cold it would be. Fortunately, I brought extra-super-thick socks. Unfortunately, my boots wouldn't fit over them. Pasha let me borrow some of his extra socks.

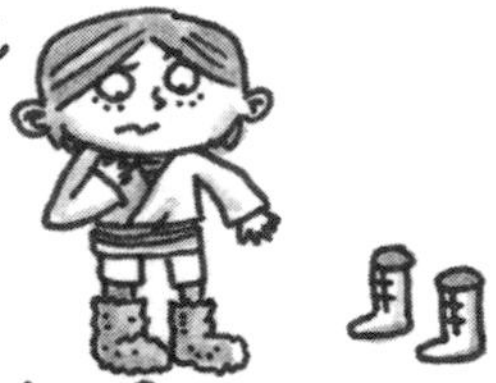

Our first activity was to look for any vegetation. Gaiana teamed up with Bill and Tegan before I could join their group. I went with Pasha, and he showed Egon and me how to follow the tauntaun trails to find where the herds have foraged for lichen. We also learned that tauntauns do get some moisture from the lichen, but they also have specially adapted tongues to lick the ice walls of their caves without getting their tongues stuck... Greer wasn't so lucky!

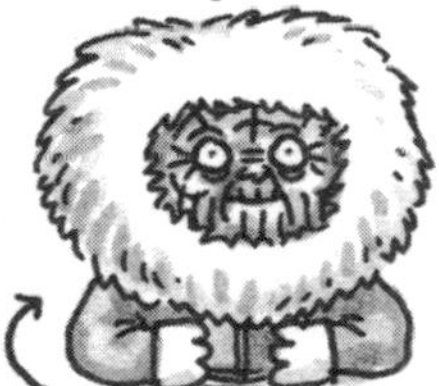

Yoda on Hoth

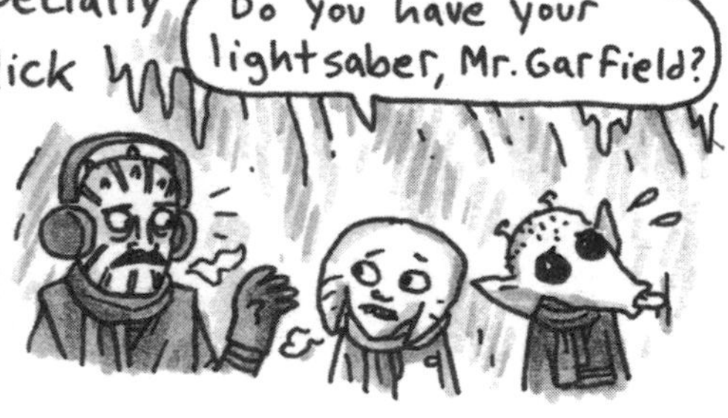
Do you have your lightsaber, Mr. Garfield?

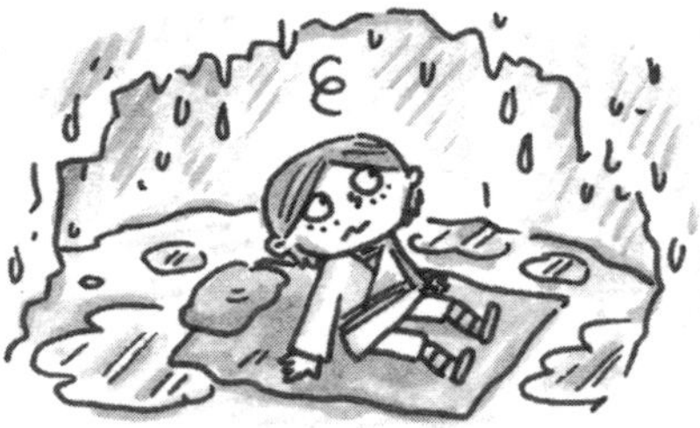

The first night, Silva turned the heat on too high, so we had to spend part of the morning drying off our clothes. Then Ronald went out before his clothes had completely dried and got frozen. We debated leaving him there while we all went sledding, but took him back inside the ice base to thaw out first.

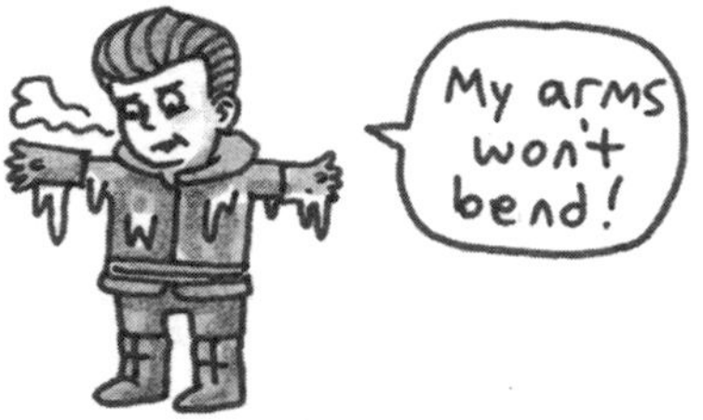
My arms won't bend!

Sledding was AWESOME. There are huge hills and some of them had jumps. Even Cyrus and Cronah were impressed by my big jump.

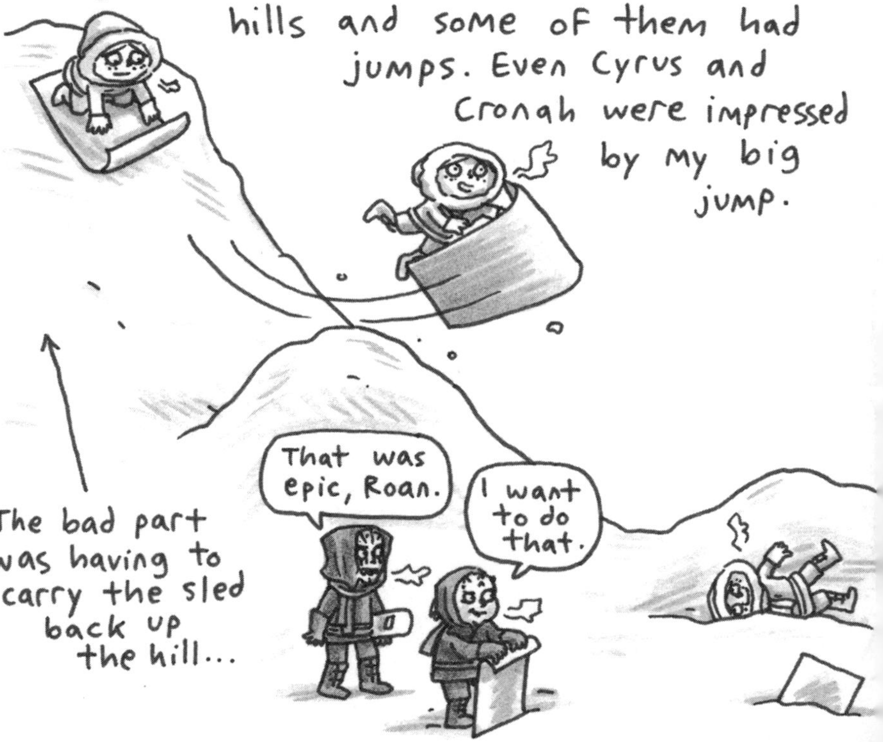
That was epic, Roan.
I want to do that.

The bad part was having to carry the sled back up the hill...

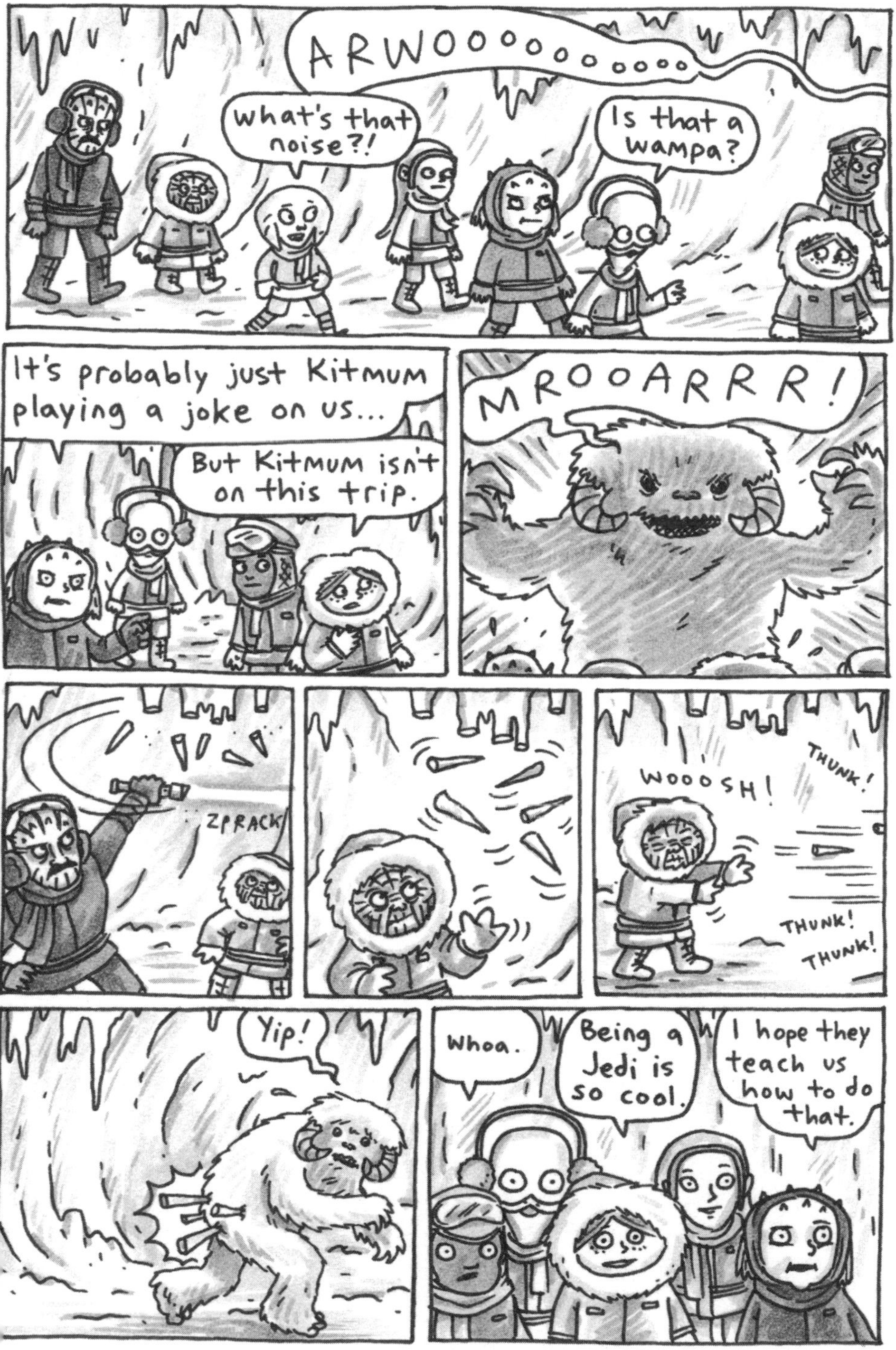
ARWOOOOOOOOOO
what's that noise?!
Is that a wampa?
It's probably just Kitmum playing a joke on us...
But Kitmum isn't on this trip.
MROOARRR!
ZPRACK
WOOOSH!
THUNK!
THUNK!
THUNK!
Yip!
Whoa.
Being a Jedi is so cool.
I hope they teach us how to do that.

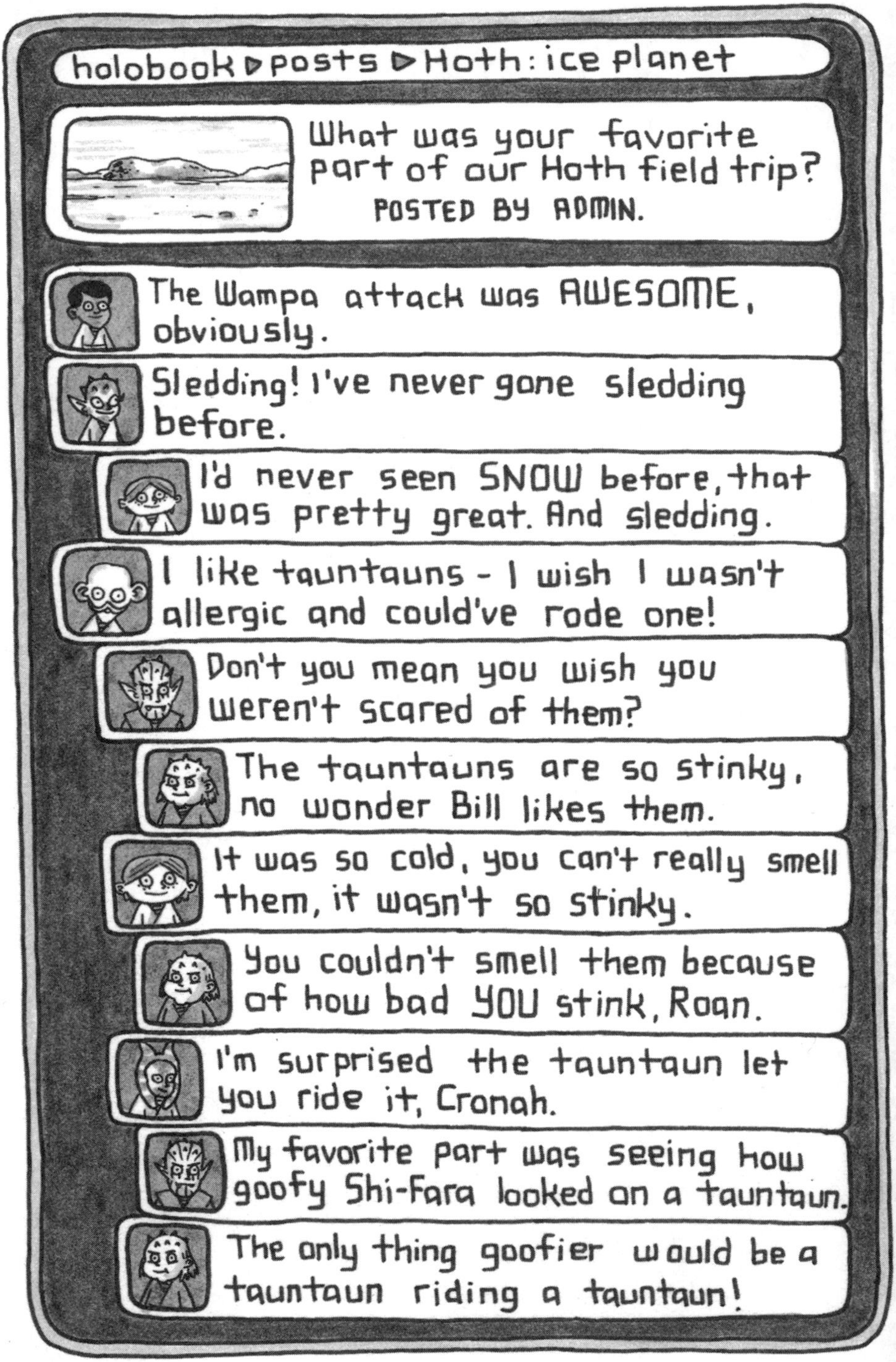

holobook ▷ posts ▷ Hoth: ice planet
What was your favorite part of our Hoth field trip?
POSTED BY ADMIN.
The Wampa attack was AWESOME, obviously.
Sledding! I've never gone sledding before.
I'd never seen SNOW before, that was pretty great. And sledding.
I like tauntauns - I wish I wasn't allergic and could've rode one!
Don't you mean you wish you weren't scared of them?
The tauntauns are so stinky, no wonder Bill likes them.
It was so cold, you can't really smell them, it wasn't so stinky.
You couldn't smell them because of how bad YOU stink, Roan.
I'm surprised the tauntaun let you ride it, Cronah.
My favorite part was seeing how goofy Shi-Fara looked on a tauntaun.
The only thing goofier would be a tauntaun riding a tauntaun!

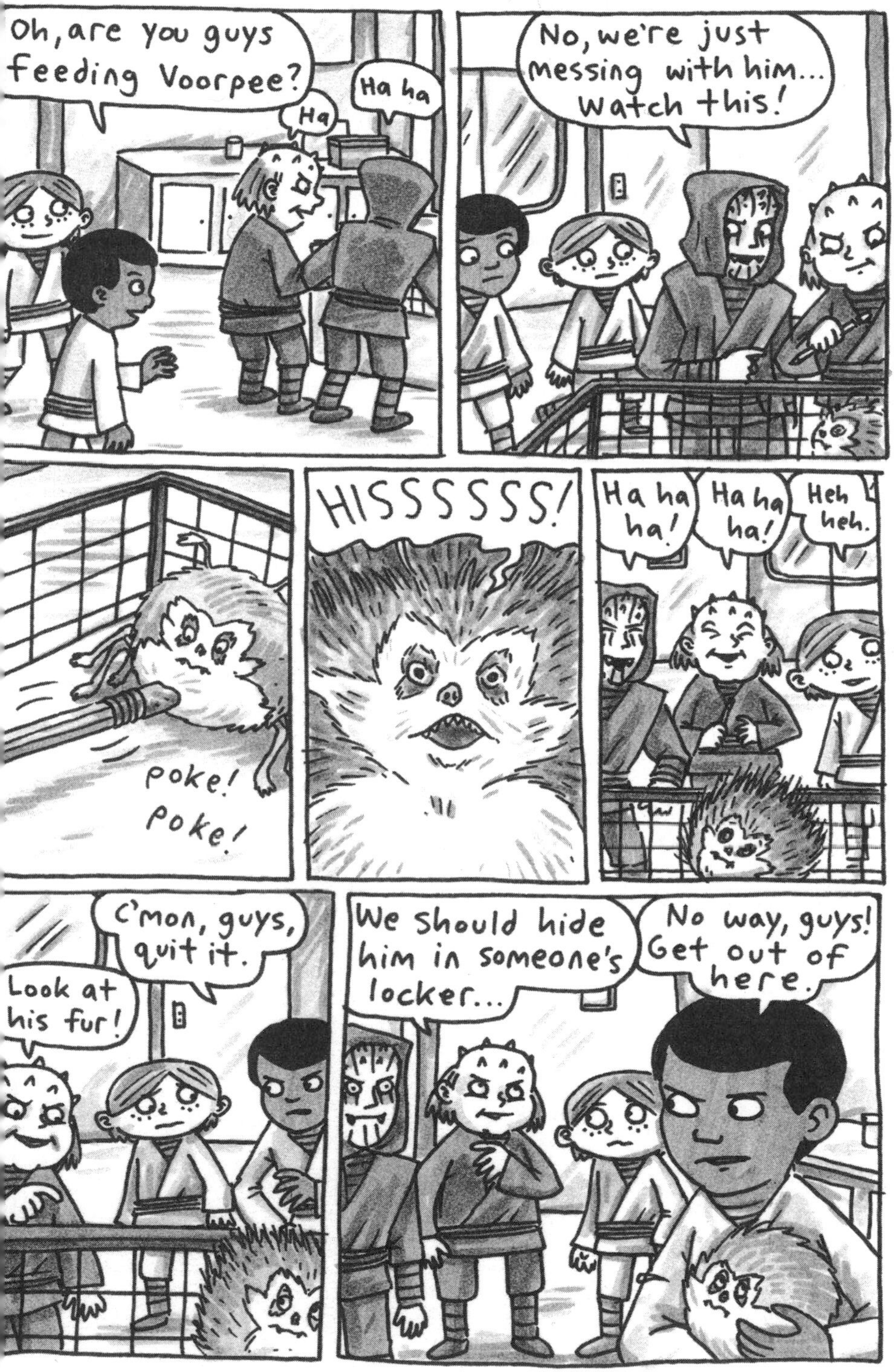
Oh, are you guys feeding Voorpee?
Ha
Ha ha
No, we're just messing with him... watch this!
poke!
poke!
HISSSSSS!
Ha ha ha!
Ha ha ha!
Heh heh.
Look at his fur!
C'mon, guys, quit it.
We should hide him in someone's locker...
No way, guys! Get out of here.

HEXADAY

Every time I post on Holobook, it seems like Cronah and Cyrus have to say something mean to me. I know they don't like me that much, but they're never that rude when they talk to me in class or wherever. They're jerks to pretty much everyone on Holobook, but if you say anything, they notice you and write even MORE mean stuff. I'm supposed to be getting homework done, anyway. I've been studying for the star pilot simulator a lot, because I want to get the high score in class. So far, Gaiana and Pasha got high scores, which is okay, but one week Cronah got it, and I can't let that happen again!

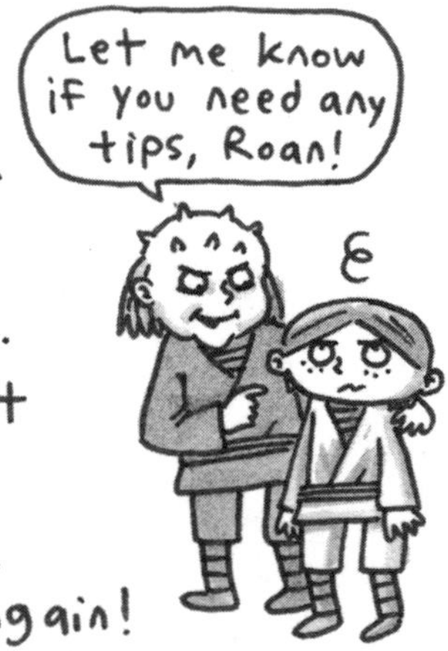
Let me know if you need any tips, Roan!

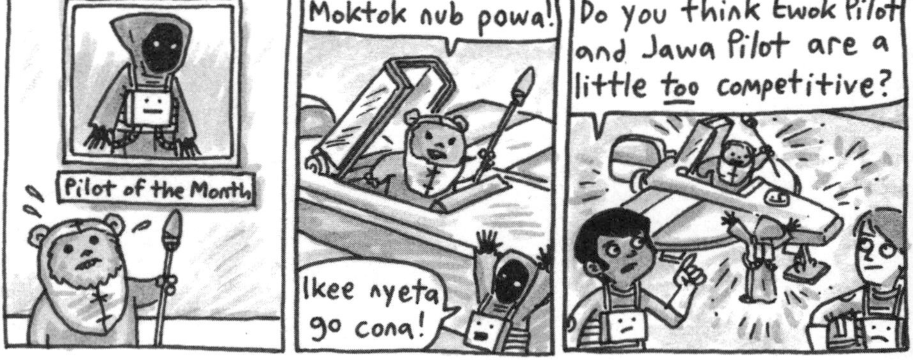
Pilot of the Month
Moktok nub powa!
Ikee nyeta go cona!
Do you think Ewok Pilot and Jawa Pilot are a little too competitive?

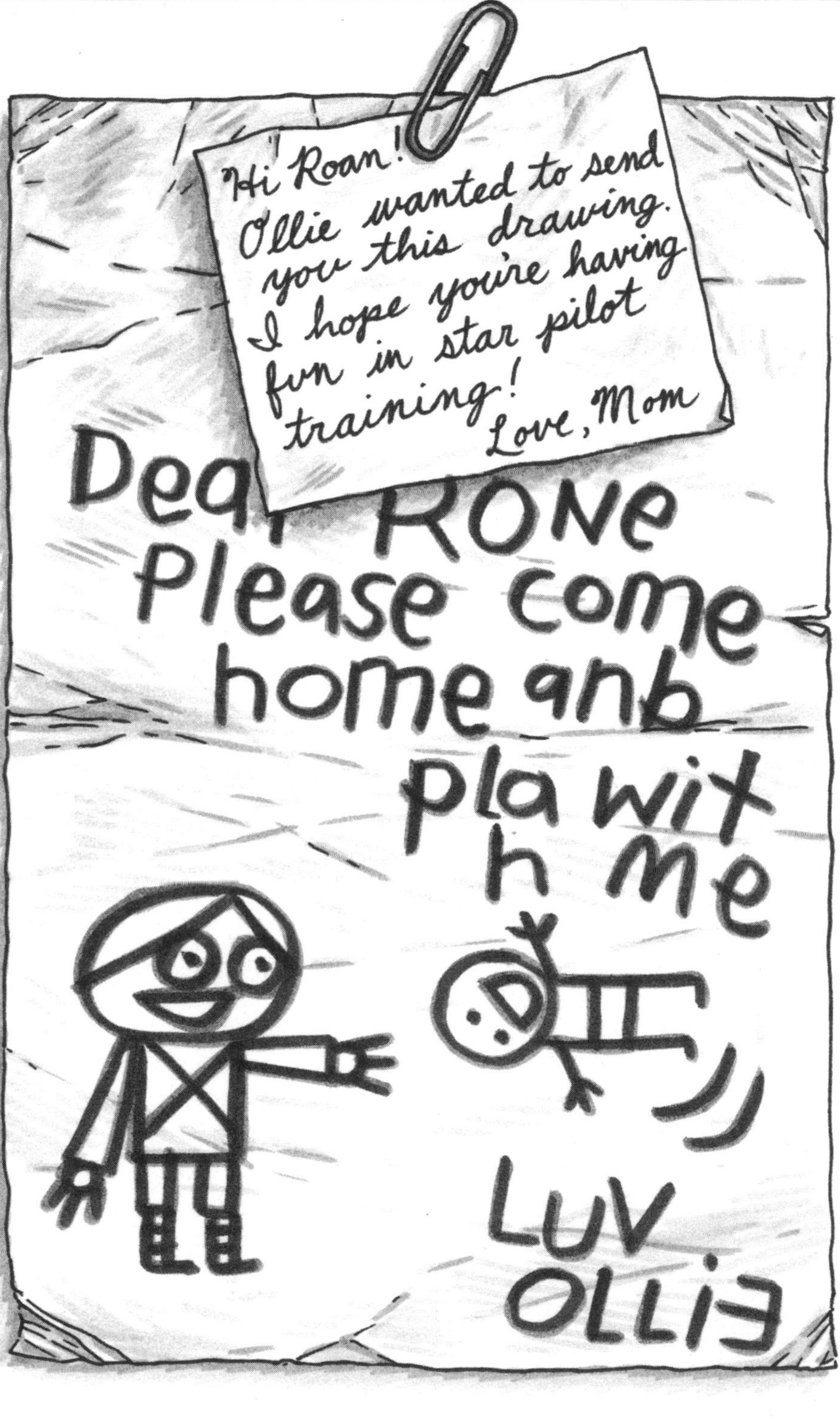
Hi Roan!
Ollie wanted to send you this drawing.
I hope you're having fun in star pilot training!
Love, Mom
Dear RONe
Please come home anb pla wit h me
LUV OLLIƎ

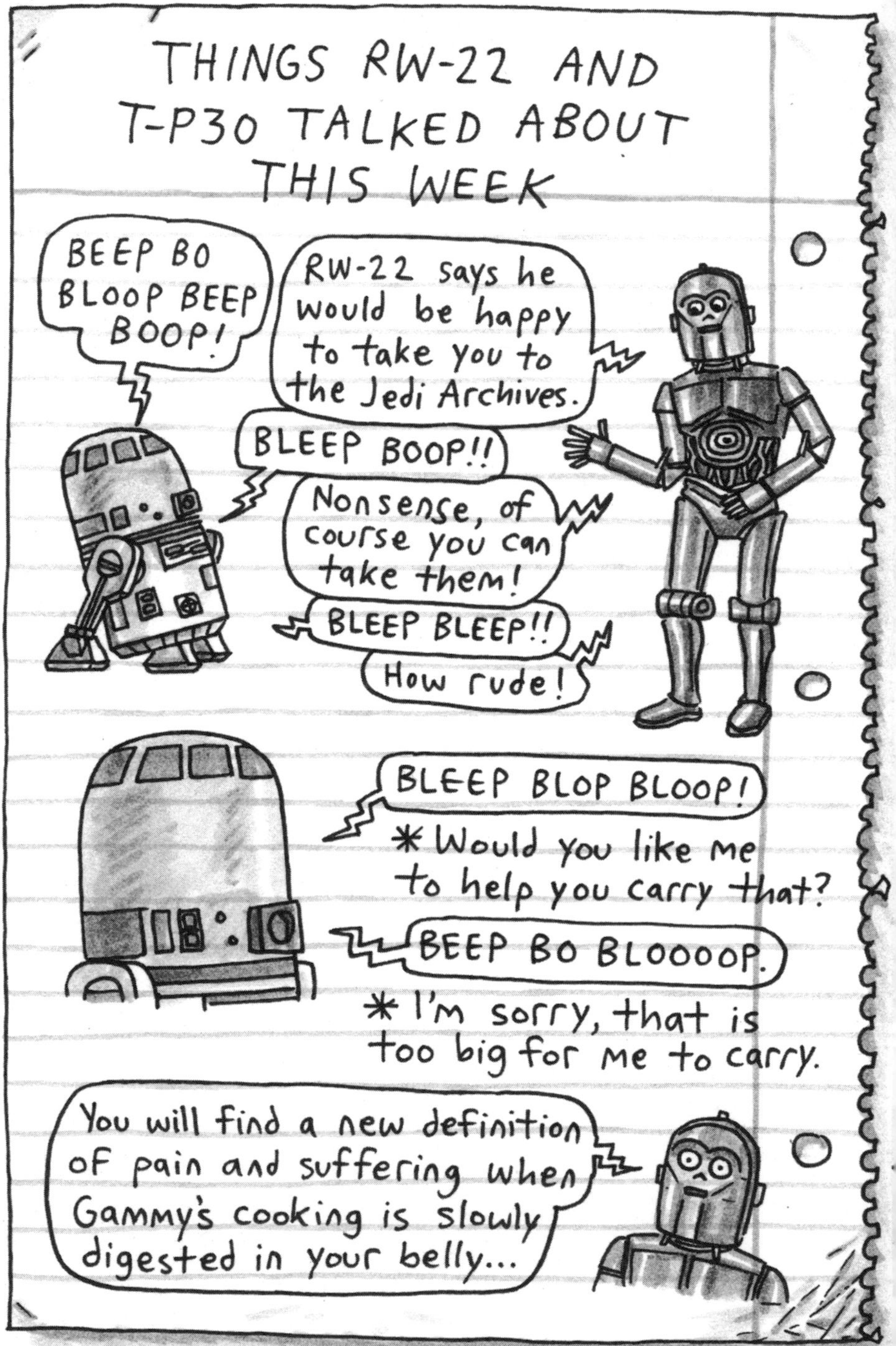
THINGS RW-22 AND T-P30 TALKED ABOUT THIS WEEK
BEEP BO BLOOP BEEP BOOP!
RW-22 says he would be happy to take you to the Jedi Archives.
BLEEP BOOP!!
Nonsense, of course you can take them!
BLEEP BLEEP!!
How rude!
BLEEP BLOP BLOOP!
* Would you like me to help you carry that?
BEEP BO BLOOOOP.
* I'm sorry, that is too big for me to carry.
You will find a new definition of pain and suffering when Gammy's cooking is slowly digested in your belly...

In range...target's coming up. Almost there...bomb's away!

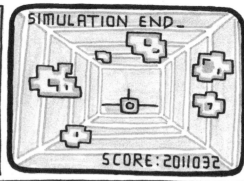

SIMULATION END.

SCORE: 2011032

Phew!

HMPH. A NEW HIGH SCORE FOR YOU, ROAN.

Yes!

Did you guys see that? I did AWESOME!

Let's see YOU beat that record!

Don't worry, Roan, your record is safe from us.

No, uh, I meant Cronah...

Snicker

TRIDAY

I've finally gotten the hang of the star pilot simulators. I would've done better from the ~~beggining~~ beginning if we had REAL starships to fly. It's hard to feel the Force as a Jedi pilot when everything you're seeing in the cockpit is a holocomputer-generated image.

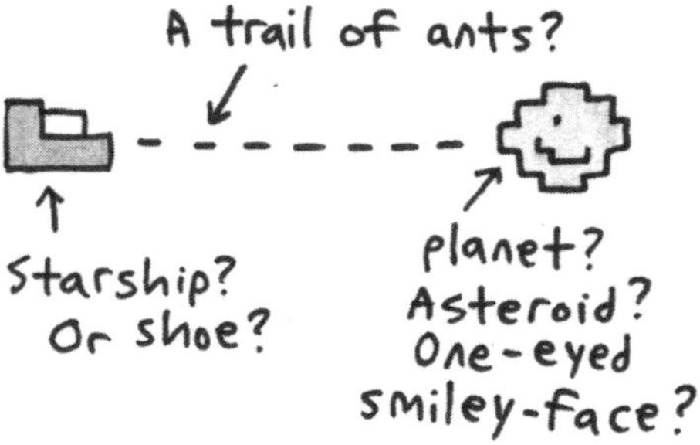
A trail of ants?
Starship? Or shoe?
planet? Asteroid? One-eyed smiley-face?

The graphics on the video screen don't even look real! Egon has video games that are more realistic. Mr. Garfield still hates me, too. I got the high score yesterday, and he made his usual grumpy face and gave me a lecture, pointing out all the things I could've done better or differently.

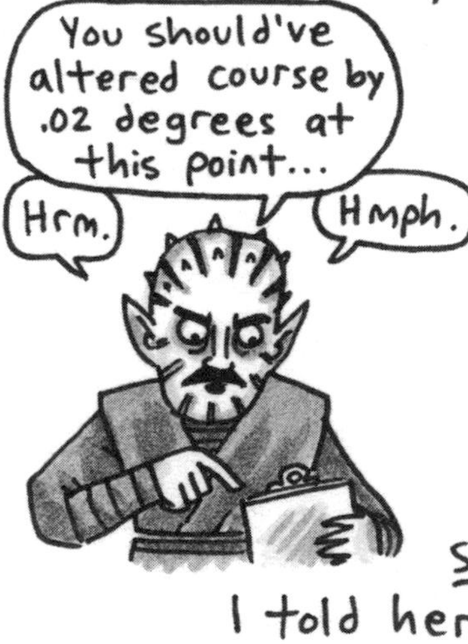
You should've altered course by .02 degrees at this point...
Hrm.
Hmph.

And then Gaiana seemed annoyed that I did better than her. When _she_ did better than me, I told her "good job" and everything.

ATTENTION PADAWANS

JEDI ACADEMY · CORUSCANT CAMPUS

Before this year's spring break, we will hold parent-teacher conferences. Parents will stay at the nearby Coruscant Hotel. As always, parents are discouraged from bringing care packages containing sugary foods or energy drinks.

Schedule For Heptaday:

0900: Parents arrive and give you embarrassing hugs!

0930: Parent-teacher conferences no hiding report cards this time

1230: Lunch at Gammy's

0130: Parents will receive tour of classrooms and messy dorm rooms

0400: Parents depart after probably crying for no reason

HEXADAY

I'm pretty excited for parent-teacher conferences tomorrow. I'll finally get to see my grades, and I know they'll be way better than my first semester at Jedi Academy. I may even be getting all "A's." Since Dad is coming, I'll get to show him how well I'm doing in star pilot flight training. It'll also be fun to show Ollie around. He gets so happy when I use the Force, he'll have his mind blown by everyone at Jedi Academy! I'm glad that Ollie's coming, because maybe Mom will be too busy taking care of him to embarrass me too much.

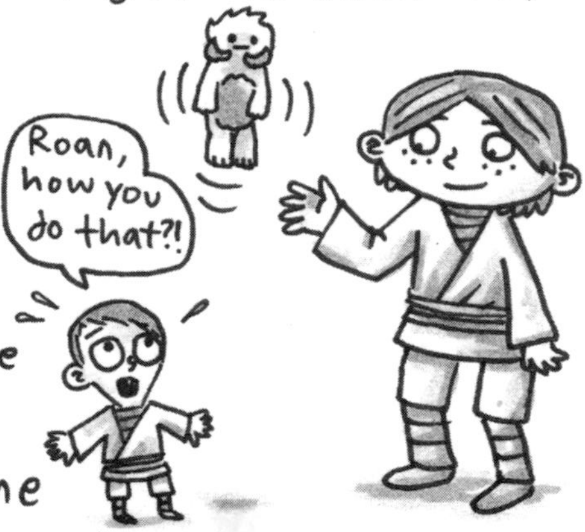
Roan, how you do that?!

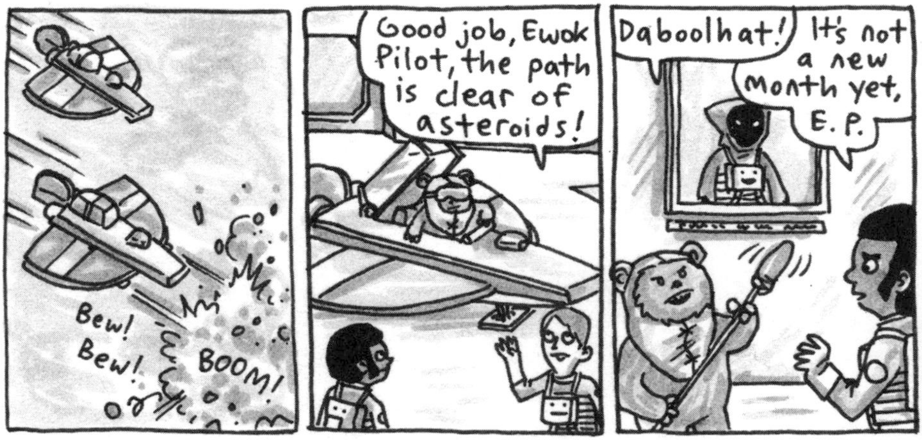
Bew!
Bew!
BOOM!
Good job, Ewok Pilot, the path is clear of asteroids!
Daboolhat!
It's not a new month yet, E.P.

CLASS	NOTES	GRADE
STUDENT: ROAN NOVACHEZ **LEVEL:** PADAWAN **SEMESTER:** THREE **HOMEROOM:** MASTER YODA **REPORT CARD**		

CLASS	NOTES	GRADE
ADVANCED USING THE FORCE [MASTER YODA]	Roan's size mattered not, this semester.	A-
HISTORY OF THE JEDI ORDER [MRS. PILTON]	Excellent, except for study of major events during the Force Wars.	B+
GALACTIC ECOLOGY [PRINCIPAL MAR]	VERY GOOD UNDERSTANDING OF INTERPLANETARY ECOSYSTEMS.	A
HYPERALGEBRA [MRS. PILTON]	Roan is very close to knowing all the basic hyperspace equations.	a
STAR PILOT FLIGHT TRAINING, PT. 1. [MR. GARFIELD]	AFTER A ROUGH START, ROAN IMPROVED, BUT IS NOT ACHIEVING FULL POTENTIAL.	C+
PUBLIC SPEAKING [LIBRARIAN LACKBAR]	Roan needs more practice and confidence.	B-
PHYSICAL EDUCATION [KITMUM]		😮

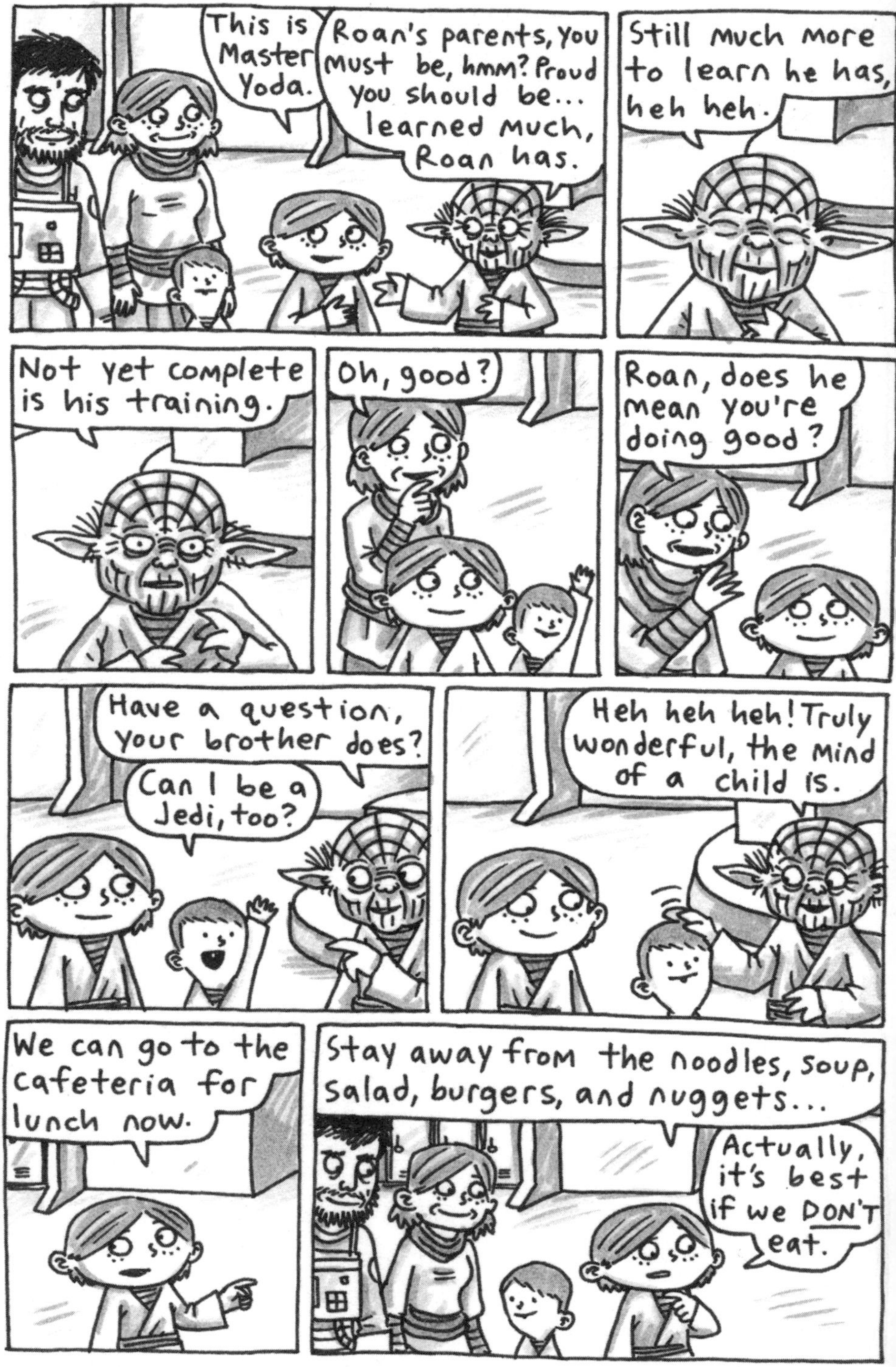
This is Master Yoda.
Roan's parents, you must be, hmm? Proud you should be... learned much, Roan has.
Still much more to learn he has, heh heh.
Not yet complete is his training.
Oh, good?
Roan, does he mean you're doing good?
Have a question, your brother does?
Can I be a Jedi, too?
Heh heh heh! Truly wonderful, the mind of a child is.
We can go to the cafeteria for lunch now.
Stay away from the noodles, soup, salad, burgers, and nuggets...
Actually, it's best if we DON'T eat.

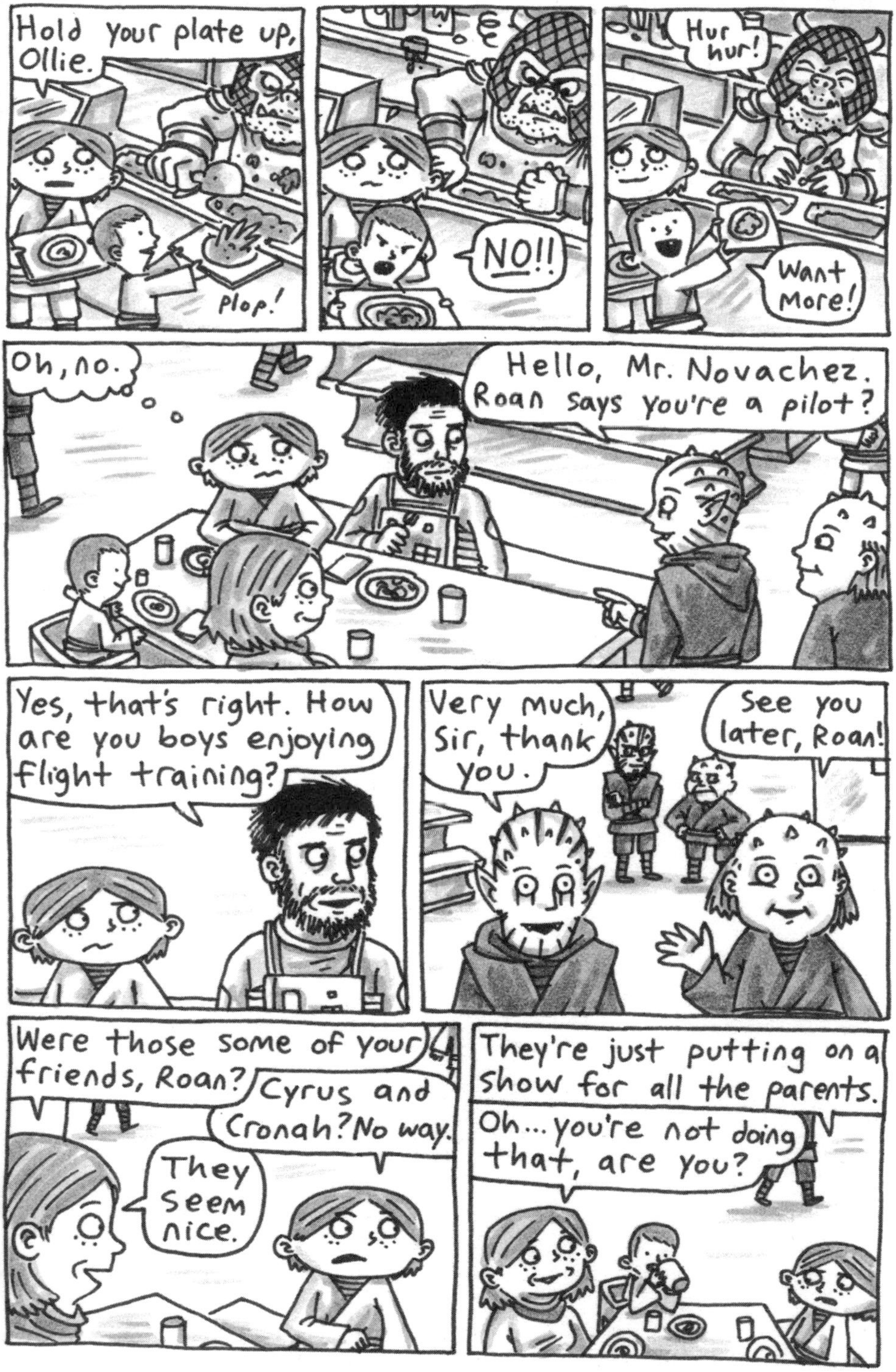
Hold your plate up, Ollie.
Plop!
NO!!
Hur hur!
Want More!
Oh, no.
Hello, Mr. Novachez. Roan says you're a pilot?
Yes, that's right. How are you boys enjoying flight training?
Very much, Sir, thank you.
See you later, Roan!
Were those some of your friends, Roan?
Cyrus and Cronah? No way.
They seem nice.
They're just putting on a show for all the parents.
Oh... you're not doing that, are you?

MONODAY

Parent-teacher conferences weren't a TOTAL disaster, at least. Of course, Mr. Garfield had to figure out a way to give me a bad grade and said I only deserved a "C+." I thought Dad would be disappointed with me (again), but he wasn't, he just gave me some helpful advice.

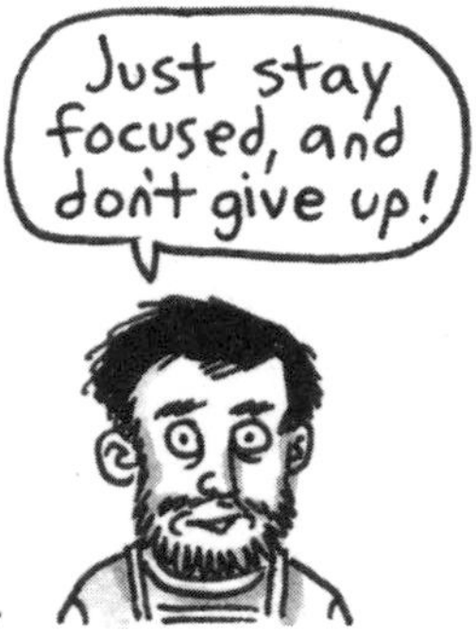
Just stay focused, and don't give up!

Everyone really liked Ollie. They thought he was adorable, especially the girls. Mom and Dad got to meet Gaiana finally, and Mom pinched me for some reason. I thought Gaiana might eat lunch with us, since her parents weren't even there, but she seemed like she was in a hurry. After lunch I found out Gaiana went home early for spring break, I wonder why she didn't say good-bye. I also got to meet Pasha's parents. They're super-nice! They invited me to come visit for spring break, and Mom and Dad

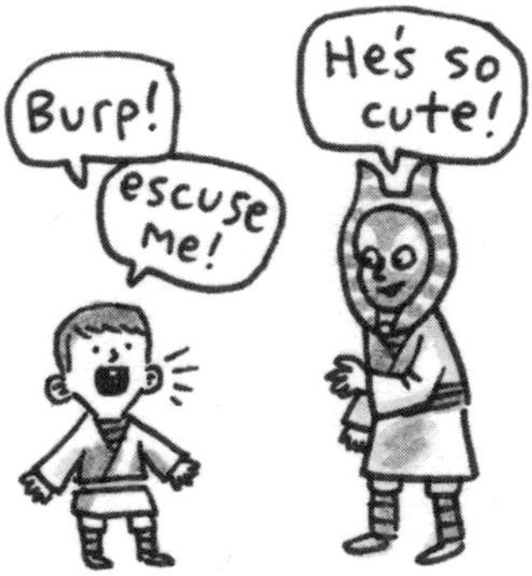
Burp!
escuse me!
He's so cute!

said that I could. So I won't even have to spend spring break doing a bunch of chores at home. Too bad for Dav, ha! This will be the first time I've taken an actual trip for spring break, which is the opposite of Pasha — he usually goes somewhere instead of staying home. Pasha's dad says he'll show us some of the different things he studies at the museum where he works. The WEIRDEST part about the day was Cronah and Cyrus. They were actually... *nice* to me. Maybe now they can see how well I use the Force, AND that I'm a better pilot? They were there when I was saying good-bye to my family and they even shook my dad's hand. I thought they were going to play some kind of joke, but they didn't. They didn't even laugh when Mom totally embarrassed me before she got on the shuttle for home!

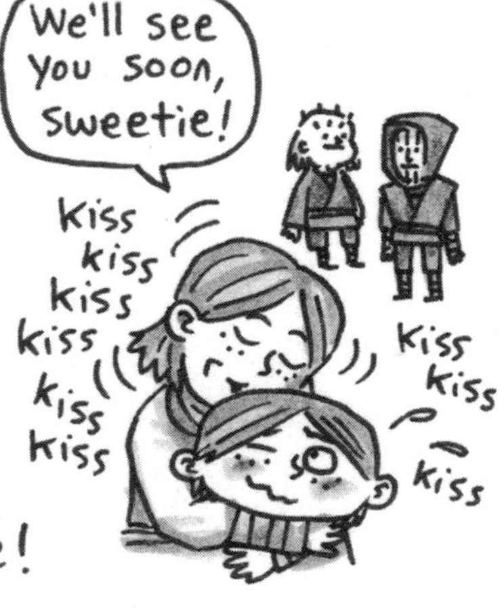
We'll see you soon, sweetie!
kiss kiss kiss kiss kiss kiss
kiss kiss kiss

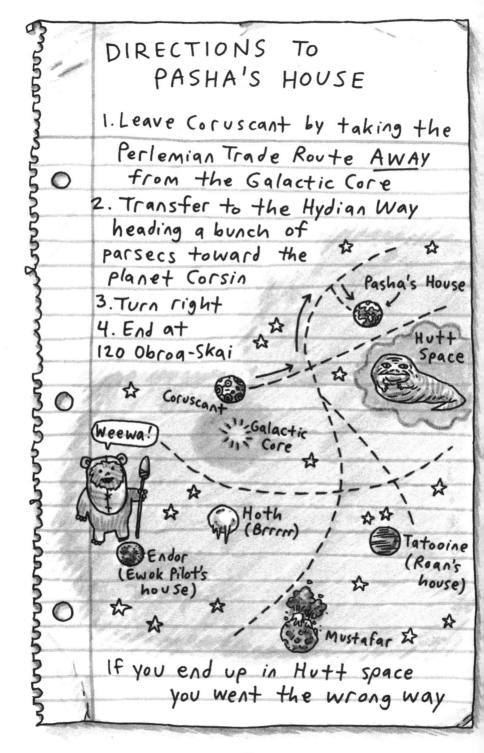

DIRECTIONS TO PASHA'S HOUSE

1. Leave Coruscant by taking the Perlemian Trade Route AWAY from the Galactic Core
2. Transfer to the Hydian Way heading a bunch of parsecs toward the planet Corsin
3. Turn right
4. End at 120 Obroa-Skai

Pasha's House

Hutt Space

Weewa!

Coruscant

Galactic Core

Hoth (Brrrrr)

Endor (Ewok Pilot's house)

Tatooine (Roan's house)

Mustafar

If you end up in Hutt space you went the wrong way

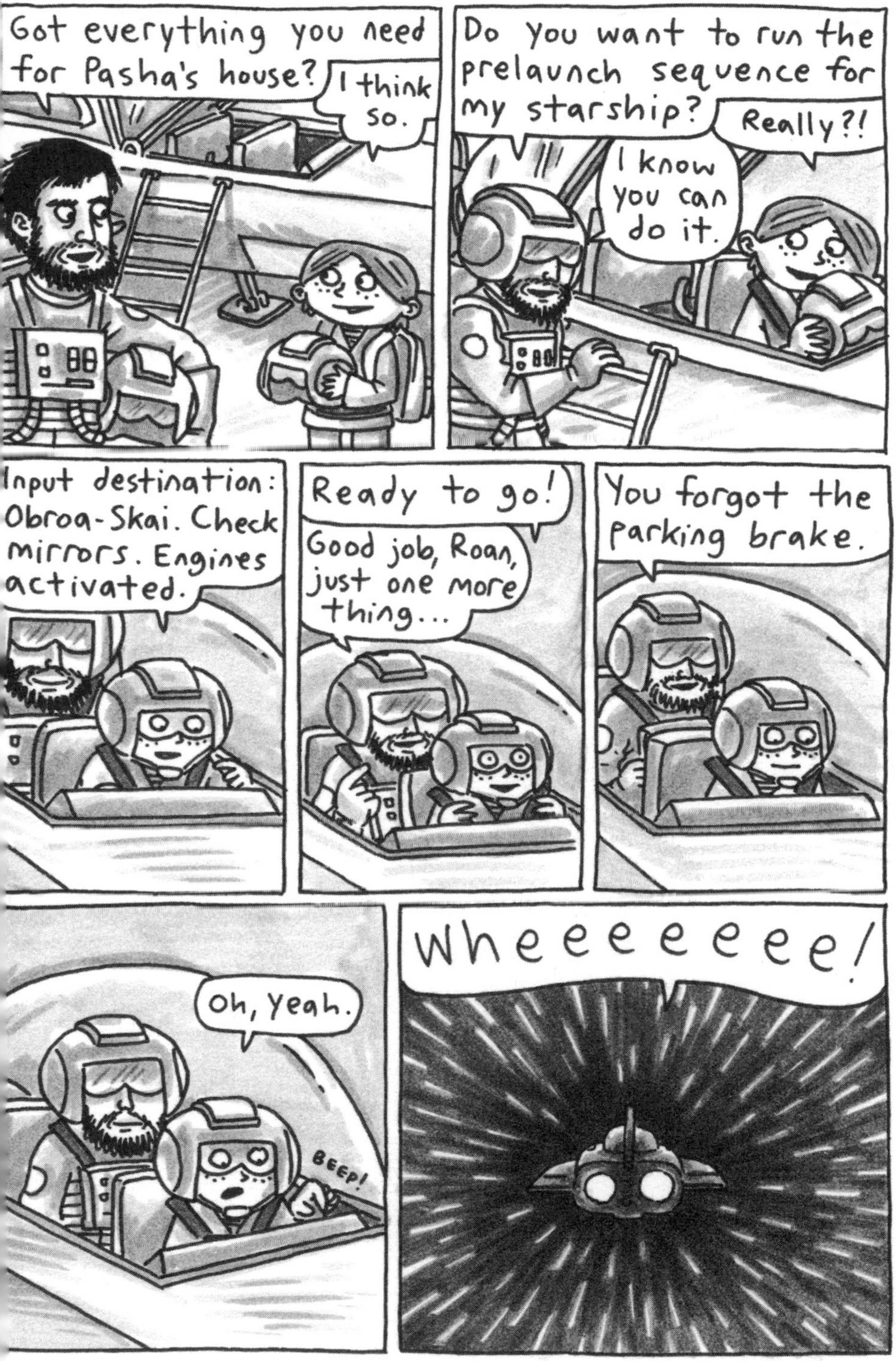
Got everything you need for Pasha's house?
I think so.
Do you want to run the prelaunch sequence for my starship?
Really?!
I know you can do it.
Input destination: Obroa-Skai. Check mirrors. Engines activated.
Ready to go!
Good job, Roan, just one more thing...
You forgot the parking brake.
Oh, yeah.
BEEP!
Wheeeeeee!

HEPTADAY

Today I was supposed to go with Pasha and his dad to visit the Museum of Applied Photonics, but there was some kind of problem and the security guard wouldn't let me in. I could only stay in the food court. Pasha offered to stay with me, but I told him he should go ahead, so Pasha went with his dad. I expected Pasha to insist on staying! Pasha's dad just needed to pick some things up, so I figured it wouldn't take too long, but then it ended up being, like, three hours. Tomorrow, we're planning on going to the Obroan Institute for ~~Archeology~~ Archaeology, where Pasha's dad works. I probably won't be allowed to go inside there, either, so I'm going to bring my sketchbook with me for sure.

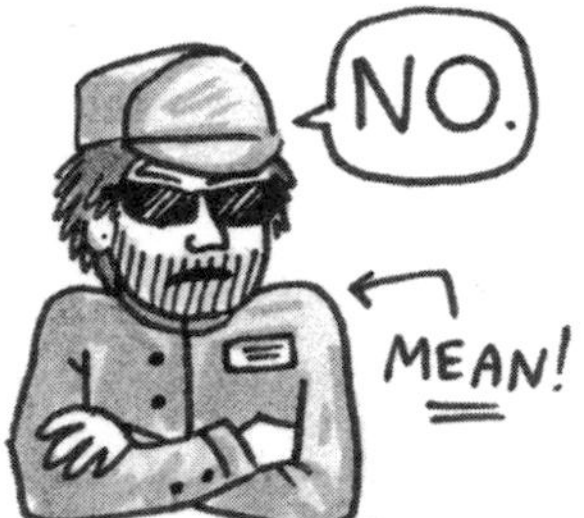
NO.
MEAN!

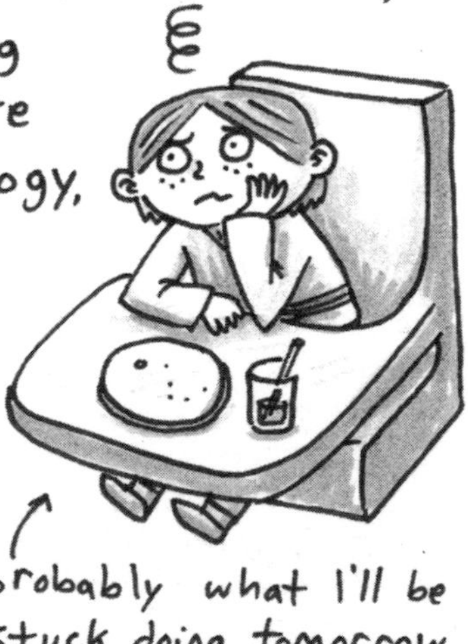
probably what I'll be stuck doing tomorrow, too

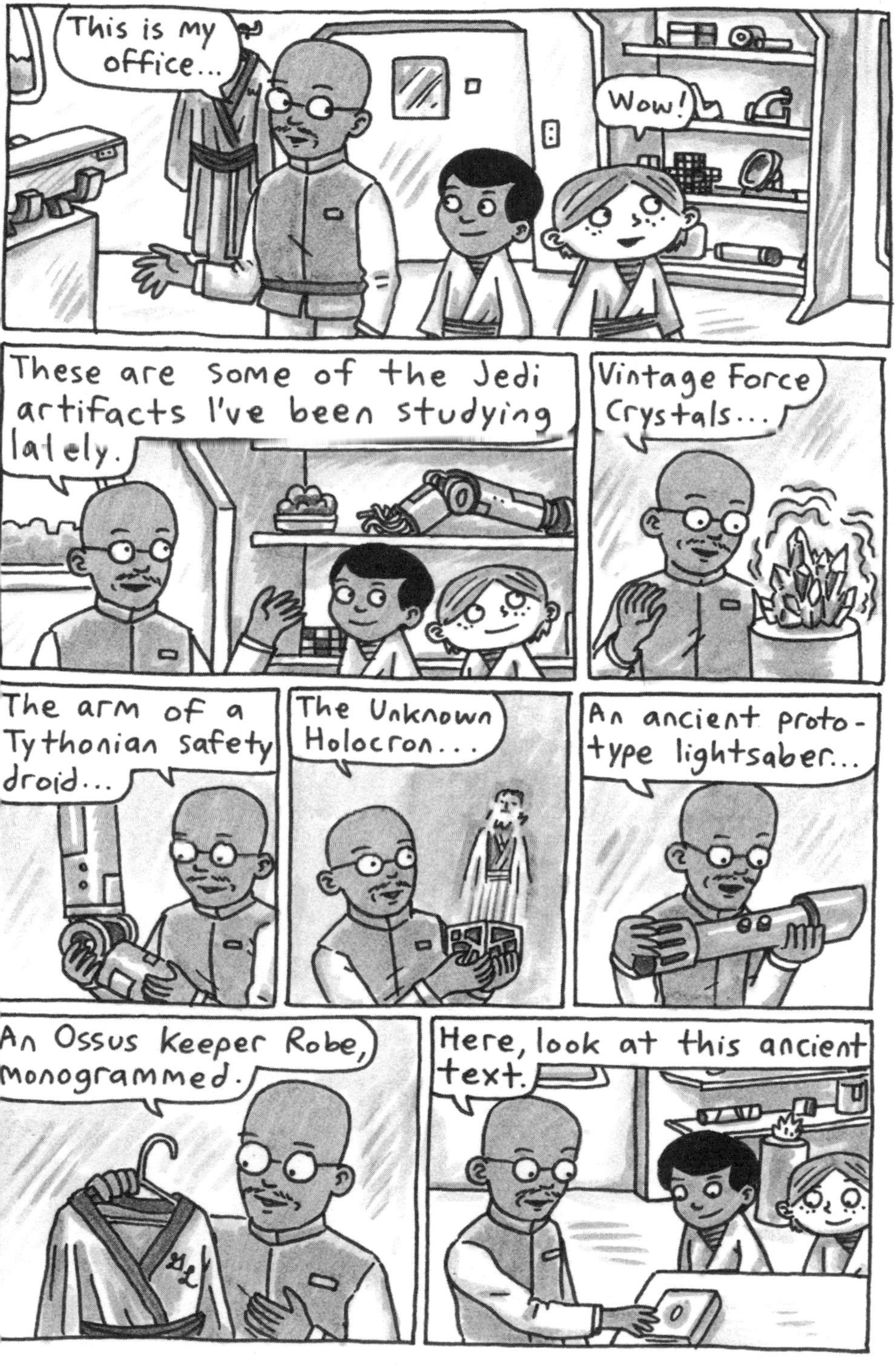
This is my office...
Wow!
These are some of the Jedi artifacts I've been studying lalely.
Vintage Force Crystals...
The arm of a Tythonian safety droid...
The Unknown Holocron...
An ancient proto-type lightsaber...
An Ossus Keeper Robe, monogrammed.
GL
Here, look at this ancient text.

Whoa, it's The Path of the Jedi!

RIPPPPppppp

Oh, no!

Here, uh, we'll just put that away.

These artifacts should be handled with extreme care.

Sorry.

Why don't we take a look at the rest of the Institute?

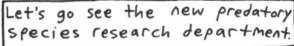

Let's go see the new predatory species research department.

Just... don't touch anything.

Why are they mad at me? It was an accident!!

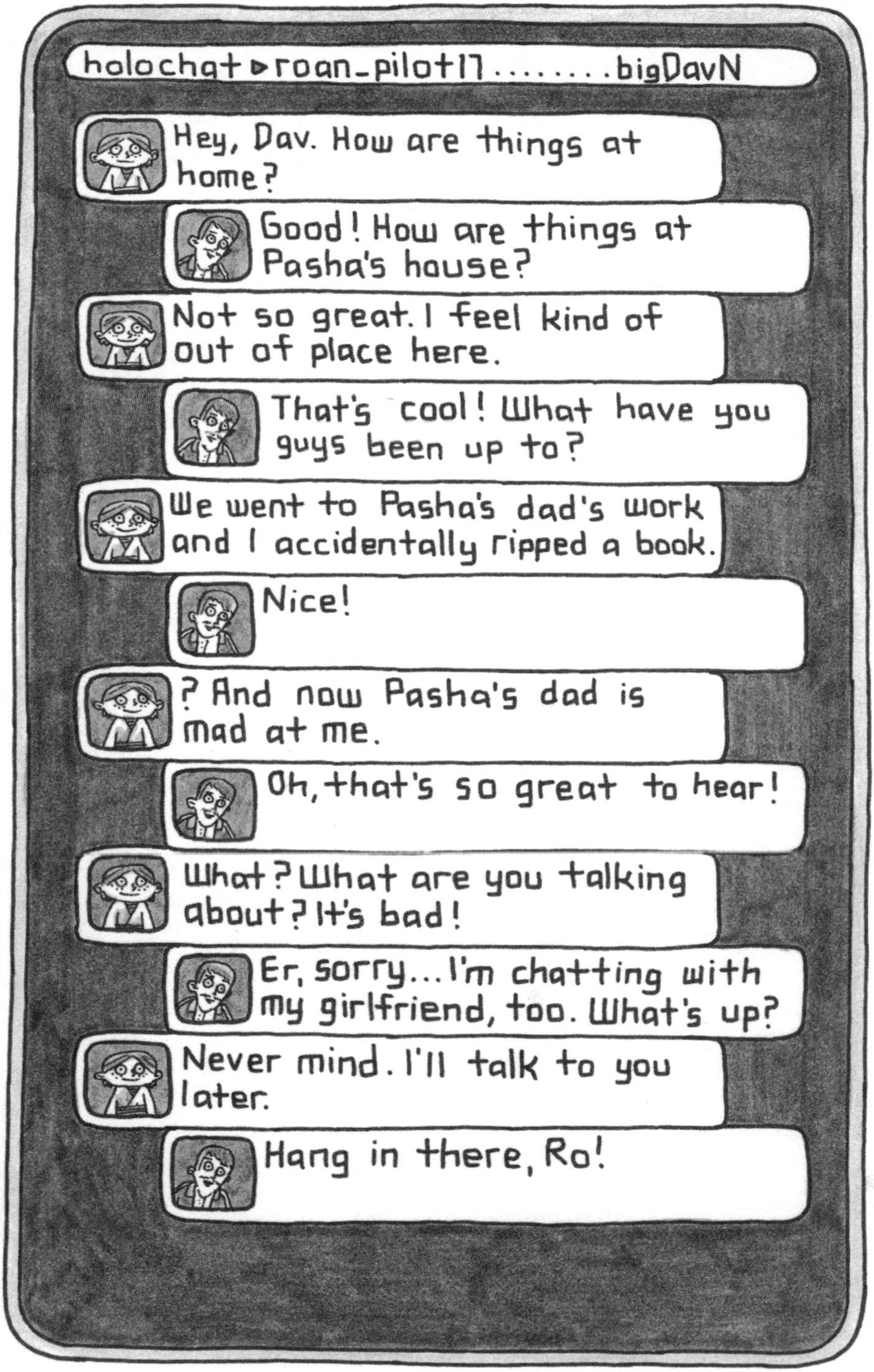
holochat ▸ roan_pilot17 .... bigDavN
Hey, Dav. How are things at home?
Good! How are things at Pasha's house?
Not so great. I feel kind of out of place here.
That's cool! What have you guys been up to?
We went to Pasha's dad's work and I accidentally ripped a book.
Nice!
? And now Pasha's dad is mad at me.
Oh, that's so great to hear!
What? What are you talking about? It's bad!
Er, sorry... I'm chatting with my girlfriend, too. What's up?
Never mind. I'll talk to you later.
Hang in there, Ro!

PENTADAY

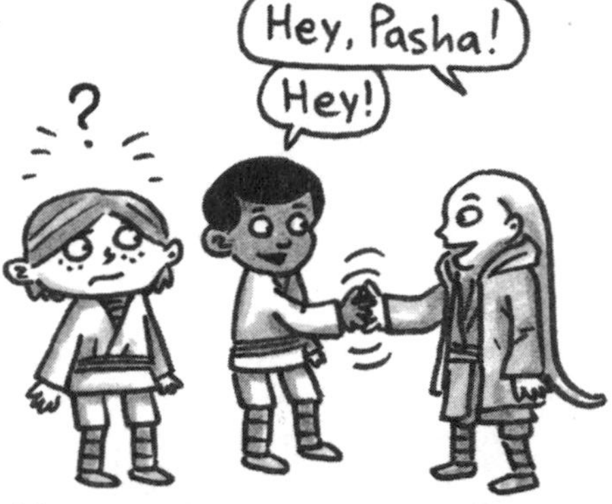
?
Hey, Pasha!
Hey!

Today I met some of Pasha's friends. They all had some kind of secret handshake, but Pasha said he'd have to teach it to me later, because it's pretty ~~complacated~~ complicated. Then they were talking about Jedi Academy, and I was confused, because I didn't know any of the teachers they were mentioning. I said something about the Archives, and they looked at me like I was a weirdo. Then Pasha laughed, because he realized I didn't know there's a different Jedi Academy on Obroa-Skai that's for Jedi Research Specialties. That's where all of his friends go. So basically I made a fool of myself. Then Pasha's friends invited him to hang out all afternoon, so I had to sit there the whole time feeling like an idiot. Especially when they started talking about their favorite holotelevision show. I don't even know what it's called because you can't see it on Tatooine.

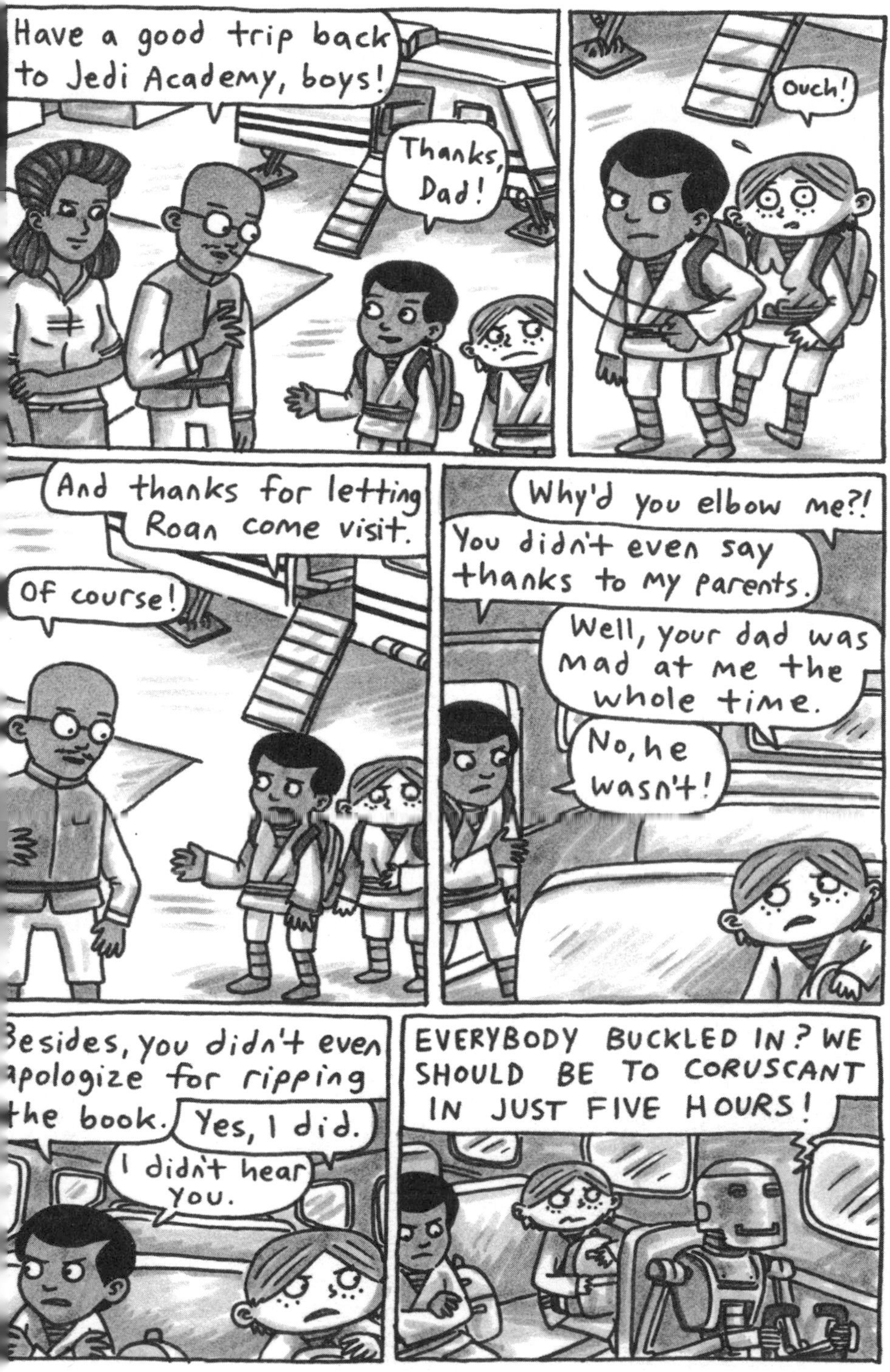
Have a good trip back to Jedi Academy, boys!
Thanks, Dad!
Ouch!
And thanks for letting Roan come visit.
Of course!
Why'd you elbow me?!
You didn't even say thanks to my parents.
Well, your dad was mad at me the whole time.
No, he wasn't!
Besides, you didn't even apologize for ripping the book.
Yes, I did.
I didn't hear you.
EVERYBODY BUCKLED IN? WE SHOULD BE TO CORUSCANT IN JUST FIVE HOURS!

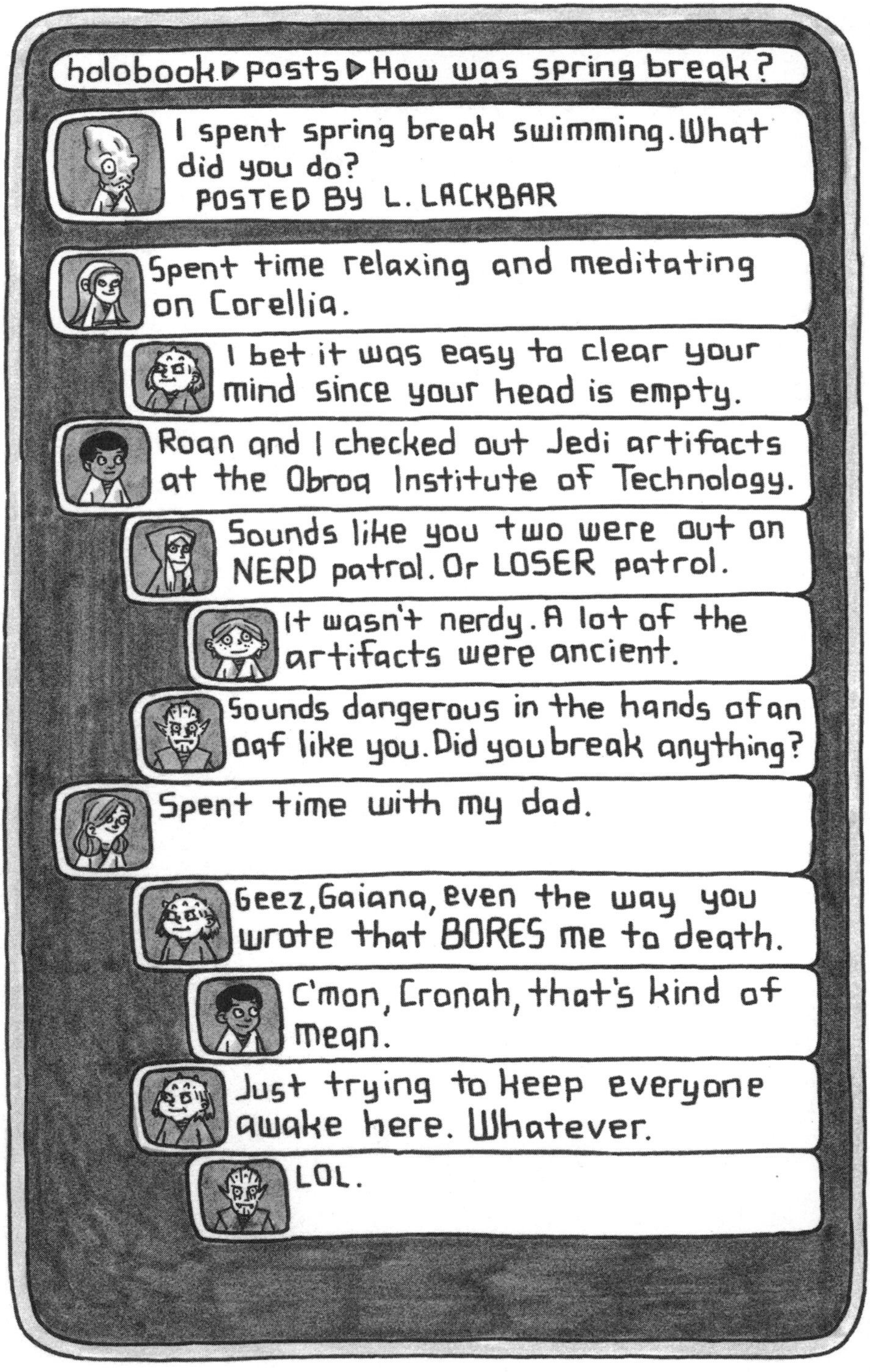
holobook ▷ posts ▷ How was spring break?
I spent spring break swimming. What did you do?
POSTED BY L. LACKBAR
Spent time relaxing and meditating on Corellia.
I bet it was easy to clear your mind since your head is empty.
Roan and I checked out Jedi artifacts at the Obroa Institute of Technology.
Sounds like you two were out on NERD patrol. Or LOSER patrol.
It wasn't nerdy. A lot of the artifacts were ancient.
Sounds dangerous in the hands of an oaf like you. Did you break anything?
Spent time with my dad.
Geez, Gaiana, even the way you wrote that BORES me to death.
C'mon, Cronah, that's kind of mean.
Just trying to keep everyone awake here. Whatever.
LOL.

STUDENT: ROAN NOVACHEZ

LEVEL: PADAWAN | SEMESTER: FOUR

HOMEROOM: MASTER YODA

CLASS SCHEDULE

JEDI ACADEMY · CORUSCANT CAMPUS ·

0730-0850: REUSING THE FORCE

MASTER YODA WILL TEACH THE CLASS A NUMBER OF LONG-FORGOTTEN FORCE TECHNIQUES.

↑ If they're forgotten, how does HE know them?

0900-0950: ART OF PHYSICS

MRS. PILTON AND LIBRARIAN LACKBAR WILL USE FAMOUS ARTWORKS TO EXPLAIN PHYSICS.

1000-1050: LIGHTSABER DUELING SKILLS

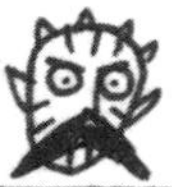

MR. GARFIELD WILL SHARPEN STUDENTS' ABILITIES WITH THIS CUTTING-EDGE CLASS. Will Mr. G. show us how he trims his mustache?

1100-1150: HOME ECONOMICS

GAMMY WILL TEACH STUDENTS TO FEED THEMSELVES WITH EDIBLE COOKING.

1200 1300: ~~LUNCH BREAK~~ Mushroom break

1300-1350: STAR PILOT FLIGHT TRAINING PART 2

STUDENTS WILL CONTINUE LEARNING TO FLY WITH MR. GARFIELD. At least this will be fun!

1400-1450: BASICS OF DROID CONSTRUCTION

PRINCIPAL MAR WILL HELP STUDENTS LEARN TO BUILD THEIR OWN DROIDS.

1500-1550: PHYSICAL EDUCATION

KITMUM WILL GUIDE STUDENTS IN VARIOUS ORGANIZED SPORTS COMPETITIONS.

And growl at us.

NEW STAR PILOT SIMULATORS ARRIVE AT JEDI ACADEMY

Just in time for the new semester, Jedi Academy has received new and improved star pilot simulators, with advanced technology

that will give students a more realistic flying experience. Mr.

OLD   NEW

Garfield stated the old simulators were "just fine" and the only reason for new ones was "politics."

EWOK PILOT   By Roan Novachez

Ewok Pilot, what are you doing to your ship? Ji?

kush drojh?!

You should ask Jawa Pilot to help you fix it. He has lots of parts.

Tyeht danti?   Yanna kuzu peekay?

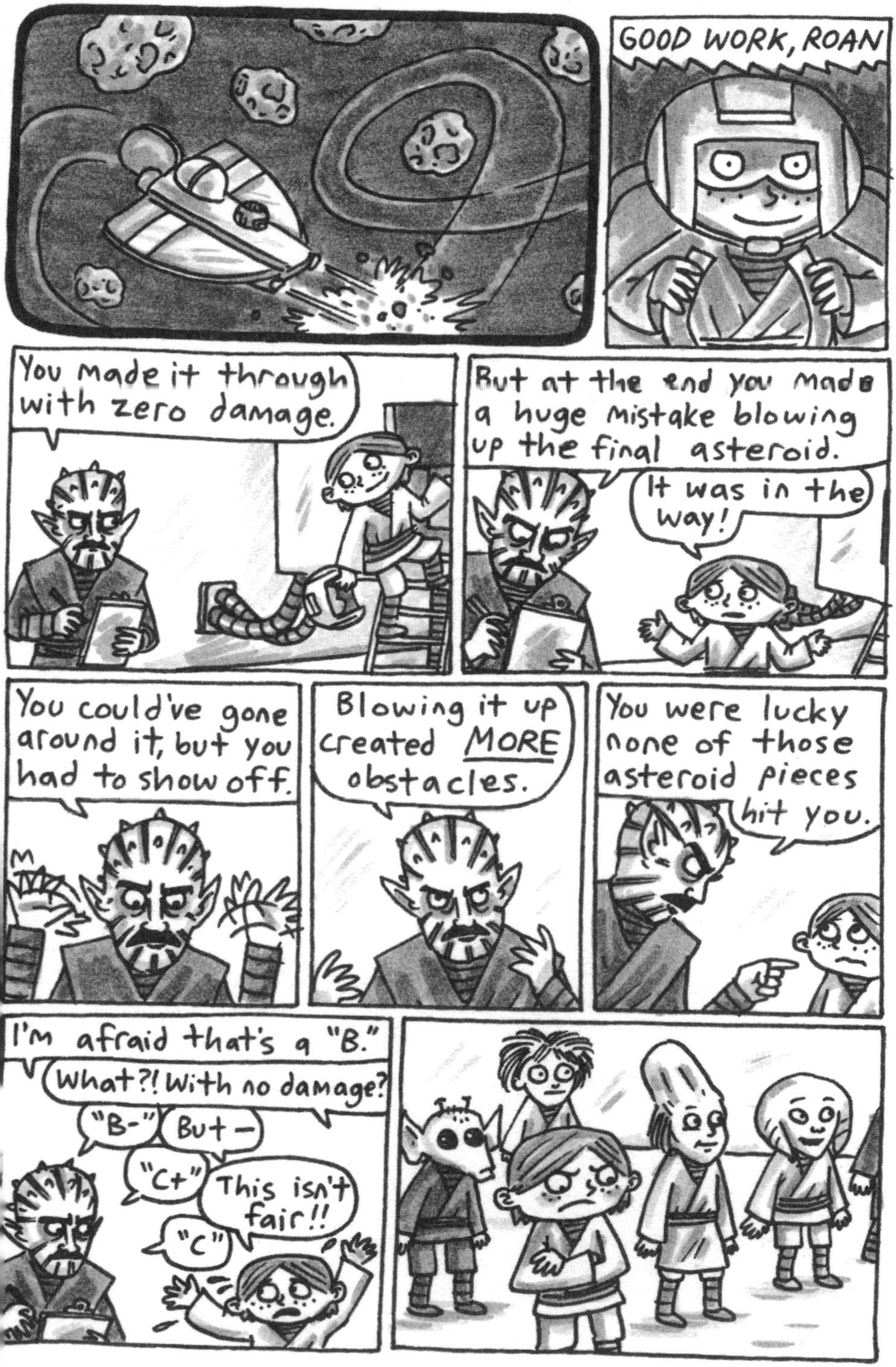
GOOD WORK, ROAN
You made it through with zero damage.
But at the end you made a huge mistake blowing up the final asteroid.
It was in the way!
You could've gone around it, but you had to show off.
Blowing it up created MORE obstacles.
You were lucky none of those asteroid pieces hit you.
I'm afraid that's a "B."
What?! With no damage?
"B-"
But—
"C+"
This isn't fair!!
"C"

STAR PILOT FLIGHT TRAINING NOTES

Avoiding Obstacles

- If you need to go faster, divert power from shields to increase power to engines. More dangerous to crash without shields, so DO NOT CRASH.
- Before avoiding obstacles by turning, make sure there isn't another obstacle where you're turning to.

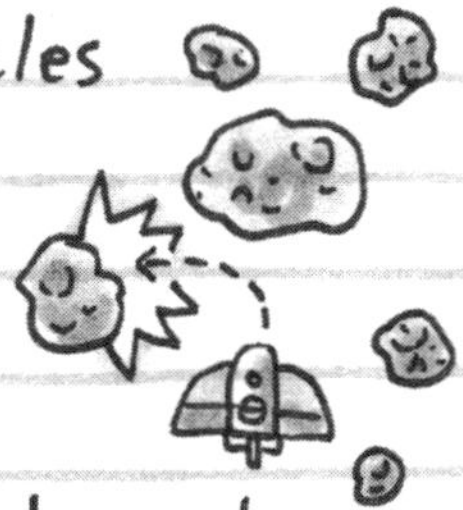

- Pay attention to onboard navigation computer. Typos are #1 cause of star pilots going the wrong direction.
- Check mirrors to make sure you're pointed AWAY from planets when entering hyperspace.
- Space is really dark so keep your lights on and make sure your starship has the proper reflective markings.

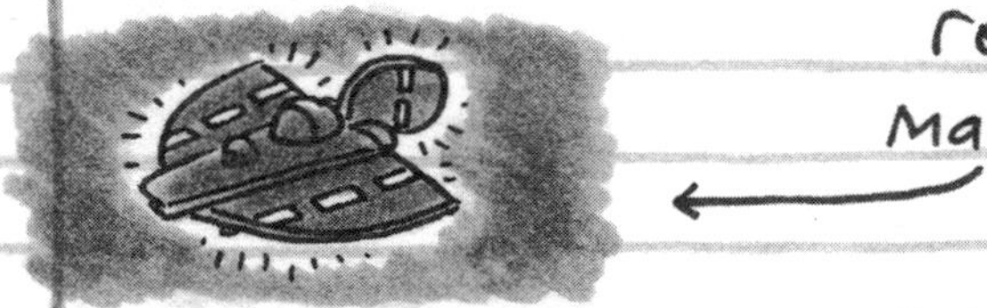

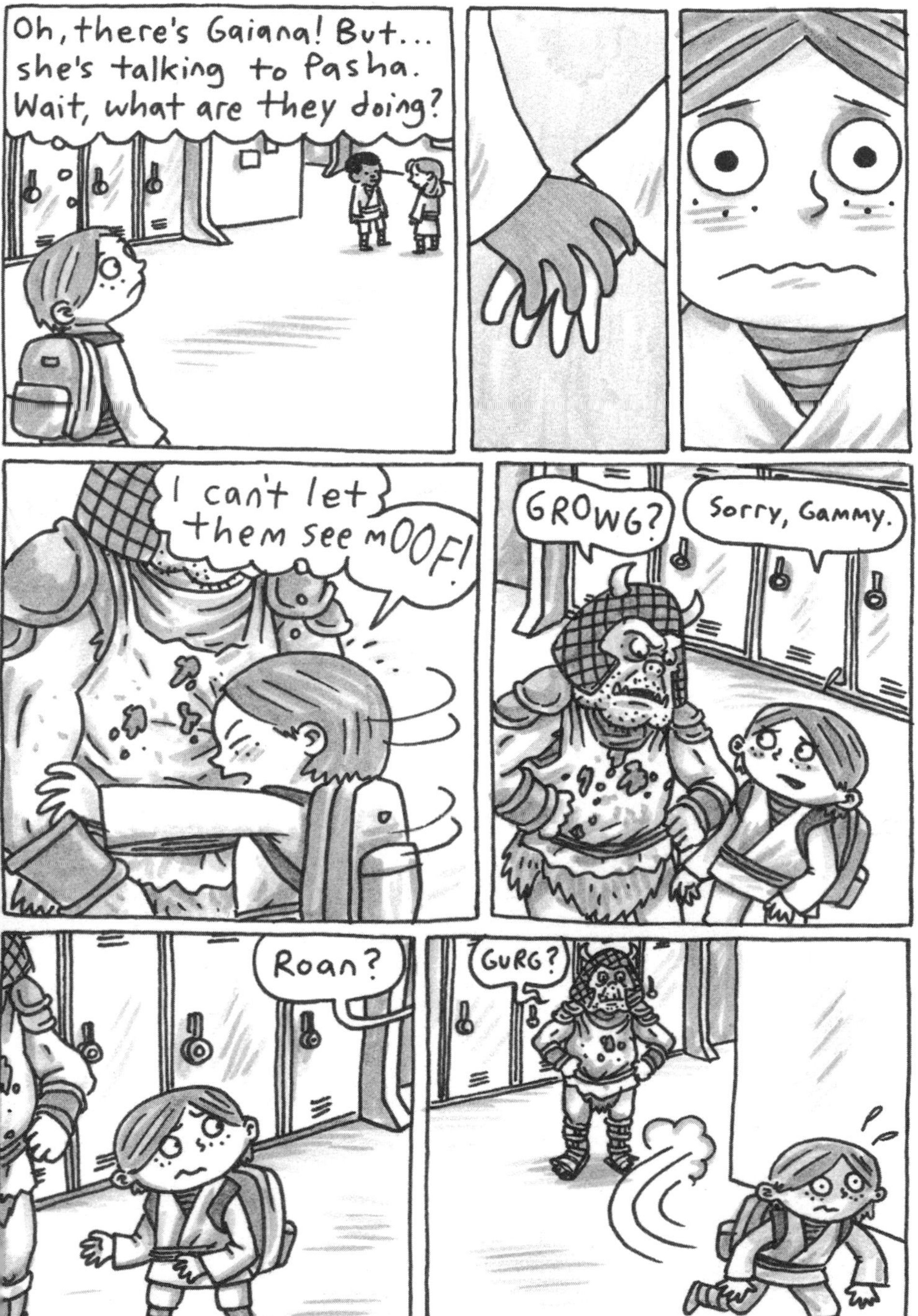
Oh, there's Gaiana! But... she's talking to Pasha. Wait, what are they doing?
I can't let them see mOOF!
GROWG?
Sorry, Gammy.
Roan?
GURG?

HEXADAY

My life is turning into a giant FAIL. After class I saw Pasha and Gaiana talking in the hallway, and Pasha was holding her hand! Maybe HE likes Gaiana now and that's why he's being weird to me since spring break. What a jerk. I'm not talking to either of them until they explain.

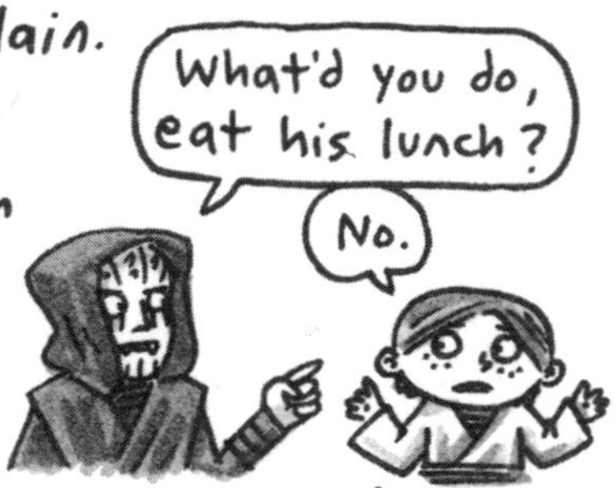
What'd you do, eat his lunch?
No.

Mr. Garfield still HATES me. Even Cyrus and Cronah think Mr. Garfield has it in for me. He always finds an excuse to mark my grade down. So even though I'm doing everything perfect, my grade will end up WORSE than last semester. The only good thing in my life is that we finally got to use the new star pilot simulators this week. They're so much better than the old ones — they even move around so it feels like you're actually flying. It's good that we have helmets to wear. With my luck, I'll probably break the new simulators, too.

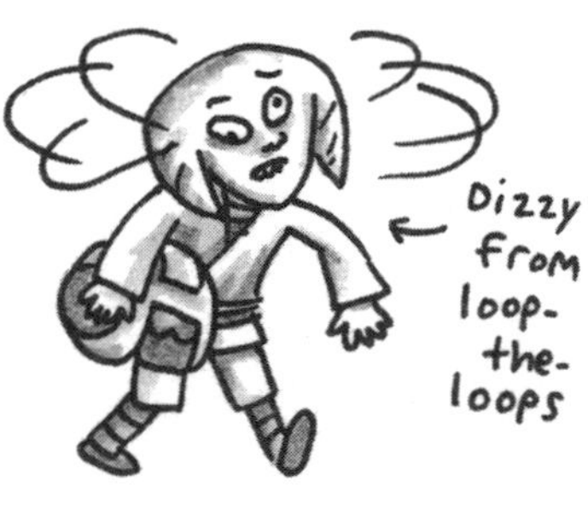
Dizzy from loop-the-loops

THINGS GAMMY SAYS

NUG UR TOG THOGK!

* Make sure you chew your food well. Especially if it's chewy.

HURG NG STUR!

*Gently spread the frosting on top of the cake and sprinkle with insect eggs.

GRN GRK TOK!

* For added taste, top with fruit.

EGRN DREG GROFKT!!

* Maybe a moldy cherry cut into starburst shape.

GRUNT!

* Don't worry about messing up a recipe, the food will still be edible. You won't starve, it'll just taste horrible.

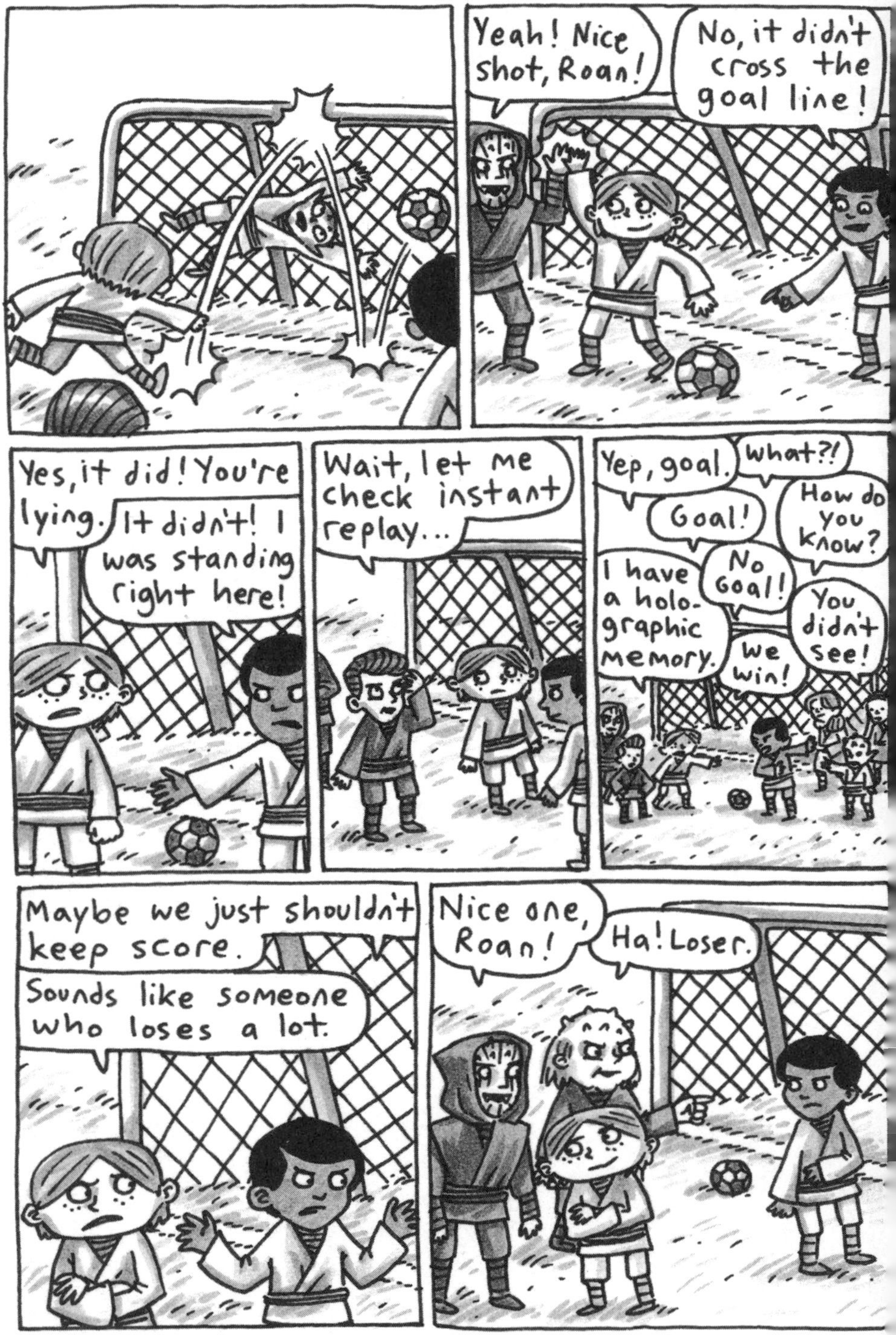
Yeah! Nice shot, Roan!
No, it didn't cross the goal line!
Yes, it did! You're lying.
It didn't! I was standing right here!
Wait, let me check instant replay...
Yep, goal.
What?!
Goal!
How do you know?
I have a holo-graphic memory.
No Goal!
You didn't see!
We win!
Maybe we just shouldn't keep score.
Sounds like someone who loses a lot.
Nice one, Roan!
Ha! Loser.

BASICS OF DROID CONSTRUCTION
PRINCIPAL MAR

CLASS ASSIGNMENT

Students will work in groups of five to build their own fully operational droids. You will be expected to work together, sharing responsibility equally. Students in each group will all receive the same grade.

- Droids are not required to communicate, but extra credit will be given to droids with multiple functions.
- Droids must have at least one primary specialized function (e.g. sweeping and vacuuming floors).
- NO WEAPONS. Any droid equipped with lasers will result in a failing grade.
- Droids will be judged on these criteria: function, design, reliability, originality, and the vague, undefinable sense of whether the droid has "it."

QUADDAY

Supposedly, the groups for our droid construction project were picked ~~randomly~~ randomly by a holocomputer, but I think the holocomputer is playing a joke on me. Not only is Cronah in my group, but none of my real friends are....

Cyrus is in my group, he's at least been cooler to me lately. I think it's partly because he met my dad, who's a real starfighter pilot and kind of a big deal. Now I'm going to have to choose between following along with what everyone else wants to do on the project, or trying to get them to listen to me, which will be impossible. This project's destiny is TOTAL DISASTER.

what our droid will end up looking like

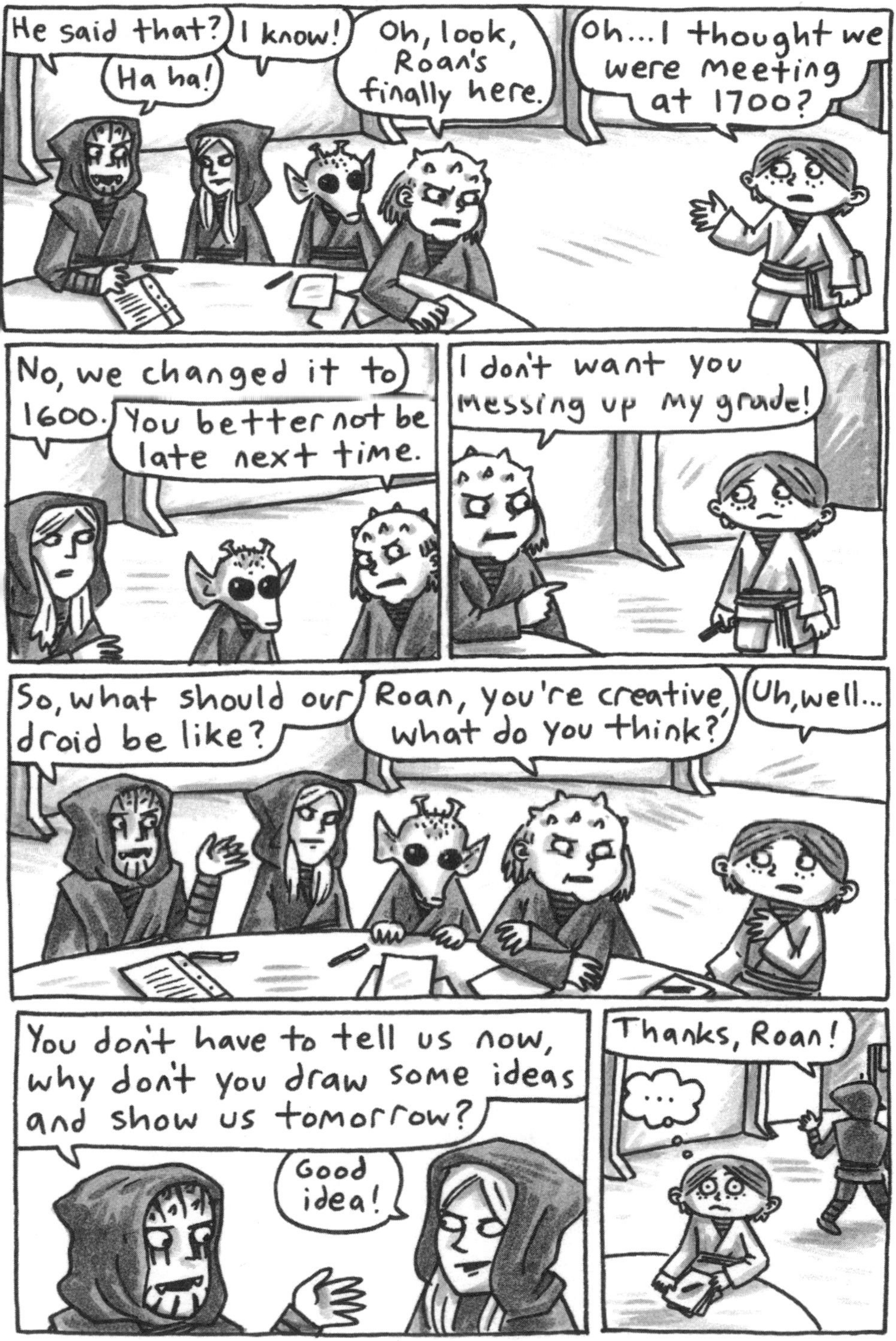
He said that?
Ha ha!
I know!
Oh, look, Roan's finally here.
Oh...I thought we were meeting at 1700?
No, we changed it to 1600.
You better not be late next time.
I don't want you messing up my grade!
So, what should our droid be like?
Roan, you're creative, what do you think?
Uh, well...
You don't have to tell us now, why don't you draw some ideas and show us tomorrow?
Good idea!
Thanks, Roan!
...

Pentaday

Home Ec.
Gammy

NOTES

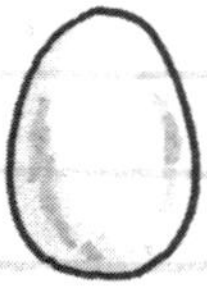

To tell if egg is ready to eat, crack open. If creature hatches and attacks you, egg should have been cooked longer.

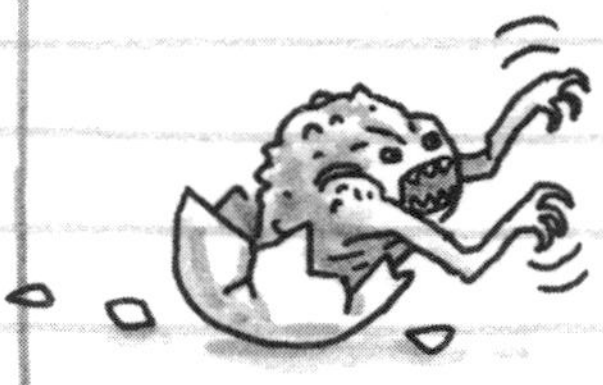

*Add mushrooms to your cupcakes so it feels like you're eating something healthy. (May taste different?!)

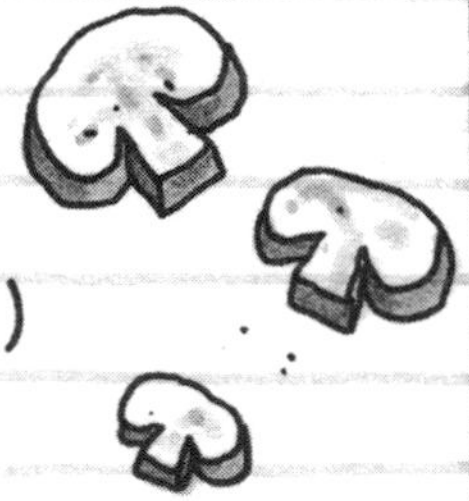

IMPORTANT!

-Lightsaber should not be used to cut butter (it tends to melt all the butter) or bread (will toast the entire loaf).

-Lightsaber CAN be used to carve turkey for dinner. Make sure to thoroughly wash lightsaber afterward.

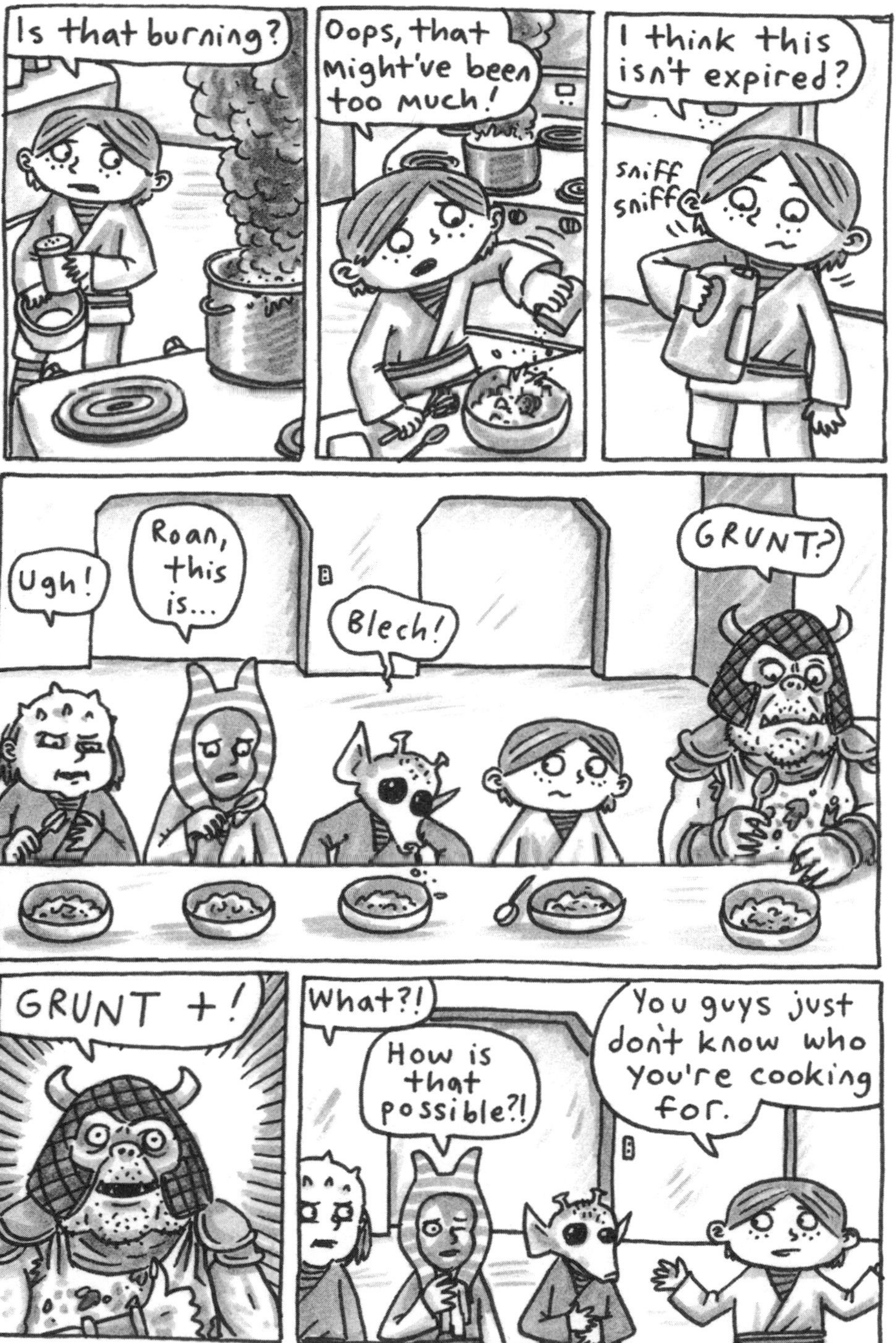

Is that burning?
Oops, that might've been too much!
I think this isn't expired?
sniff sniff
Ugh!
Roan, this is...
Blech!
GRUNT?
GRUNT +!
What?!
How is that possible?!
You guys just don't know who you're cooking for.

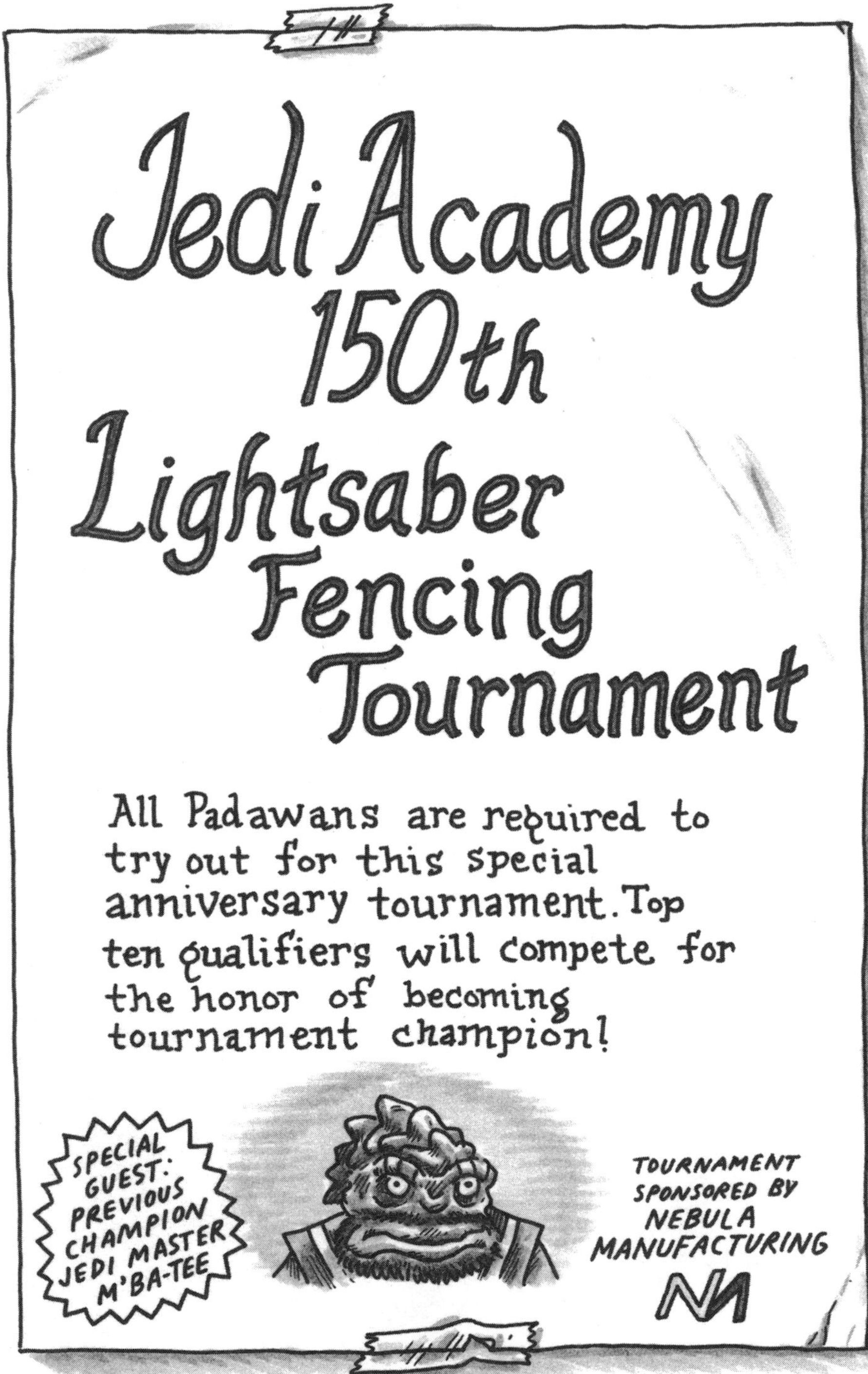
Jedi Academy 150th Lightsaber Fencing Tournament
All Padawans are required to try out for this special anniversary tournament. Top ten qualifiers will compete for the honor of becoming tournament champion!
SPECIAL GUEST: PREVIOUS CHAMPION JEDI MASTER M'BA-TEE
TOURNAMENT SPONSORED BY NEBULA MANUFACTURING
NM

TRIDAY

I'm going to start training more at lightsaber fencing. If I practice enough in secret, everyone will be surprised when I do well at the tournament. Maybe I can even win the whole thing? I've been trying to find someone to train with, but I'm still not talking to Pasha so he's out. But now I figured out a way to practice while my group is making the droid — we're going to build a training droid for lightsaber fencing. It's actually been okay working with Cyrus and Cronah. They're kind of letting me be the "idea guy." So I won't have to do as much of the ~~tedios~~ tedious work of putting the droid together.

The only plan Ewok Pilot came up with is smashing their spaceship between two logs...

Go mob un loo? M'gasha.

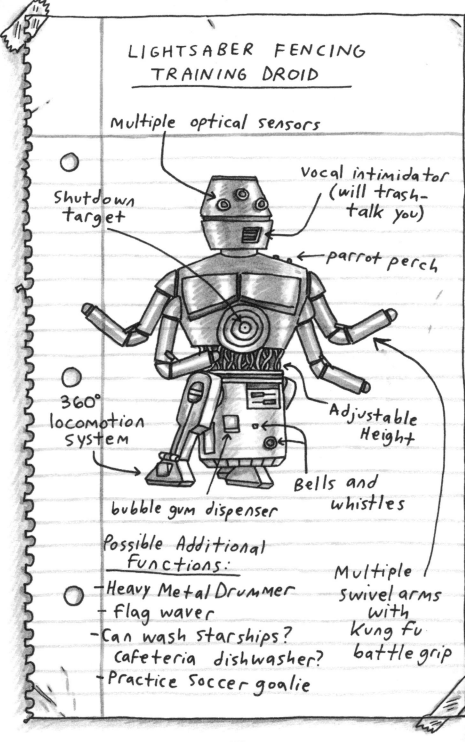

LIGHTSABER FENCING TRAINING DROID

Multiple optical sensors
Vocal intimidator (will trash-talk you)
Shutdown target
parrot perch
360° locomotion system
Adjustable Height
Bells and whistles
bubble gum dispenser
Multiple swivel arms with Kung Fu battle grip

Possible Additional Functions:

- Heavy Metal Drummer
- Flag waver
- Can wash starships? Cafeteria dishwasher?
- Practice Soccer goalie

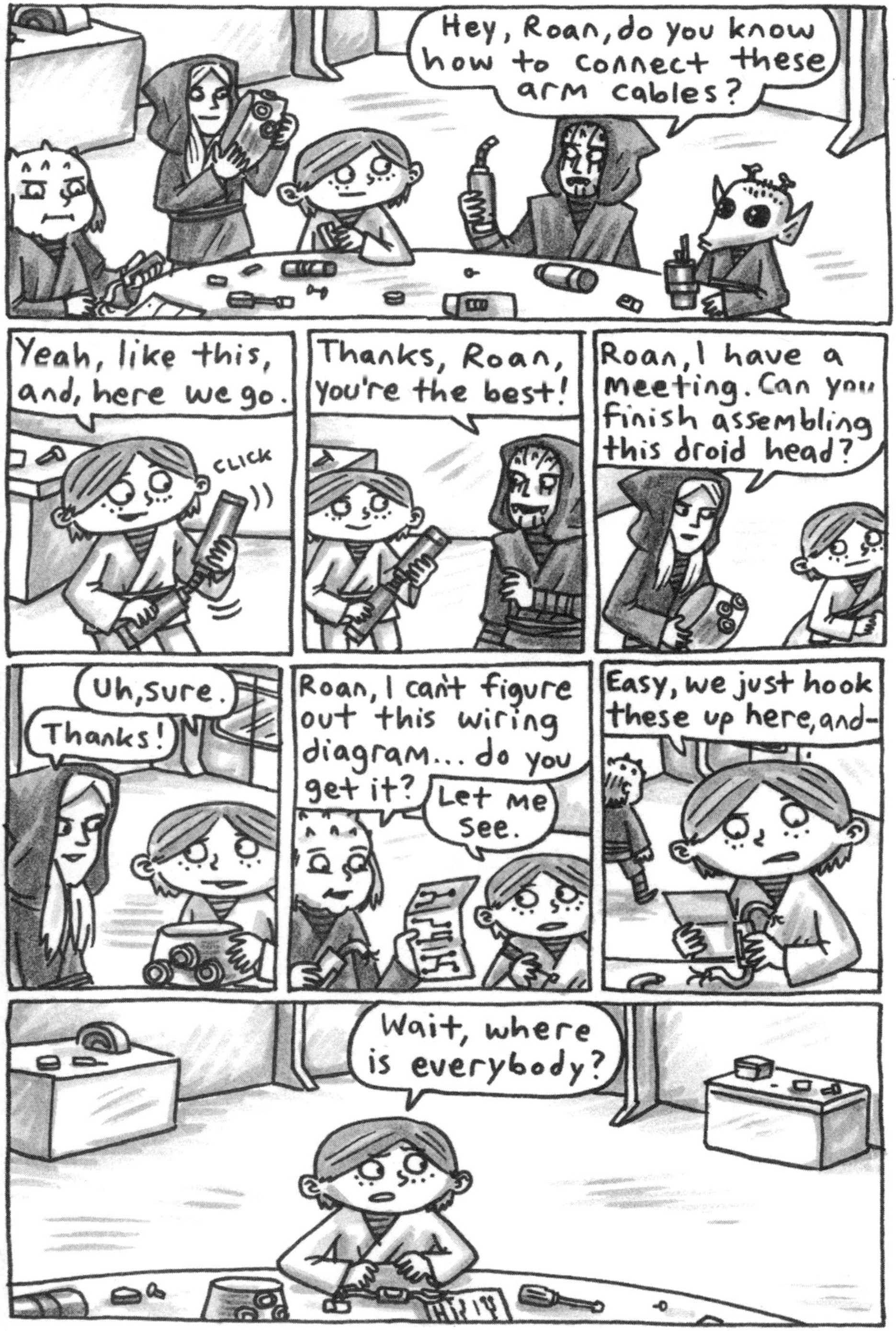
Hey, Roan, do you know how to connect these arm cables?
Yeah, like this, and, here we go.
CLICK
Thanks, Roan, you're the best!
Roan, I have a meeting. Can you finish assembling this droid head?
Uh, sure.
Thanks!
Roan, I can't figure out this wiring diagram... do you get it?
Let me see.
Easy, we just hook these up here, and-
Wait, where is everybody?

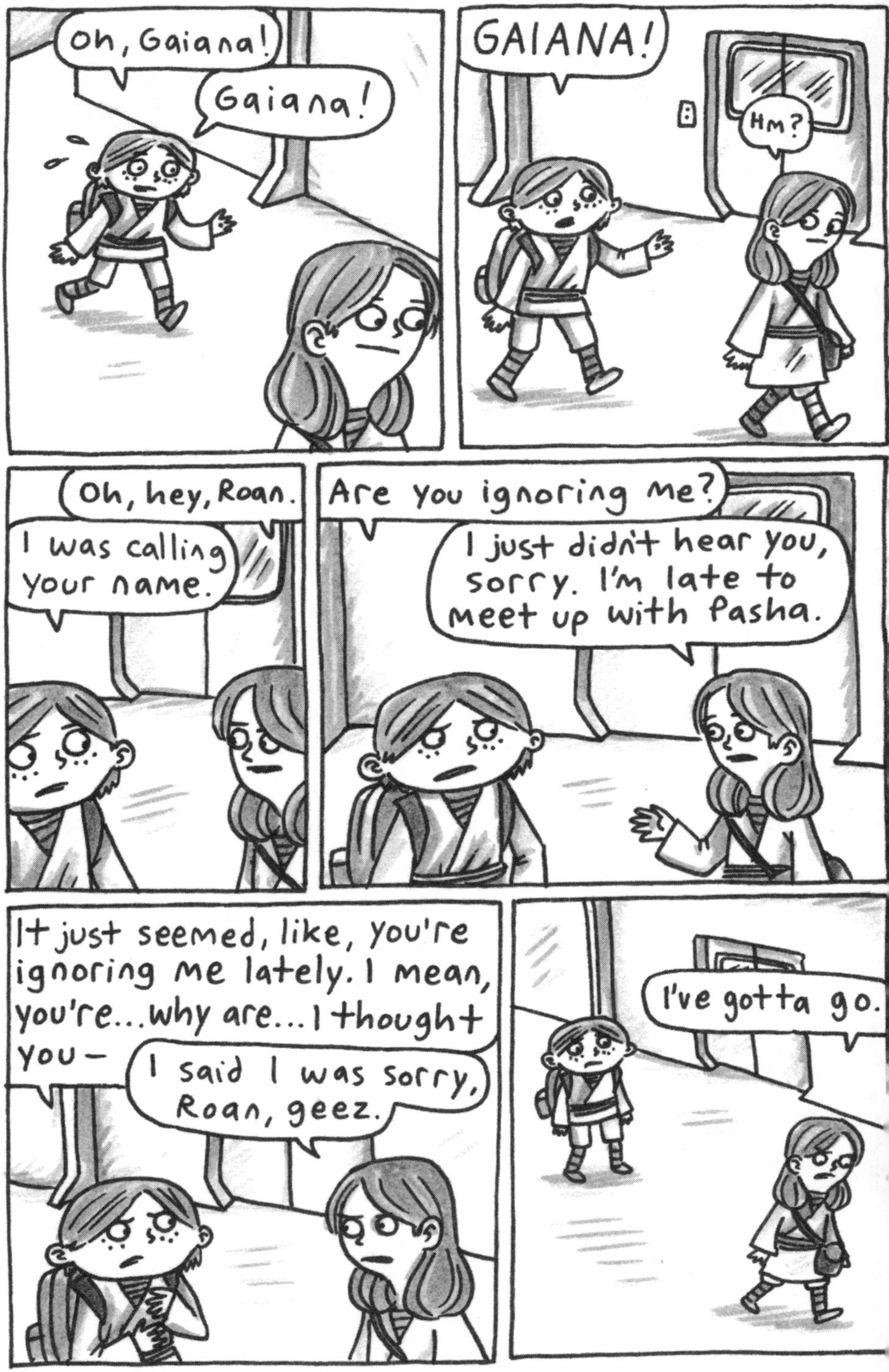
Oh, Gaiana!
Gaiana!
GAIANA!
Hm?
Oh, hey, Roan.
I was calling your name.
Are you ignoring me?
I just didn't hear you, sorry. I'm late to meet up with Pasha.
It just seemed, like, you're ignoring me lately. I mean, you're...why are...I thought you—
I said I was sorry, Roan, geez.
I've gotta go.

PENTADAY

Lately, every time I try to hang out with Bill or Egon it seems like they're busy. Actually, we DID have plans to hang out yesterday, but after waiting an hour I gave up. Bill made it sound like it was just a mistake, but it wouldn't surprise me if Pasha is trying to turn them against me, too. I've hardly talked to Gaiana this semester and I bet she's just hanging out with Pasha, and he's probably telling her how awful I am. I was going to ask Tegan what she thought Gaiana was thinking, but Tegan would just tell me to talk to Gaiana, which I tried. It was a big disaster. At least I'll get better grades this semester, since all I do is study, and not hang out with my friends.

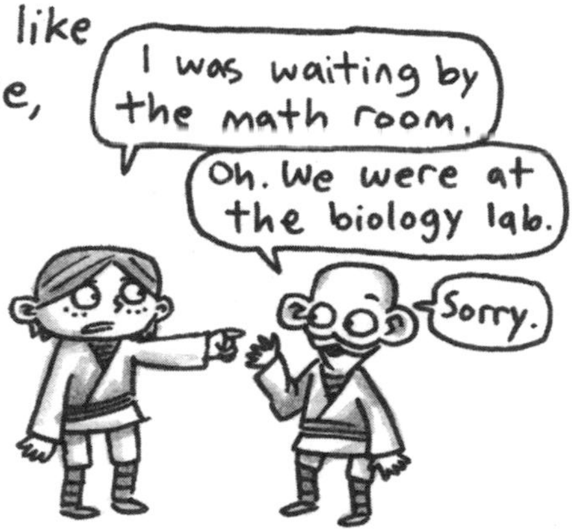
I was waiting by the math room.
Oh. We were at the biology lab.
Sorry.

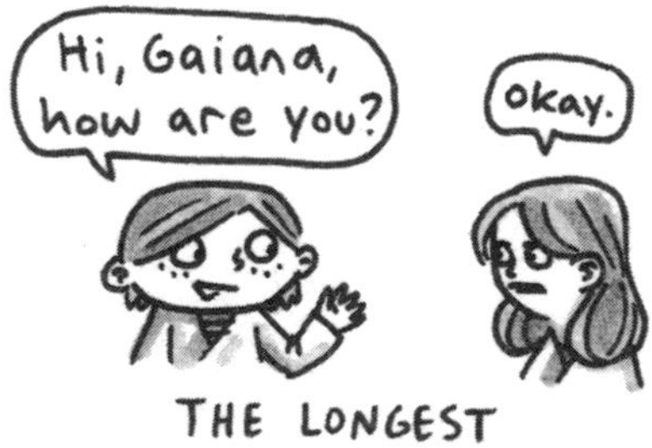
Hi, Gaiana, how are you?
Okay.
THE LONGEST CONVERSATION I HAD WITH GAIANA LAST MONTH

I have been hanging out with Cyrus and Cronah a little, mostly because we've been working on our group droid project. The droid is looking good! They let me basically design the whole thing. At the start of this year I never would've imagined working on something with them, let alone me leading

I wish I could shrug like that

them all on the whole project. Cyrus said I should hang out with him and Cronah tomorrow. I asked him what they were doing and he just shrugged. It's cool— they don't even need to have a plan of what they're going to do. Cyrus and I also had a really long conversation, about Corellian starfighter ~~mano maneuvers~~ maneuvers.

I guess I just needed to get to know him and Cronah to realize they aren't ALWAYS total jerks. We're going to practice lightsaber fencing... I'll bet I can learn some new techniques from them.

I'm not sure we can use this method, Ewok Pilot.

Dangar!

ART OF PHYSICS
IMPORTANT EXAMPLES

Lackbar/Pilton

The Hyperspace Night

Painting shows how perception of astronomical objects changes when a starship enters hyperspace

The Great Wave Off Naboo

Shows behavior of water molecules when a sando aqua mon~~~~ approache~

ROAN —
LET'S SKIP
MR. G.'S CLASS.
CRONAH AND
I HAVE
SOMETHING TO
SHOW YOU.
—CY

Monoday Afternoon On Yavin 4

~~~t style of drawing ~~~ptical illusion using ~~~d distance

~~~e Rhythm

~~~al chaos could represent interactions of atomic particles affected by the Force

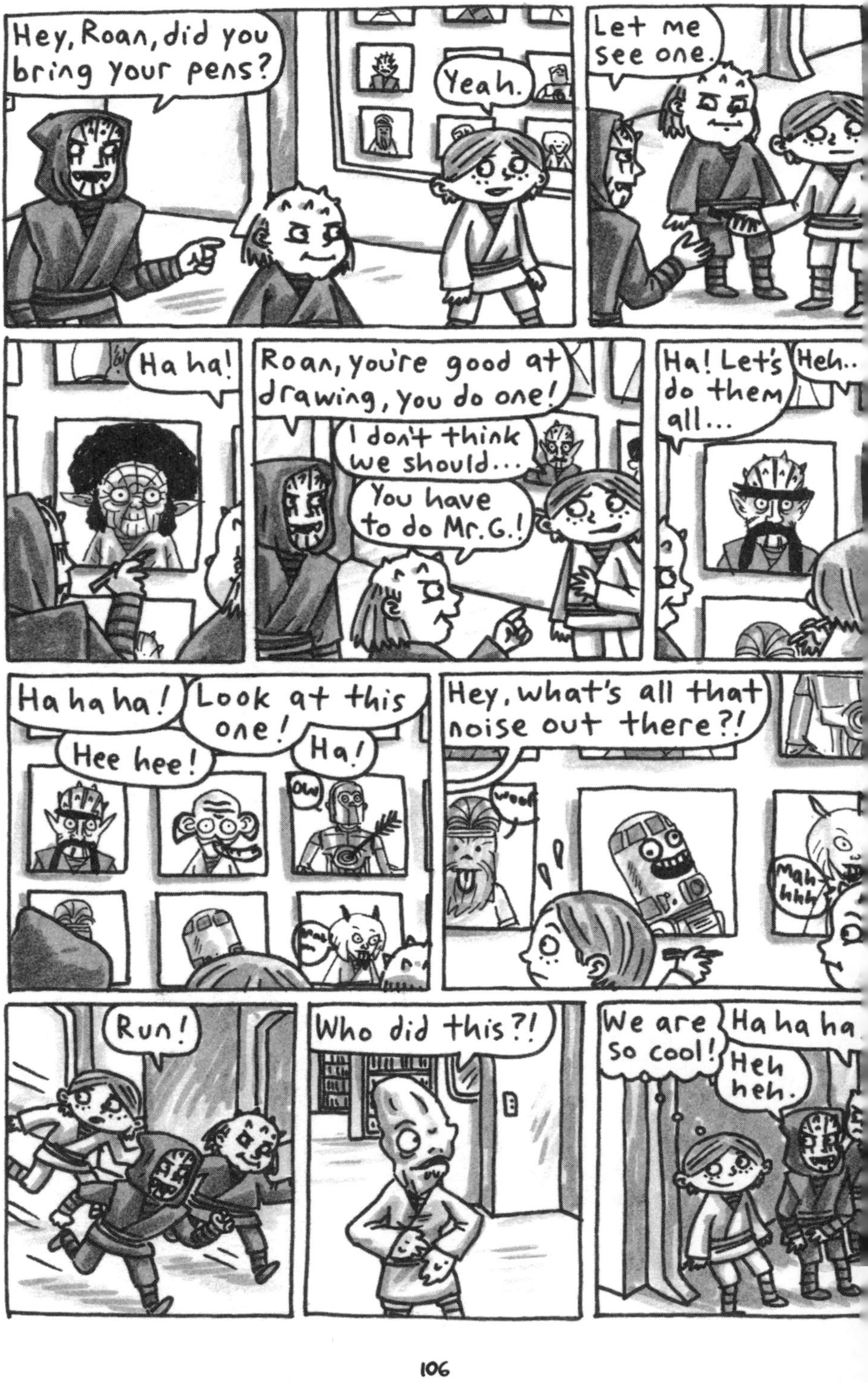
Hey, Roan, did you bring your pens?
Yeah.
Let me see one.
Ha ha!
Roan, you're good at drawing, you do one!
I don't think we should...
You have to do Mr. G.!
Ha! Let's do them all...
Heh..
Ha ha ha!
Look at this one!
Hee hee!
Ha!
Ow
Hey, what's all that noise out there?!
Woof
Run!
Who did this?!
We are so cool!
Ha ha ha
Heh heh.

TRIDAY

Tomorrow we present our group droid construction projects. I'm going to look over ours one last time tonight. It turned out well! We'll even be able to use it to train for the lightsaber fencing tournament. Since everyone else in my group usually wears dark robes, we thought I should wear a dark robe for the presentation, so we all look the same. Cyrus had some old robes that

Hood = ✓ Awesome!

didn't fit him anymore, and he said I could just keep them. I think I look pretty cool in them, actually. I mean, they're a little big, but everyone wears robes that are a little big. That was nice of Cyrus, and then Cronah suggested that I get to name the droid, since it was my design. I decided we should call it the Multi-Armed Dueling Simulator droid. So we call him M.A.D.S.

I WILL DESTROY YOU!

I WILL DEFEAT YOU!

MADS

That was a most interesting cafeteria droid we just saw...

Cyrus, Jo-Ahn, Roan, Cronah, and Greer...would you like to present your droid?

Thank you, Principal Mar. As you can see, this Multi-Armed Duel Simulator droid — or "M.A.D.S." — is designed for training and preparation in lightsaber dueling.

It's full of specialized design functions.

Each arm is covered with lightsaber-resistant foam padding.

The multiple optical sensors can detect a full 360° of movement.

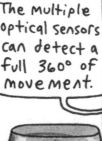

By combining a swivel torso and wheeled feet, the droid is super mobile.

And the center target tracks points earned in fencing.

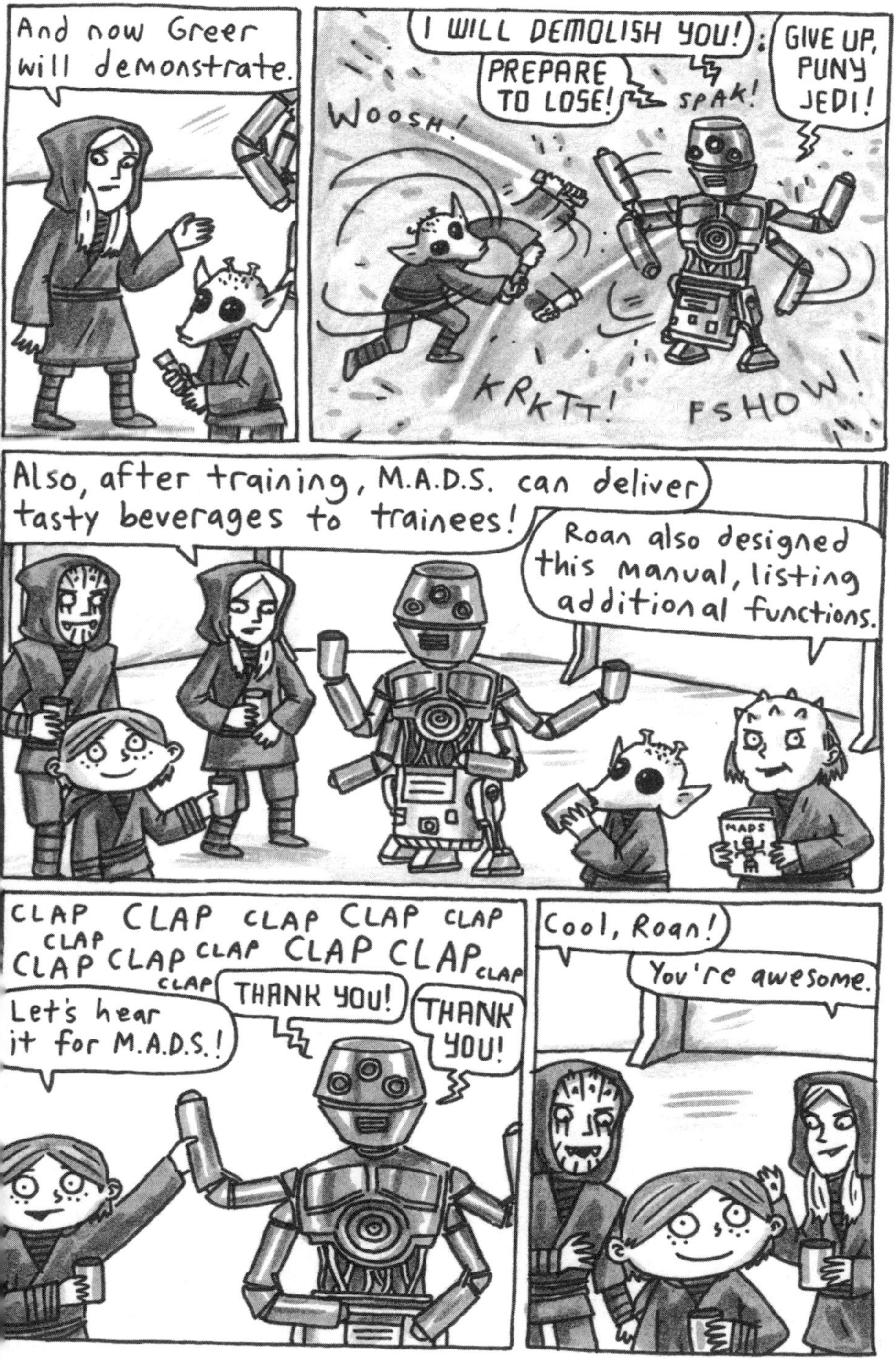
And now Greer will demonstrate.
I WILL DEMOLISH YOU!
PREPARE TO LOSE!
GIVE UP, PUNY JEDI!
WOOSH!
SPAK!
KRKTT!
FSHOW!
Also, after training, M.A.D.S. can deliver tasty beverages to trainees!
Roan also designed this manual, listing additional functions.
MADS
CLAP CLAP CLAP CLAP CLAP CLAP CLAP CLAP CLAP CLAP CLAP CLAP CLAP
Let's hear it for M.A.D.S.!
THANK YOU!
THANK YOU!
Cool, Roan!
You're awesome.

HEPTADAY

Our droid got the best grade in class Principal Mar seemed impressed by how much work we put into it. Of course, I think the other droids weren't that great. Pasha and Bill made a "Class Schedule Assistant" droid that basically leads you to your next class. I think you'd only need it the first day of class and after that it'd just trip you. I've been having a lot of fun hanging out with Cyrus and Cronah. They're pretty cool — they even have some video games I'd never seen. Way cooler than the games Egon is usually showing us. If Pasha played them he'd probably make a big deal about them being too violent. He's probably jealous of my group, because he had to do extra work with his group since their droid malfunctioned. Cyrus says that the only people who think school grades are a competition are the people who aren't doing as well.

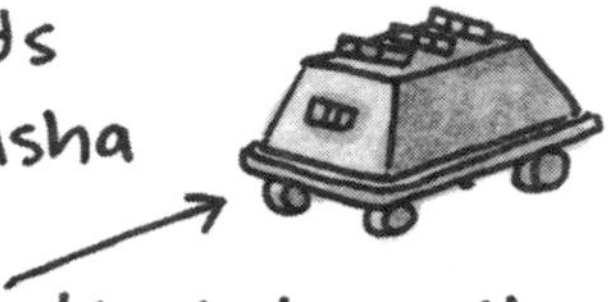

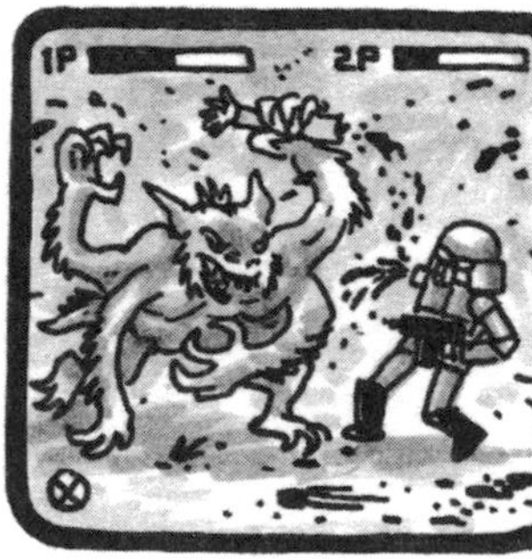
1P
2P

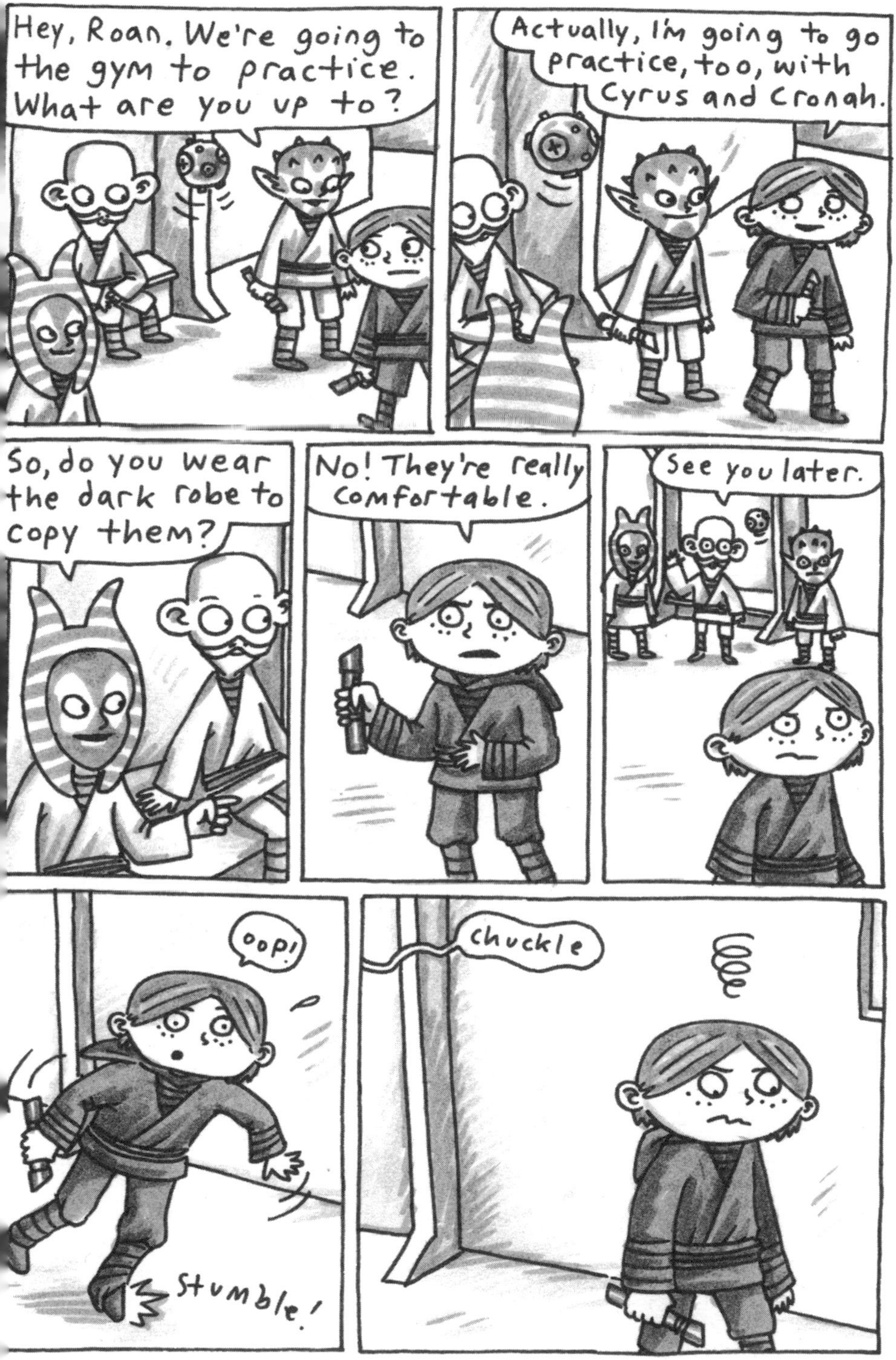
Hey, Roan. We're going to the gym to practice. What are you up to?
Actually, I'm going to go practice, too, with Cyrus and Cronah.
So, do you wear the dark robe to copy them?
No! They're really comfortable.
See you later.
oop!
Stumble!
chuckle

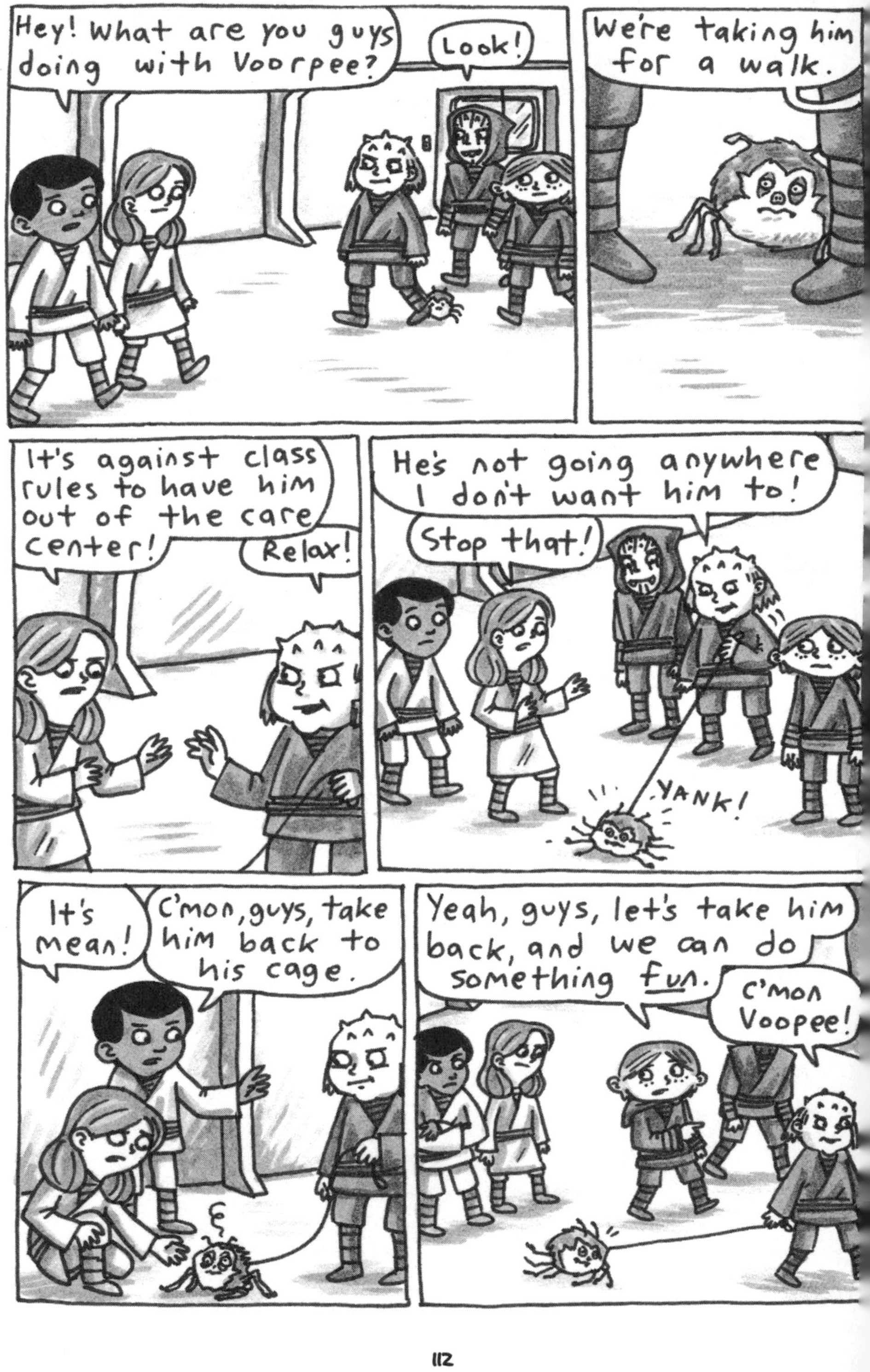
Hey! What are you guys doing with Voorpee?
Look!
We're taking him for a walk.
It's against class rules to have him out of the care center!
Relax!
He's not going anywhere I don't want him to!
Stop that!
YANK!
It's mean!
C'mon, guys, take him back to his cage.
Yeah, guys, let's take him back, and we can do something fun.
C'mon Voopee!

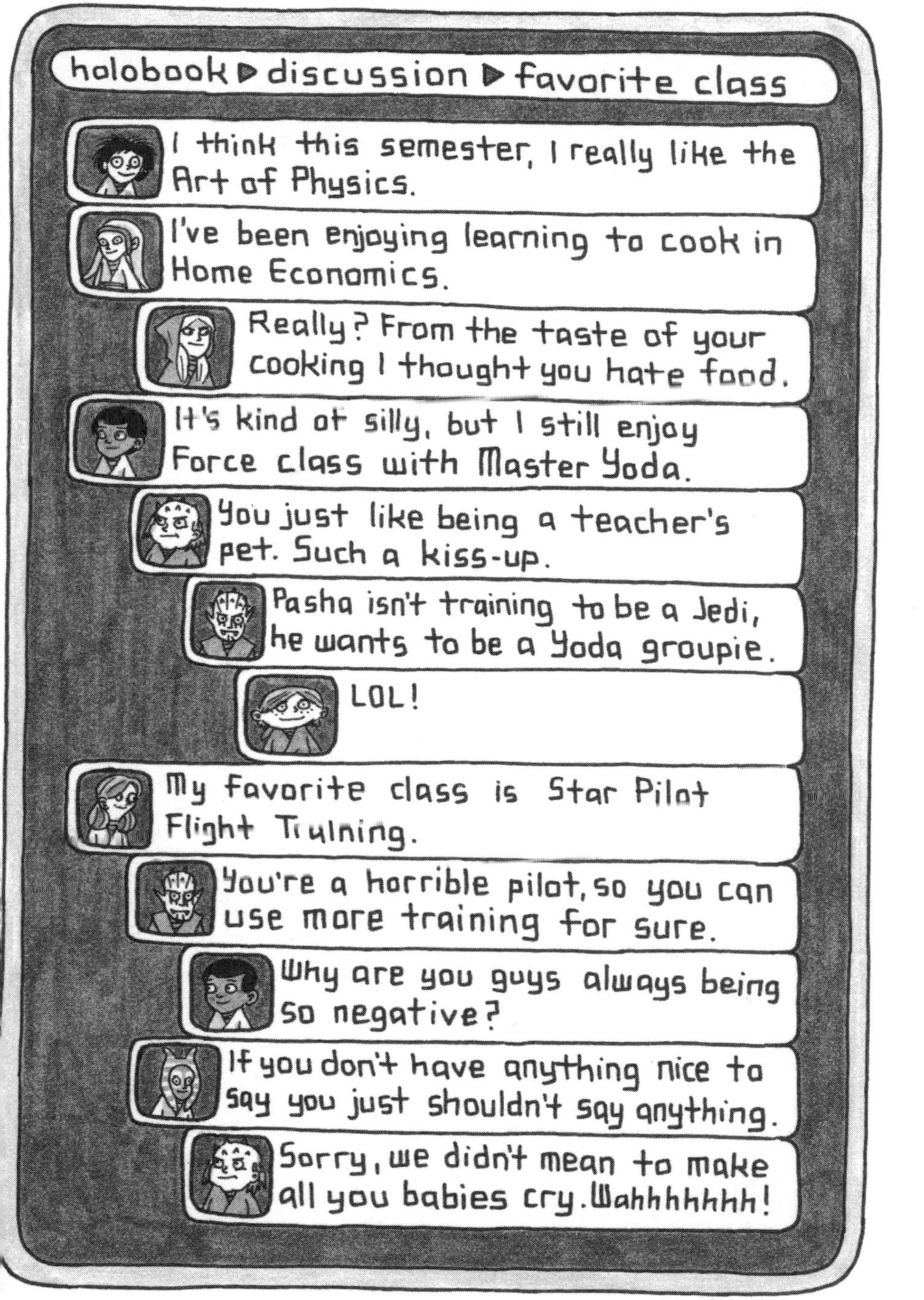
holobook ▶ discussion ▶ favorite class
I think this semester, I really like the Art of Physics.
I've been enjoying learning to cook in Home Economics.
Really? From the taste of your cooking I thought you hate food.
It's kind of silly, but I still enjoy Force class with Master Yoda.
You just like being a teacher's pet. Such a kiss-up.
Pasha isn't training to be a Jedi, he wants to be a Yoda groupie.
LOL!
My favorite class is Star Pilot Flight Training.
You're a horrible pilot, so you can use more training for sure.
Why are you guys always being so negative?
If you don't have anything nice to say you just shouldn't say anything.
Sorry, we didn't mean to make all you babies cry. Wahhhhhhh!

The Padawan Observer

EDITED BY THE STUDENTS OF JEDI ACADEMY · VOL. MXIII #8

MASTER YODA SHUTS DOWN HOLOBOOK DUE TO COMMENTS

In an unexpected move, Holobook has been completely shut down by Master Yoda, due to the large number of mean and insulting comments appearing recently. "Behave like this, Padawans should not. Off, Holobook will be, until better manners, the Padawans have." Master Yoda warned that although writing mean comments may flow easily for some, they can lead to the dark side. Students may still use Holomail.

MISSING!

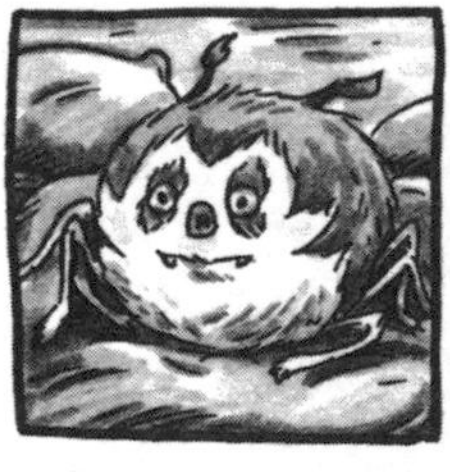

"Voorpee," the class pet voorpak, has gone missing!

- Does not actually answer to "Voorpee" but may come if you make cute noises.
- May look like a piece of dirt or lint, so be careful to not sweep up.
- Please help find Voorpee!
- Also, watch your step.

INSIDE:

HEXADAY

Voorpee is lost, but it's not my fault. Some of the other students think it is anyway. I heard that Pasha told Gaiana he thought that someone said I made a joke about losing Voorpee or something. Just because I was with Cronah and Cyrus when they took Voorpee out of his cage doesn't mean I'm the one who lost him. I know Gaiana didn't take him, but why didn't anyone think it was her, since SHE likes Voorpee so much? Plus, she's been acting weird all semester, especially to me. Whatever, I don't care. I used to, but not anymore. Not really. I think.

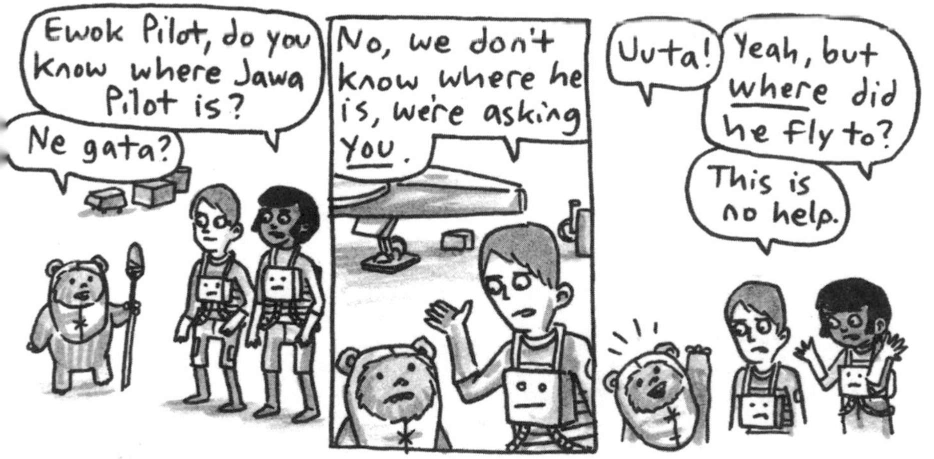
Ewok Pilot, do you know where Jawa Pilot is?
Ne gata?
No, we don't know where he is, we're asking YOU.
Uuta!
Yeah, but where did he fly to?
This is no help.

The other thing that happened is that Master Yoda shut off access to Holobook because people were being too mean. Maybe it got a little out of hand, but I think some people just don't know how to take a joke. Pasha has been mean to me, too, not on Holobook but in REAL LIFE. He still hasn't said anything to me about Gaiana, and when he found out I pretended to be sick to get out of some homework he started lecturing me. It kind of hurts that he didn't even realize that's the first time he talked to me in, like, a month! I just ignored him. The only problem with ignoring Pasha is that our Marksman-H Combat Remote is missing,

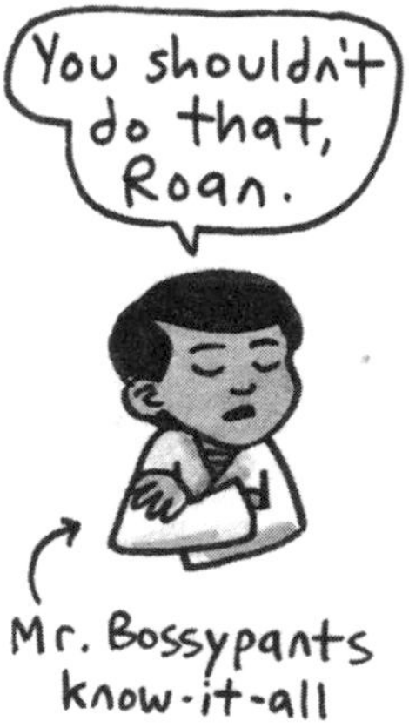
You shouldn't do that, Roan.
Mr. Bossypants know-it-all

and I can't ask him where it is. He must be hiding it from me on purpose. Unless Voorpee took it. (NOT likely.)

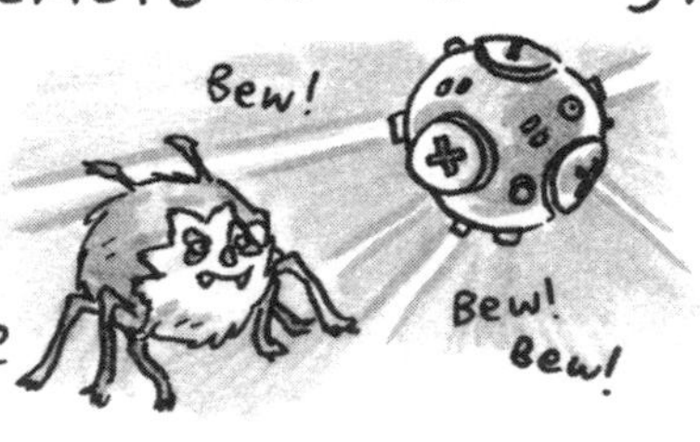
Bew!
Bew!
Bew!

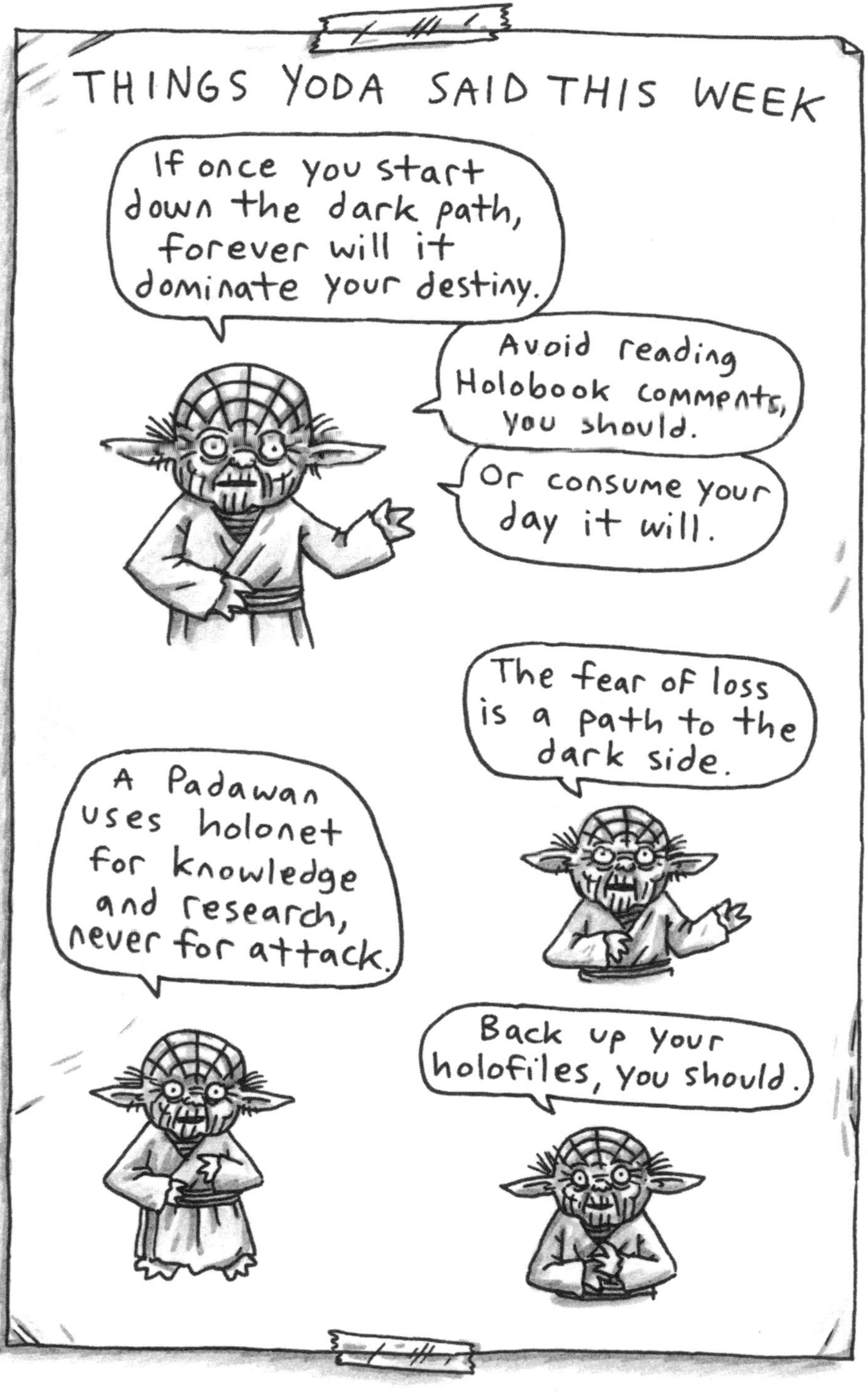
THINGS YODA SAID THIS WEEK
If once you start down the dark path, forever will it dominate your destiny.
Avoid reading Holobook comments, you should.
Or consume your day it will.
The fear of loss is a path to the dark side.
A Padawan uses holonet for knowledge and research, never for attack.
Back up your holofiles, you should.

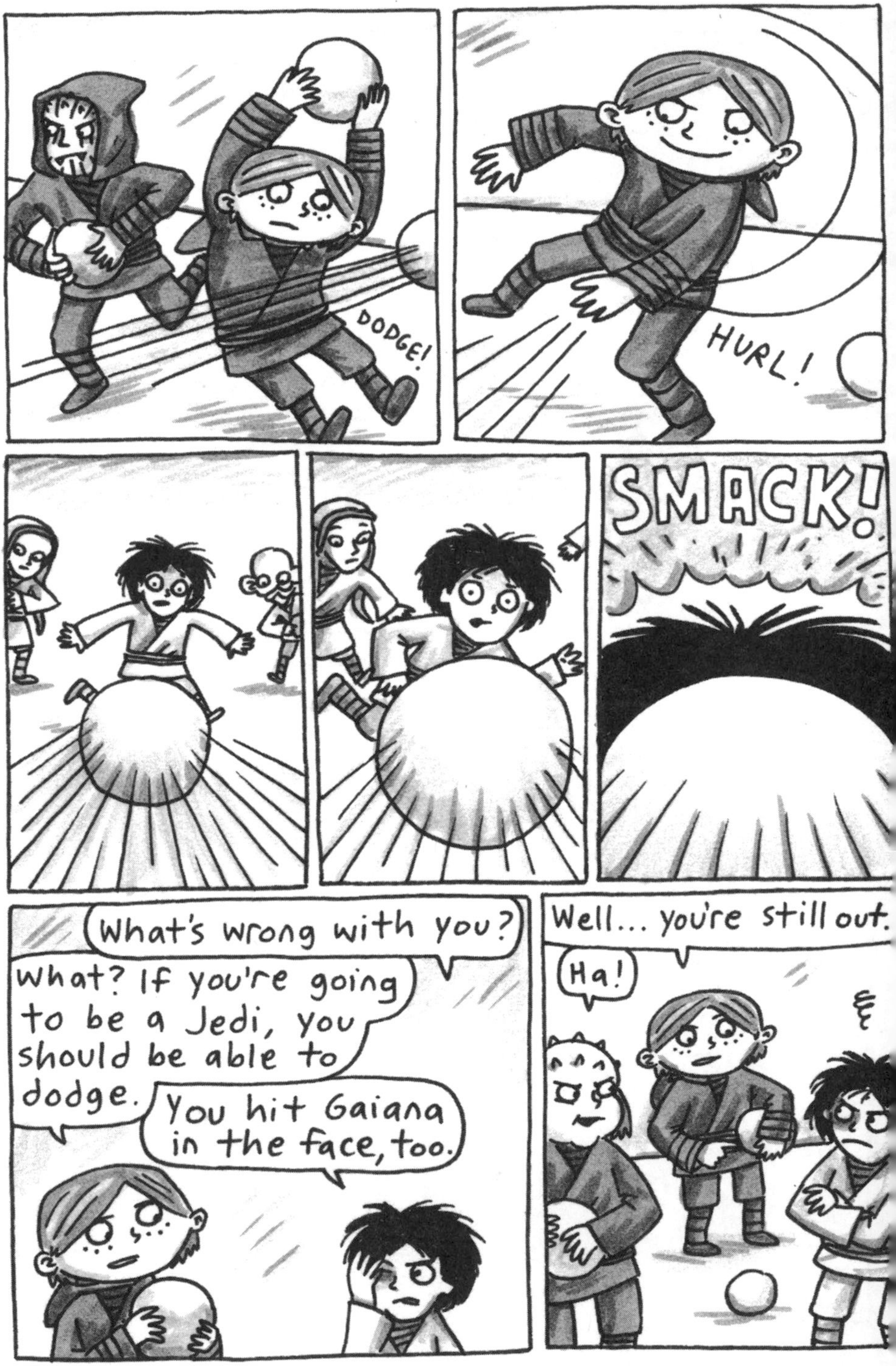
DODGE!
HURL!
SMACK!
What's wrong with you?
What? If you're going to be a Jedi, you should be able to dodge.
You hit Gaiana in the face, too.
Well... you're still out.
Ha!

LIGHTSABER DUELING SKILLS
TAKE-HOME QUIZ

(B)

STUDENT: <u>Roan Novachez</u>
INSTRUCTOR: <u>Mr. Garfield</u>

1. Fill in the missing movement for basic lightsaber forms.

A SIMPLE STICK FIGURE WOULD BE ENOUGH HERE, ROAN!

2. What three moves should be used together in Form IV?

   <u>rapid spin, somersault, cartwheel</u>

~~3.~~ What is the first Form to use in a real-life lightsaber duel?

Form II - Makashi Form

NO- FORM ZERO: FIND A NONVIOLENT SOLUTION

119

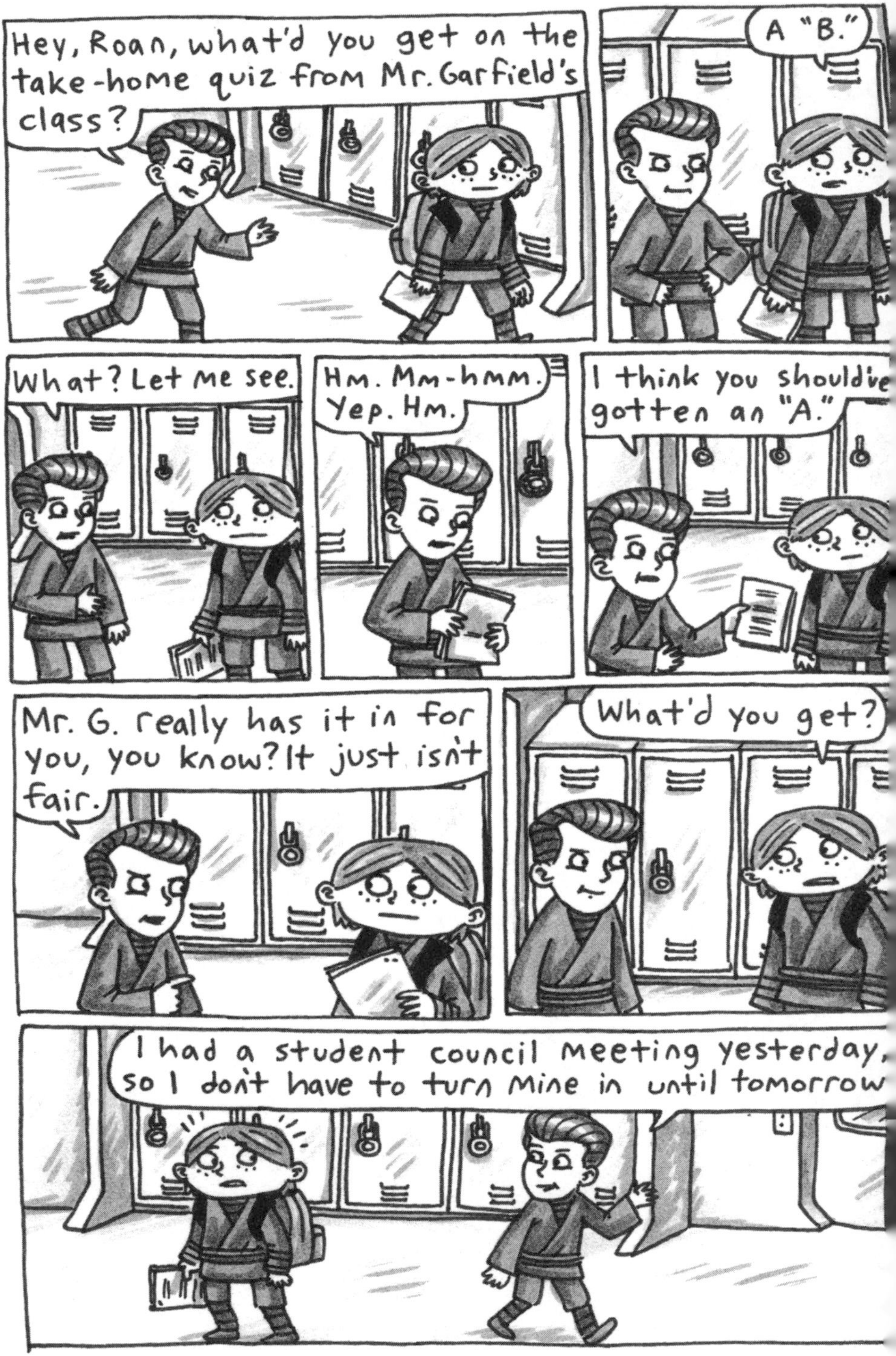
Hey, Roan, what'd you get on the take-home quiz from Mr. Garfield's class?
A "B."
What? Let me see.
Hm. Mm-hmm. Yep. Hm.
I think you should've gotten an "A."
Mr. G. really has it in for you, you know? It just isn't fair.
What'd you get?
I had a student council meeting yesterday, so I don't have to turn mine in until tomorrow

DUODAY

I've been getting a lot more training for the lightsaber fencing tournament, thanks to M.A.D.S., Cyrus, and Cronah. The other day they told Ronald he could come with us, which annoyed me. They seem to like him, but he's always cheating and just seems slimy to me. Cronah says Ronald actually has some good ideas for st~~ratag~~y strategy but I don't want to have to listen to Ronald just to win in lightsaber fencing.

Fortunately, the height adjustment got stuck on M.A.D.S. so we spent the whole time fixing that and didn't have to practice with Ronald.

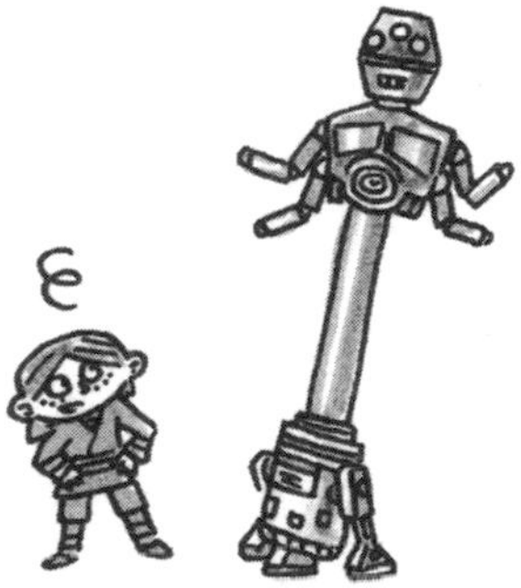

Unfortunately, I couldn't get the storage space (where we've been keeping M.A.D.S.) unlocked. So I ended up keeping M.A.D.S. in my room last night, which made it hard to sleep, because I swear he was staring at me all night!

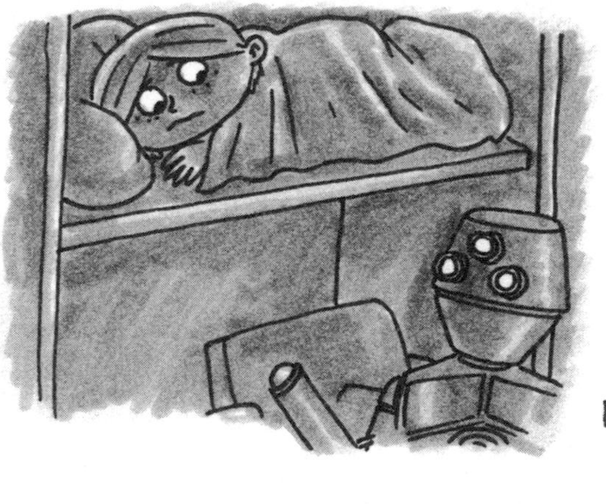

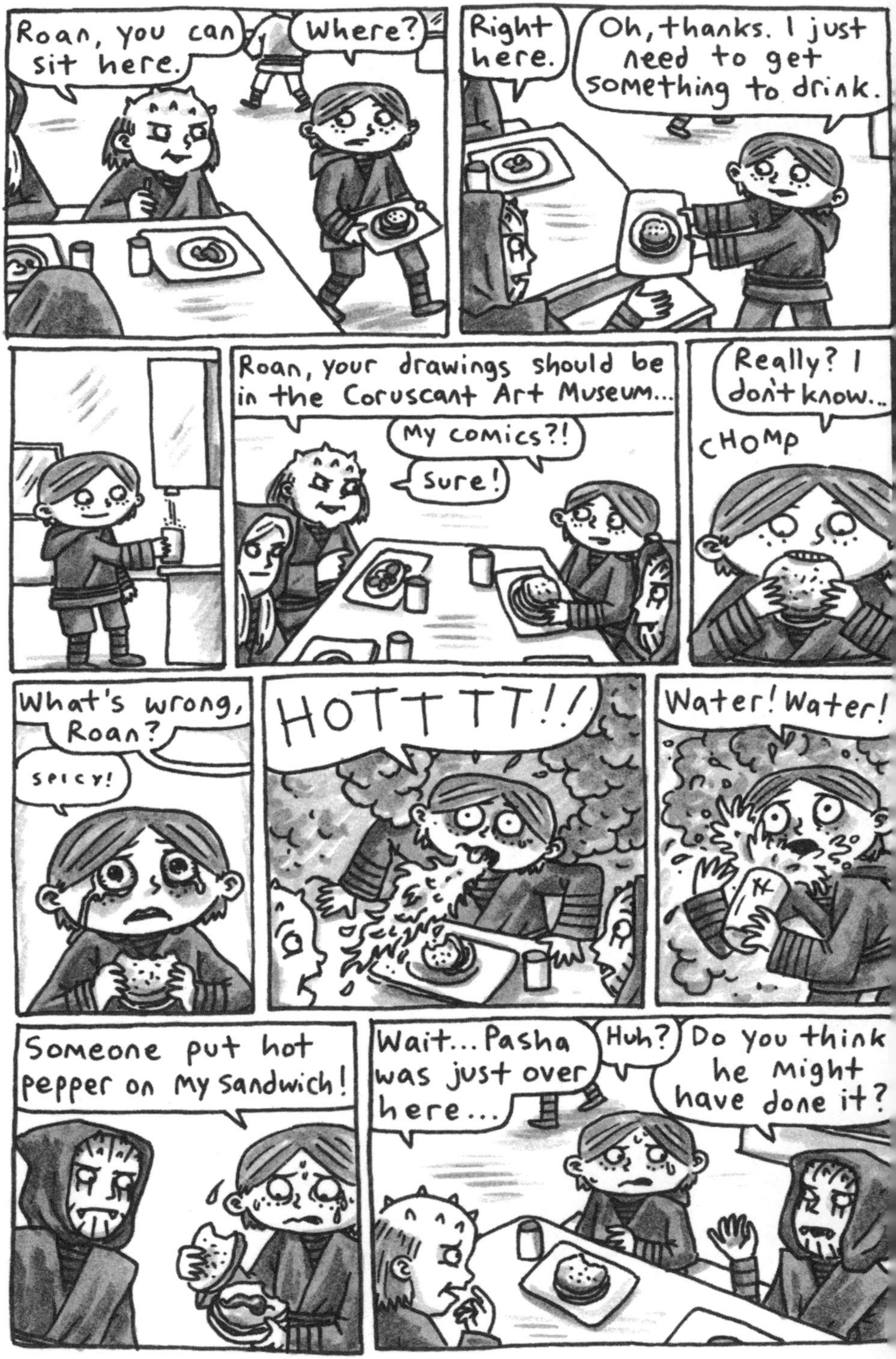
Roan, you can sit here.
Where?
Right here.
Oh, thanks. I just need to get something to drink.
Roan, your drawings should be in the Coruscant Art Museum...
My comics?!
Sure!
Really? I don't know...
CHOMP
What's wrong, Roan?
SPICY!
HOTTTTT!!
Water! Water!
Someone put hot pepper on my sandwich!
Wait... Pasha was just over here...
Huh?
Do you think he might have done it?

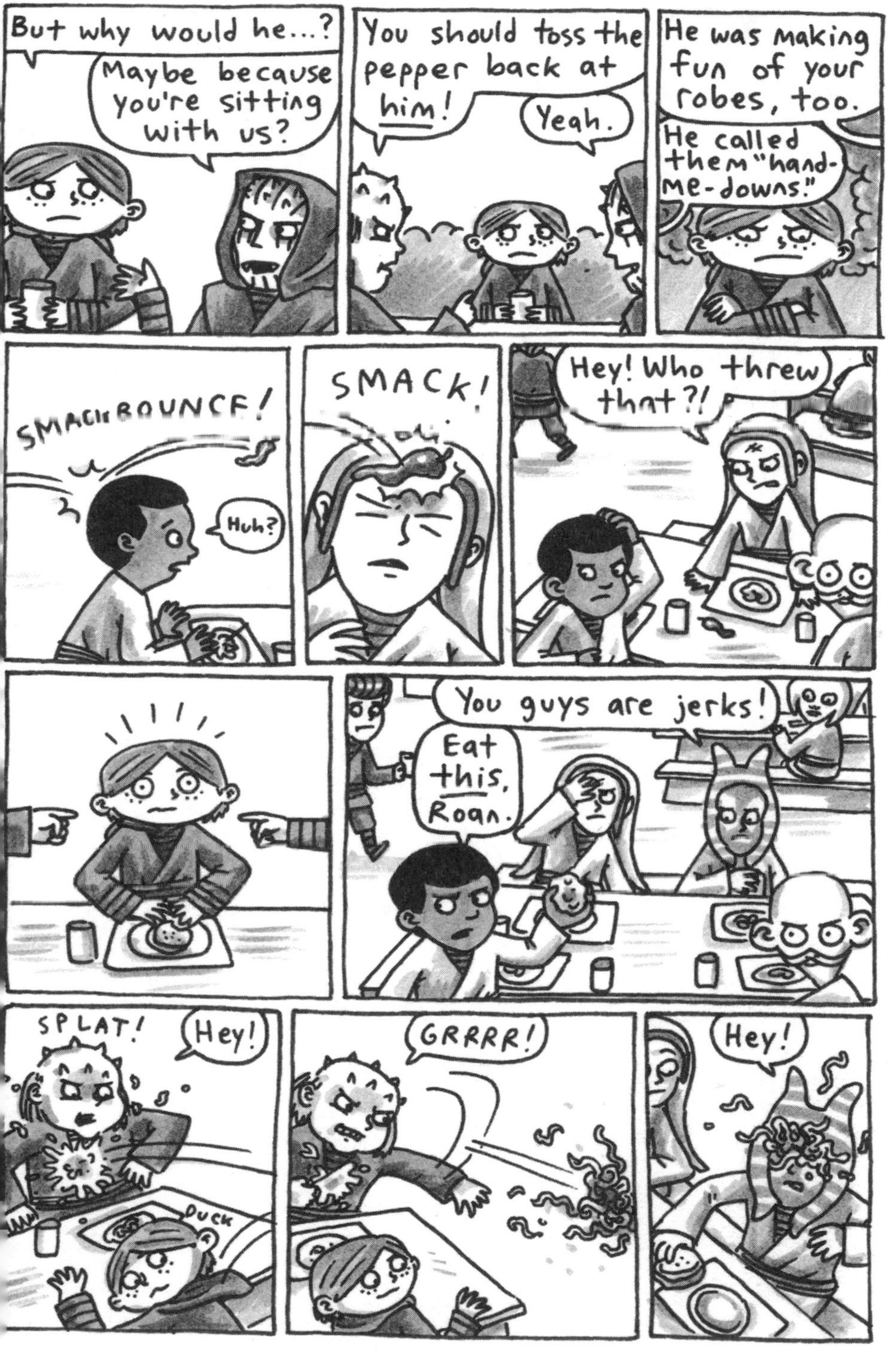
But why would he...?
Maybe because you're sitting with us?
You should toss the pepper back at him!
Yeah.
He was making fun of your robes, too.
He called them "hand-me-downs."
SMACK BOUNCE!
Huh?
SMACK!
Hey! Who threw that?!
You guys are jerks!
Eat this, Roan.
SPLAT!
Hey!
DUCK
GRRRR!
Hey!

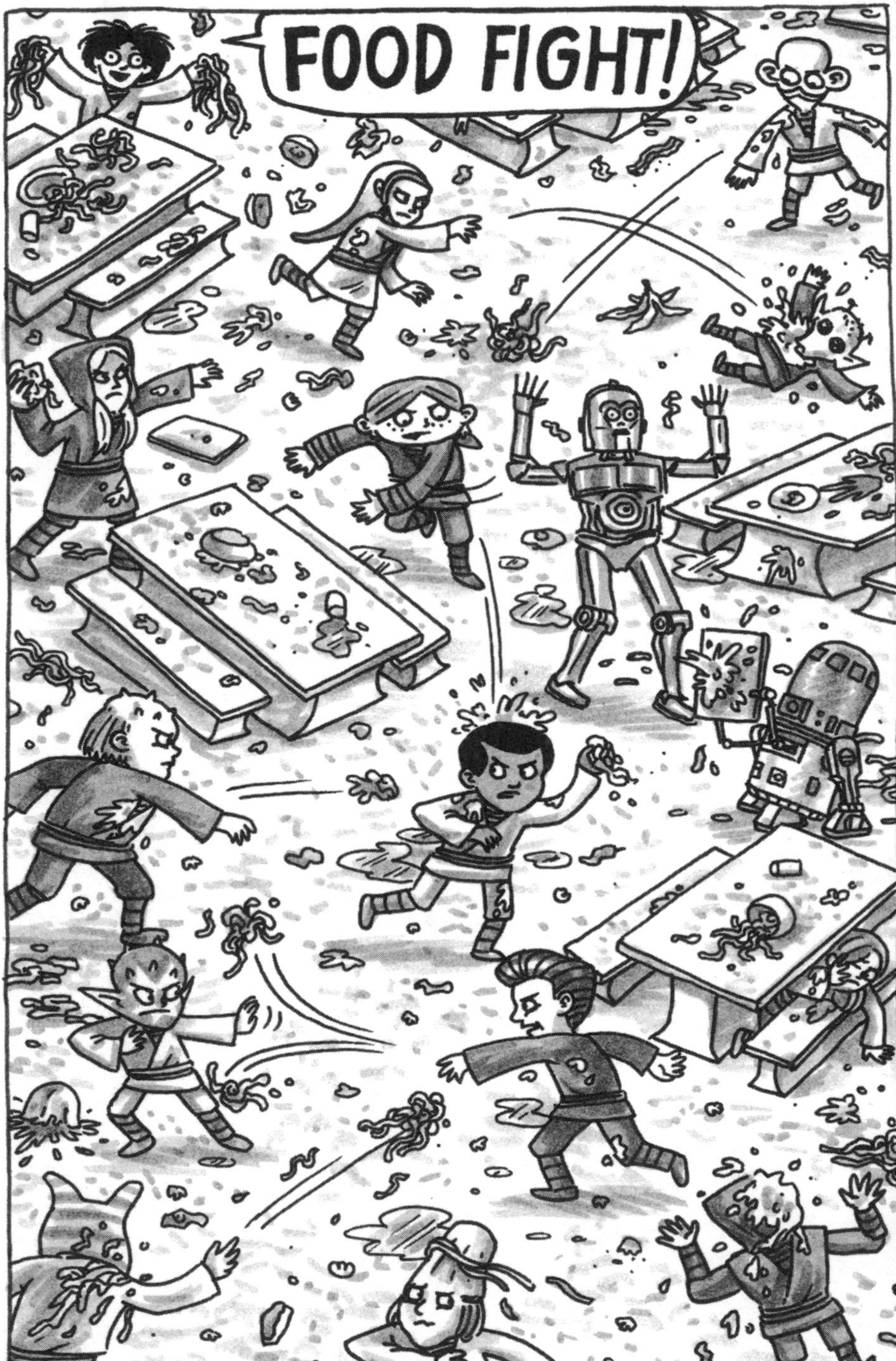
FOOD FIGHT!

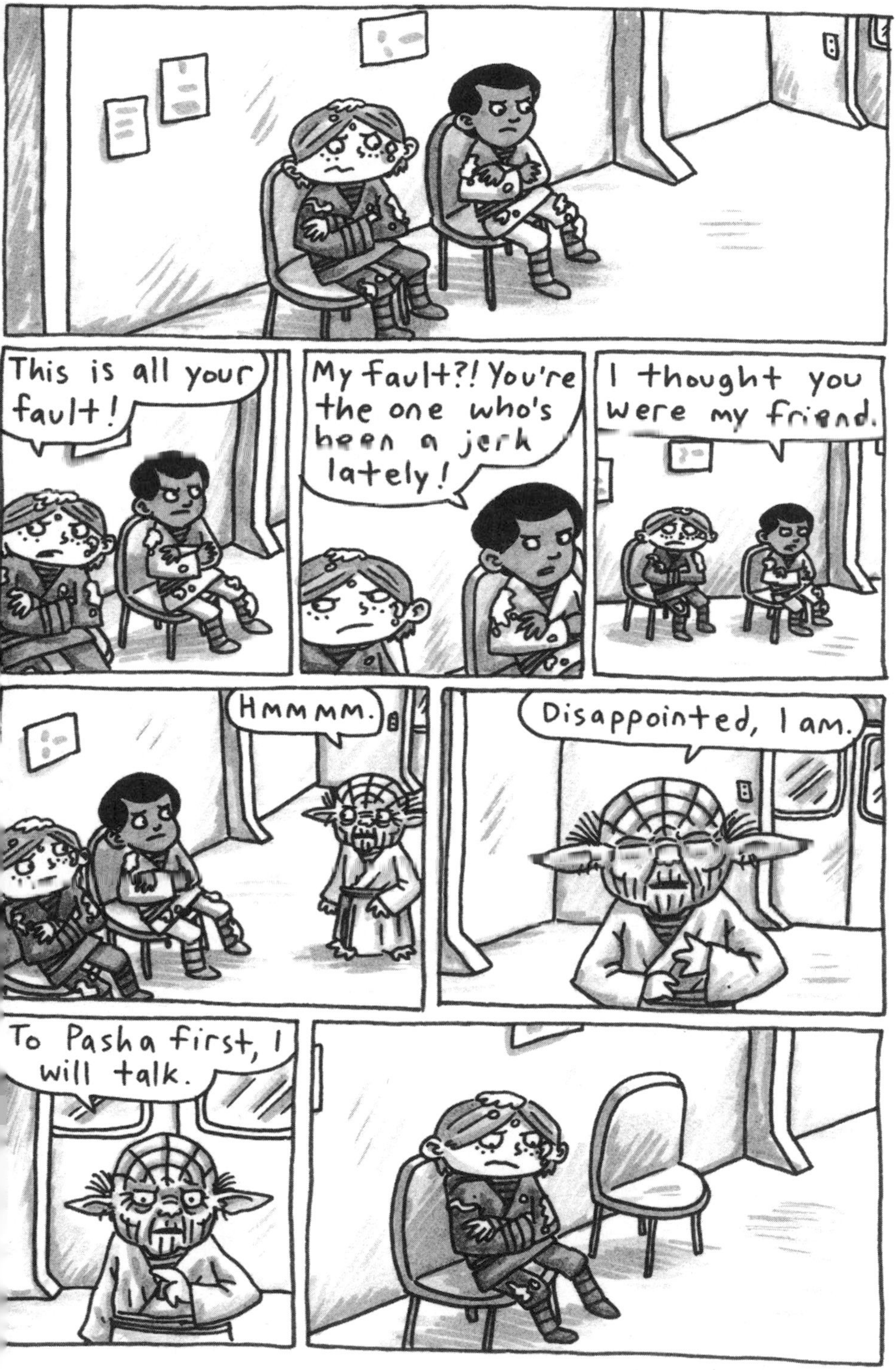
This is all your fault!
My fault?! You're the one who's been a jerk lately!
I thought you were my friend.
HMMMM.
Disappointed, I am.
To Pasha first, I will talk.

QUADDAY

Yoda is making me go on a totally boring field trip to watch the Galactic Senate as part of my punishment for the food fight. He said something like "learn peaceful solutions, you must." The teachers think I started it. Even though Cyrus and Cronah told them what happened, I guess, NO ONE believed me when I said Pasha was the one who really started it. I thought at first maybe Pasha was lying, and I was getting angrier, because Master Yoda and Principal Mar wouldn't listen to me. But Master Yoda said they knew what happened and that was the end of it. Master Yoda gave me this look like he was REALLY disappointed in me and I felt really stupid.

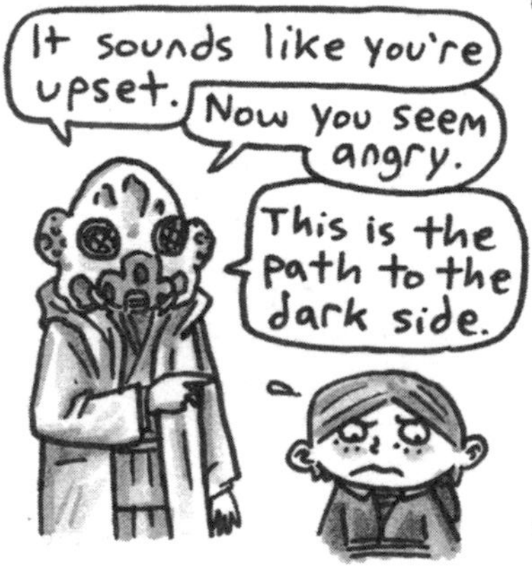

It sounds like you're upset.
Now you seem angry.
This is the path to the dark side.

Even seeing the food in Ronald's hair after the food fight didn't cheer me up, and the more I think about it, the more I wish I hadn't thrown any food. At least my dodgeball skills came in handy.

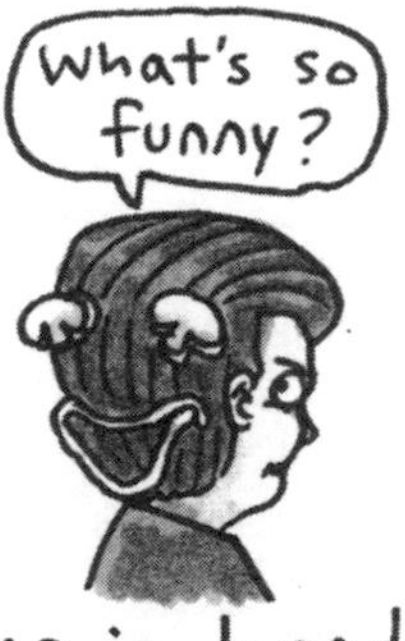

What's so funny?

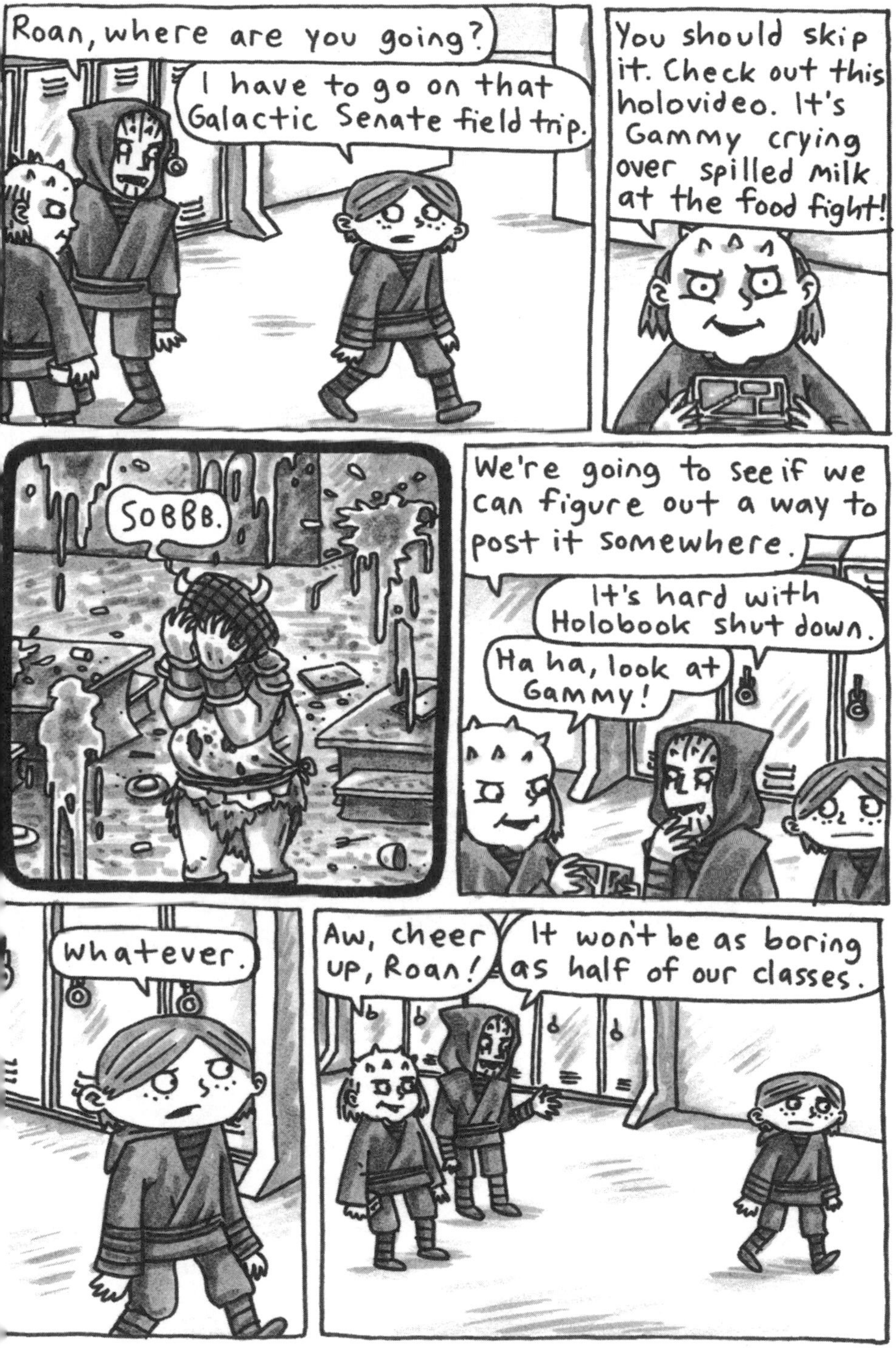
Roan, where are you going?
I have to go on that Galactic Senate field trip.
You should skip it. Check out this holovideo. It's Gammy crying over spilled milk at the food fight!
SOBBB.
We're going to see if we can figure out a way to post it somewhere.
It's hard with Holobook shut down.
Ha ha, look at Gammy!
Whatever.
Aw, cheer up, Roan!
It won't be as boring as half of our classes.

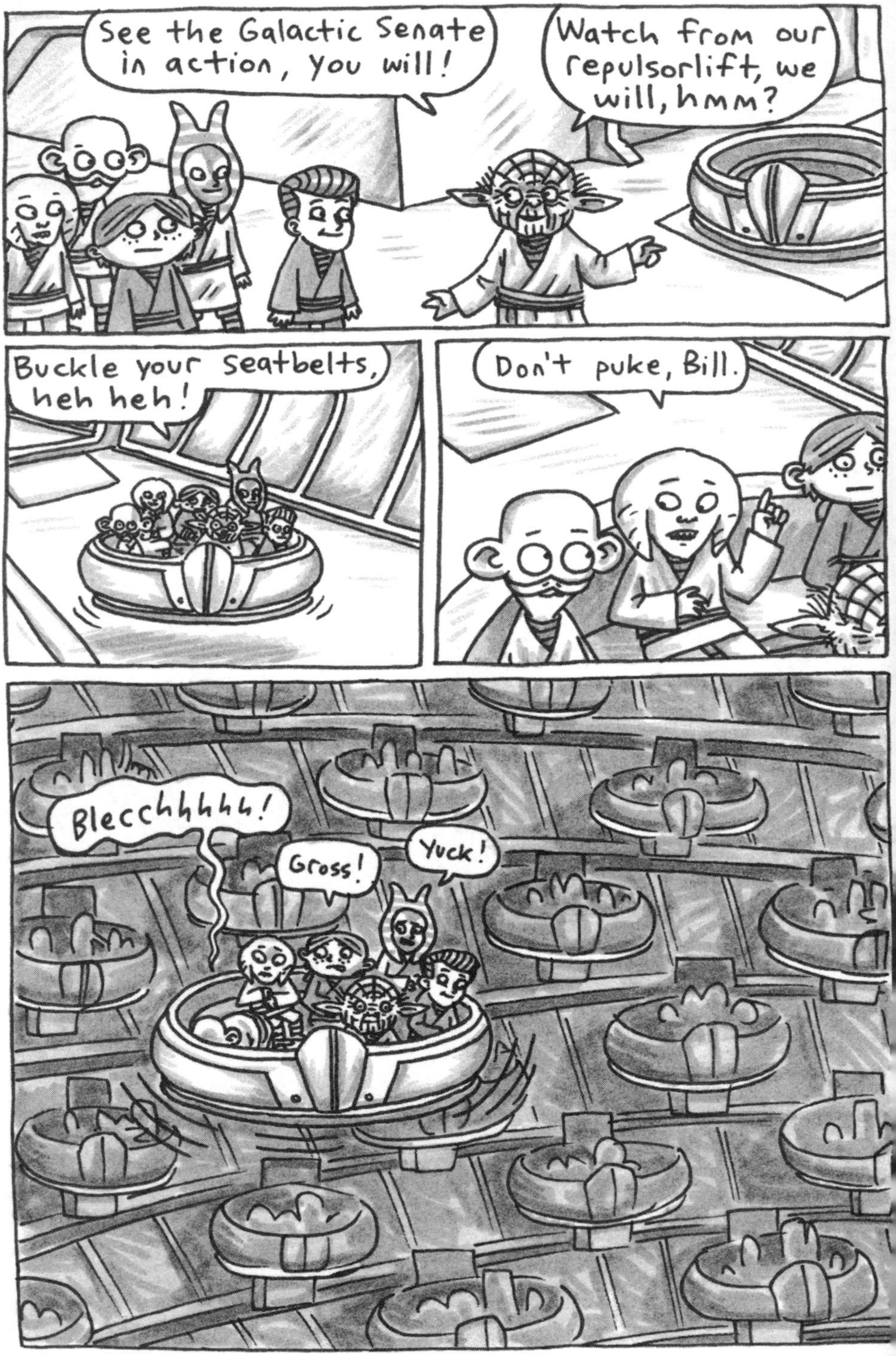
See the Galactic Senate in action, you will!
Watch from our repulsorlift, we will, hmm?
Buckle your seatbelts, heh heh!
Don't puke, Bill.
Blecchhhhh!
Gross!
Yuck!

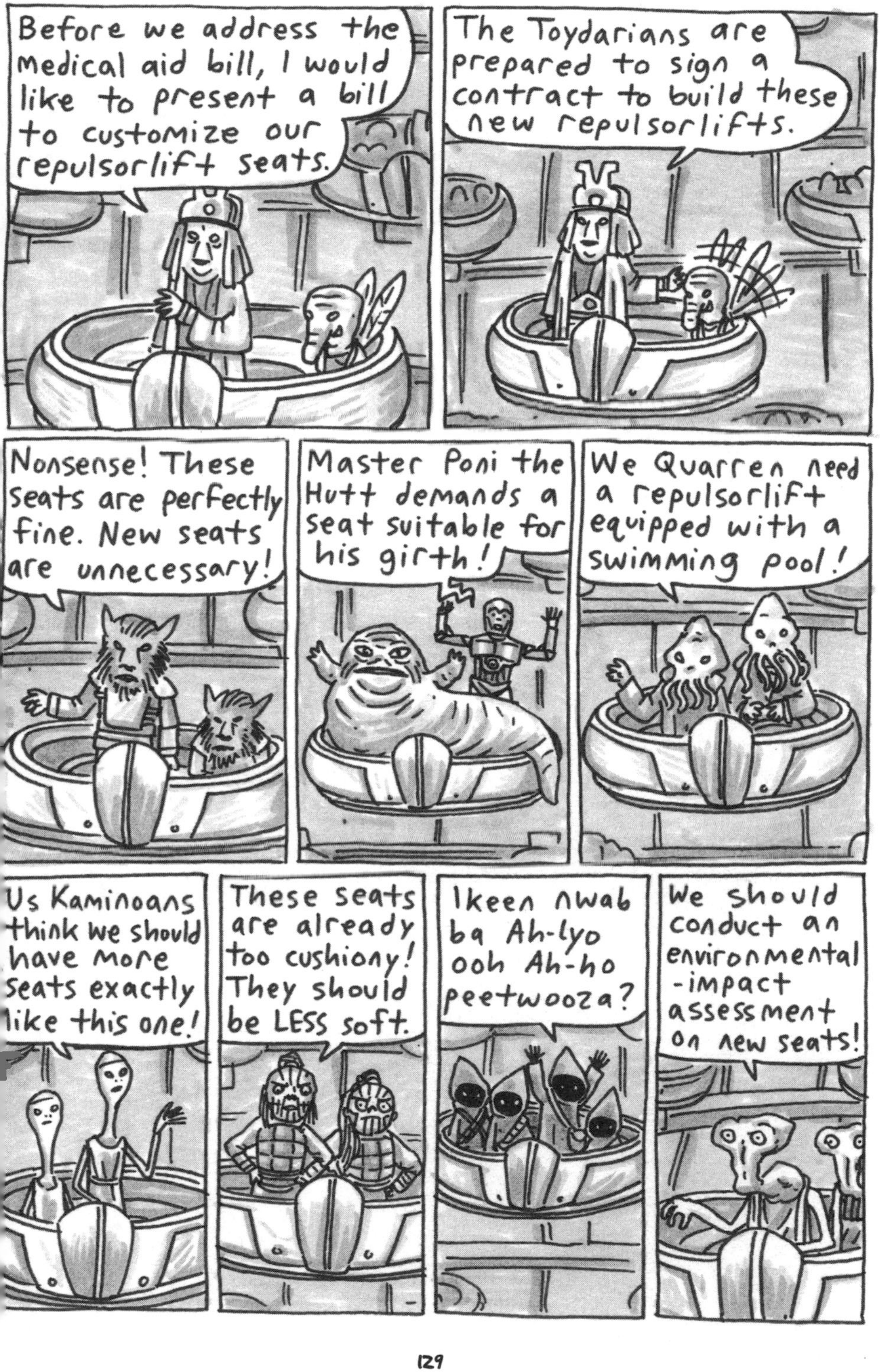

Before we address the medical aid bill, I would like to present a bill to customize our repulsorlift seats.
The Toydarians are prepared to sign a contract to build these new repulsorlifts.
Nonsense! These seats are perfectly fine. New seats are unnecessary!
Master Poni the Hutt demands a seat suitable for his girth!
We Quarren need a repulsorlift equipped with a swimming pool!
Us Kaminoans think we should have more seats exactly like this one!
These seats are already too cushiony! They should be LESS soft.
Ikeen nwab ba Ah-lyo ooh Ah-ho peetwooza?
We should conduct an environmental-impact assessment on new seats!

Master Yoda, why are the Senators wasting their time on chairs? So worried about themselves, miss the big problems for everyone, they do.

They should work on the medical aid bill. That would help Gaiana's dad...

Gaiana's dad?

Yeah, you know, because he's been sick all year.

What?!

That's why she didn't come on this field trip. She and Pasha were making a care package.

Her dad is sick?!

Pasha even made a special box to send everything to Gaiana's dad. I have the sweetest boyfriend.

Wait, what? Boyfriend?

So, anyway, it'd be great if they passed the medical aid bill.

Sick? Boyfriend?

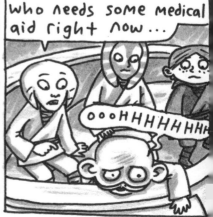

I think Bill is the one who needs some medical aid right now...

oooHHHHHHHH

GALACTIC SENATE NOTES

didn't see any Ewoks?

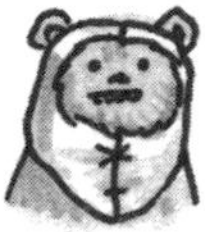

- Senators represent inhabited planets from across galaxy, like to talk
- Senate responsible for regulating trade, maintaining galactic maps, try to solve intergalactic problems without causing more intergalactic problems
- Led by Supreme Chancellor and Vice Chair. "Vice Chair" is not actually a chair but position of authority

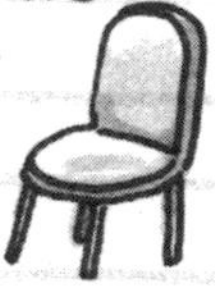

- Senator Blagotine introduced bill to change how bills are introduced by Senators

(not that kind of Bill)

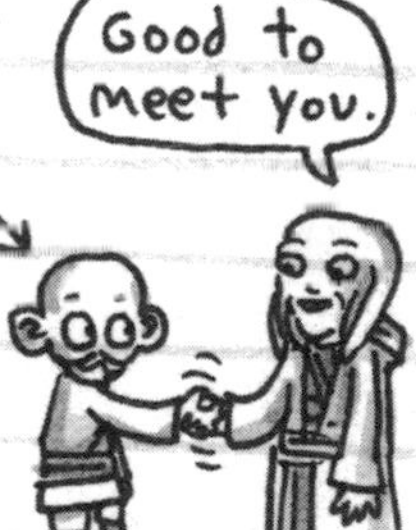
Good to meet you.

MY LIFE NOTES

- How did I not know Gaiana's dad was sick?
- Pasha is dating Shi-Fara?!
- I am such a moron!

HEPTADAY

So, I'm an idiot. And a jerk. I mean, I'm totally NOT an idiot or a jerk, but I guess I have kind of acted like one lately. The whole semester I've been thinking Gaiana was acting weird about me when really her dad was sick. But now she doesn't really want to talk to me. I don't think Pasha does, either. I thought he was trying to date Gaiana, but he was just helping her, which is what I should've been doing. When Shi-Fara told me what Pasha was really doing, I almost puked like Bill. Now I need to figure out how to fix things, but I can't really talk to anyone. The only people still talking to me are Cyrus and Cronah, but I feel like they don't really care. They would probably just laugh if I told them what I was thinking about. Especially since they can't give anyone a hard time on Holobook right now. Maybe if I can talk to Pasha, he

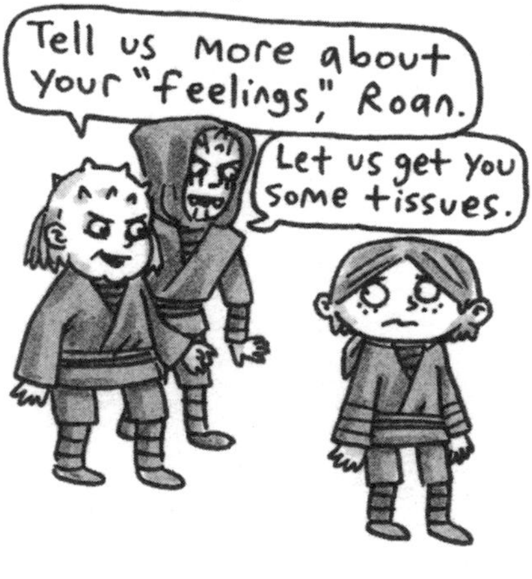
Tell us more about your "feelings," Roan.
Let us get you some tissues.

can explain stuff to Gaiana. Maybe I'll get on the same lightsaber fencing tournament team as Gaiana and Pasha, and then I'll have an excuse to talk to them. That would be too easy. It's like the Senators— they have a reason to talk, and all they do is argue. It was ~~frustecating~~ frustrating to watch them. Afterward, I was talking to Master Yoda, and he made it sound like I was actually complaining about Myself, and not the Senators...

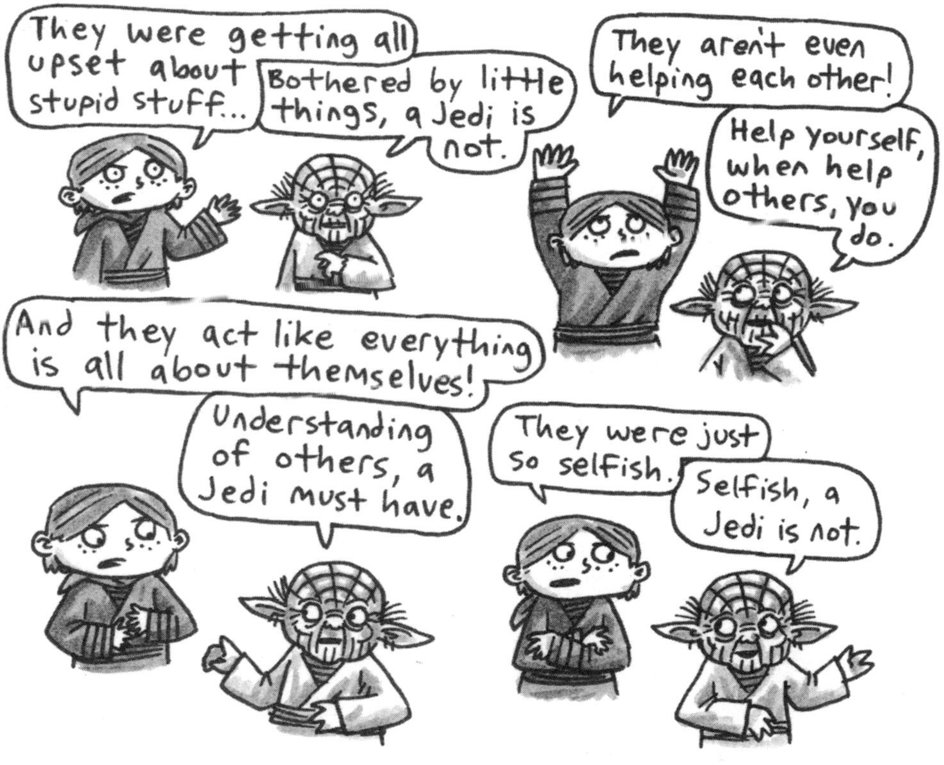

They were getting all upset about stupid stuff...
Bothered by little things, a Jedi is not.
They aren't even helping each other!
Help yourself, when help others, you do.
And they act like everything is all about themselves!
Understanding of others, a Jedi must have.
They were just so selfish.
Selfish, a Jedi is not.

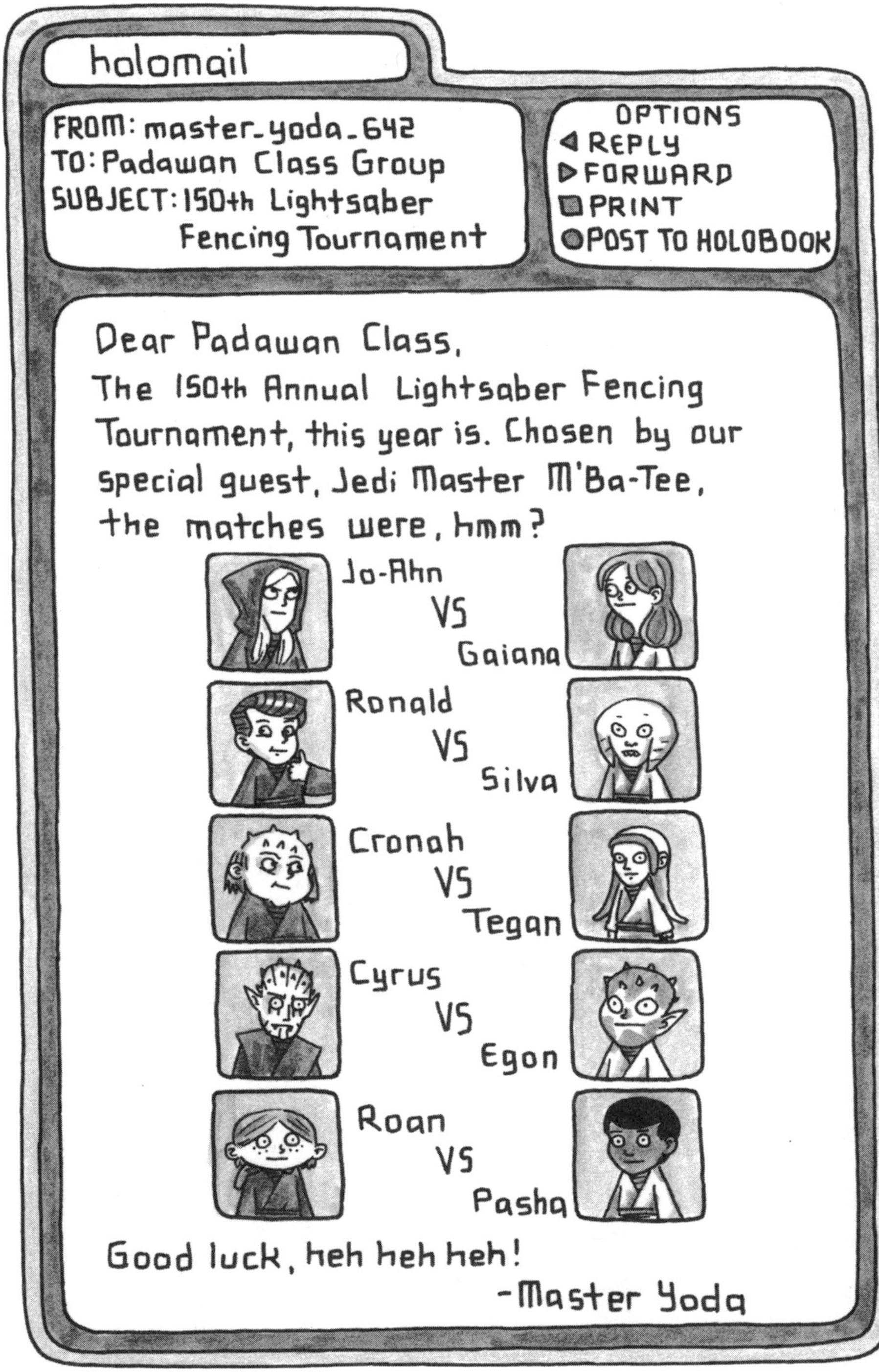
holomail
FROM: master_yoda_642
TO: Padawan Class Group
SUBJECT: 150th Lightsaber Fencing Tournament
OPTIONS
REPLY
FORWARD
PRINT
POST TO HOLOBOOK
Dear Padawan Class,
The 150th Annual Lightsaber Fencing Tournament, this year is. Chosen by our special guest, Jedi Master M'Ba-Tee, the matches were, hmm?
Jo-Ahn VS Gaiana
Ronald VS Silva
Cronah VS Tegan
Cyrus VS Egon
Roan VS Pasha
Good luck, heh heh heh!
-Master Yoda

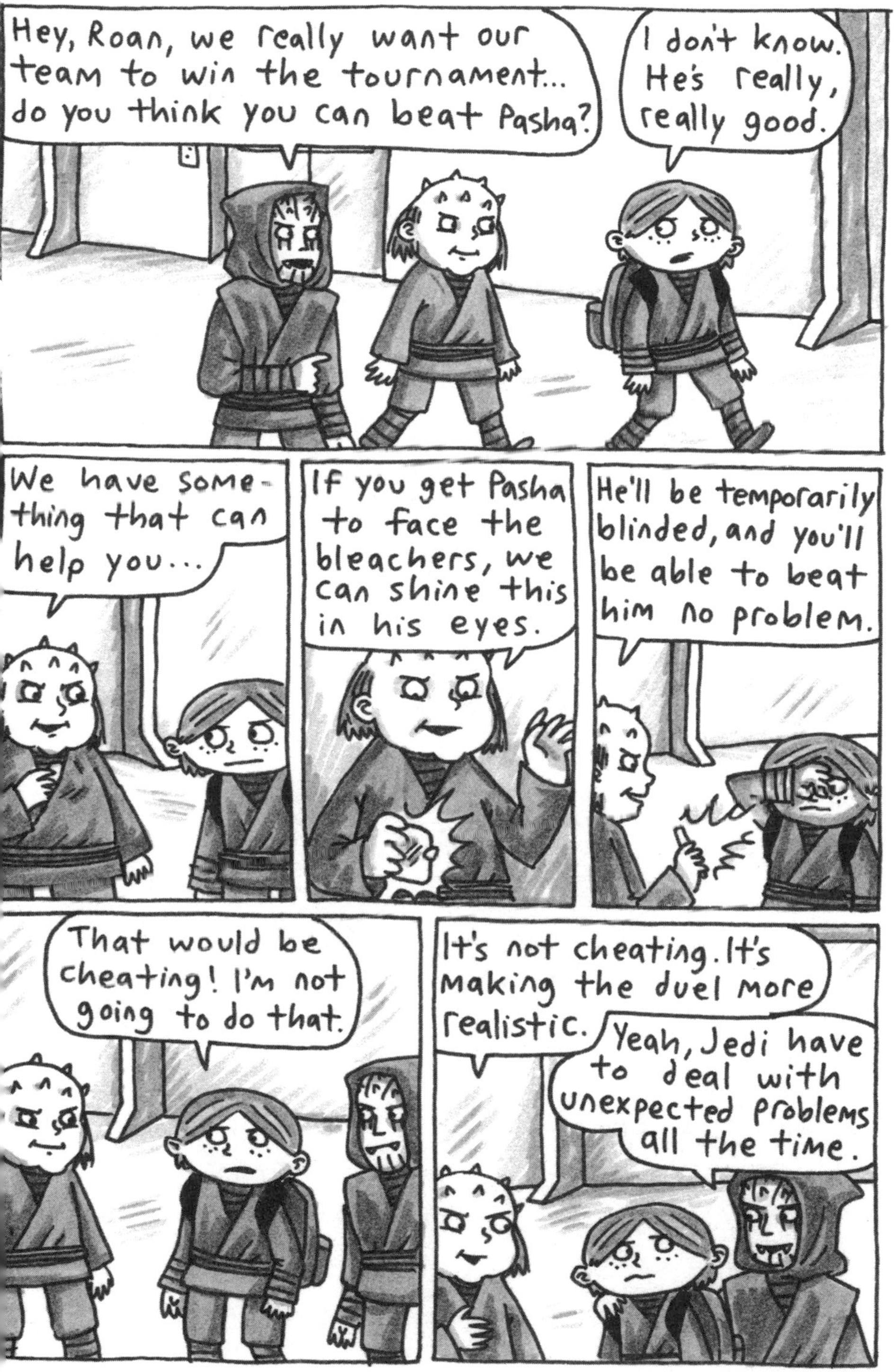
Hey, Roan, we really want our team to win the tournament... do you think you can beat Pasha?
I don't know. He's really, really good.
We have something that can help you...
If you get Pasha to face the bleachers, we can shine this in his eyes.
He'll be temporarily blinded, and you'll be able to beat him no problem.
That would be cheating! I'm not going to do that.
It's not cheating. It's making the duel more realistic.
Yeah, Jedi have to deal with unexpected problems all the time.

HEXADAY

The lightsaber fencing tournament is tomorrow, and it's turning into a disaster already. First of all, I'm matched up against Pasha. How am I supposed to make up with Pasha when I have to fight him? And to make things worse, Cronah and Cyrus are trying to make me cheat.

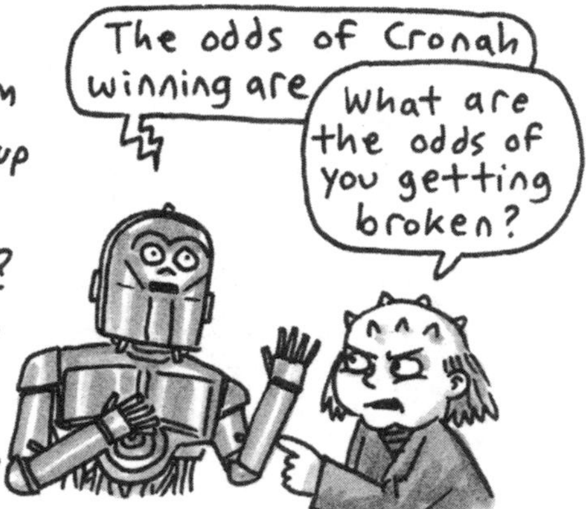
The odds of Cronah winning are
What are the odds of you getting broken?

I told them I wouldn't but now they're threatening to tell Master Yoda that I took Voorpee, when I know it was Cronah who did something. I can't say anything now, because it'll look like I was part of it anyway and I'll still get in trouble. All Cronah and Cyrus care about is winning. I don't know why I cared so much about what they think of me. If I tell on them now, I'll have zero friends. Maybe I deserve no friends, since I've been such a bad friend. All I've done lately is mess things up, but at least I can TRY to stop messing things up.

NEBULA MANUFACTURING PRESENTS

150th ANNUAL CORUSCANT JEDI ACADEMY LIGHTSABER FENCING TOURNAMENT

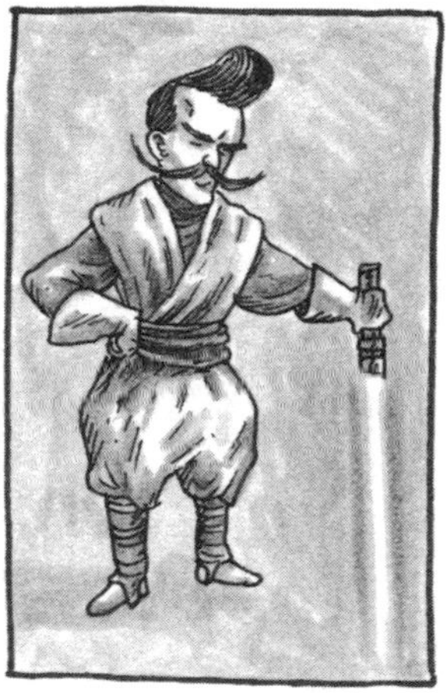

The Coruscant Jedi Academy Lightsaber Fencing Tournament began when Jedi Master Jan Mincénte would challenge each of his Padawan students to lightsaber fencing duels. He quickly grew tired of winning easily, and decided it made more sense for students to test their skills against one another. Since the first tournament, many of our most well-known Jedi Knights have competed in, and won, the tournament. This includes Jedi Master M'Ba-Tee, whose skills made him the champion of the 12th Annual Tournament.

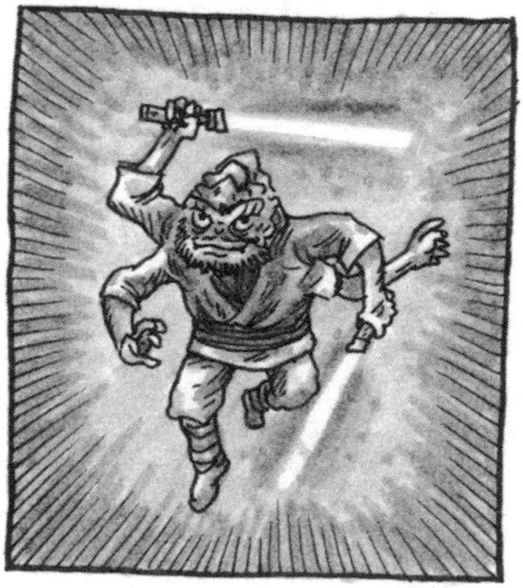

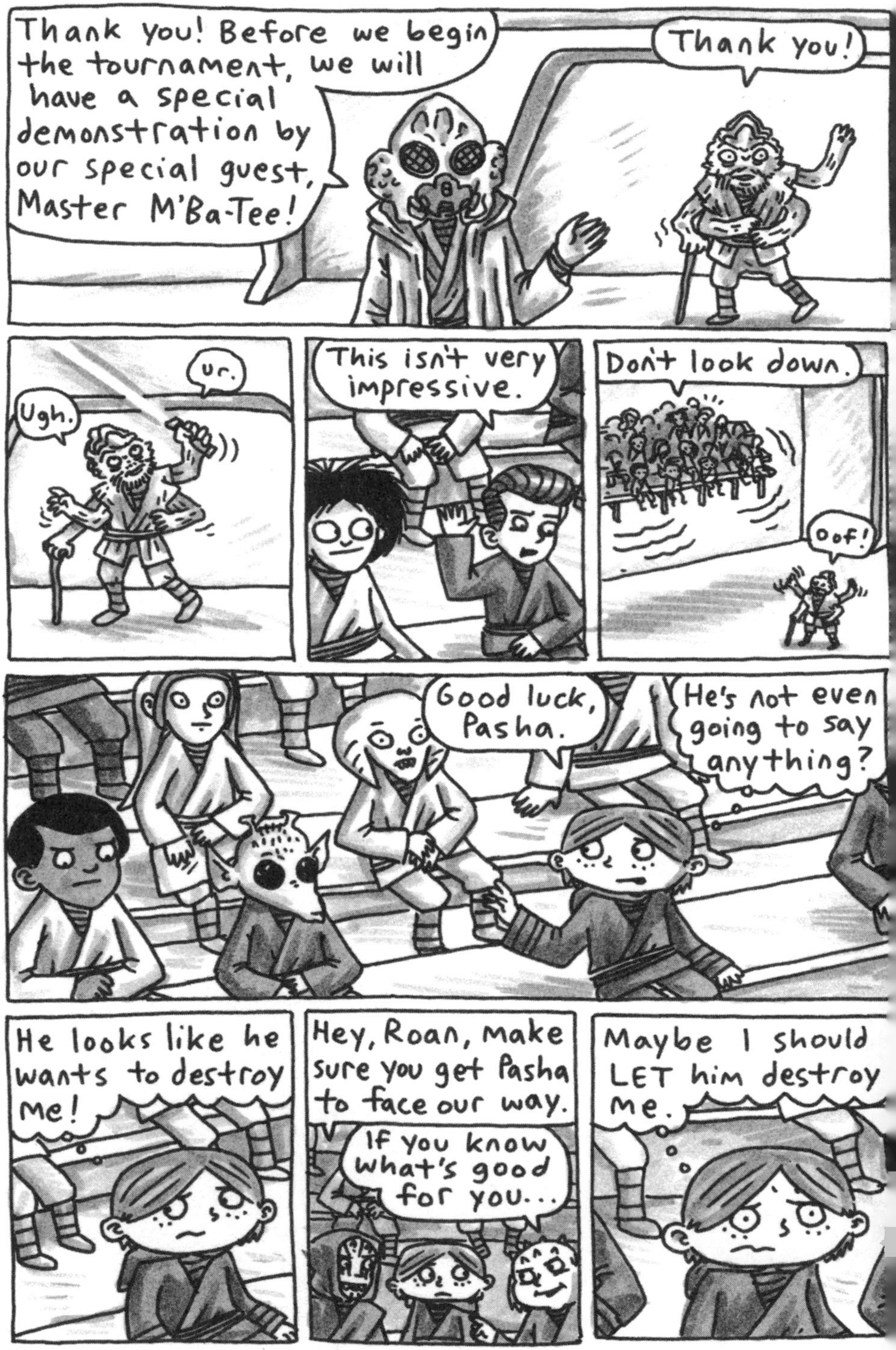

Thank you! Before we begin the tournament, we will have a special demonstration by our special guest, Master M'Ba-Tee!
Thank you!
Ugh.
ur.
This isn't very impressive.
Don't look down.
Oof!
Good luck, Pasha.
He's not even going to say anything?
He looks like he wants to destroy me!
Hey, Roan, make sure you get Pasha to face our way.
If you know what's good for you...
Maybe I should LET him destroy me.

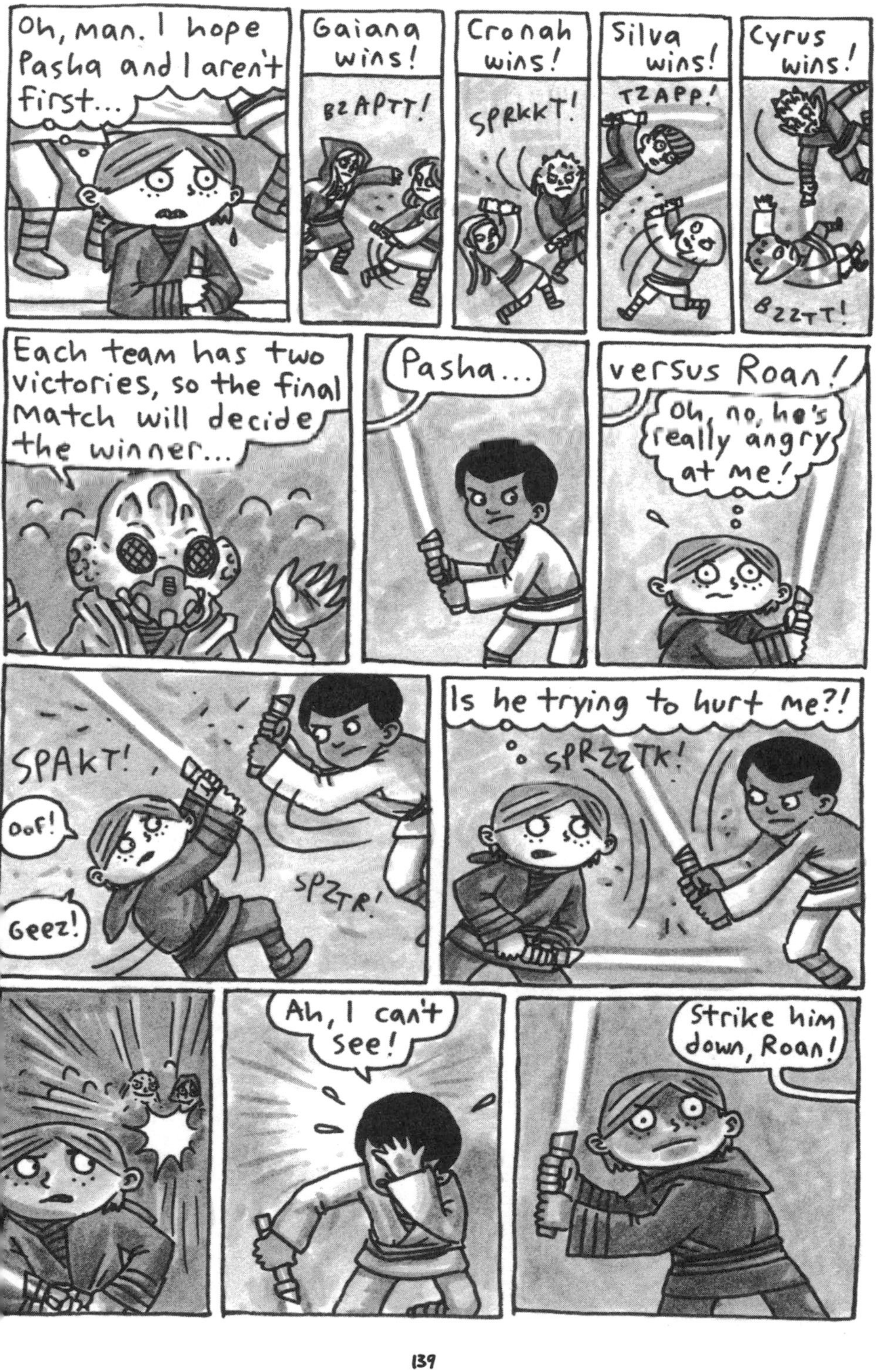
Oh, man. I hope Pasha and I aren't first...
Gaiana wins!
BZAPTT!
Cronah wins!
SPRKKT!
Silva wins!
TZAPP!
Cyrus wins!
BZZTT!
Each team has two victories, so the final match will decide the winner...
Pasha...
versus Roan!
Oh, no, he's really angry at me!
SPAKT!
OOF!
Geez!
SPZTR!
Is he trying to hurt me?!
SPRZZTK!
Ah, I can't see!
Strike him down, Roan!

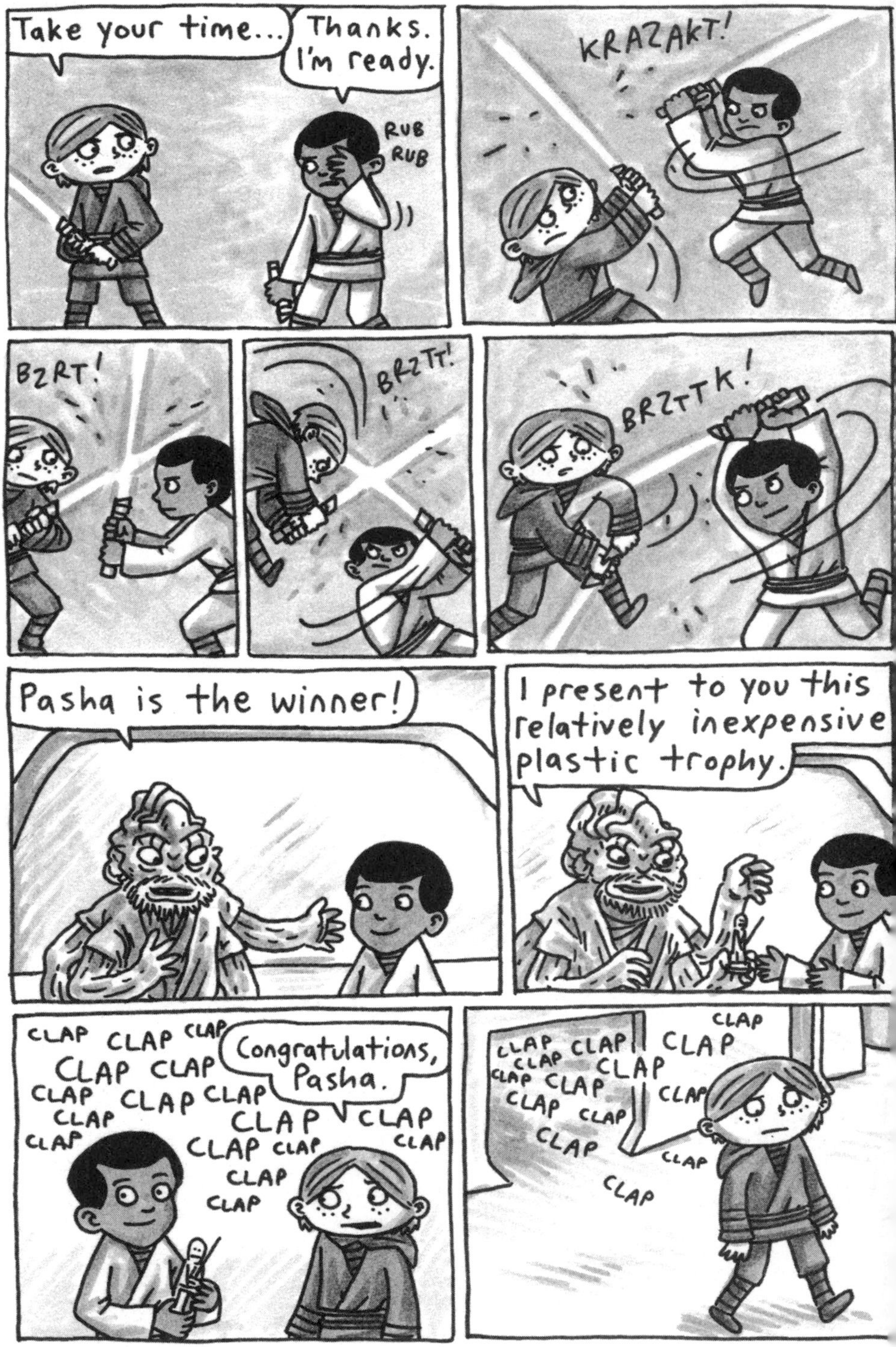
Take your time...
Thanks. I'm ready.
RUB RUB
KRAZAKT!
BZRT!
BRZTT!
BRZTTK!
Pasha is the winner!
I present to you this relatively inexpensive plastic trophy.
CLAP CLAP CLAP CLAP CLAP CLAP CLAP CLAP CLAP CLAP CLAP
Congratulations, Pasha.
CLAP CLAP CLAP CLAP CLAP CLAP CLAP
CLAP CLAP CLAP CLAP CLAP CLAP CLAP CLAP CLAP CLAP CLAP CLAP CLAP

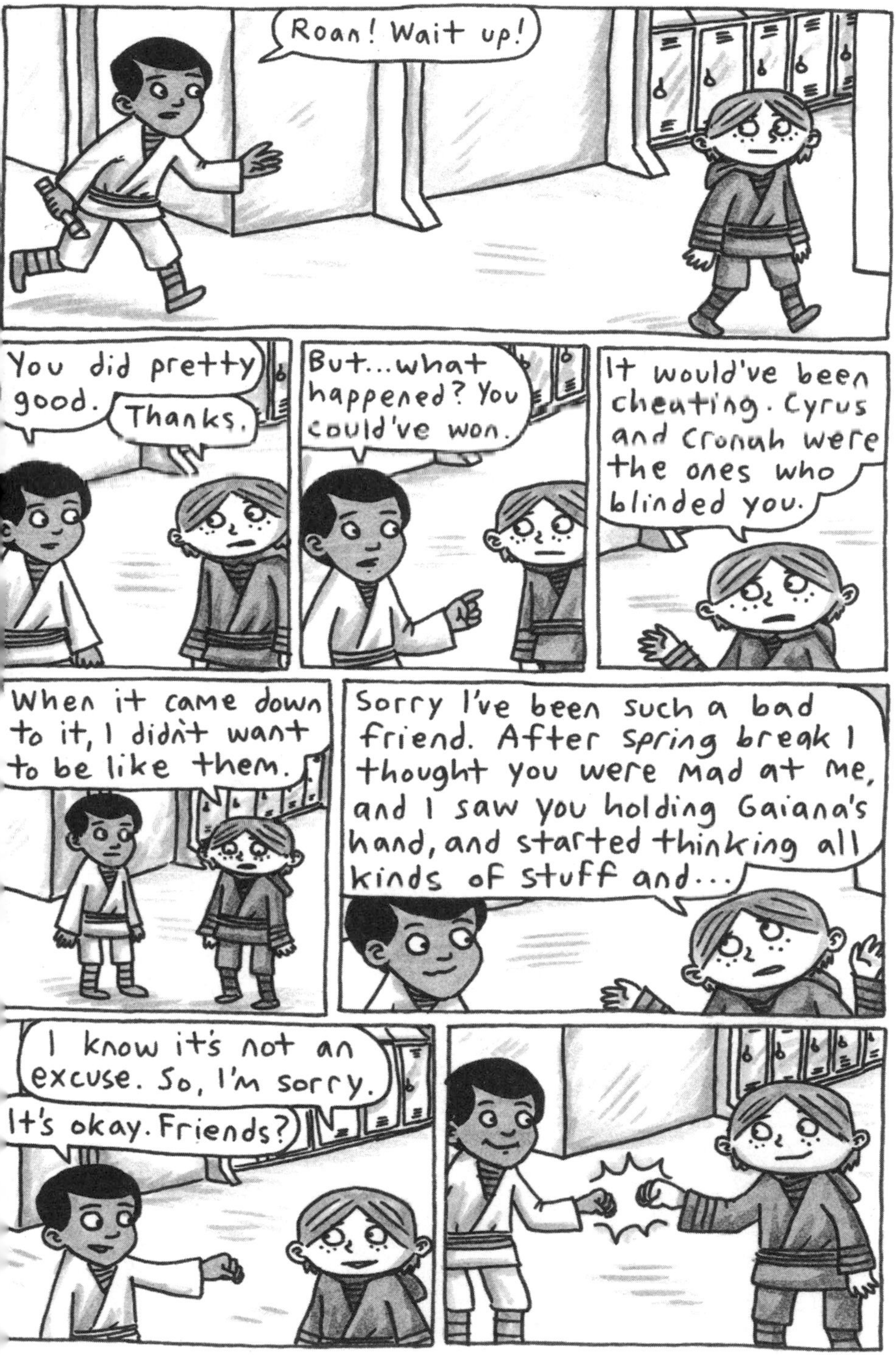
Roan! Wait up!
You did pretty good.
Thanks.
But...what happened? You could've won.
It would've been cheating. Cyrus and Cronah were the ones who blinded you.
When it came down to it, I didn't want to be like them.
Sorry I've been such a bad friend. After spring break I thought you were mad at me, and I saw you holding Gaiana's hand, and started thinking all kinds of stuff and...
I know it's not an excuse. So, I'm sorry.
It's okay. Friends?

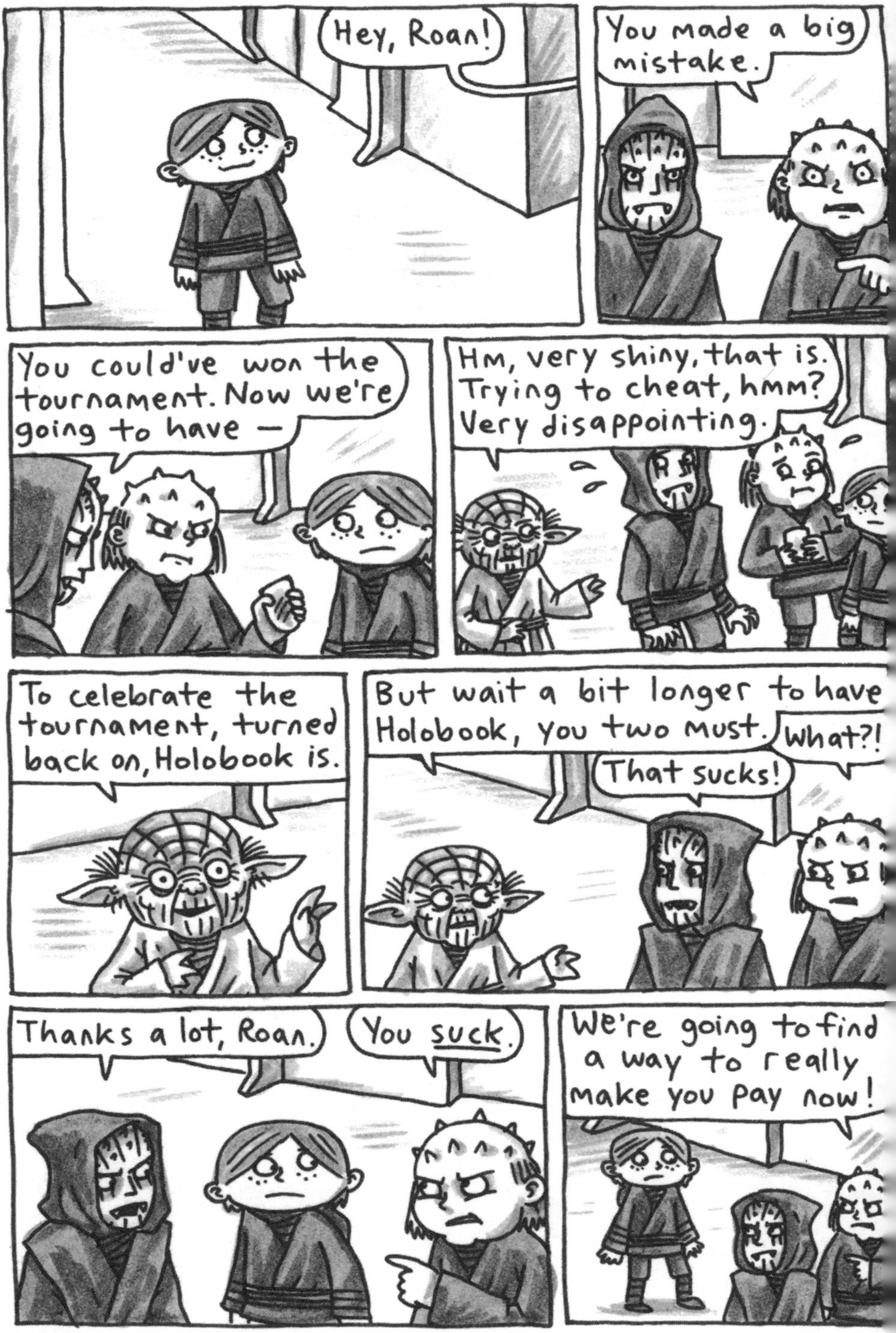
Hey, Roan!
You made a big mistake.
You could've won the tournament. Now we're going to have —
Hm, very shiny, that is. Trying to cheat, hmm? Very disappointing.
To celebrate the tournament, turned back on, Holobook is.
But wait a bit longer to have Holobook, you two must.
What?!
That sucks!
Thanks a lot, Roan.
You suck.
We're going to find a way to really make you pay now!

MONODAY

I was really proud of Pasha winning the tournament, but I'm also proud of myself. I mean, I think I did well, even though I lost, but I didn't cheat. Best of all, I managed to make up with Pasha. We were feeling so good after the tournament that Pasha didn't even mind they spelled his

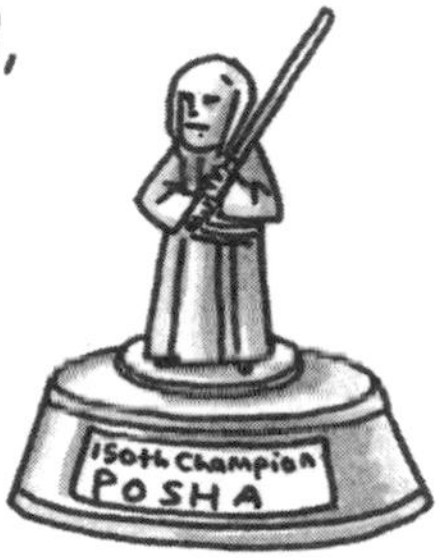
150th Champion
POSHA

name wrong on his trophy. Then Pasha invited me to come with his team for their victory dinner. Gaiana was sitting across the table from me, and since I was

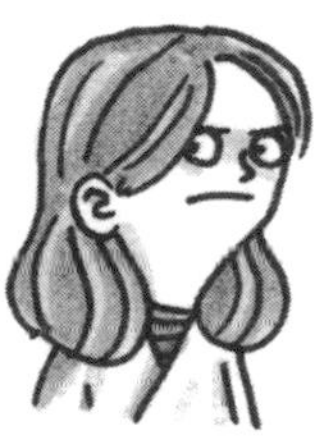

feeling so good, I thought I'd try to talk to her. She just gave me a kind of angry look and said she didn't really want to talk to me.

So I still need to find a way to apologize to her.

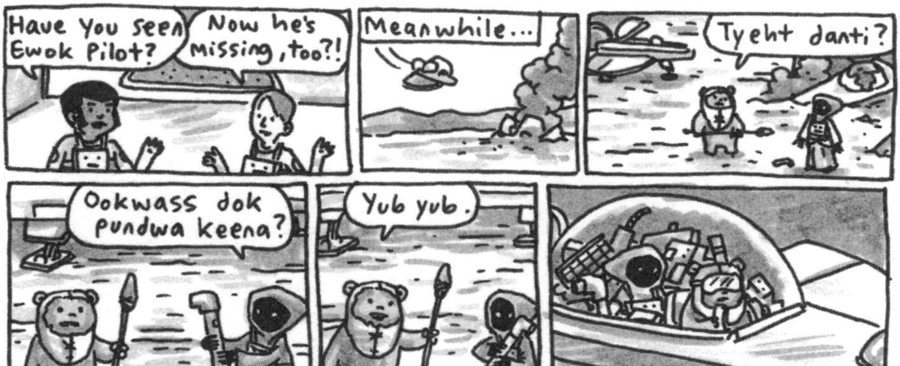
Have you seen Ewok Pilot?
Now he's missing, too?!
Meanwhile...
Tyeht danti?
Ookwass dok pundwa keena?
Yub yub.

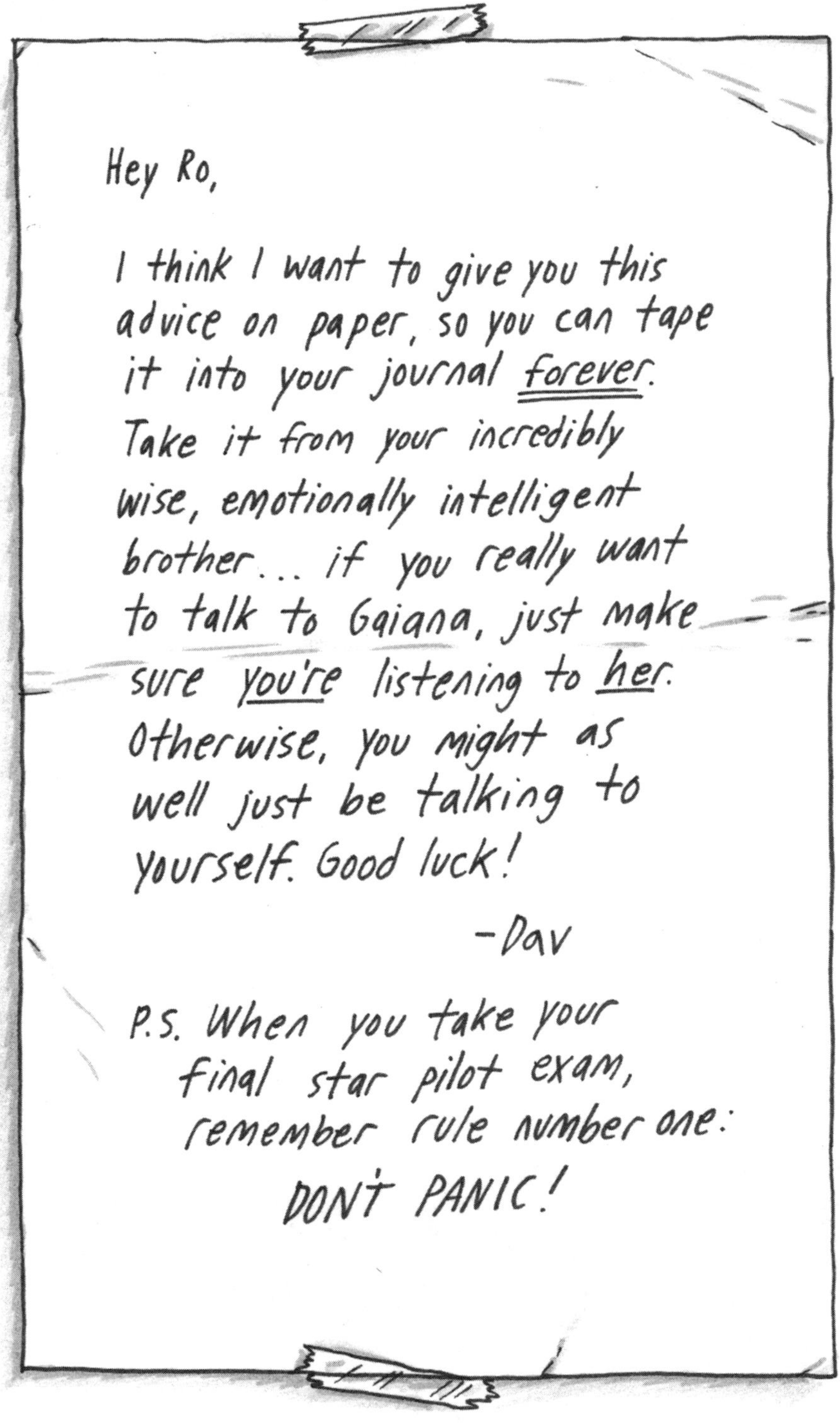

Hey Ro,

I think I want to give you this advice on paper, so you can tape it into your journal forever. Take it from your incredibly wise, emotionally intelligent brother... if you really want to talk to Gaiana, just make sure you're listening to her. Otherwise, you might as well just be talking to yourself. Good luck!

-Dav

P.S. When you take your final star pilot exam, remember rule number one:

DON'T PANIC!

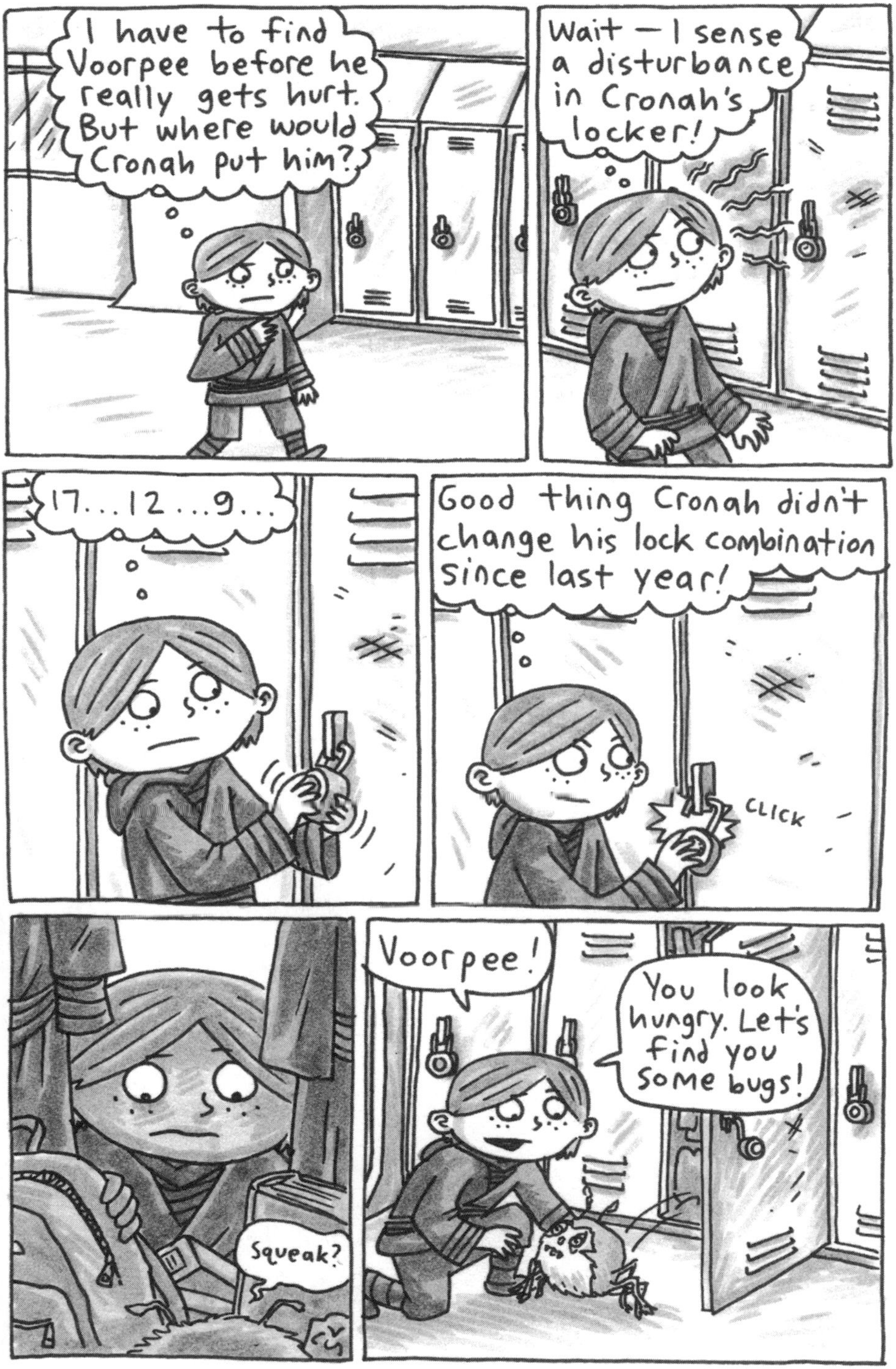
I have to find Voorpee before he really gets hurt. But where would Cronah put him?
Wait — I sense a disturbance in Cronah's locker!
17...12...9...
Good thing Cronah didn't change his lock combination since last year!
CLICK
Squeak?
Voorpee!
You look hungry. Let's find you some bugs!

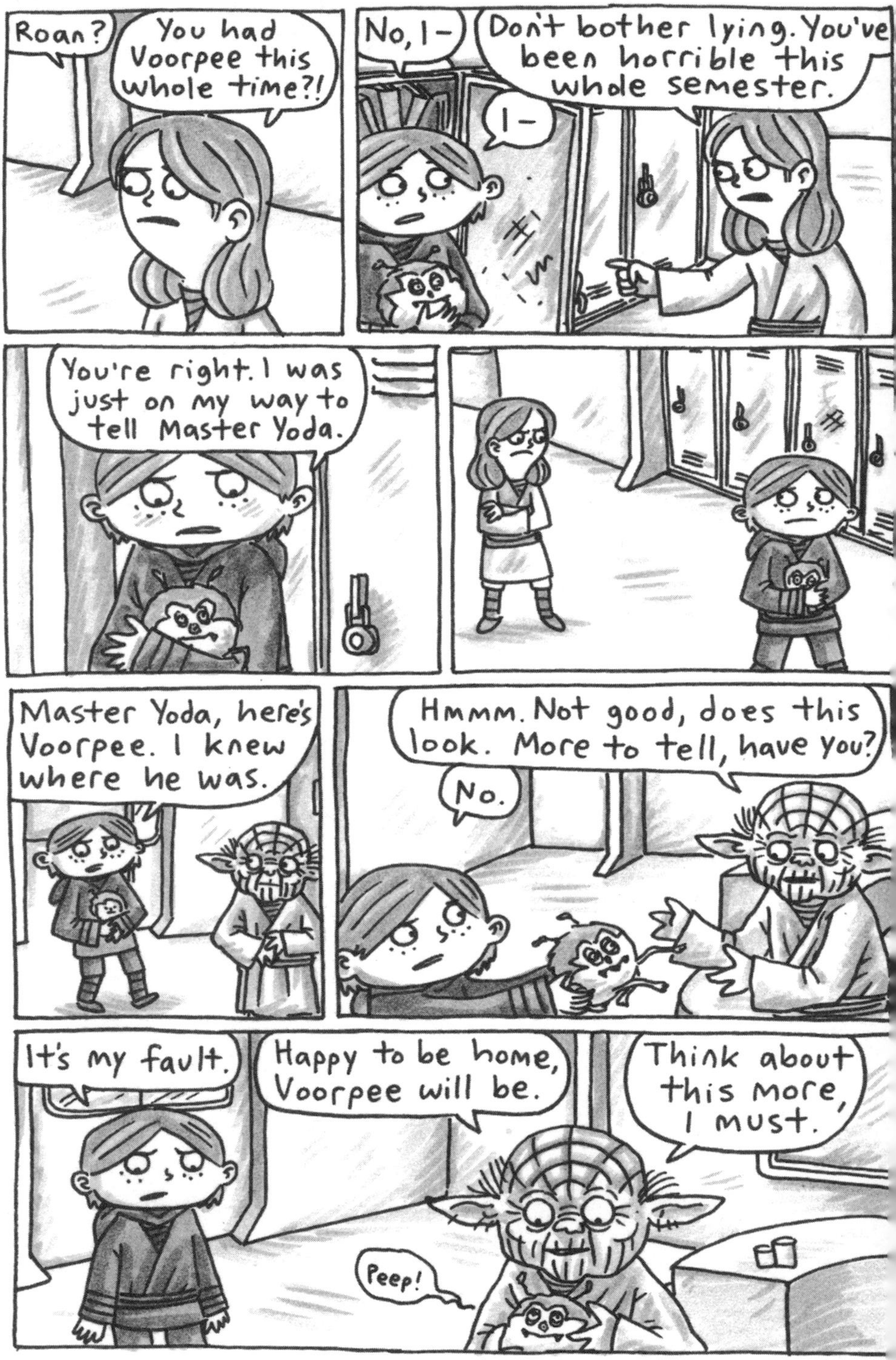

Roan?
You had Voorpee this whole time?!
No, I–
Don't bother lying. You've been horrible this whole semester.
I–
You're right. I was just on my way to tell Master Yoda.
Master Yoda, here's Voorpee. I knew where he was.
Hmmm. Not good, does this look. More to tell, have you?
No.
It's my fault.
Happy to be home, Voorpee will be.
Think about this more, I must.
Peep!

TRIDAY

Master Yoda decided I would have to write an apology to the Naboo Zoo for what happened with Voorpee. I think he may think there was someone else involved. Maybe I just should've told Master Yoda about Cronah and Cyrus anyway, since they both think I told on them, even though I didn't. They were already mad at me about not cheating to help them win the lightsaber tournament, and now they're super mad at me. But I didn't want to be a snitch. The important thing is that Voorpee is okay. Gaiana is also super mad at me. She won't even talk to me. Even if I told her the whole truth, I don't think she'd believe me anyway. I haven't gotten much sleep, because I'm trying to think of a way I can make her understand. Now I need to get back to studying for the star pilot flight training exam. If I don't pass that, I might as well quit Jedi Academy....

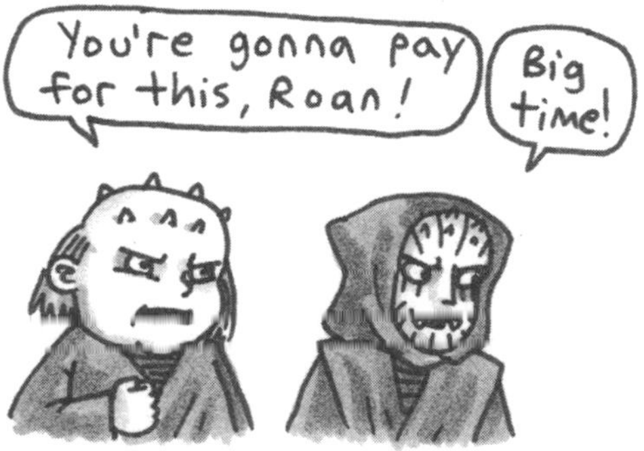
You're gonna pay for this, Roan!
Big time!

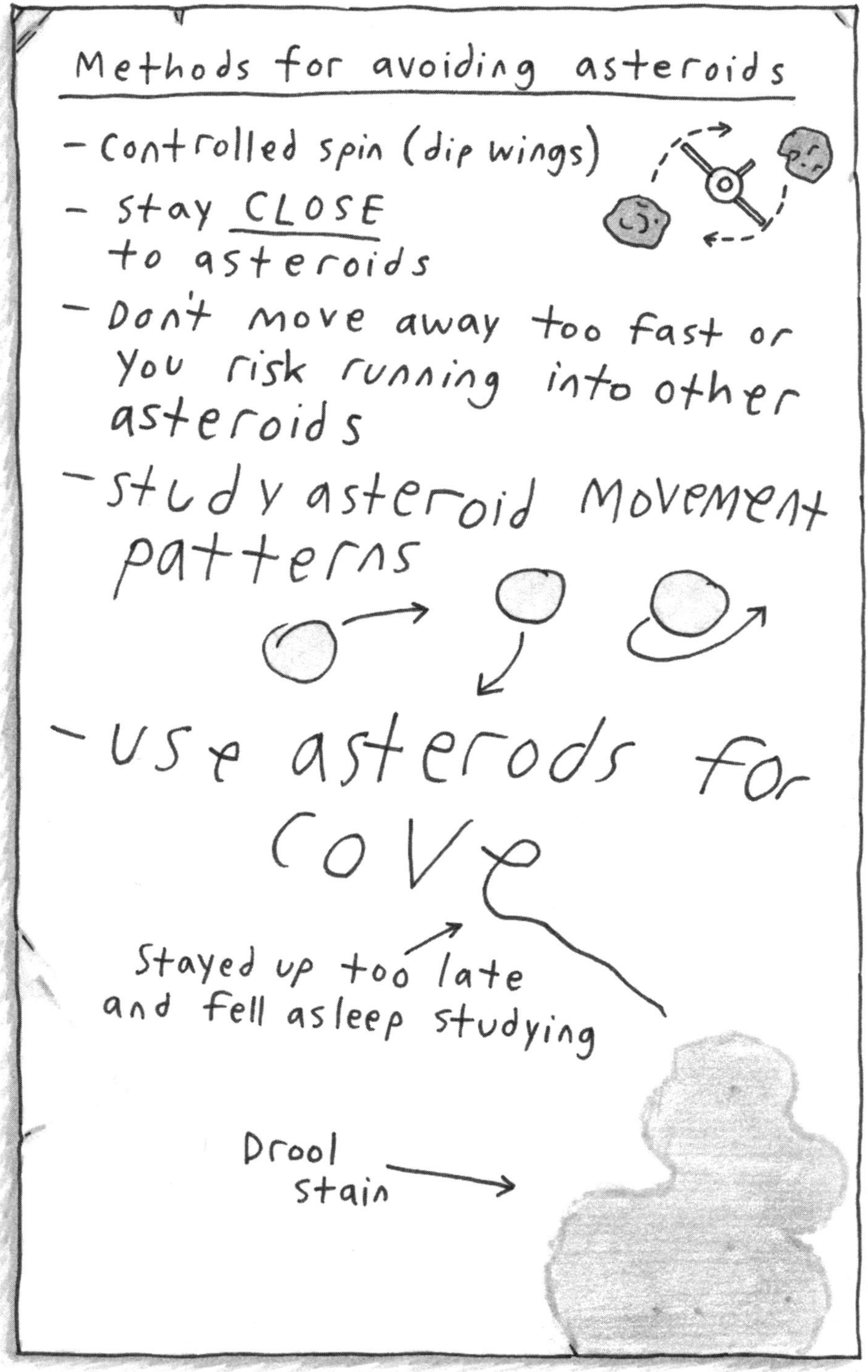
Methods for avoiding asteroids
- Controlled spin (dip wings)
- stay CLOSE to asteroids
- Don't move away too fast or you risk running into other asteroids
- study asteroid movement patterns
- use asterods for cove
Stayed up too late and fell asleep studying
Drool stain

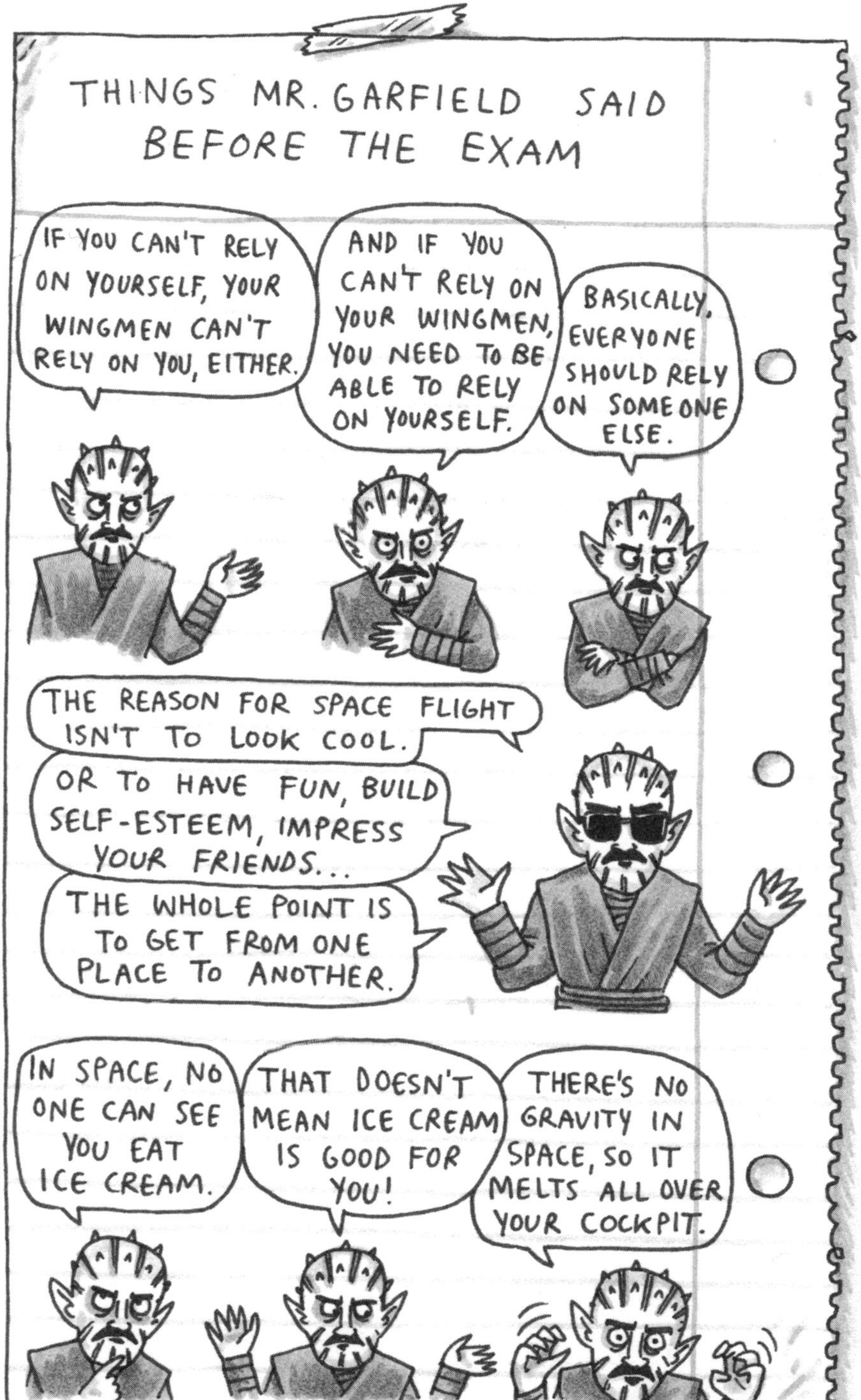
THINGS MR. GARFIELD SAID BEFORE THE EXAM
IF YOU CAN'T RELY ON YOURSELF, YOUR WINGMEN CAN'T RELY ON YOU, EITHER.
AND IF YOU CAN'T RELY ON YOUR WINGMEN, YOU NEED TO BE ABLE TO RELY ON YOURSELF.
BASICALLY, EVERYONE SHOULD RELY ON SOMEONE ELSE.
THE REASON FOR SPACE FLIGHT ISN'T TO LOOK COOL.
OR TO HAVE FUN, BUILD SELF-ESTEEM, IMPRESS YOUR FRIENDS...
THE WHOLE POINT IS TO GET FROM ONE PLACE TO ANOTHER.
IN SPACE, NO ONE CAN SEE YOU EAT ICE CREAM.
THAT DOESN'T MEAN ICE CREAM IS GOOD FOR YOU!
THERE'S NO GRAVITY IN SPACE, SO IT MELTS ALL OVER YOUR COCKPIT.

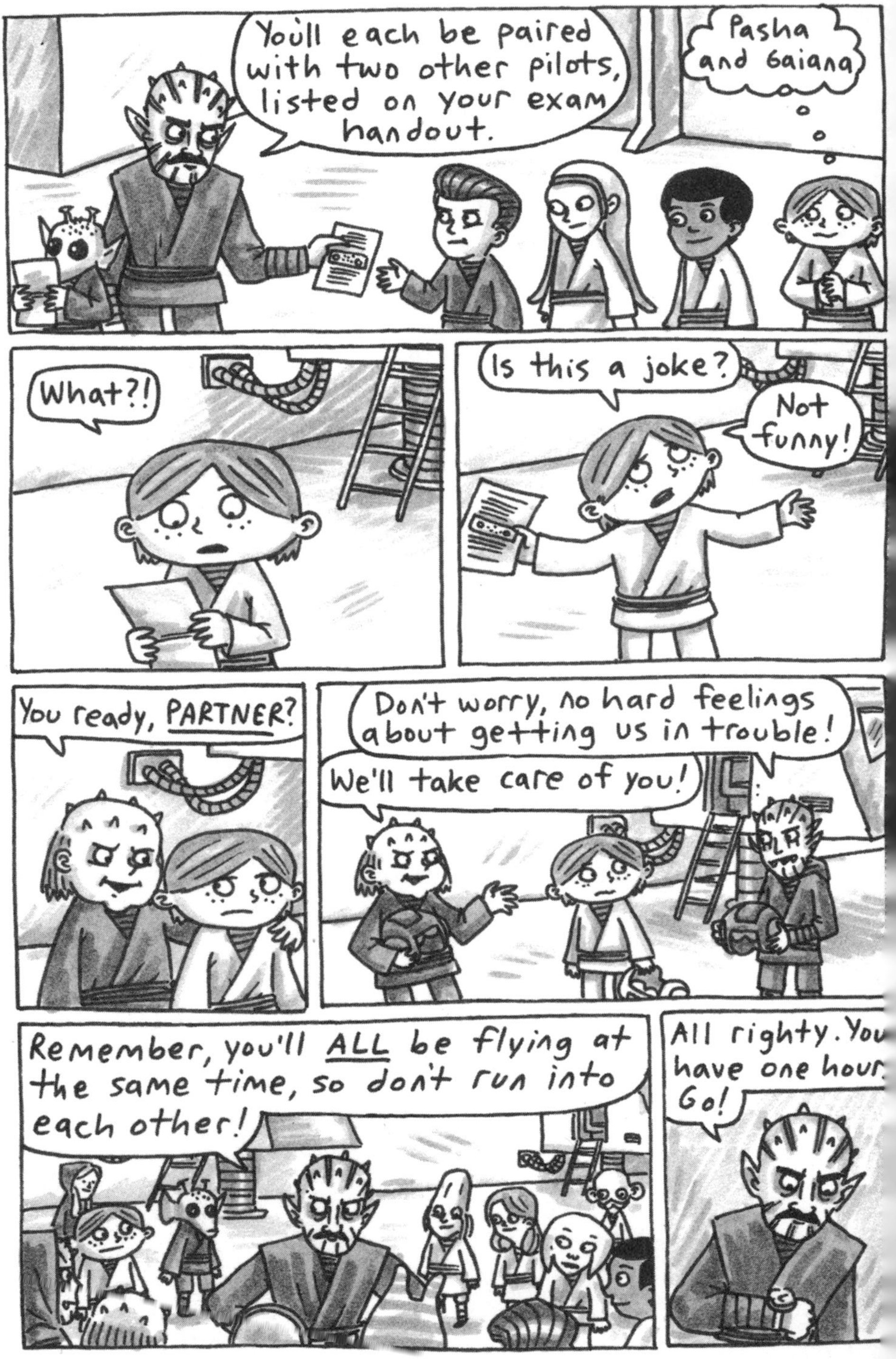
You'll each be paired with two other pilots, listed on your exam handout.
Pasha and Gaiana
What?!
Is this a joke?
Not funny!
You ready, PARTNER?
Don't worry, no hard feelings about getting us in trouble!
We'll take care of you!
Remember, you'll ALL be flying at the same time, so don't run into each other!
All righty. You have one hour. Go!

STAR PILOT FLIGHT TRAINING
FINAL EXAM

This test requires each student to complete a flight path through an asteroid belt from Planet "A" to Planet "B." Grades will be determined by distance, duration, and damage.

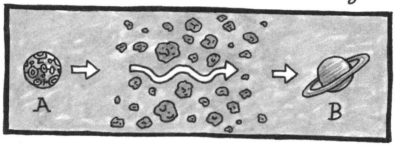

While grades are assessed individually, it is expected you will work together to remove obstacles, cover one another, and warn of potential dangers. Students will be able to track one another's progress, and should maintain awareness of their Health/Damage Meter status.

FLIGHT LEADER: _ROAN_
WINGMEN: _CYRUS_
CRONAH

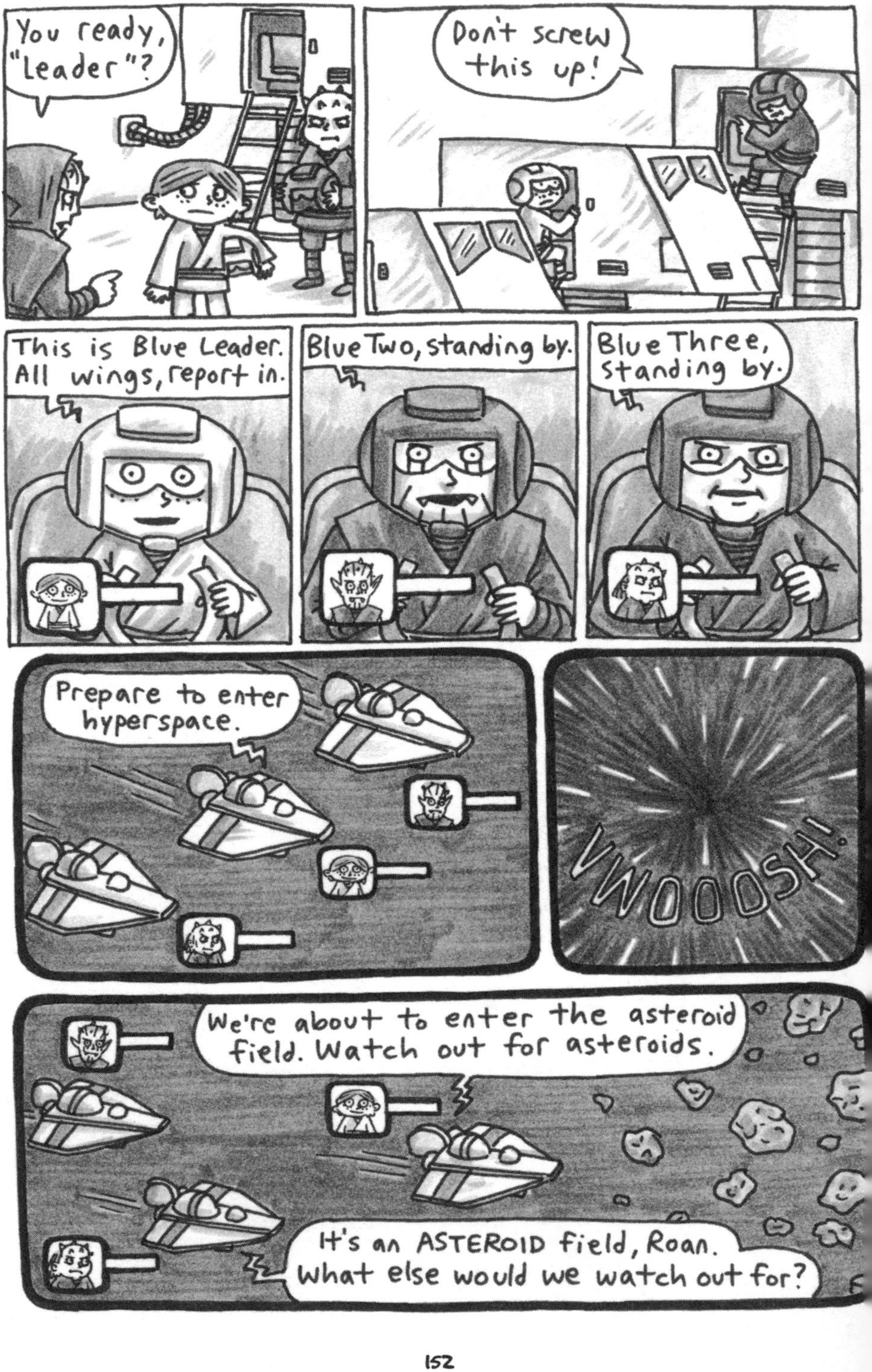
You ready, "Leader"?
Don't screw this up!
This is Blue Leader. All wings, report in.
Blue Two, standing by.
Blue Three, standing by.
Prepare to enter hyperspace.
VWOOOSH!
We're about to enter the asteroid field. Watch out for asteroids.
It's an ASTEROID field, Roan. What else would we watch out for?

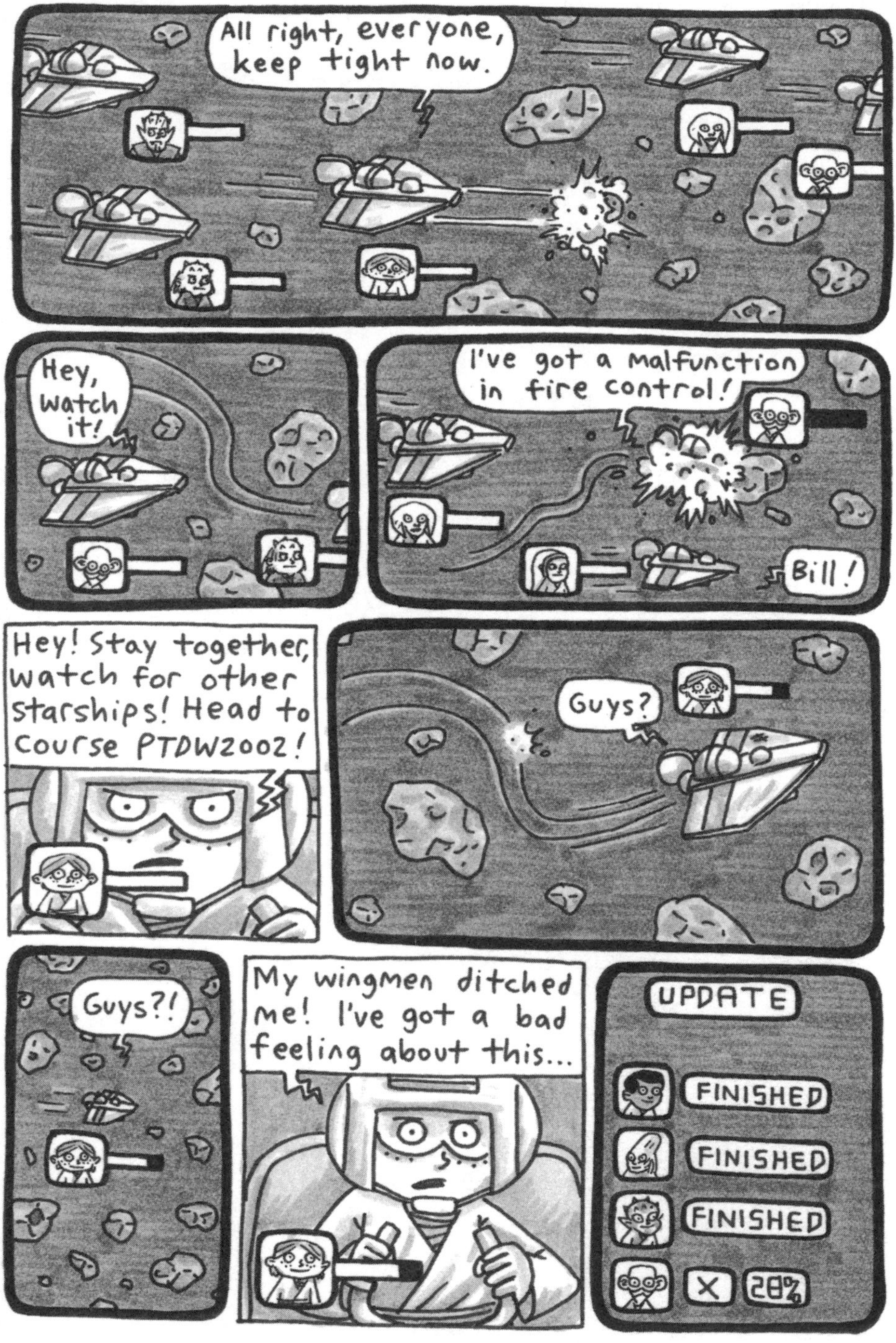
All right, everyone, keep tight now.
Hey, watch it!
I've got a malfunction in fire control!
Bill!
Hey! Stay together, watch for other starships! Head to course PTDW2002!
Guys?
Guys?!
My wingmen ditched me! I've got a bad feeling about this...
UPDATE
FINISHED
FINISHED
FINISHED
X
28%

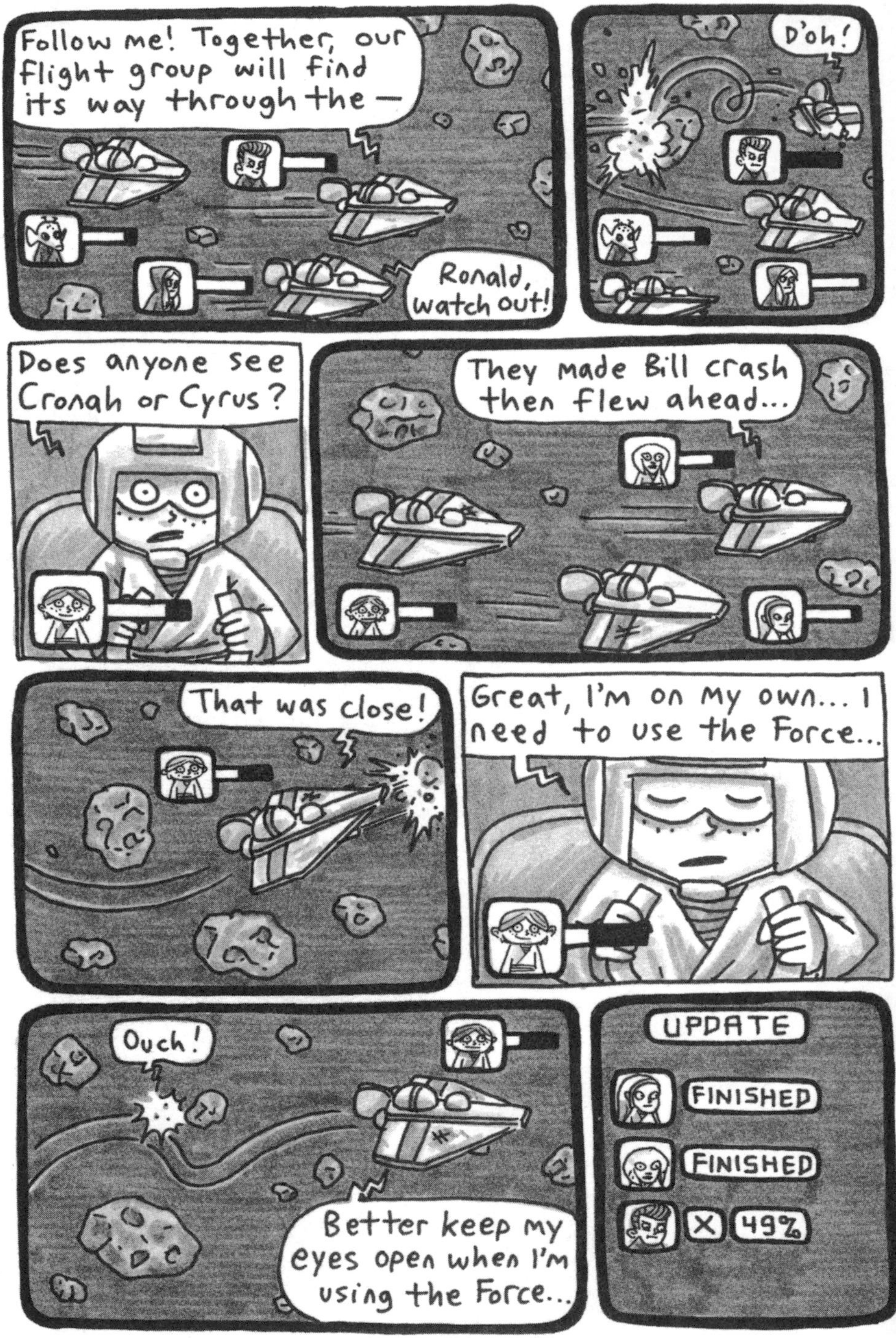
Follow me! Together, our flight group will find its way through the—
Ronald, watch out!
D'oh!
Does anyone see Cronah or Cyrus?
They made Bill crash then flew ahead...
That was close!
Great, I'm on my own... I need to use the Force...
Ouch!
Better keep my eyes open when I'm using the Force...
UPDATE
FINISHED
FINISHED
X
49%

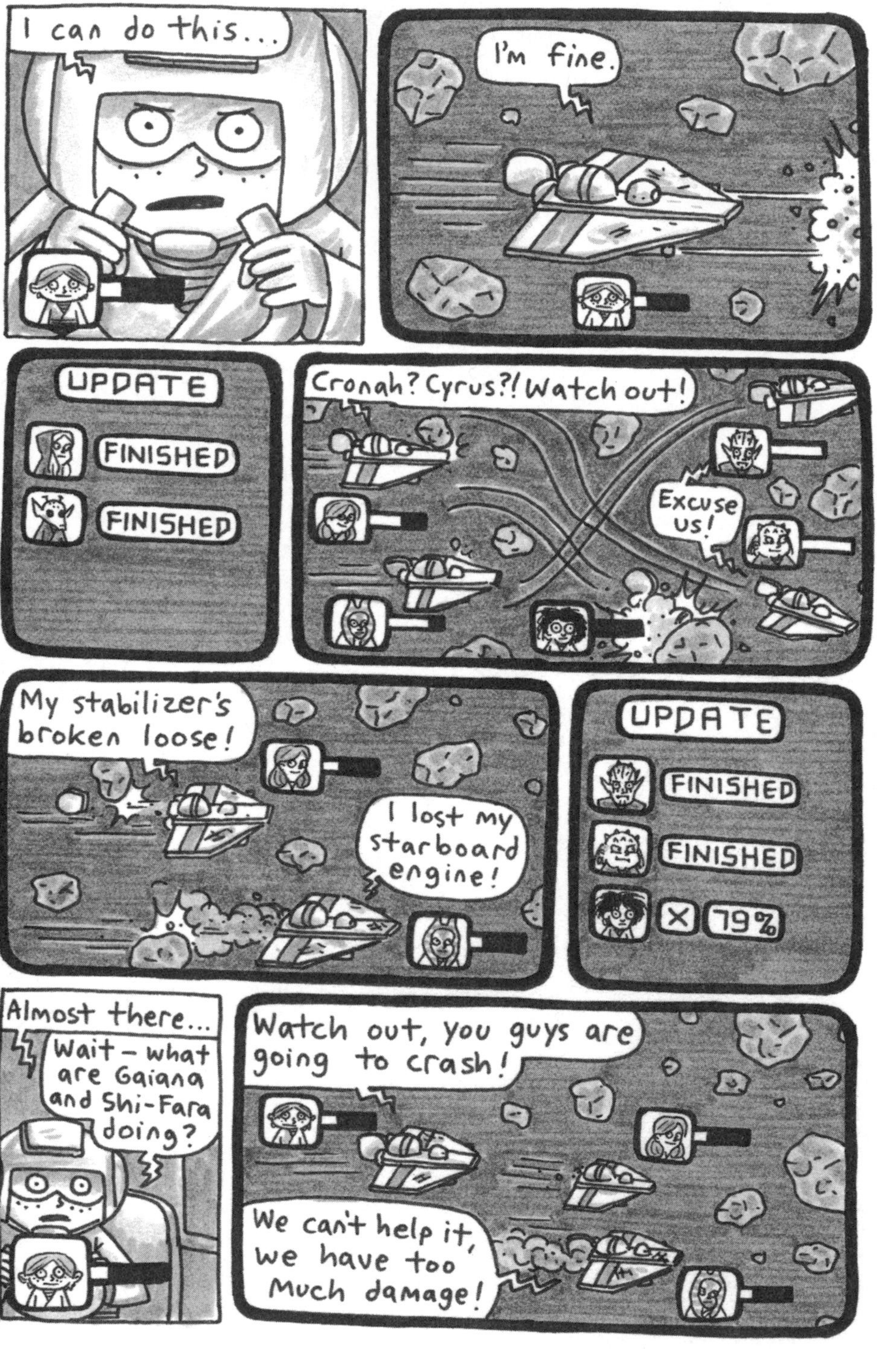
I can do this...
I'm fine.
UPDATE
FINISHED
FINISHED
Cronah? Cyrus?! Watch out!
Excuse us!
My stabilizer's broken loose!
I lost my starboard engine!
UPDATE
FINISHED
FINISHED
X 79%
Almost there...
Wait – what are Gaiana and Shi-Fara doing?
Watch out, you guys are going to crash!
We can't help it, we have too much damage!

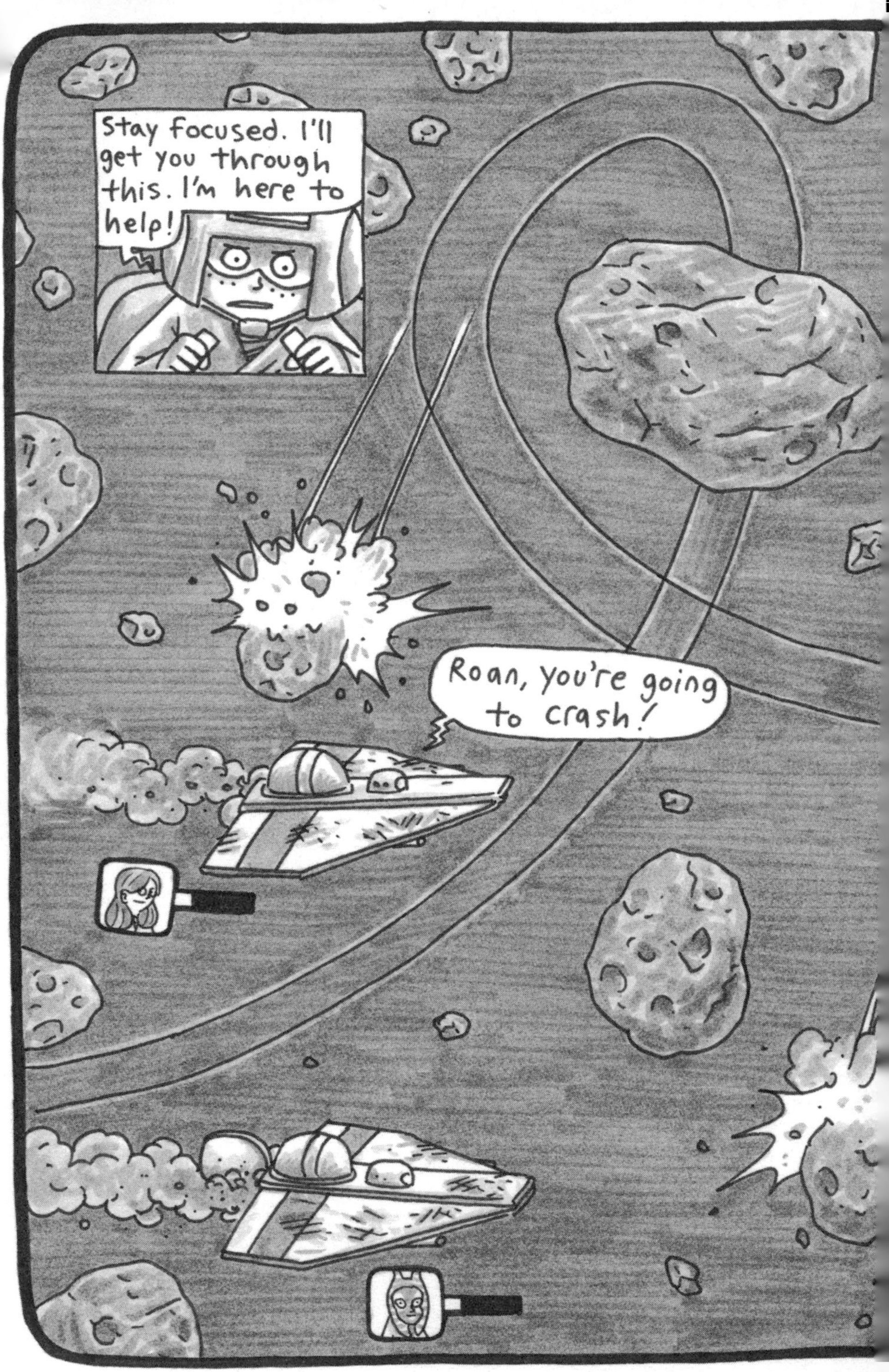
Stay focused. I'll get you through this. I'm here to help!
Roan, you're going to crash!

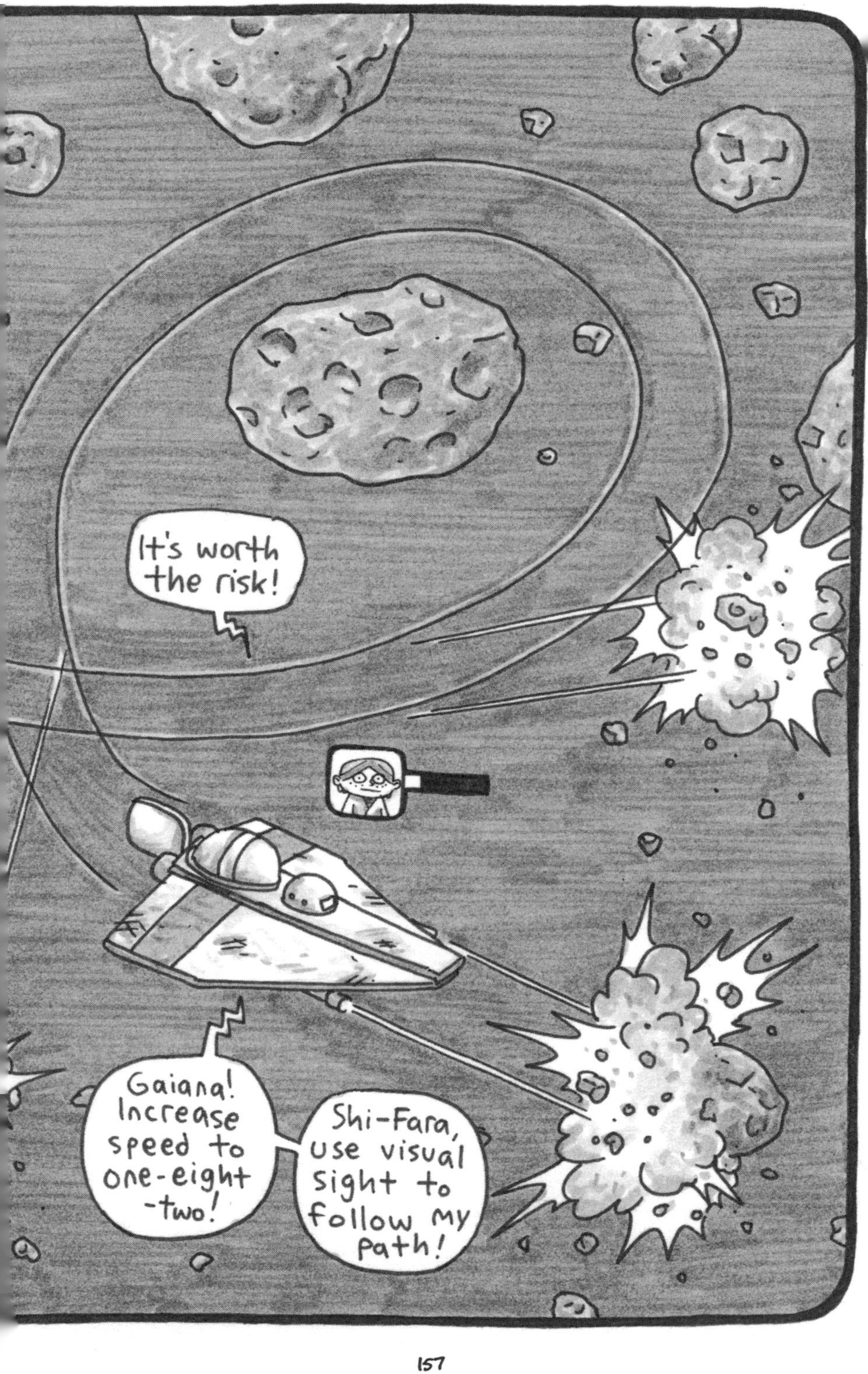
It's worth the risk!
Gaiana! Increase speed to one-eight -two!
Shi-Fara, use visual sight to follow my path!

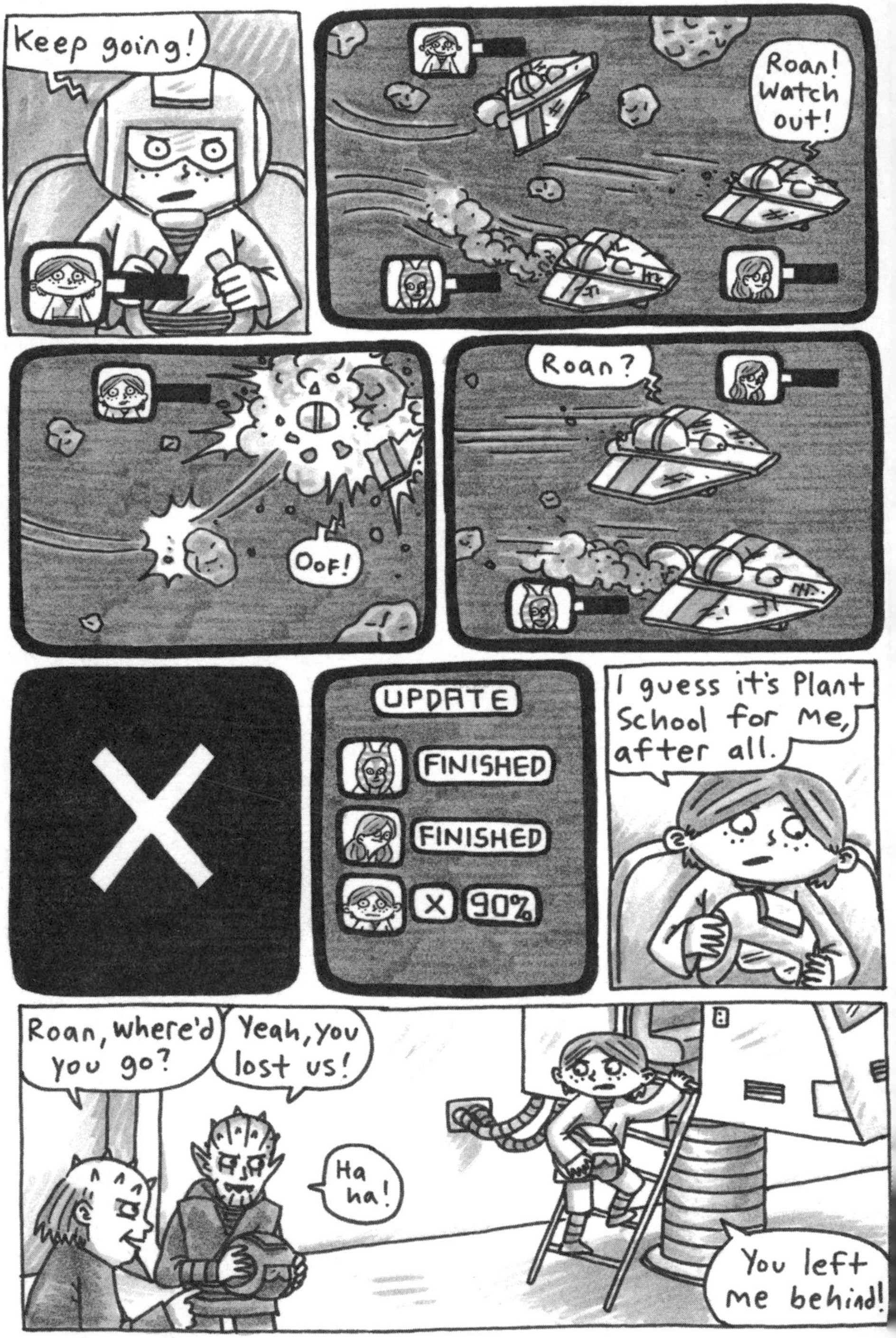
Keep going!
Roan! Watch out!
OOF!
Roan?
UPDATE
FINISHED
FINISHED
X 90%
I guess it's Plant School for me, after all.
Roan, where'd you go?
Yeah, you lost us!
Ha ha!
You left me behind!

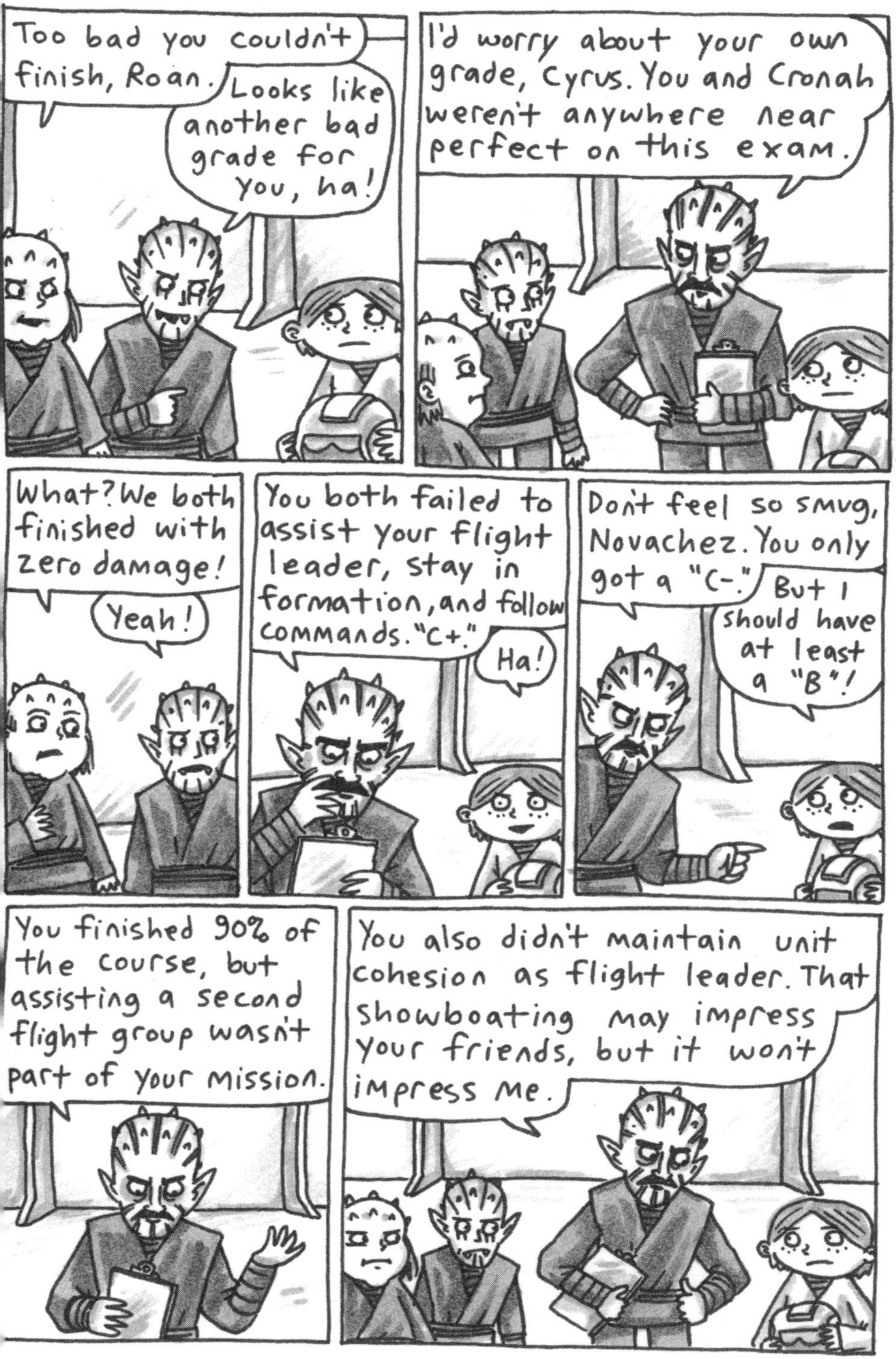
Too bad you couldn't finish, Roan.
Looks like another bad grade for you, ha!
I'd worry about your own grade, Cyrus. You and Cronah weren't anywhere near perfect on this exam.
What? We both finished with zero damage!
Yeah!
You both failed to assist your flight leader, stay in formation, and follow commands. "C+."
Ha!
Don't feel so smug, Novachez. You only got a "C-."
But I should have at least a "B"!
You finished 90% of the course, but assisting a second flight group wasn't part of your mission.
You also didn't maintain unit cohesion as flight leader. That showboating may impress your friends, but it won't impress me.

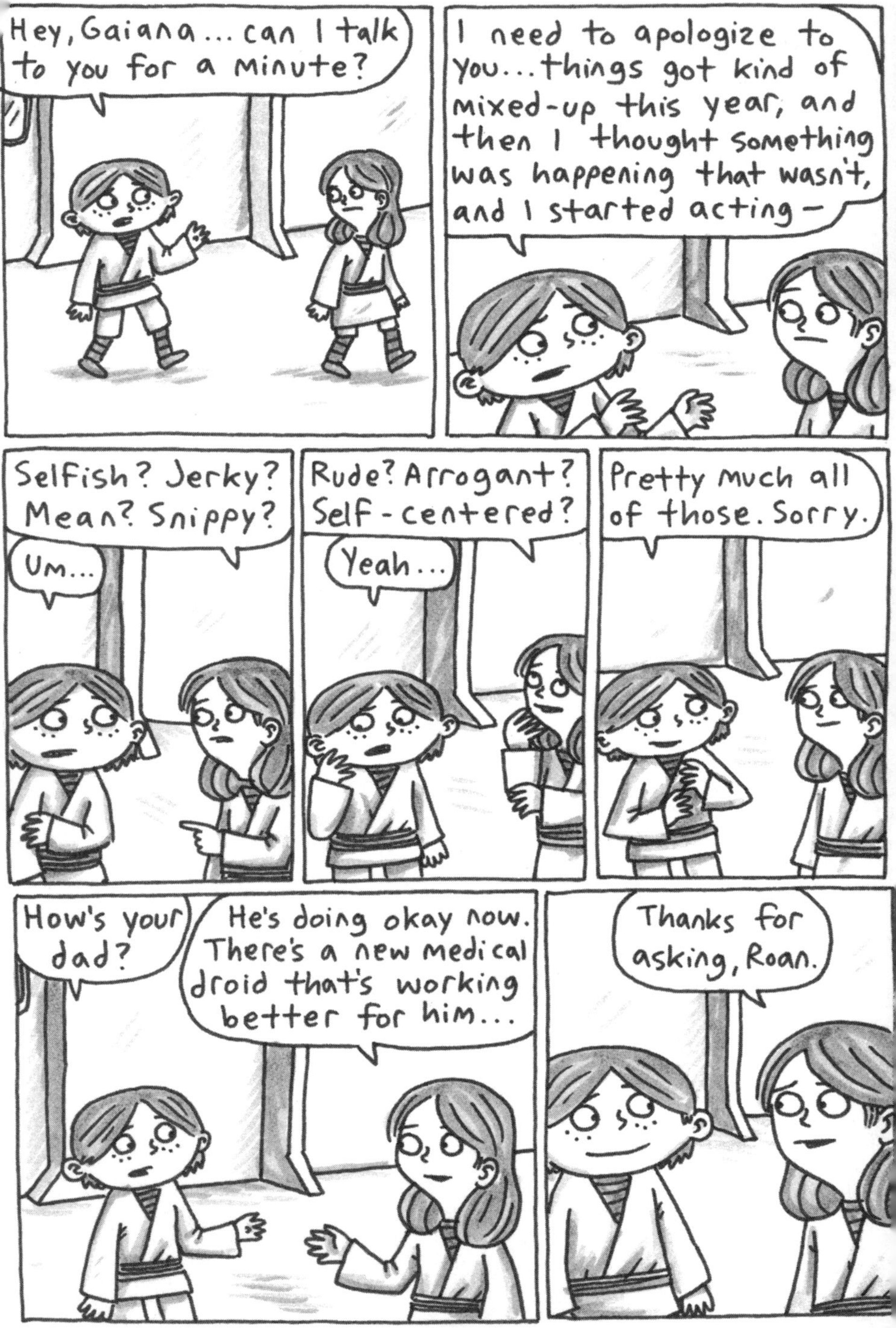
Hey, Gaiana... can I talk to you for a minute?
I need to apologize to you... things got kind of mixed-up this year, and then I thought something was happening that wasn't, and I started acting—
Selfish? Jerky? Mean? Snippy?
Um...
Rude? Arrogant? Self-centered?
Yeah...
Pretty much all of those. Sorry.
How's your dad?
He's doing okay now. There's a new medical droid that's working better for him...
Thanks for asking, Roan.

PENTADAY

The way this year started, I wasn't sure I was going to pass star pilot flight training. By the time this semester was half over, I wasn't sure I'd have any friends left. So it felt good to help Gaiana (and Shi-Fara), even though I didn't end up with that good a score at the end of the exam.

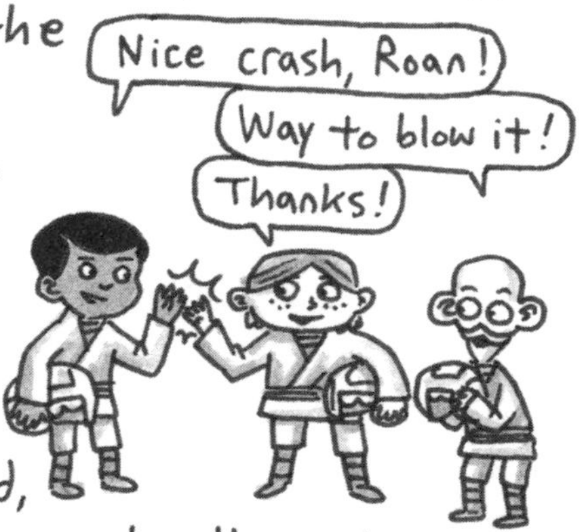

Nice crash, Roan!
Way to blow it!
Thanks!

Mr. Garfield had a hard time deciding what grade to give me. He likes to give me bad grades. Even though I crashed, I figured he might actually give me an "A" because of <u>HOW</u> I crashed. I was even thinking maybe he doesn't <u>WANT</u> to like me, but he does. He was

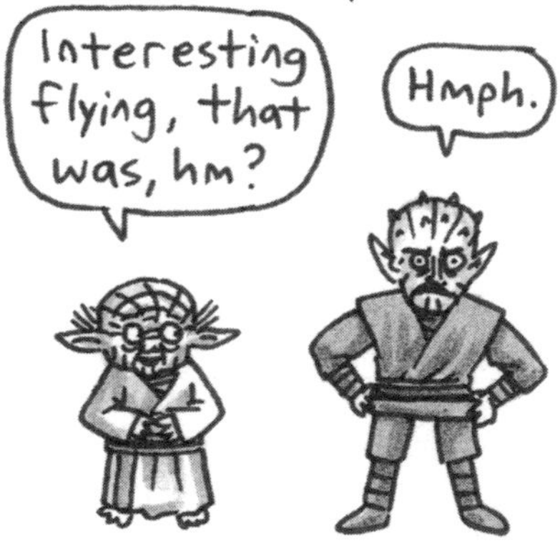

Interesting flying, that was, hm?
Hmph.

only going to give me a "C-" until Master Yoda talked him into giving me a "B-." Getting a better grade than Cyrus and Cronah REALLY made them mad, though.

Not that I thought Cyrus and Cronah were going to be my friends after the flight exam, but I didn't think they would HATE me. Master Yoda put them on academic probation for next year's first semester because of what happened with Voorpee. Now they really think I snitched on them, but I didn't. The only person who I told what really happened was Pasha, and I made him promise to not tell ANYONE. Master Yoda is really smart, so maybe he used the Force to figure it out? Or he can talk to animals and Voorpee told him what happened? Maybe Cyrus and Cronah told on each other.

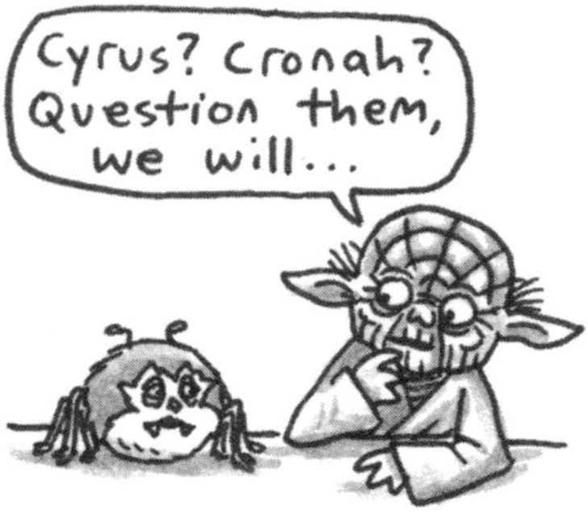
Cyrus? Cronah? Question them, we will...

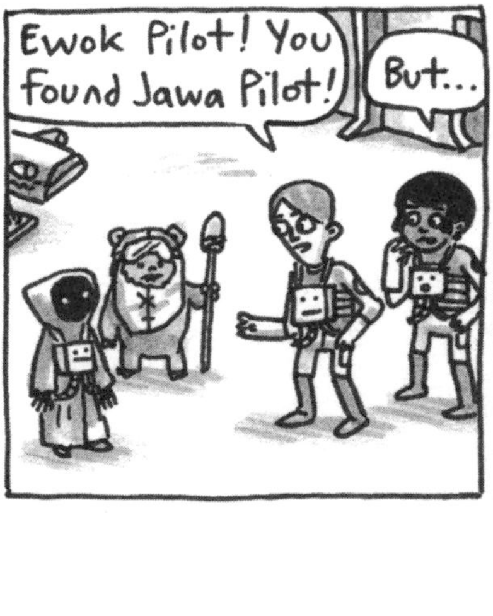
Ewok Pilot! You found Jawa Pilot!
But...

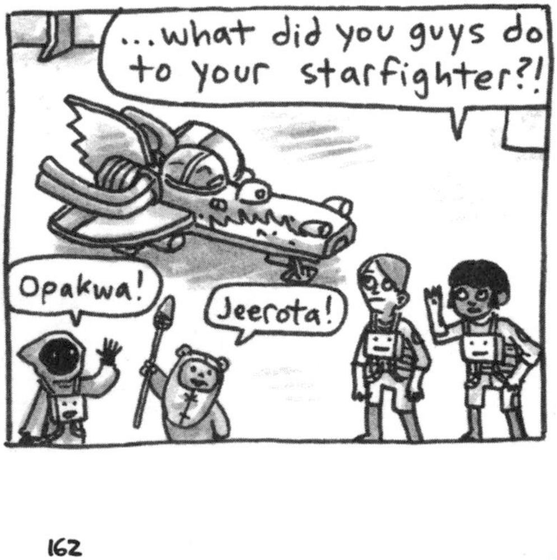
...what did you guys do to your starfighter?!
Opakwa!
Jeerota!

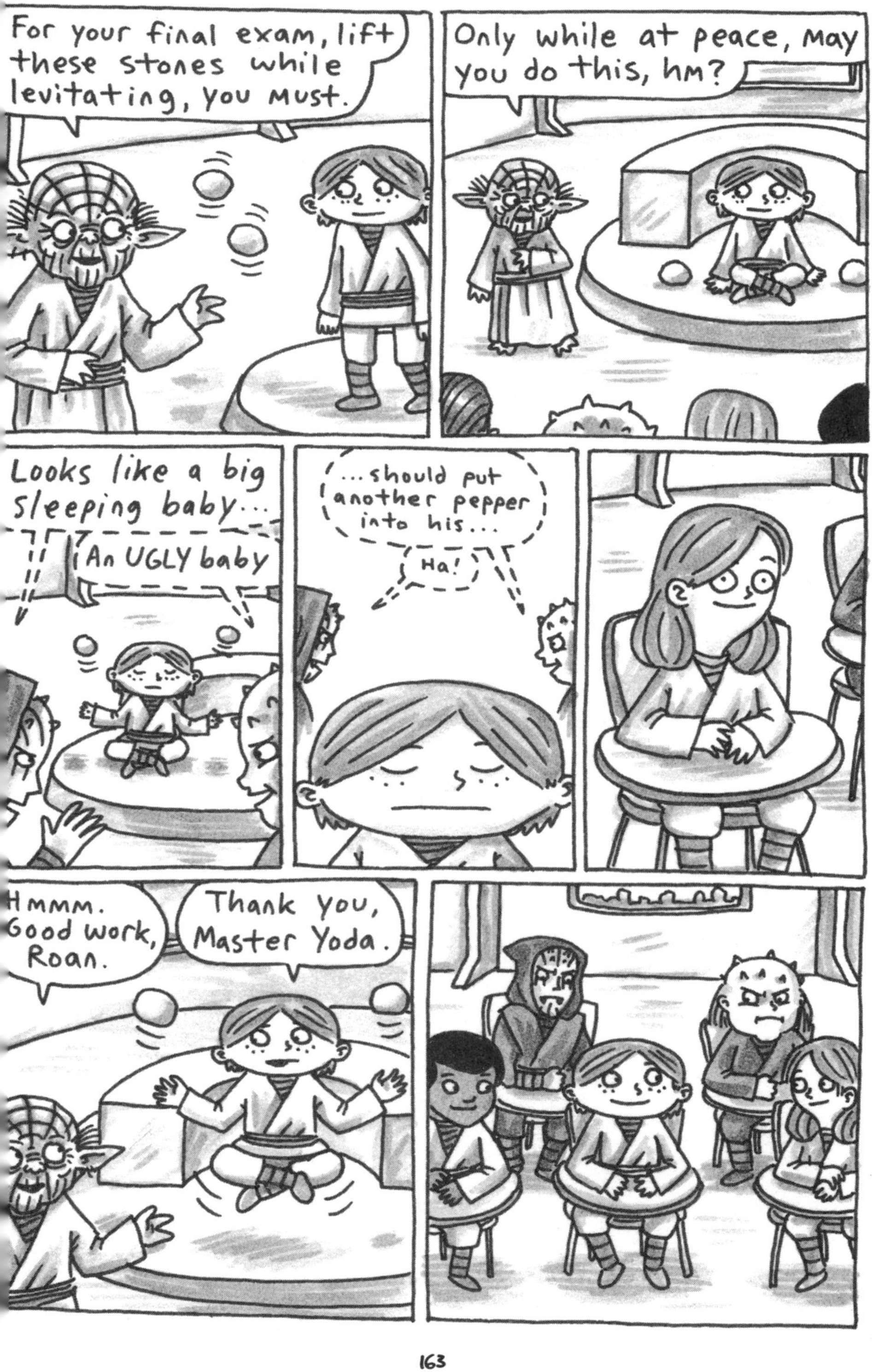
For your final exam, lift these stones while levitating, you must.
Only while at peace, may you do this, hm?
Looks like a big sleeping baby...
An UGLY baby
...should put another pepper into his...
Ha!
Hmmm. Good work, Roan.
Thank you, Master Yoda.

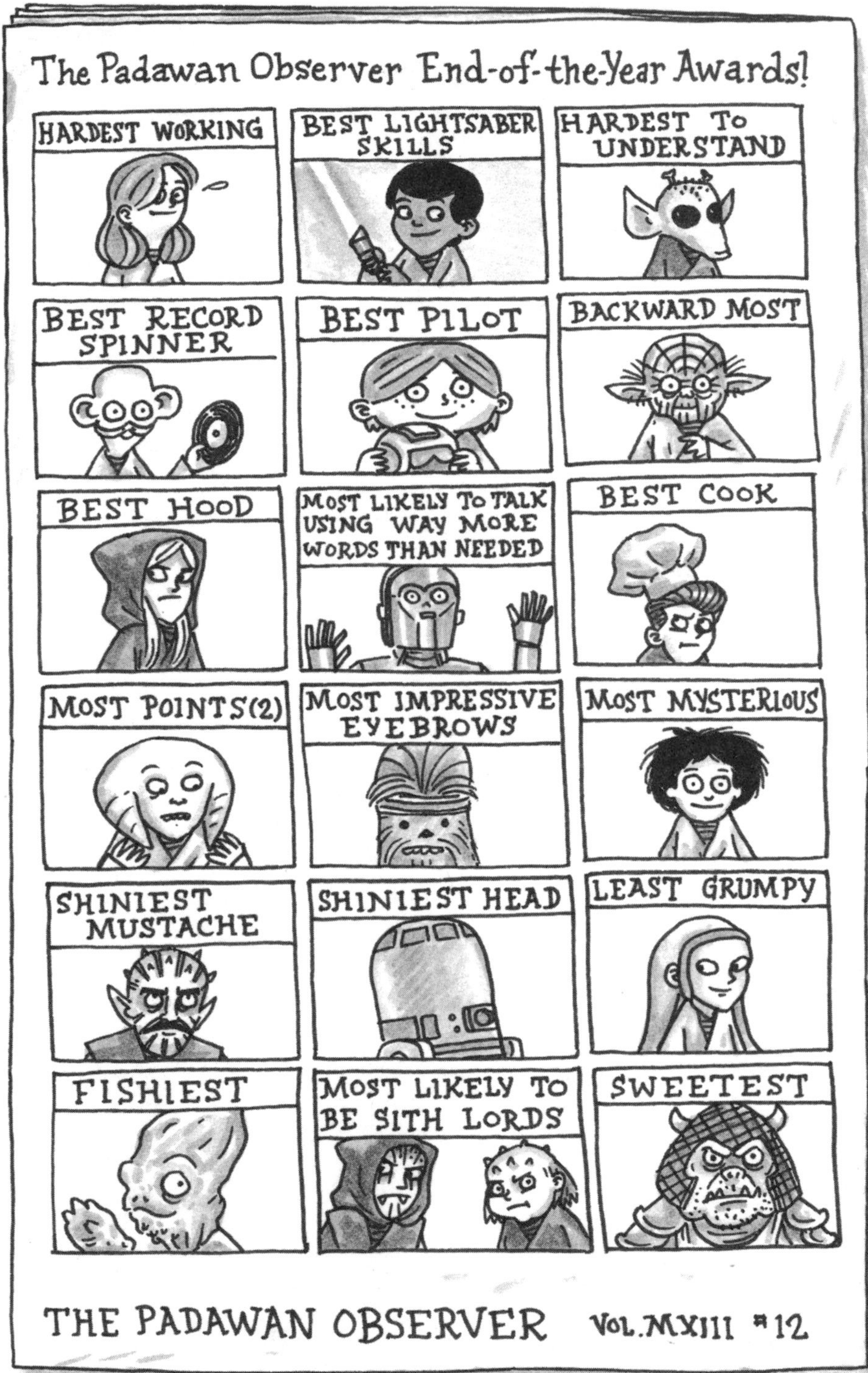
The Padawan Observer End-of-the-Year Awards!
HARDEST WORKING
BEST LIGHTSABER SKILLS
HARDEST TO UNDERSTAND
BEST RECORD SPINNER
BEST PILOT
BACKWARD MOST
BEST HOOD
MOST LIKELY TO TALK USING WAY MORE WORDS THAN NEEDED
BEST COOK
MOST POINTS (2)
MOST IMPRESSIVE EYEBROWS
MOST MYSTERIOUS
SHINIEST MUSTACHE
SHINIEST HEAD
LEAST GRUMPY
FISHIEST
MOST LIKELY TO BE SITH LORDS
SWEETEST
THE PADAWAN OBSERVER VOL. MXIII #12

STUDENT: ROAN NOVACHEZ
LEVEL: PADAWAN | SEMESTER: FOUR
HOMEROOM: MASTER YODA

REPORT CARD

JEDI ACADEMY · CORUSCANT CAMPUS

CLASS	NOTES	GRADE
REUSING THE FORCE [MASTER YODA]	Use the Force outside of class more, Roan should, hm?	A
ART OF PHYSICS [MRS. PILTON/ LIBRARIAN LACKBAR]	Roan's thoughts were an excellent addition to this class	a-
LIGHTSABER DUELING SKILLS [MR. GARFIELD]	ROAN'S SKILLS IMPROVED, BUT HE NEEDS MORE FOCUS	A-
HOME ECONOMICS [GAMMY]	[illegible]	[illegible]
STAR PILOT FLIGHT TRAINING, PT. 2 [MR. GARFIELD]	ROAN HASN'T REACHED HIS FULL POTENTIAL, MUST WORK HARDER	B-
BASICS OF DROID CONSTRUCTION [PRINCIPAL MAR]	ROAN COULD BE MORE ASSERTIVE WITH VOCAL DROID COMMANDS.	A
PHYSICAL EDUCATION [KITMUM]		

DUODAY

I learned a lot this year, but not the way I expected to. Like, being in pilot training taught me about being a good friend. Or maybe learning to be a good friend made me a better pilot? Something like that. Mr. Garfield never really got around to liking me this year.

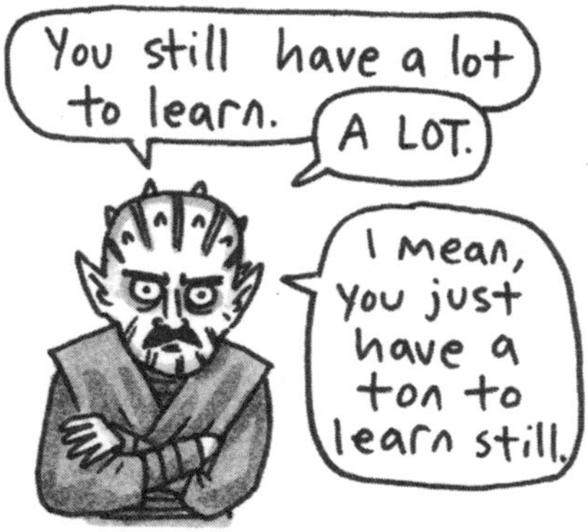
You still have a lot to learn.
A LOT.
I mean, you just have a ton to learn still.

Even when I did good, he would list a bunch of things I did wrong. I thought maybe Mr. Garfield was finally going to start liking me, because I've become a really good pilot, but he just doesn't care. I also thought Cyrus and Cronah were starting to like me, too, but they ended up being jerks and tried to make me look stupid. I'm even okay that Pasha beat me in lightsaber fencing, now that things are back to normal with us.

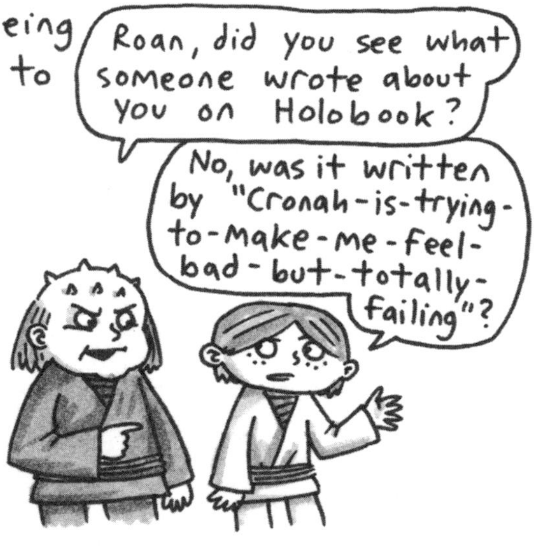
Roan, did you see what someone wrote about you on Holobook?
No, was it written by "Cronah-is-trying-to-make-me-feel-bad-but-totally-failing"?

So even though I thought it was silly how Kitmum always wants to tell us that winning isn't important, maybe she has the right idea. I don't know how these teachers all know so much, except Master Yoda. If I were six hundred years old, I'd know EVERYTHING, too. But then Yoda goes and says things like this. → I wonder if Master Yoda ever messed things up with his friends? Last year, I was worried about having any friends here, but it ended up being easy. This year, I wasn't worried at all, and I almost ended up losing ALL of my friends. That's another thing, I learned—if you want to find something out, sometimes you just have to ask. That seems really obvious when I write it down now. Gaiana isn't still mad at me, at least, but I don't know if she likes me the same. Maybe I can ask her. Sometime.

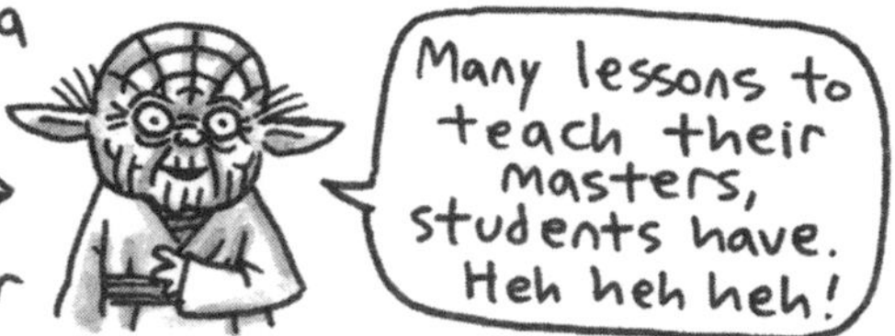
Many lessons to teach their masters, students have. Heh heh heh!

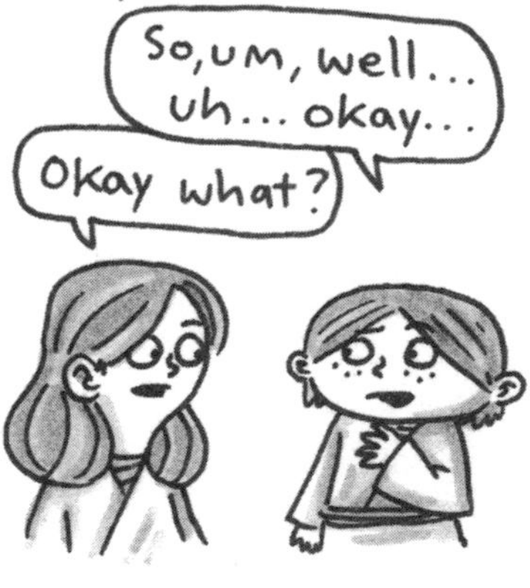
So, um, well... uh... okay...
Okay what?

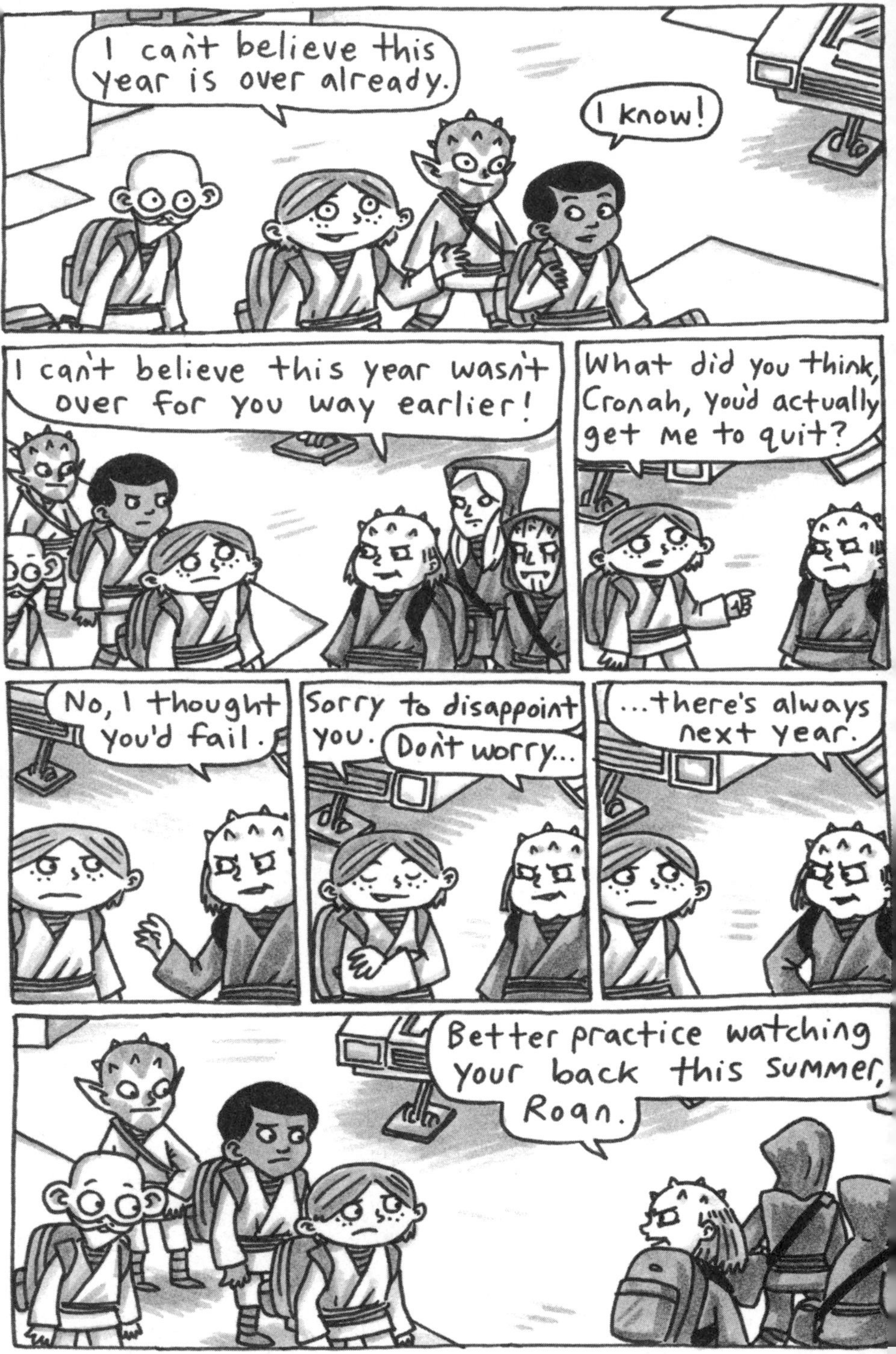
I can't believe this year is over already.
I know!
I can't believe this year wasn't over for you way earlier!
What did you think, Cronah, you'd actually get me to quit?
No, I thought you'd fail.
Sorry to disappoint you.
Don't worry...
...there's always next year.
Better practice watching your back this summer, Roan.

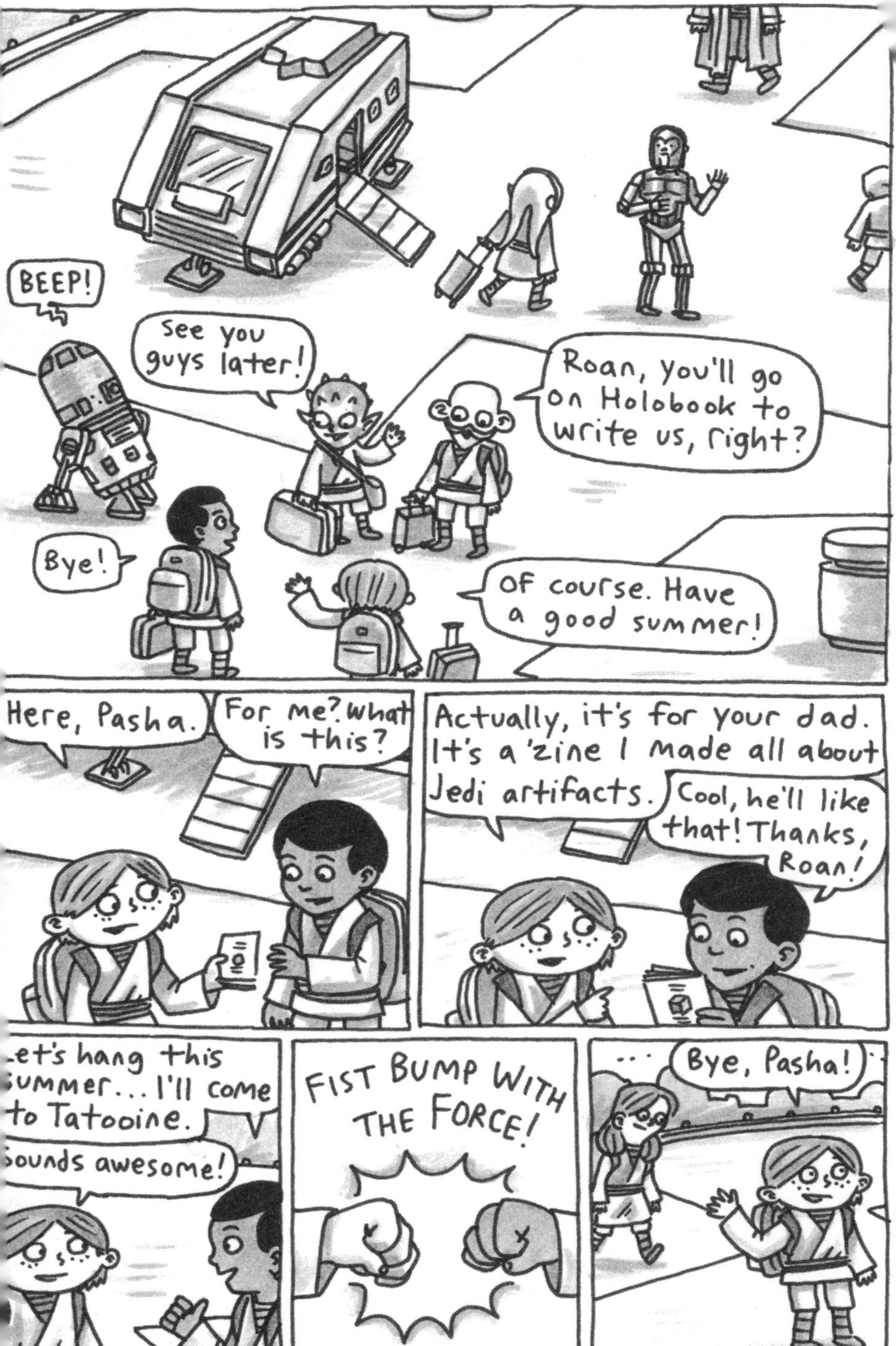
BEEP!
See you guys later!
Roan, you'll go on Holobook to write us, right?
Bye!
Of course. Have a good summer!
Here, Pasha.
For me? What is this?
Actually, it's for your dad. It's a 'zine I made all about Jedi artifacts.
Cool, he'll like that! Thanks, Roan!
Let's hang this summer... I'll come to Tatooine.
Sounds awesome!
FIST BUMP WITH THE FORCE!
...
Bye, Pasha!

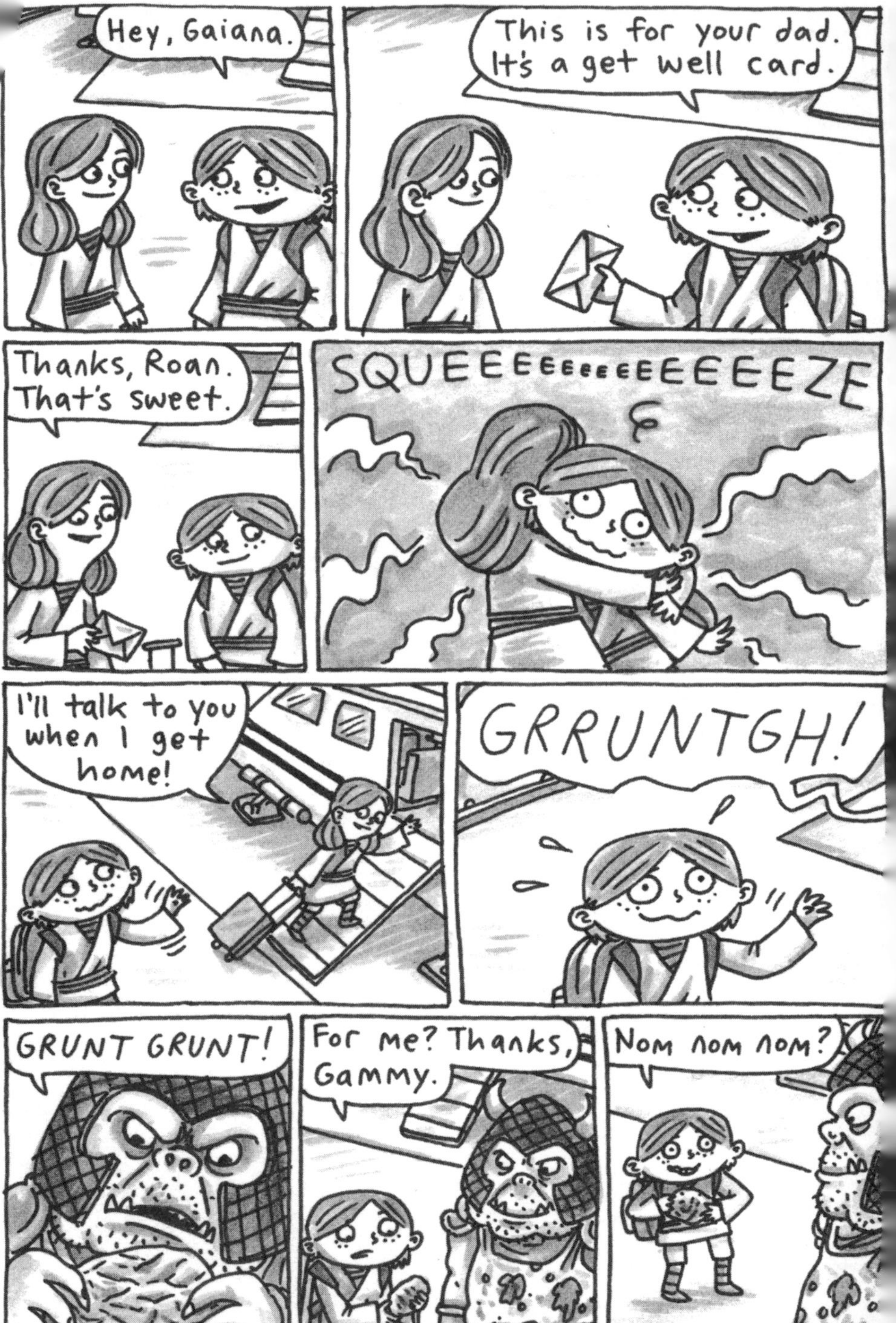
Hey, Gaiana.
This is for your dad. It's a get well card.
Thanks, Roan. That's sweet.
SQUEEEEeeeeeEEEEEZE
I'll talk to you when I get home!
GRRUNTGH!
GRUNT GRUNT!
For me? Thanks, Gammy.
Nom nom nom?

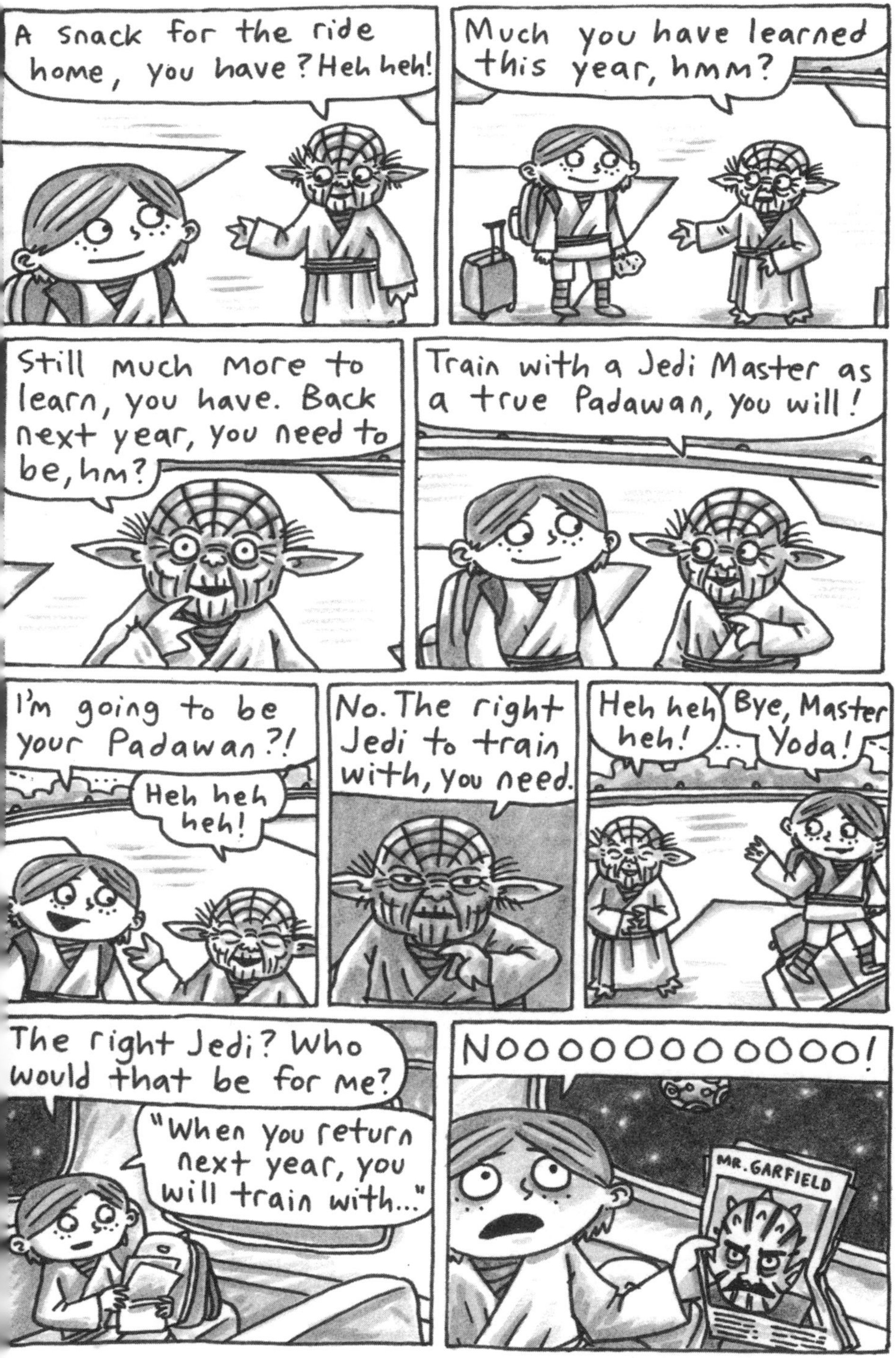
A snack for the ride home, you have? Heh heh!
Much you have learned this year, hmm?
Still much more to learn, you have. Back next year, you need to be, hm?
Train with a Jedi Master as a true Padawan, you will!
I'm going to be your Padawan?!
Heh heh heh!
No. The right Jedi to train with, you need.
Heh heh heh!
Bye, Master Yoda!
The right Jedi? Who would that be for me?
"When you return next year, you will train with..."
NOOOOOOOOOOOO!
MR. GARFIELD

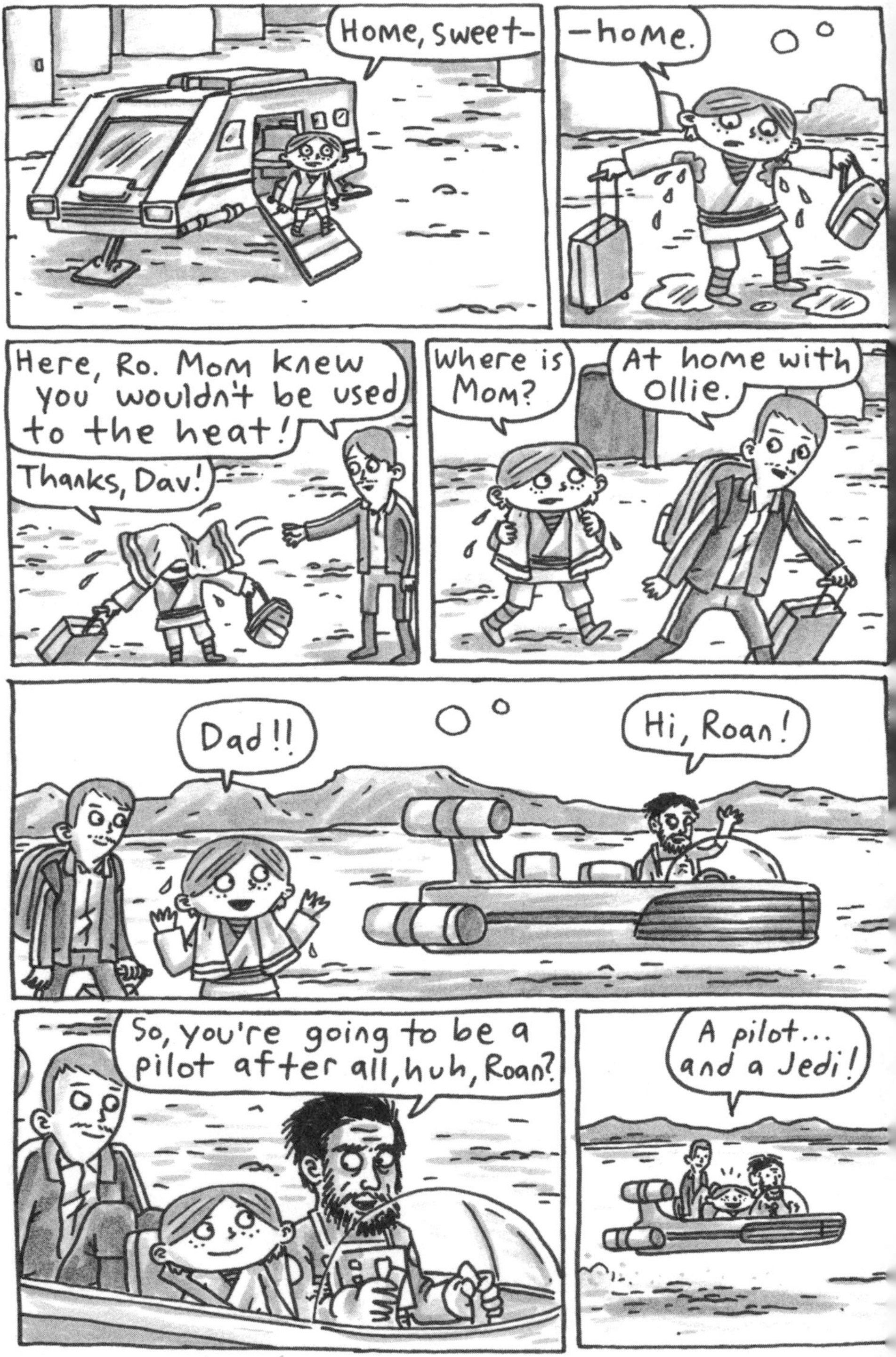
Home, sweet-
-home.
Here, Ro. Mom knew you wouldn't be used to the heat!
Thanks, Dav!
Where is Mom?
At home with Ollie.
Dad!!
Hi, Roan!
So, you're going to be a pilot after all, huh, Roan?
A pilot... and a Jedi!

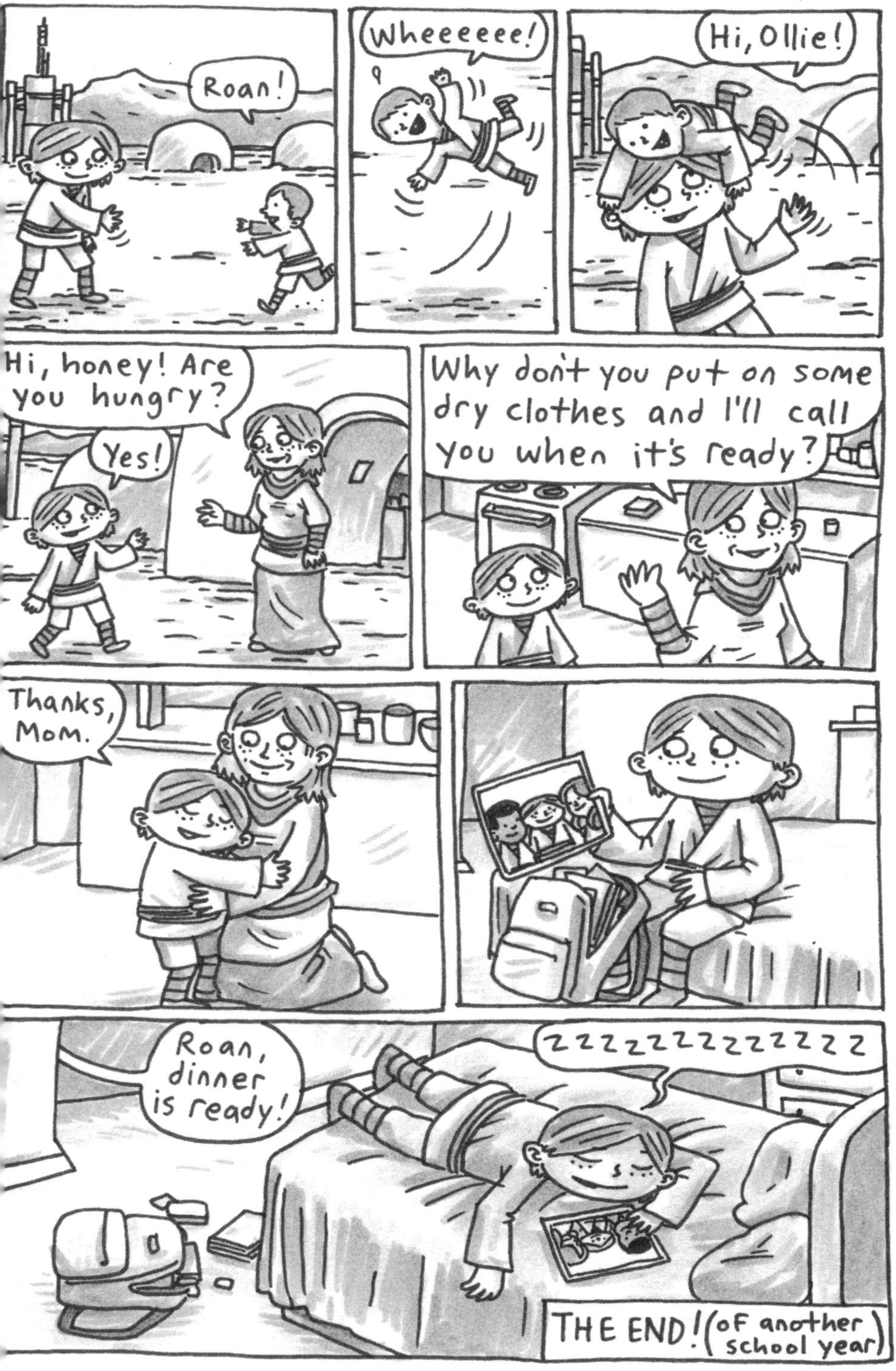
Roan!
Wheeeeee!
Hi, Ollie!
Hi, honey! Are you hungry?
Yes!
Why don't you put on some dry clothes and I'll call you when it's ready?
Thanks, Mom.
Roan, dinner is ready!
ZZZZZZZZZZZZZZ
THE END! (of another school year)

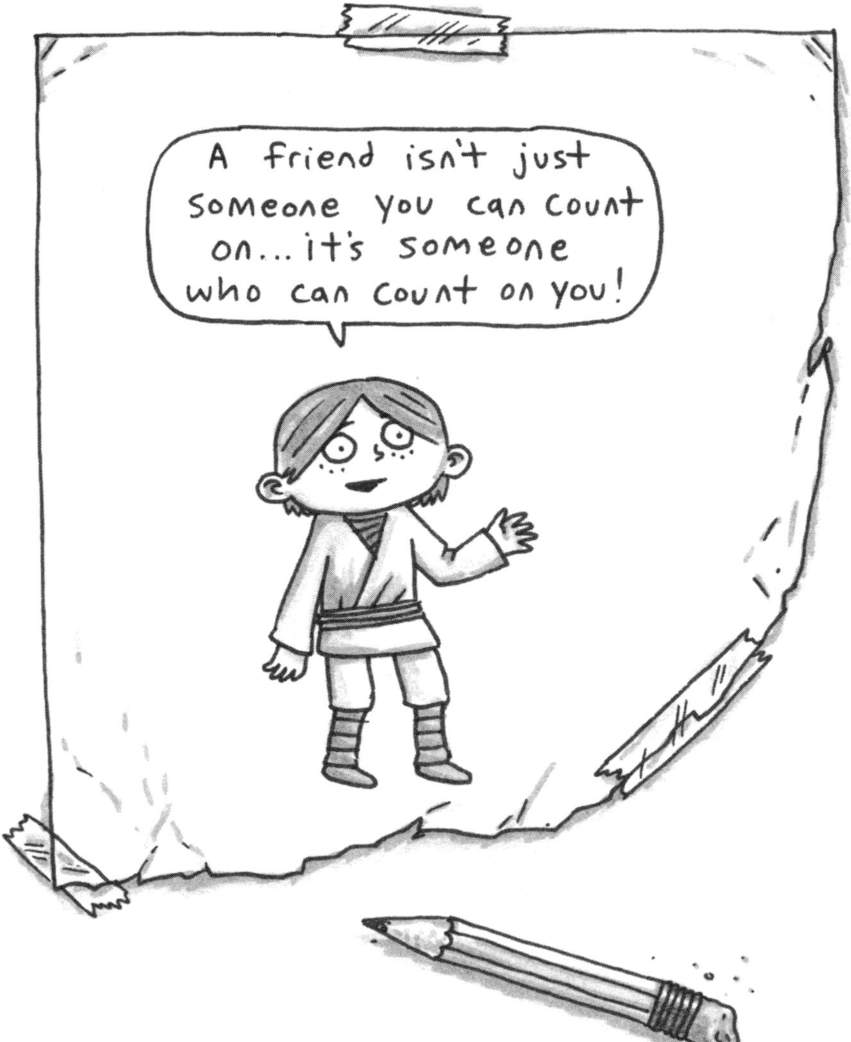
A friend isn't just someone you can count on... it's someone who can count on you!

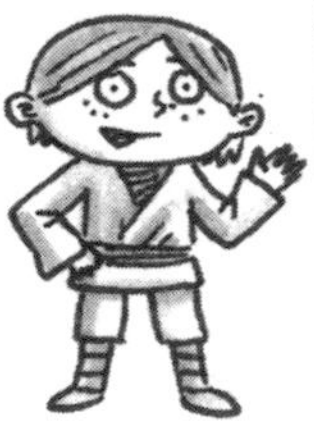

WRITE YOUR OWN STORIES!

Use your favorite characters, make up new ones, or have you and your friends be the heroes!

Decide where your story is happening — on Earth or in a galaxy far, far away?

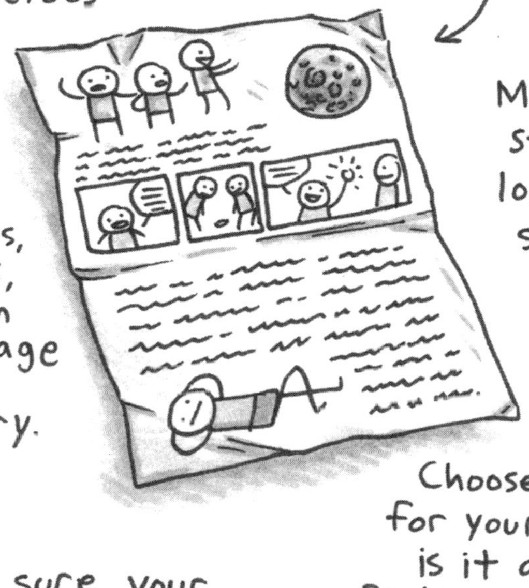

Make your story as long or as short as you want.

Use words, pictures, or even photo collage to tell your story.

Choose a theme for your story — is it about finding something? Winning a competition? Escaping danger? Or just telling a funny joke?

Make sure your story has a beginning and an end.

Share your stories with your friends!

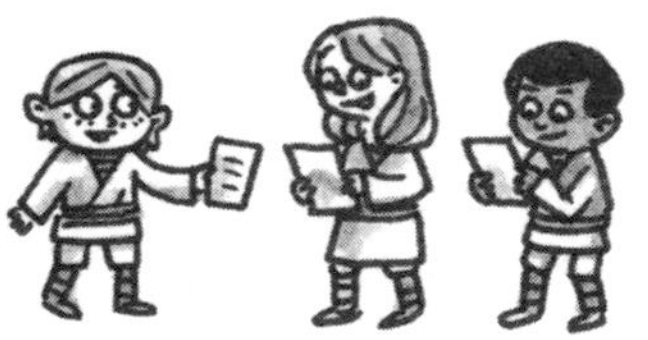

Jeffrey Brown is a cartoonist and author of the bestselling DARTH VADER AND SON and its sequels VADER'S LITTLE PRINCESS, GOODNIGHT DARTH VADER, and DARTH VADER AND FRIENDS as well as the STAR WARS: JEDI ACADEMY series. He lives in Chicago with his wife and two sons. Despite being a lifelong Star Wars fan, he still can't use the Force, but sometimes he likes to imagine that he can.

P.O. BOX 120   DEERFIELD, IL 60015-0120   USA